THE
SOUTH
LAWN
PLOT

THE
SOUTH
LAWN
PLOT

RAY O'HANLON

GEMMA

Boston

First published by GemmaMedia in 2011.

GemmaMedia
230 Commercial Street
Boston, MA 02109 USA
www.gemmamedia.com

Printed in the United States of America

15   14   13   12   11   1   2   3   4   5

978-1-934848-87-6

Library of Congress Cataloging-in-Publication Data: O'Hanlon, Ray.
    The South Lawn plot / Ray O'Hanlon.
        p. cm.
    Summary: "An international thriller that explores long-simmering religous conflict and modern-day territory disputes"—Provided by publisher.
    ISBN 978-1-934848-87-6
    1. Journalists—Fiction.   2. Presidents—United States—Fiction.   3. Prime ministers—Great Britain—Fiction.   4. Conspiracies—Fiction.   5. Political fiction.   I. Title.
    PS3615.H355S68 2011
    813'.6—dc22

                                                          2010054379

For my family, in America and Ireland.
And for my father, Frank O'Hanlon (1926–2005)

1

BAILEY WATCHED as the smoke spiraled upwards and merged into the fog. Though it was officially spring, the temperature was purest January. He shivered. The light from the building and the street lamps by the dock gave the murk a yellowish hue. It was impossible to see beyond a few yards. Bailey sucked hard on his cigarette. He glanced at his watch and pressed the tiny knob that ignited the timepiece's internal light. It was twenty minutes to midnight. He would be done with his shift before the nicotine took full effect. For about ten seconds he ignored the vibrating of the cell phone in his pocket. He knew it had to be Henderson.

It was.

Henderson said nothing other than Nick Bailey's surname. That was all he needed to say.

Bailey drew his last satisfaction from the eroding stump of his filter tip, itself an insult to past generations of tabloid reporters who had turned newsrooms into toxic harbingers of global warming. Bailey wasn't impressed by the climate change theory. London, lately at any rate, seemed to have missed the phenomenon completely.

Turning into the doorway, he waved his security card in front of the scanner. The door opened, and he stepped into a foyer that was so brightly lit it might have been using half the city's electrical power supply. Bailey's eyes narrowed in the glare.

Beyond the lone security guard in his booth the place was empty. The front office, as it was called, had recently been redone. It was a homage to plastic; plastic tables and seats where people could wait to meet people from the offices on the upper floors and, of course, the newsroom, which was off limits to general visitors, yet another limit on the relaxed freedoms of a bygone time in the new age of security.

Framed front pages of the paper lined the walls. Some of them were undoubted classics, some dubious, and just a few plain tacky. The latest was inspired by a simmering crisis between the western powers and China over Taiwan.

Beijing's foreign minister had recently been in London to meet his British counterpart. Britain had been told in no uncertain terms where it could consign its indignation. One of the paper's columnists had suggested, not entirely in jest, that Hong Kong should be retaken.

Bailey stared at the headline, a take on the Chinese minister's name. Not for the first time he smiled at "Chou Mean."

Glancing at his watch, Bailey walked by the security guard. The man's eyes were fixed on a small television set that was showing an adult movie. Bailey shook his head. Godzilla could have been scampering around in the eight security monitors, and it would have made no difference.

Bailey covered the few paces to the elevator and pressed the button for the fifth floor. He cursed silently as, moments later, he stepped into the small hallway with the door leading into the newsroom of *The London Morning Post*.

As newsrooms went, the *Post's* was modest in size. Nevertheless its occupants considered themselves to have the edge over the city's rival tabs. But that edge had been sadly lacking on this night.

The first edition had carried a worthy but lackluster lead about health service cuts. The headline, "Hellth On Earth," had been dreamed up in an effort to lift the story a bit. But Henderson had been muttering about the big one that was out there and had been clearly missed, not just by the *Post*, but by all the other tabs.

There was always an elusive big one as far as Henderson was concerned. And usually this Holy Grail of front-page spectaculars would be taking form between ten and midnight on a weeknight.

He wasn't always wrong. Throughout a career spanning more than forty years, Henderson had been proven correct in his assertion more times than any other tabloid deskman in London. He was sixty now and entitled to kick back a bit, but his energy for the mega scoops appeared undiminished.

Bailey was not alone in considering Henderson a little mad.

He had passed the lines of reporter's desks and was now standing in the little corral that housed the news editors, the beating heart of the *Post's* corpus.

It was also referred to by several other sobriquets, none of them polite. Right now, as far as Bailey was concerned, it was the rattrap. And he was playing the only rodent in sight. Percy Grace had somehow vanished.

Henderson was eyeballing the rival tabloid first editions. Bailey quickly dismissed their front-page leads from consideration; all but one. This one was trouble.

Henderson had scant time for the royal family. He was the newsroom's nearest thing to a resident republican and was never shy about showing his contempt for the monarchy, though he had sometimes displayed a softer spot for the dearly departed queen mum.

Henderson's antipathy towards matters royal had been attributed by those who cared to his birth in Quebec. Though he was not French Canadian, it was the common view that Henderson had been infected by French Canadian Anglophobia at an early age. Why else, it was asked, would he drink nothing but Cognac and keep a small plaster bust of Napoleon Bonaparte on his desk?

Yes, Henderson was just waiting for a chance to storm Buckingham Palace with a mob in tow and burn the pile to the ground. At the same time, and this was crucial to understanding what made the man tick, he was like a rabid dog when it came to royal stories, the more scandalous the better.

Henderson had the look of a man who had been sent to the newsroom by a kind of journalistic central casting. He was stocky, of middle height, balding and ruddy-faced. His sleeves, as far as Bailey could tell, had never been rolled down. His tie, his only tie, had a crest of a rugby club that had faded into history with the arrival of the professional game.

An older colleague had once told Bailey that Henderson was London's answer to Lou Grant. Bailey had nodded in the affirmative before checking out on his computer who the hell Lou Grant was.

No matter who he was like, or not like, Henderson had sniffed out some of the tabloid world's greatest hits on the royal family. In another time he would have long ago lost his head to the executioner's axe.

The only punishments he had suffered, however, was a dearth of invitations to royal events and a lengthy list of disdainful rebuttals from the palace to the scandals and affairs, some of them undoubtedly true, that he had splashed across the front page.

So here was the problem. It stared back at the glaring Henderson and now it reached out to the reluctant Bailey. *The Sun* had a whopper. One of the young royals, admittedly a second tier member of the family, was seemingly pregnant. And out of arranged wedlock.

The headline was no surprise in itself. It had probably taken a deskman at the rival tab about three seconds to come up with "Princess Preggars." The front page did not name the unfortunate royal. Finding out that gem would require lifting up the paper and turning inside. And that, of course, was a copy sold.

Oh, shit, Bailey thought.

The storm, however, did not follow. Henderson stared at the headline for a few moments and drummed the fingers of both hands on the desk. Then he turned, looked up at Bailey and delivered what passed for one of his rare smiles.

"We might have something better," he said.

Bailey glanced at his watch. Whatever better was it would have to be already in the basket, more or less. Perhaps, he thought, old Percy Grace, the night reporter, and a man who looked like a survivor from the era of Lord Northcliffe, was working on the story this very minute.

Henderson let the moment linger. And then he let it out.

"Friend of mine on the force," he said before pausing.

Oh, Christ, here we go, Bailey thought.

Henderson always referred to the police as the force. Not the plod, peelers coppers or filth. No such disrespect ever poured forth from the man's mouth. He had the utmost respect for the Metropolitan Police. And in fairness, the respect was returned from time to time. He seemed to have an army of sources in the ranks and the result had been occasionally startling.

"Yes," Bailey said, a note of extreme caution in his voice. He had an idea what was coming next. It was something in the way that Henderson was leaning out of his chair towards him.

"A source," Henderson said. "In the force." He seemed pleased with the rhyme.

"Lestrade, perhaps?" Bailey was salvaging a smidgen of pleasure in referring to the bumbling inspector from the Sherlock Holmes stories. But he knew he was cornered.

Henderson ignored the jibe.

"There's a body hanging from Blackfriars Bridge," he said. "A friend of mine, a source, is on the scene. His name is Tim Plaice. Detective Superintendent Tim Plaice."

Bailey was momentarily surprised. Henderson did not usually put names on his sources. But then he understood. He, Nick Bailey, off home in a handful of minutes, was expected to plunge into the fog in search of this Plaice guy so as to lay claim to a body dangling from a bridge over the Thames.

"Somebody topped himself on the bridge," said Bailey flatly. "Happens all the time. Three paragraphs on page nine."

Henderson took in a breath that for a split second sounded like it might be his last.

"Think, Mr. Bailey, for God's sake," he said. "A body on Blackfriars Bridge. Looks like a suicide, but a suspicious policeman has another idea swirling about in his highly attuned head"

"Okay, fine," Bailey said in response, trying not to sound exasperated. "Six or seven pars on page four, no five, right hand page. It's late. There won't be much room for any more than that."

Henderson leaned back. He was closing in for checkmate.

"Not if we ditch the lead, turn it into an inside short, open up the front page and run the new piece onto page two," he said.

"All right," said Bailey giving up. "You have me. What in the name of God is so big about a body hanging from a bridge? People throw themselves off bridges all the time. Bringing along a rope for the ride is a little unusual, I grant you, but not unknown. What are you sitting on?"

Henderson moved his queen, and Bailey, stuck fast and playing the role of cornered king, steeled himself for the *coup de grâce*.

"The deceased is a priest," he said. "And he's hanging off Blackfriars Bridge."

"What?" said Bailey, not bothering to conceal his disbelief. "Stop the bleedin' presses for a pun! Have you been on the sauce?"

Bailey knew full well that Henderson was on nothing at the minute other than the printing ink that flowed through his veins.

"God give me strength." Henderson almost snorted. "Where have you been all these years, Nick? Blackfriars Bridge. Nineteen eighty-two. Roberto Calvi. God's bloody banker."

"Oh," said Bailey. And that was all he could manage.

He suddenly felt very hungry. A vision of hot curried chips. It lingered for a split second before being blown away by Henderson who was now presenting him with a piece of paper with a scribbled headline.

"Nineteen eighty-two," said Bailey. "I was still sucking my thumb. But the name Calvi does ring a bell. There's an Italian restaurant in Chelsea called Calvis I think, or maybe it's West Ken."

Bailey had long ago learned never to admit to total ignorance. Every name rang a bell, especially if it came up in an exchange with Henderson.

Henderson, elbows on his desk and hands clasped, nodded.

"Every name rings a bell in your head, Nick. Think I didn't notice? You hear more bells than Quasimodo. Must be driving you round the bend by now."

Bailey raised his eyes to heaven, or at least the strip lights that burned in the newsroom ceiling around the clock.

"Right," said Henderson, "a quick lesson, so listen. And by the way I won't mind if you call in sick tomorrow night. I do owe you some hours."

"Thanks," said Bailey, though with little enthusiasm.

"Roberto Calvi, God's banker. Found hanging from Blackfriars Bridge, June of that year."

Henderson had launched into one of his famous short hand briefings, the full intake of which was expected of all reporters at the *Post*, regardless of experience and tenure.

"Chairman of Banco Ambrosiano which was in much the same shape at the time as Calvi was after his leap. Huge debts in part due to murky dealings with the Vatican's version of the Bank of England, the Institute for Religious Works. Questions at the time of his death swirled around the Vatican, Mafia, freemasons, dodgy bankers and politicians and anyone in the building brick business."

"The what?" said Bailey.

"Calvi's pockets and pants were stuffed with them. The force figured a suicide, but a few years ago there was a murder trial in Rome. So now you can see it, can't you? A priest dangling from Blackfriars. Chance to pad story from bottom with Calvi business. I'll get Percy to dredge it up. A new head, 'Deadfriars,' or something on those lines. Better lead than health cuts. The taxi is waiting outside. Get something from the scene by one, one thirty at absolute latest, then piss off home."

Bailey glanced at his watch.

"I'll call Percy on my mobile and just read over whatever I can get. He is here somewhere?"

Henderson nodded towards the gents.

"You said your friend's name was Plaice, Detective Superintendent Plaice?"

Henderson nodded again and returned to scanning the rival papers.

Bailey moved quickly towards the door. He looked at his watch again. It was two minutes after midnight. He was walking into a new day.

And, though he did not suspect it, another time.

2

Near Colchester, England, 1606

It was, at long last, only a few minutes before cock-crow.

The night had finally passed. Richard Cole drew the blankets closer about himself. He shivered in the dawn chill.

Cole had wondered if his humors, so troubled these past few months, had given him a fever. But not on this occasion for in what remained of the darkness, it was simply the cold. This, he thought, had to be a blessing of sorts.

Cole had nevertheless passed a very uneasy night. There had been noises, scratching and shuffling under his bed. He had considered investigating but thought better of it. He imagined it might be the spirit of Saint Anselm, a blessed soul to whom he had lately directed a good deal of prayer and beseeching. But the noises had been just a mouse going about his night's work. Cole was finally convinced of this less wondrous truth because he had heard the creature squeak.

Cole was well used to the chill, a constant presence that seeped through the walls and wrapped itself around his bed, a wide four-poster. It had never been a warm house. There was the matter of its elevation. It caught whatever cold air there was about. And the walls, though apparently thick and strong, seemed to part on chilled nights such as the one just now passing. Where once it had disturbed Cole little, the coldness of the room now seemed to clutch at his very heart.

But it hadn't been just the chill that had disturbed Cole's rest. Nor had it been the latest manifestation of what he fervently believed to be his failing health. Rather, it had been his mind turning over and over the expectation of a visit, not from some spectral saint, but a man he had not seen in many years.

Now, in the moments before daybreak, Cole felt a growing anticipation. This, at last, would be the day.

Outside the great house a dog barked. It was followed by a whelping sound. The fox had won, Cole thought. Perhaps it had been a badger.

Inspired momentarily by the activities of warm living things, Cole sat up. He yawned, glanced at the ash pile where the fire had been at his bedtime. He resolved to speak later in the day with the house servant charged with keeping the fire fueled through the night. The knave had clearly fallen asleep and neglected his duty.

Cole thought about slipping under his bed covers again. However cold it was within their embrace, it was a far grimmer prospect without. Nevertheless, he decided to rise and pushing his legs to one side and downwards his stocking feet made contact with the course woolen rug lately donated for his comfort by an old friend.

Cole regarded his legs and feet. It occurred to him that he had not changed his stockings for three days and three nights and that they had all but become part of him. He resolved to put on a new set once the day was advanced enough to permit exposure of his skin.

With a little more purpose, Cole stood and, with a blanket about his shoulders, walked towards the faint glimmer of light that signaled the morning of the fourteenth day of the month.

Cole stood with his face almost touching the window. He pulled his fingertip in a line through the frost covering the inside of the pane. He repeated this with another chilled finger. He brought his face to the glass and stared beyond it. His warm breath only succeeded in clouding the glass and his narrow lines of view once more. So he blew hard again and rubbed the window vigorously with his sleeve. Now he could more easily see the world outside.

The moon, a creamy ball of light, was slipping away to the west. The sky to the east was fast brightening. The sun would soon win its battle with the night. Half a full glass at most and it would be fully light, Cole thought.

"Another day, and where might you be, sir?" he said in a whisper.

Outside, a wispy blanket of mist covered the fields that spanned the half-mile of open ground between the moat surrounding the great house to the boundary wood. Essex still slumbered, though both county and broader England would shortly rise with all the confidence and bluster that was, even Cole would reluctantly admit, the legacy of Elizabeth though not, he was certain, the rightful inheritance of her successor, James.

Cole gazed down the narrow road leading from the front of the house to the point where it met the wider highway to Colchester. It was deserted though some would be out by this hour.

He was conscious now of a bird, a redbreast, which had started to sing in the bush beneath his room. He leaned forward and rubbed against more of the glass, this time with his blanket. Tiny flecks of ice fell to the floor.

In this way he had stood for mornings stretching back almost to the day that the great plot had been discovered and the fate of Fawkes and his fellow patriots sealed. But this morning would be different. The messenger he had sent out in search of the man had brought advance word.

Cole turned and looked back to the bed. The woman lay still and coiled. She made a soft whistling sound as the air escaped her partly opened mouth. Cole stared at her for a moment, but his eyes returned to the window, the open ground, the road and the trees that were just beginning to show signs of awakening from a long winter.

His one-handed grip on the blanket tightened as the pain moved again through his body. He no longer knew where it started. It mattered little anyway. It could find no way out.

The dawn light was beginning to reach the corners of the room. It was a spacious chamber, one that displayed trappings of a prosperous life.

Cole shuffled slowly back to the bed and sat down heavily. He regarded his feet, now numb, and sniffed. The clamor of birds outside was rising. He raised his right hand and pulled his left arm closer to his body.

It would no longer move of its own accord. He would rub some compound into it later. With an effort, he pulled himself back into the bed. The woman stirred. She muttered a few words he could not quite decipher.

She was carrying his child. A child he would never live to see.

Cole had concluded, with no sense of particular fear, resentment or anger that he would be dead by May. His life of forty-six years would be taken by the relentless turbulence in his humors that was, even in the dawn stillness, causing him to press his eyes shut and close his good hand into a fist so tight that his finger bones cracked.

He had seen the signs before, more than once, in the company of his uncle, a leading London physician. Cole took in a slow, deep breath. The pain eased a little.

He turned his head and stared across the room. About twenty paces away, by the wall close to the bedchamber door, there was a writing desk in front of which was a long-backed chair. He watched as the first rays of the sun reached the edge of the desk and began spreading light over its surface.

Cole rose again and shuffled across the island of woven wool to the desk long ago purchased by his father, a man who had taken as great an interest in business and profit as had his own brother in the medicinal arts.

The room had once been a library and scriptorium before being adapted to its present function and the desk was well used. There were scratches in abundance and in one or two places previous users had carved signs and letters.

Cole eased himself into the chair. A carved figure of the sun with a smiling face adorned the apex of the chair's back. Cole reached for a calamus and dipped it into a small wooden jug full of ink. There was paper in abundance and he began to scratch out words on a page. He was close now to finishing the document and for that he gave silent thanks to God. His eyes passed over the neatly arranged pile of pages written yesterday, the day before, and the days before that.

Together, they amounted to what he believed was a most judicious indictment of James, the man who called himself king. The tract would conclude with a reasoned justification for the king's abdication or, if necessary, death at the hands of noble and patriotic Englishmen loyal to the true, mother church.

The tract was intended for publication and dissemination only when James was removed from the throne. Cole felt he had more than justified in his writing what would be nothing less than a revolution. He had summoned all his power with words to join together the strands of argument that would surely convince England's nobility that the kingdom's rightful destiny was to be found by following the path laid down by the Church of Rome.

This he believed with his heart, his soul; his very life. Others believed it too and one among them, the man who would carry the plan to its fruition, was close, very close, perhaps even now riding over the last miles to the house that stood where once a Norman keep, and before it a Saxon fort, had held sway over the fields and fens of this corner of Essex.

Cole, lost in thought of what would soon reshape England's destiny, did not immediately notice the knock on the door. But the woman, now sitting up in the bed, coughed. He turned his head. The door opened slowly and the boy from the stables pushed his head into the room.

"A horseman, my lord, on the Colchester road."

Cole dismissed the child with a nod. With a nimbleness that caused him some surprise he rose from the chair and made again for the window.

Indeed there was a man, though not on a horse. He was walking his mount slowly towards the house. Cole recognized immediately the man's height, the purposeful, certain stride.

"Christ and his virgin mother be praised," he said.

"Richard." The woman said no more. But her complaint was clear. Cole ignored her nevertheless.

He clapped his hands together in delight and stared intently at the approaching figure, his feet lost in ground fog. The rising sun was casting light on the man. It seemed to Cole as if the light was bursting forth from his very body. It seemed as if this man was the Messiah himself.

Cole bowed his head. More quietly now he spoke lest he disturb the woman who seemed to have returned to her slumbers. He did not care a whit how he spoke in her presence. But lately he had to consider other matters, one of them being that she was carrying his child.

"Thy will be done," he said. And he repeated the incantation until he heard the noise from the horse's hooves as it walked across the drawbridge.

3

THE TAXICAB MOVED EASILY through the mostly deserted streets that crisscrossed the expanse of London between the *Morning Post* building and Blackfriars Bridge.

Bailey had kept his counsel for the first few minutes of the ride. He wanted to see if the cab driver was the chatty or silent type. He was the latter. He was also Sikh, young and, by dint of the few words he had uttered in response to Bailey's initial directions, more Putney than Punjab.

At roughly half way in the journey, Bailey probed with a comment on the weather. The driver responded. By the time they were on the last stretch before Blackfriars, the two men were holding a sparse conversation on the thorny issue of relations between India and Pakistan, the problem of Kashmir and the desire, still kept alive by some Sikhs, for a homeland.

Bailey's knowledge of India and Pakistan was accidental. It was a byproduct of his interest in cricket. Still, he gave the driver his silent grade. An A.

"I work for the *Morning Post*," he said.

"I know; that's where I picked you up," the driver replied.

"Here's my card," said Bailey. "You're on the town and all over the town. Ever come across anything you think might be of interest do me a favor and give me a bell. There might be a few quid in it for you."

"No need for money," the driver replied. "If I come across anything of interest I'll call."

Misplaced bleeding pride, Bailey thought.

The cab pulled up at the end of the bridge that reached the north bank of the Thames.

"This will do fine, said Bailey. I think I can just about see them. I can walk from here."

Bailey paid the driver and added a generous tip. He made a mental note to pad his expenses accordingly.

"Have a good night, my friend," he said as he stepped out of the taxi and on to the damp pavement.

The driver nodded and drove off. Within a couple of seconds the cab's tail lights had been sucked in by the fog.

Bailey pulled the collar of his inadequate coat up as high as it would go and began to walk across the bridge. Traffic, what there was of it, was moving both ways on the far side. The police had closed the southbound lanes.

Several vehicles were lined up along the closed stretch, a couple of them with flashing emergency lights that sent darts of light into the fog, a pea-souper that seemed to be drawing endless replenishment from the waters of the river.

Bailey reached into his coat pocket for his press pass. A young woman constable stood between him and the center of activity that, Bailey concluded, had passed its peak. An ambulance was pulling slowly away, presumably with the body.

"Evening all," said Bailey. It was a little joke, a line from a long ago police drama on the BBC. The young officer didn't seem to get it.

"Nick Bailey from the *Morning Post*. DS Plaice is expecting me," he said.

The constable looked doubtful. "Wait here," she said. And by way of rein-forcement, "Don't move."

She walked to the rear of the yellow tape crime scene line that was now holding back a crowd of precisely one. Bailey lifted his watch. He had enough time to get over his story. It had better be up to snuff, he thought.

The constable was now talking to a tall man in a green raincoat with a rather incongruous looking baseball hat on his head. She turned and walked briskly back to the crime scene line.

"Go ahead sir," she said.

Her formality was a good sign. He was being taken seriously.

He stepped over the tape and walked purposely towards the small knot of officers huddled in what was an abutment that broke up the otherwise lin-ear aspect of the bridge. There were a number of them spaced out at intervals where the supports of the bridge reached up from the ooze at the bottom of the Thames.

"DS Plaice?" said Bailey from a distance of a few feet.

The tall man turned. Bailey extended his hand. The gesture was returned.

"Henderson said you might have something of interest for us," Bailey said. "And given the fact that a detective superintendent has stepped out on a night like this I imagine that it is interesting indeed."

Bailey half-smiled. He was pushing a bit but was determined not to walk away with stuff that he could have picked up on the phone.

"First of all," Plaice replied, "the ground rules. No attributions, no names. Make it look as if you just happened on this business by way of a random check. And do me a favor, also make it look as if the story was written in the office, not based on what you see here. Not that there's very much at this point anyway."

Plaice was about his business for sure, Bailey thought. Knew how to handle the press. No bullshit, straight to the point.

"No problem with that, Superintendent. Half the story has already been written in the office anyway. All the Calvi stuff and I'll bet a few lines on the history of the bridge."

"Come over here," Plaice said.

The two men walked over to the stone wall beyond which was a straight drop to the water.

"Right now we're simply treating this death as suspicious. It looks like a suicide at first glance, but given what happened here before, we're keeping an open mind."

"Why so?" said Bailey.

Plaice turned to face Bailey, rammed his hands into his pockets and pulled his shoulders forward.

"I wasn't particularly au fait with the Calvi affair," he said.

"It was a long time ago. I was just out of the army and new on the force, more concerned with getting little old ladies across pedestrian crossings in one piece than with international intrigue."

Bailey nodded and Plaice smiled, clearly seeing himself for a moment again in his early days as a green young copper.

"But I had to do some pretty quick homework tonight. Thank the gods for computers. No doubt it makes your job a lot easier."

Bailey was paying closer attention. Plaice was drawing some link between the Calvi business and the death just a few feet from where they were standing and only a short while before. This might be something, he thought.

"I hadn't put two and two together but one of my sergeants mentioned Calvi and Blackfriars, the manner of his death and the apparent way in which the man died here tonight."

Hanging from the bridge. Maybe with stones in his pockets, Bailey thought. He wasn't going to interrupt the man now.

"By the way," said Plaice. "How well do you know Henderson?"

Bailey was a little taken aback by the question. Plaice was clearly checking himself, considering how much he should give this emissary from his newspaper friend. Or maybe Henderson was just an acquaintance.

"Well," said Bailey, not quite sure how to handle the question. "We've had our differences. But I think we see eye to eye most times. And he does seem to send me out on big stories. Like this one."

Bailey's tone was that of the supplicant. Plaice was checking him out. He might throw him a line and only that. Or he might let him in on something that would only be imparted here, on the bridge, face to face and not over the line by some faceless press officer to an equally indistinct reporter.

Bailey took a chance. "He was priest," he said. And then by way of a not so subtle addendum. "Henderson told me."

"Yes," said Plaice. "Yes, a priest. Are you Catholic?"

"Not much of anything," the journalist replied. "My mum and dad used go to a little church, one of those gospel places, but it didn't much rub off on me I'm afraid. I guess I'm a bit of a heathen."

Plaice seemed not to hear.

"It doesn't make much sense," he said. "Priests don't commit suicide, or at least it's such a rare event as to be extraordinary. It was a mortal sin for Roman Catholics, you know, not anymore though. The church realizes now that someone who takes their own life really isn't capable of sinning. So this really doesn't add up at first glance."

"You Catholic yourself, then?" said Bailey, sensing that he had Plaice going somewhere, though he could not quite figure out where.

Plaice pulled himself back.

"My faith isn't the issue here," he said. "His fate is what it's all about," he added glancing at the ambulance which was now turning off the far end of the bridge, lights on, siren off.

Bailey silently cursed. He wasn't going to get a look at the body now. It did not matter for the literal telling of the story so much as the sense of it that he would hold in his mind for a possible follow up; an interview with family members perhaps.

"How do you know Henderson?"

Bailey felt the rapport with Plaice, if there had been any to begin with, slipping a bit. Henderson, for want of someone, or something, better, seemed to be the common ground between them, something to warm up the descending chill.

Bailey knew from experience that the relationship between the police and the press was far from being a love affair. Each needed the other and would use the other to the utmost if the circumstances demanded. Other than that there was a wariness bordering on outright mistrust and occasional hostility.

And then there was the matter of the type of paper and the type of copper. Some of the higher ranks were tabloid inclined, while others were serious broadsheet sorts. Plaice didn't seem to fit either category.

"We were in the army together," Plaice said.

"Well now, that's a surprise. Henderson never mentioned the fact that he served queen and country," Bailey replied.

He hoped that Plaice had failed to detect the now bubbling curiosity in his response. The fact that Henderson had once worn army uniform was genuine news. Bailey wondered if anyone else in the newsroom knew, because Henderson had never mentioned it. And for sure never came across as a military type. He didn't seem quite organized enough.

"Which regiment?" said Bailey. But before there was any reply, a detective who had been standing nearby suddenly sprang to life.

"Excuse me a moment," Plaice said. He turned and walked over to the subaltern. The two men huddled and spoke in low tones. Bailey tried to catch what they were saying but even the still, damp air failed to carry the substance or even sense of what the two men were talking about.

Bailey looked both ways, up and down the river. Somewhere a clock chimed and, almost in unison, his stomach growled. He had not eaten for hours. He thought of smoking a cigarette, but thought better of it. Some people took offense. Lestrade here might be one of them.

Plaice returned to where Bailey was contemplating his longed for curried chips.

"Well, this is what we've got that we can give you," he said.

"We can't release his name right away until we are sure all his family has been informed. But you know that. He's a priest all right, Roman Catholic. A member of a rather small and obscure order called the Order of Saint Anselm."

Bailey's eyes narrowed. "Never heard of them," he said.

"Neither have I," Plaice replied. "I had someone back at the office look them up. They are an English order, founded in the early seventeenth century. A bit of a hard bunch, Jesuits with an extra edge, my man described them.

But there's hardly any of them left, no more than a couple of dozen, maybe fewer than that."

"Where do they hang out? Do they have a monastery or something like that?"

Plaice folded his arms and looked at his shoes. "Essex," he said. "Near Colchester, some big old Tudor pile. Seems they managed to hang on to the place when their brethren were being kicked out of everywhere else. Apparently they didn't let on what they were and managed to keep below the radar even during the Cromwell years. That's about it, really."

"Was this guy based in Essex?"

"No," said Plaice quickly. "He was actually working at a parish just a few miles from here, south side of the river. Saint something or other."

Bailey raised his watch close to his eyes and hit the light button. His sight, he thought, must be fading because he was doing this more and more of late. Too much damn time in front of computers.

"Well, that's not bad at all, Superintendent," he said. "Henderson will be happy; mysterious order of near extinct priests and now one less of them. 'Deadfriars' might be the headline on this one. You wouldn't mind if I sit in one of your cars to send the story over my mobile? I'm freezing."

"Not at all, go ahead," Plaice replied. "'Deadfriars.' Not bad. And absolutely appropriate in the literal sense, too. It's a play on the bridge's name, I assume."

"Bingo," said Bailey.

Plaice stared straight at Bailey in a way the reporter could not ignore.

"Well, it's less a play and more the literal truth," he said.

"What do you mean?" Bailey said.

"This reverend, the one who did a Calvi tonight. I'm not saying he was murdered. We're still working on suicide."

Plaice paused.

"Yes?" Bailey said invitingly.

"He's not the only one."

"What?"

"Our dead Padre is not the only member of his order to meet his maker recently. There was another one, a couple of months back. Looked like a suicide for sure but two priestly suicides in a short space of time, same order. You're the reporter, work on that one."

Plaice had a slight grin on his face now. He had the sense that if he asked Bailey to jump in the river for another installment the reporter might just make a move for the parapet.

Bailey snatched the cigarettes from his pocket and pulled one from the pocket. "Smoke?" he said, offering one to the man who had just handed him a chance at the Henderson hall of fame.

4

A LITTLE OVER FOUR HUNDRED MILES to the north west of Blackfriars Bridge, a man who knew a thing or two about big stories was savoring at close hand the power of the Atlantic Ocean.

He had checked the light, estimated the wind speed and, as best he could, the time lapse before the next squall.

The man decided that the light was his most immediate concern. It was changing so rapidly that taking the right shot would be mostly luck, regardless of the sophistication of the equipment he had balanced precariously on the stony shingle.

It was, he decided, all rather exquisite. If only it wasn't so damn bone chilling.

He pulled aside the waterproof cover and placed his right eye to the viewfinder. Through it he stared intently at the plumes of spray being blown off the tops of the waves. The rollers were six or seven feet at least, despite the sheltering headland at the northern end of the bay and the great mountain looming over its southern approaches.

He closed his right hand into a little ball in an effort to restore some feeling to its extremities. He slowly wrapped his fingers around the trigger and squeezed his forefinger lightly against it.

The Leicaflex whizzed and clicked.

Steven Pender raised himself. He was in better physical shape than he had been in months, but his back protested. He looked to his left and right, taking in both ends of the deserted stone beach. Had he the advantage of a gull's eye view he would have seen a spit of land not unlike a cocked thumb. He was standing at the end of it, where the stones and shingle fell into the bay.

Pender fired off the camera a few more times to bring his day's work to a close. He well understood that all his efforts might be for naught. The difference between good and outstanding was not really in his hands on a day like this.

He had lodged his backpack and camera bag behind an outcrop of rocks about a hundred yards back down the beach. Folding his arms about the tripod and nestling the camera under his chin, Pender began to make his way back to the rocks. They seemed to be miles away. His mind wandered ahead of his feet. It embraced memories of Africa and the steamy heat that had made him dream longingly about places like this: the Lake District, the Shetland Islands, west of Ireland. Somewhere in the world, he thought, there just had to be a happy medium.

Pender reached the rocks and slumped against the largest of them. It offered some protection from the wind though not the rain, now more intense than the earlier drizzle. Pender tucked his head as deeply into his upturned collar as he possibly could and corkscrewed his rear end into the stones.

Every fraction of an inch counted. Quickly, and expertly, despite his numbed hands, he broke down the tripod, packed the camera into its bag and pulled both backpack and bag to each side of him. He was facing inwards, towards the land. The alternating shadows and shards of light raced over the shoreline on the far side of the channel, upwards over the stone walled fields and beyond them up the bare slopes of the mountain.

Pender scanned the channel's landside beach, a sandier affair than the one on which he was huddled. His eyes rested at the point where the path began. It snaked its way through rocky outcrops before ending abruptly at a line of stunted trees, the grizzled sentinels marking out the garden.

He narrowed his eyes against the wetness and could just about make out the house. The lights were on. Or at least one was, in the living room, the one with the big window.

Pender picked up a gray colored stone about the size of his palm and turned it over. It would probably be still here a hundred years from now, he thought.

He tried to keep his thoughts focused on the stone, a simple thing. But it was useless of course. Jonas Sem was close by, his body all twisted and bloodied.

They had taken no chances with Sem. At least half a dozen AK47 magazines had been unloaded into the room. It was as if the bastards were trying to kill the entire building.

Pender's photos of the assassinated rebel leader had been sensational. Not surprising since the man's blood was still flowing when he had taken them. The shots had appeared in just about every significant newspaper and magazine on the planet. They had sealed his growing reputation as the man who got the big ones.

Prizes and awards had followed. Someone else always had to collect the bronze cameras and framed certificates on his behalf, because Pender was invariably lost in some war-crazed hellhole, daily witnessing death so seemingly casual that it had become just that.

Sem had been the start of the casual phase. He had no regrets. The bastard had died too quickly, really. And his death had probably saved hundreds of lives, maybe thousands. It had been a good thing. So why was he thinking of it again now? Here in this rain purified place.

Pender shivered, stood up, gathered his gear and began to walk back to the house. Fifteen minutes later he stood in the doorway gazing into the main room of the cottage.

There was no sight or sound of Manning. He had, Pender remembered, mentioned something about a walk up the mountain. And they laughed at mad dogs and Englishmen, he thought.

Figuring that he had a few minutes to himself, Pender walked straight to the writing desk against the far wall. Manning kept a diary. Over the past couple of nights Pender had noticed that the last thing that the Irishman did before bed was to write for about three or four minutes in a leather-bound journal.

Pender flicked through the pages. Most of them referred to mundane events in Washington. There were, as was to be expected, frequent references to his host's wife and daughter and several to his work at the embassy. The first secretary and political officer at the Irish Embassy was, by dint of his own words, clearly a little restless. Promotion to ambassadorial level, it seemed, had not quite come quickly enough.

Pender opened the pages for the last couple of days. Manning referred to his presence in the house, but there was no indication as to how he felt about his English guest. No criticism, no praise, no pithy observation. Perhaps he expected his visitor to spy. There was, at various points in the diary, mention of a man named Michael who appeared to be linked to the cottage in some way. Pender had met no one else since his arrival. He rubbed his palm over his chin as his eyes fixed on the stranger's name. He needed a shave.

Pender closed the diary and placed it back exactly as he had found it. He had noted that it had been placed with the text facing out from the desk, so upside down from his perspective. It might have been nothing, but he had employed tricks himself from time to time when he wanted to be sure that eyes were not prying. One of them was to place an object at a particular angle, or in a specific position relative to others.

He walked across the room to the wall that served as a picture gallery. Here there were several dozen framed photographs arranged in what appeared to be chronological order, oldest on the left and most recent on the right. This had been only one aspect of the overall order and neatness that Pender had observed seconds after his arrival in the cottage. But he also had the sense that it was someone else's order. Manning's late father.

The oldest photographs were of Victorian ladies and gentlemen staring at the lens as if it were the barrel of a gun. There were several of soldiers dressed in British uniform, the bellhop variety. They were from the ranks though one appeared to have been a junior officer. Moving to the right, Pender crossed the threshold of the twentieth century.

One of pictures was of a group posing with an early model automobile. And then there were more uniforms, a couple still British but several of stern young men in the dress of the Irish Republican Brotherhood.

Before he was posted to Northern Ireland, a time when the place could dish up dramatic photos as if on a conveyor belt, Pender had taken a crash course in Irish history. It served him well now as he could distinguish between the IRB boys and a lone member of the Irish Citizen Army.

The photos to the right of the soldiers were all of civilians, family groups and the occasional individual. There were three photos of a man in barrister garb. The father. Pender knew of him, or at least of him. Manning senior had been famous, or infamous, for his ability to get IRA men off the hook, even in the non-jury special court in Dublin. His death, fortunately for many of his likely future clients, had come after, and not before, the Provo ceasefire.

Pender's version of a sixth sense told him that something had changed in the room. He turned and stiffened. A man was standing in the door, an old man. He was bareheaded and wore no coat. He looked at least eighty though he had a thick and wavy head of white hair.

But it was the eyes that Pender was drawn to. They did not betray age. They were a grayish-blue and not in the least bit inquisitive.

"You must be Michael," Pender said with a half smile. The old man said nothing. The nod was barely discernible. The old man was carrying a couple of plastic bags. He turned, and with surprisingly agile steps, went into the adjoining kitchen. Pender glanced at his watch. It was a few minutes shy of four thirty. The old man had apparently brought dinner and, from the banging of pots now coming from the kitchen, was also intending to cook it.

"Splendid," Pender said to himself. "A batman for the old legal eagle."

He decided to pour himself a small whiskey to warm up his damp bones. This entailed stepping into the kitchen and retrieving both the bottle and a glass from an old pine dresser.

"I was down on the beach taking photographs and the damp went right through me," Pender said by way of making conversation.

The old man was holding potatoes under a thin stream of water flowing from the faucet and scrubbing them with bony hands.

"I'm going to have a drop; fancy one yourself?"

"Later," said the old man.

There was no arguing.

Pender was determined not to retreat. A high stool was backed up against the wall at the opposite end of the narrow kitchen from where the old man stood.

Pender poured himself a generous measure of whiskey. He reached into the ancient refrigerator's icebox and chipped out a couple of cubes. He sat on the stool and watched the old man who was now cutting up a thick piece of steak he had taken from one of the plastic bags.

"Making an Irish stew?" said Pender.

The old man was cutting the steak into squares. "Just a stew," he said.

Pender stared into his glass.

"Eamonn must have gone for a walk up the mountain," he said.

"Mr. Manning likes his walks," the old man replied, more quickly this time.

The old man was cracking a bit, Pender thought.

"I suppose his father liked to walk the mountain as well," he said.

"Did," came the reply.

That was about it. The old man made a fuss of digging out a large cooking pot from the space below the sink.

Pender decided to retreat into the living room. He stood and considered the kind of job he had been given. If it required the use of a diplomat based in Washington he imagined that his target would be either political or diplomatic; hopefully not his host but, of course, what could one do if it was?

Then again, it might be a business type. Diplos met all sorts of people. Manning would more likely be the means of access and introduction, the Trojan Horse.

Would the horse have to be disposed of at the end of the operation? He stared intently at his hand holding the glass. Not a tremor. The liquid was absolutely still. He was curious as to what was coming next. But for now he would just relax and enjoy a little Irish hospitality.

5

MANNING STARED THROUGH THE WINDOW. His guest was somewhere out in the murk. The ambassador had asked him to entertain Pender. And so he had, for two long days.

It wasn't that Pender was dull, or uneasy company. But Manning had not flown the Atlantic to socialize.

He had planned the visit to the house for months. It was to be a final immersion in his father's private space before the place was put on the market. But it hadn't been so simple. He had been foolish to think that simply because of his father's death the old man's presence would somehow evaporate. Adjourning to the town and considering matters from the safe distance of a hotel would have been an alternative.

But now there was Pender, lost somewhere below in the gloom.

Still, Manning thought, his guest would be gone tomorrow and he could manage to wangle another couple of days leave from the embassy, time enough to make final plans. And besides, there was the sudden complication. The thought of it made him look again at his watch. What the hell did they want now?

He tried to clear his mind by thinking of other things, of Rebecca, Jessica, even work at the embassy. But he had found solace only by turning his mind back, to his father, here in this place, and earlier still to the boarding school in the midlands, the one with the farm, ivy covered walls and scholar monks who were either three quarters genius, or two thirds mad.

The place had been his home for six years. There had been days of late when he wanted to be back there, closeted behind the muscular traditions and the embracing certainty of history essays and Latin preparation.

But thoughts of schools days had faded, and Manning was again staring out of the window towards the bay and its hidden islands and islets.

His hands were in his pockets. His father would have scolded him.

Hands were tools, weapons, Joe Manning would have said. You could turn a jury, sometimes even a judge, with the proper use of hands.

A sudden flash of sunlight banished thoughts of the father and focused the son's eyes on the world outside. One by one, the islands in the bay below the house were popping into view. The squall, easing now, had been the heaviest of the day. It had unleashed itself over the bay, smacking its turreted edges with great sheets of water. But now the rain had galloped inland and was soaking the upland bogs and walled fields of Mayo's wild interior.

A wood pigeon glided across the lawn on a collision course with the hedge. Just before the crash, the bird's wings began to flap furiously. It rose over the top before dropping down the far side. Flying away and vanishing had its merits, Manning thought.

He walked around the pine dining table that doubled as a work desk and sat himself down. His tea, stewing away in the chipped mug, was still warm. He picked up the cup and swallowed a gulp of the stuff. His eyes rested on the table and the assortment of items that were the afternoon's primary concern.

Before him, neatly arrayed, was a stack of papers, a leather-bound diary, a radio with short wave capabilities, Japanese make, and a pistol.

It was an old gun, a Browning of considerable vintage but still in good working order. His father had taken good care of the weapon. The wily senior counsel, friend of the politically oppressed, one side anyway, had his enemies. He was presumed to be a target for loyalists from the North. This had been his personal protection firearm though Manning had been unable to find a permit.

The gun's presence in the house had been a secret for all the years that his father had used the place as his refuge. Not that there had ever been much chance of someone finding it. Old Joe had kept even his law library cronies at a distance. The house was his world and his alone. His mother had only been in it about three times in their entire marriage.

About three days before his death, Joe had muttered something about hidden treasure under the floorboards. Manning had only to rummage for a few minutes to find it. There were four bullets. It was hardly much of an arsenal, but Manning well remembered the times when his father's life had been threatened and he had gone to bed only after spending endless minutes staring out his bedroom window into the darkness. More often than not, a police car was stationed on the street outside the house. But the fear remained. It had been the price for his father getting so many hard men on one side off.

Manning fingered through the papers and letters, looked again at his watch. He took a pencil in hand but just as quickly put it down. The clock chimed. It was two o'clock. His appointment, if it could be described as such, was at three. The bastard could wait in the rain, he thought.

He sat back in the rickety chair and swallowed another mouthful of tea. Would he miss the place if he went ahead and sold it? Sure he would. But he had never quite felt that it belonged to him. Even now, with his father gone, it could never be really his, or his mother's. It would always be Joe's retreat, or the hiding place of a complete stranger, someone who could start from scratch and, like his father, invest an entirely new thirty years of contemplation, scheming and late night solitary tippling behind its foot-and-a-half thick walls.

Manning shivered. He rose from his chair and stretched out his arms. On wet days such as this, he always felt his bones shrink a bit. It was the inescapable bloody damp. He walked the few paces to the fireplace. The turf fire in the iron grate was in need of immediate replenishment.

Dropping to his knees, he took a sod from the basket and threw it on the still glowing ash. He loved the smell of burning turf.

He grabbed a second sod and threw it on to the now reviving fire. A cloud of turf dust exploded in the grate and an ember reached his eye. In the few moments of pain he was back in history class, final year in school and old Clinch rambling on about the Fenians and Pearse. The teachers who marked the exams were all patriots, he said. They all spelled their names in Irish and wanted to see good students pay homage to Ireland's martyred dead. He had laughed at Clinch, they all had. But, as it later turned out, neither the martyrs nor their propagandists were to be so easily dismissed.

He got up and stepped slowly along the wall crowded with the framed photographs, old Joe's hall of family fame.

Long dead relatives stared at him from their formal poses. One was dressed in a uniform, British army. He was a family legend from his mother's side, a token amid all the Manning greats. Great Uncle Willie. Lost up the Khyber Pass. Dead at the hands of the Pathans. Never seen again. But mentioned in dispatches. Brave Uncle Willie.

Uncle Willie stared down at Manning. Manning stared back. God bless Uncle Willie, he thought. Died for king and country, they had said. But really, as his father has never failed to point out, it had been the king of another country. He needed air. He covered the few steps to the door and pulled down his father's battered Barbour coat. Even at close to six feet tall and over 200 pounds, Manning still swam in the rainproof. His father had been larger than life, and large in it.

Throwing on the coat, he opened the door and stepped into the drizzle. He sucked down a deep gulp of saturated air and zipped up the Barbour as far as it would go. He would walk up the mountain, find out what they wanted and tell them to go to hell. Get it over and done with, see Pender off in the morning and make his final decision on the house. It was simple, really.

Then he saw her again.

Manning had been unable to sleep much despite the cool evenings and the ocean air. He had remained awake into the early hours thinking of his father, dearly departed, more or less, a year now.

But it wasn't just that. There was the matter of the young woman, her smile, her puzzlement, the question in her eyes, the moment of absolute realization. And there she was now, standing by the gate, waiting for him, smiling.

She watched Manning as he hunched his shoulders. He did his best to ignore the apparition but slowly turned his eyes. She smiled, looked puzzled, concerned and then fixed him with the question. Manning rubbed his fingers into his eyes and stamped his feet. She was gone. He comforted himself with the thought that at least the ghost, memory, vision or whatever it was, was confined to his native soil. She, it, had made no appearances in Washington. No visa, he thought, and laughed out loud.

He covered the few steps to the rusty gate and pulled it open. To the left, the stone pocked lane ran down the hill to a point where it met asphalt. To the right, it became narrower as it cut through a run of fields surrounded by stone walls before giving way to heather and tussock covered upland and the upper reaches of the mountain.

Manning turned right and walked past dripping fuchsia and hawthorn bushes towards the mountain track. One more day, maybe two, and he would head back to Dublin, stay with his mother for a night and catch a flight back to the States. There was no need to consider any longer. He had a wife, child and career to take care of. What was past was past.

As if to confirm the soundness of his plan, Manning quickened his pace. The thicker vegetation gave way to open pasture in which a few soaked sheep nibbled at grass that was already reduced almost to the roots. His father had often lectured the idiotic animals on the evils of overgrazing and had complained of the negligence of farmers who seemed more phantom around these parts than human flesh.

These hills had been his father's personal court, nature his judge and jury. As a younger man, a boy, Manning had, on those rare visits that included his mother, walked behind the great man as he jabbed his finger at a meandering seagull or scampering rabbit.

Not a few cases had been won in court with arguments perfected on walks from the house to the top of the mountain and back. Manning could hear his father now, loquacious even in his isolation, hammering home the final nails into the prosecution's coffin as twelve angry rabbits looked on from a safe distance.

Manning made quick time up the slope. He was in his early forties but that, he would remind himself almost daily, was merely his extra late thirties. He still managed to get up a head of steam over the last half mile of his twice-weekly five-mile run. And now he was pumping his arms and pushing against the stony track with quads honed hard on muddy football fields. He could still do it, he thought, the mountain in one continuous stretch, no rest stops.

He was close now to the top and paused only momentarily at the flat rock that topped the Hag's Tailbone, a slope that fell about a hundred feet and then curved upwards briefly only to give way to nothing but air and a straight plunge to a jumble of rocks another three hundred feet below, rocks that had been in place since the death throes of the last ice age.

The track turned to the left and was now a clearly visible strip of trammeled earth leading all the way to the summit, its rock pile and the small white wooden cross that was painted every summer, and replaced every four or five, for as long as any of the locals could remember.

Manning poured it on. His heart was doing double time. But this was good, a needed purgative. His father would have approved of the tempo, if not the silence of the climber.

A final few yards, a last push and he had reached the summit. This was not a high mountain by world standards. It looked big because it rose its almost 2,000 feet starting from sea level. Its summit afforded an uninterrupted view north to the bay and the distant town, south towards Galway, east towards the uplands of Mayo and west, well, west was America, his home for almost two years, and at least a couple more.

It was on this piece of ground that Manning had once stood motionless and at rapt attention as his father recited, word for word, Robert Emmett's speech from the dock, only to follow it with the Gettysburg Address and the best lines from Kennedy's inauguration speech.

The last time they had been together here, Joe Manning had spoken of history. Consider, he had said, if the theory about the butterfly flapping its wings on one side of the world and causing a hurricane on the other was applied to history. Consider an action in one century and its possible effects in another. What if someone had been in the book depository and had disarmed Oswald? What if someone had shot Hitler dead in Munich? The key thing, he had said, was in the knowing that someone, or something, was destined to have significant historical ramifications. You had to spot history's titans while still in chrysalis form.

"And then what?" the son had asked the father.

"Just get out of the bloody way," his father had replied.

The son's mind had wandered just as it was doing now as a cloud rolled in from the ocean and wrapped itself around the summit. Manning wanted to believe that this moisture on his face was a gift from nature, but he could not for long ignore his tears. He had held it in for all the months. But they were coming freely now, his very own Atlantic squall.

Manning allowed himself the release though he knew that not all his tears were for his father. He bowed his head and quickly rubbed his eyes dry when he heard the cheerful salutation from behind him.

He glanced over his shoulder. The bent figure of the man was traversing the last few meters of the mountain's south slope.

Looking north again and down towards the house, Manning could just about make out another figure approaching the garden gate. Pender.

He lifted his eyes and stared at the horizon, visible again after the shower.

But if one squall had passed another was about to hit. This one, he knew, would not be born over an ocean, though it would most assuredly spring from a sea of troubles.

6

NICK BAILEY WAS EARLY AT HIS DESK, earlier than he could remember, earlier than anyone in the newsroom who noticed cared to remember.

Bailey was not known for precise time keeping. The news editors would have little bets as to whether or not he would show up in this fifteen-minute interval or the next. Nick Bailey didn't quite fit into the *Post's* ordered shift system. But he was a good reporter, good enough for his tardiness to be tolerated, more or less.

His presence at such an unusual hour naturally raised a few eyebrows. And Trevor Worth was the one colleague who moved rapidly beyond facial expression and asked questions.

Worth, after all, was Bailey's mate. Which is to say they shared cigarettes.

Worth opened his probe with a suggestion that Bailey must be hiding from either a woman demanding his body, or the landlord demanding the rent. Bailey countered with a few seconds of silence. His eyes leaned closer to his computer screen.

"Sod off, Trev," he said, punching the keys harder still with his forefingers.

Worth tried another tack.

"Nice lead this morning Nick. Must have sold a bundle."

This was true, Bailey thought. He had taken his usual underground train, though at the now record earlier hour. This presented an opportunity to check out his fellow tube riders.

A rough survey of their newspapers gave up a dominant combination of the *Sun's* royal rubbish, a *Mirror* lead on a drunken soccer star, and the *Post's* Deadfriars exclusive.

And it was indeed such a thing. Bailey scanned the few remaining broadsheet titles and noticed nothing that would take away from the fact that the *Post,* and more importantly he himself, had actually bagged a good one.

The text of the story ran on page five. Bailey's top was propped up by Henderson's background material on the Calvi affair.

There were, in addition, a couple of paragraphs at the bottom giving something of the history of Blackfriars Bridge. *Post* readers had been offered the intriguing fact that the bridge had been given a cameo mention by H.G. Wells in *The War of the Worlds*. This little gem was Percy's contribution. And given that he was the last reporter to handle the story there had been nothing to stop him from slipping in a byline for good measure.

And this he had done, the old codger.

"So why are you here now?" said Worth.

Bailey leaned back in his chair. He had slept little and was feeling the effect. Still, what the inspector had told him was more than enough for a follow up. Bailey had allowed his imagination to run a bit. He had started dreaming up all manner of conspiracies that would lead to a string of front-page exclusives. But Trevor Worth had shattered the moment.

"If I tell you I'll have to kill you," said Bailey. "But if you get me a coffee, maybe I'll tell you and yet spare your miserable life."

"On it. Crude or refined?"

Nobody in the newsroom had quite worked out the mystery of the office coffee. Either some small furry creature had upped and died in the coffee machine, or it was simply the London tap water, already consumed too many times over and recycled before it hit the bottom of a *Morning Post* coffee mug.

"Crude mate," said Bailey. "Like one of your better jokes."

Worth went off to carry out his mission. Bailey stared at his screen. Plaice had said that he would have a name on the dead priest for tomorrow's edition. But it would naturally go out to everyone else through normal channels.

The other death was still a mystery. And still his if he had read Plaice correctly. He wasn't all the way to linking the demise of one priest in London and another down in the sticks. There was a possible tie-in, but Plaice was a long way from being certain. He had suggested to Bailey that what information he had, and what he could add to it today, would be his to run with for a day or two.

There was nothing certain, nothing openly stated. But Plaice, and Bailey was certain of this, was clearly forming the idea in his mind that there was a connection between the two dead padres.

"Coffee's up." Worth had returned with reinforcements. Deb Smith and Charlie Chilton grabbed chairs and crowded around.

"Nick pulling a late one and up with the lark. Have they tested you for banned substances?"

"Only the coffee, Charlie," Bailey replied.

Deb Smith said nothing but stared at Bailey with a slightly amused look. Bailey was certain, or thought he was, that she fancied him. But he was off the ladies for the moment. That moment being all of two weeks since his last relationship floundered, rather publicly, in a Chinese restaurant.

"Look, everybody," said Bailey, "I appreciate the congratulations and all that but really there's nothing much else to tell right now. The best part of the whole bloody story was the Calvi bit. Right now we've got some old monk who had a bad day, an even lousier night and somewhere along the line a severe lapse in faith. It might be a three par follow up tomorrow morning and nothing more than that, right?"

Nobody said a word. Charlie Chilton saw a light flashing on his phone and was fast out of his seat. Deb Smith folded her arms and kicked her feet out. Trevor Worth asked him for the zillionth time if he wanted sugar with his tar.

"Okay," said Bailey. There might be a link to another death that just might be suspicious. Now that's all I know. Go do your work."

Triumphant, Deb Smith got up and walked in what could only be described as a provocative fashion over to Charlie Chilton's desk.

Trevor Worth nodded, apparently satisfied. "I'll watch this space," he said before heading back to his cubicle.

"This place is bloody unbelievable," Bailey said loudly enough for more than his immediate inquisitors to hear.

He took a mouthful of the foul brew, grimaced and leaned closer to his screen. Henderson would be here in less than an hour. Plaice had better call soon with something, anything.

Tim Plaice was not thinking of calling anyone. He had been fussing around his office for much of the afternoon, moving his bits and pieces into new formations. He was more than a little tired. It had been a late night.

Plaice's quarters were small for an officer of his rank. His office was precisely half of what had once been a room twice the size. Budgetary requirements had precluded an extension to the station, so offices had been consolidated or partitioned. He had been promised a bigger space. The promise was now close to two years old.

Plaice had long since noticed that no matter how dire the financial reali-
ties for the Metropolitan Police, there seemed to be an endless supply of funds
for sheetrock.

Plaice was not a particularly tidy man. Indeed some of his colleagues considered him sloppy. But today he had things in order. Or so he thought.

His office knickknacks were in rows, triangles and squares, military style.
The wall to his right held various books and files. He had blown off clouds of
dust and propped them up. The wall to his right was dominated by a notice
board with more pins than notices on it, and the obligatory photograph of the
queen. Beside this was a smaller portrait of Princess Diana. It was Tim Plaice's
slightly defiant gesture. He had always fancied himself a bit of a rebel.

Right behind Plaice's desk was the single window. Straight ahead was the
door, and standing in it was Detective Sergeant Samantha Walsh.

"Step in, Sam, take a seat," said Plaice.

Walsh nodded and covered the couple of steps to one of the two chairs
in front of Plaice's desk.

"Be with you in a moment," said Plaice, pretending to scan a piece of
paper.

He gave up the pretense and looked up at Walsh.

"You've read the file, and probably the paper. The priest, the dead priest,"
he said.

"Oh yes, guv, both of them. It's an odd one for sure. Do we have anything
nailed down?"

"Not really," Plaice said. "But there's a whiff of something about it. I'm not
quite sure, but I have a strong feeling there might be more."

Walsh nodded.

"Sam," said Plaice, "you've got a few days coming haven't you?"

Walsh shrugged, then nodded.

"You can say no, of course, but I'm going to ask you a favor."

"Yes," said Walsh.

"The other priest, the one who fell over the cliff in Cornwall a while back.
I want to run that one over again, be sure that it was an accident."

"You would like me to go down and sniff around," said Walsh.

"Just for a couple of days. It's very nice down there. My parents took my
sister and I there for holidays in the summer once or twice in that very area."

Walsh smiled.

"Indeed, Plaice went on, "I remember the cliffs rather well. My father was always warning me to stay away from the edge. And that was easy enough because the pathway was some yards from it."

"Are you going where I think you're going with this?"

"Well, it's a funny thing," said Plaice. "The cliffs where this priest took a tumble are dangerous enough, but you really have to go out of your way to put yourself in harm's way."

"Perhaps he meant to die, took his own life," said Walsh.

"Two suicides by priests in almost as many months? I just don't think so," said Plaice.

"And yet the accident theory doesn't quite do it either," he said.

"No, it doesn't, does it?"

"I'll get on it. I'll give you a call when I get down there. Should I contact the locals?"

"No, better not. Keep this very quiet. I don't want to be stirring anything up. Not now anyway."

Samantha Walsh stood up. Plaice was about to compliment her on her perfume but thought better of it.

"I'll bring you back a stick of rock," she said before turning for the door.

"Detective Sergeant," said Plaice, with a tone of formality in his voice. "Be careful."

"You have a feeling about this," she said. "A real feeling. One of those."

"Yes I do," said Plaice. "And a stick of rock would be nice. Peppermint."

Plaice had not called. Bailey was going to give him another ten minutes and then he himself would try to contact the head of the investigation into God only knew what. Bailey reckoned that by at least making the call he would cover himself should Henderson arrive at work ready to eat children, as he not infrequently did.

He glanced at the clock on the newsroom wall. Forget the ten minutes, he thought.

He picked up the phone and punched in the numbers. He put the phone down just as quickly as Henderson strode into the view.

Bailey couldn't believe his eyes. The man seemed to be singing to himself. And he definitely, yes, was smiling.

7

THE MAN WHO IN THREE DAYS would seem a messiah to Richard Cole was coping with the very worldly problem of foul smelling Englishmen.

He was surrounded and hemmed in by his reeking countrymen. Their Englishness was in itself no bad thing, and he took some comfort in familiar accents and speech. But John Falsham was also being asphyxiated by their pungent homespun. It had rained as it often did this time of year, and the throng had been greatly doused.

Added to this cloying, wooly dampness was the yield of several hundred unwashed bodies, the tinge of fear that even the most boastful felt at an execution, and, most loathsome of all, that peculiar air given off by a mob lusting for the blood of the wretch soon to be put to death. The entire concoction was enough to fell a man.

Falsham, hemmed in on all sides, could do little but wrap his silken scarf around his face and hold fast in his imagination the memory of warm and scented winds from North Africa. He wished now, most fervently, to be back in Spain. But he had been summoned home to England and his native city of London. He had no power to refuse.

It was a very different land to the one he had bade farewell seven years earlier. There was a different ruler on the throne. And the great plot to unseat the present usurper had come and gone. Some of Falsham's friends had paid with their lives for the failure of Fawkes and the others. Though he did not know the man who was about to die on the raised scaffold rising one hundred souls to his front, Falsham was keenly aware that his mission could easily lead to the same grim end.

As he strove to ignore the rankness all about, Falsham turned his mind to what the old priest in Spain had once told him in reply to a question he had posed. At what precise point in passing from this life did the faithful man or woman see or perceive God?

In the moment before death, the priest had replied. Balanced on this fulcrum between life and eternity, the good man, being in a state of God's sanctifying grace, would enjoy the supreme privilege of seeing God while yet in the physical world. If the man were to be a martyr, the sighting of God would last a longer while, though exactly how long the old priest could not state with any certainty.

Looking to the sky, now clear of the rain clouds, Falsham could see no God. But of course it was not he who was about the enter paradise. It was the priest.

He had become very quickly aware that the man about to die was in Holy Orders. It was the talk of the crowd that a papist, a heretic priest, had been caught by the watch, interrogated by the rightful authorities and found to be possessed of evil power not found in any truly Christian man. And now this priest was to meet his end in accordance with the just laws of the state, and the new church.

Falsham frowned as he considered the priest's fate, now just minutes hence. He shifted his stance and stood on his toes in an effort to better see the scaffold. He was a tall man, a head above all but a few in the crowd, head and shoulders above most. He could clearly see that those atop the scaffold charged with the coming work were making their final preparations. The crowd was so great now that it was difficult to imagine how anyone could actually approach the wooden structure.

Off to one side, meanwhile, a raised platform had been erected for those prepared to pay for a guaranteed view of the spectacle. Standing in the yard of St. Paul's cost nothing. But eight pennies for each pair of eyes were required for the platform that included chairs perched at a slightly higher level than the scaffold. Comfortable proximity to flowing blood, as ever, had its price.

Falsham eyed the seated crowd with disgust. A small gap opened in the throng, and he stepped into it. A man cut across his path, and he used his elbow to heave him aside. The man turned and was about to say something in anger. But the sight of the tall and broad-shouldered man with the Moorish looking face silenced his protest before it was given vent.

Falsham's left hand was clapped atop the grip of his sword, a formidable weapon made of superior Spanish steel. The man had also noticed the length of the weapon. There were two reasons, so, for his silence.

The chatter of the crowd was rising. A great clamor arose from somewhere to Falsham's rear. The prisoner was on his way. A crone suddenly stepped in front of Falsham, hand outstretched, her toothless mouth opening and closing.

No words were spoken. Falsham reached in his pocket for a coin. The old woman took it and without acknowledging the gift moved on through the crowd.

Falsham wondered for a moment if he had just seen God in the guise of this base creature. God did indeed appear to people, but not always in the manner or form expected.

A great cheer rose from the gathering, and his thoughts returned to the matter at hand. No, he thought, the crone had been just what she seemed. There would be no miracles here. Only murder.

Falsham now became aware of a man close by talking above all the rest. He was telling those around him that the priest about to be drawn and quartered had been overheard praying to the devil himself in his prison cell. He knew of this because his wife's brother was a jailer.

Falsham's eyes, brown, deep set and habitually narrowed after years in the sun, rested on the man. Those around the man were asking questions, demanding to know more about the papist's sacrilegious rites. Falsham thought of his blade cutting the fool's throat.

A shout went up but just as quickly subsided. The entire assembly seemed to push forward as one. There were more cries from one side of the scaffold. People on the raised benches stood up. Urgings, commands and curses were heard from the direction of the great church, demands for a way to be made clear. Someone was heard urging the priest to repent.

And then Falsham caught his first glimpse of the man who was to die. He was on his back, tied to a litter being pulled by a nervous horse.

Falsham raised his eyes to the sky again. White clouds moved quickly across the heavens from the west to the east. There was no heavenly host, just a pair of kites wheeling in circles, wings outstretched to catch the warm updraft, sensing in their nostrils the decay below.

Falsham inched through the crowd closer to the scaffold. He knew what the priest would say when asked if he wished to recant and beg forgiveness of the king. There was nothing to recant, and the priest would only ask forgiveness of God. That was if he managed any words at all. If torture had been applied in full measure, the man's mind might already be in another place.

The litter had reached the steps of the scaffold. Several men were attempting to hold the horse still. The prisoner was untied and pulled from the litter. Unable to stand, the blood having drained from his feet, he had to be pushed, prodded and partly hoisted up the steps.

Once atop he was left to stand for a moment. He did not fall and after a few seconds was able to walk the few paces to the shadow of his rope. It was a curious thing, thought Falsham, but he had seen this before. Once a condemned man had reached the final moments it was if he was given the absolute freedom of his confined realm. The scaffold was now a stage. It was as if the priest was an actor expected to play his part. And he did.

He turned and faced that part of the crowd to the immediate front of the scaffold. As best he could he straightened his back and began to speak. Several at the front of the assembly shouted for silence and a great shushing sound flowed across the yard. The priest, though weak, seemed to sense his moment and raised his voice. It was high pitched with an accent of the West Country.

The priest paused, and when certain of the crowd's attention, resumed his oration. Falsham could see no evidence of holy office in the priest's clothing. It was ragged and probably belonged to another prisoner now dead. The priest was speaking of the king. He had not, he said, ever conspired to bring harm to the king or any member of the royal household. He wished all in it long life and happiness, but, and here he raised his voice to a higher pitch, in the faith of the one, true, holy Catholic church.

A great hissing rose from the crowd. Falsham's eyes darted in a semi-circle behind him. He discerned a few who did not hiss or issue forth with curses, cries of papist and traitor, or calls for a slower, more painful death.

In all likelihood, the silent ones were recusants.

Falsham turned his eyes again to the scaffold. He admired the priest's courage. His defiance, however, would be rewarded by a longer turn on the rack, a more imprecise disemboweling.

Two priests of the new church who were standing directly behind the condemned man shook their heads in resignation. Some in the crowd were laughing now. Defiance from the prisoner had eased much of the tension. The condemned man would truly deserve all his pain. One of the new church clerics leaned over and spoke to the priest, but his words went seemingly unheard.

The priest raised his right arm. He motioned his hand in a sign of the cross over all, and then, turning, made the same sign to those on the scaffold with him. More cries of protest went up, but Falsham, his eyes darting one side to the other, noticed some in the seething mass momentarily bowing their heads.

Falsham fixed his eyes on the priest's frail form and consigned the man's all too obvious fear and agony to memory. He wondered if the man harbored doubts about God in his last seconds in a world that here and now, in this place, seemed so utterly godless.

No matter. He would not be a witness to any hanging, to any drawing of a man's body, to any butchery. Turning on his right boot's heel, Falsham pushed past the people now gaping open-mouthed as the priest's head was placed through the noose.

Falsham's hand reached inside his long coat to his doublet and into a pocket containing a few Spanish coins and a set of wooden praying beads. His finger and thumb ran rapidly over the beads and the gold chain connecting them. He prayed for the priest, even as he left him to his enemies.

"Rest with God," he said.

Falsham uttered his prayer aloud but the triumphal roar of the crowd, its praise of violent death in the shadow of a saint's church, overwhelmed all individual sound.

8

THE TWO MEN had stood side by side for several minutes. Not a word had been exchanged.

It was the Englishman who spoke first.

"Splendid view," he said, not really inviting an answer. The splendor of the view was a given.

"Why are you here? I thought I had finished with all this," Manning said.

"Splendid," said the man Manning knew as Roger Burdin. Jolly Roger Burdin.

"Well, I could say that I was a tourist interested in a little local knowledge, but you know me, a little is never enough."

"Oh, I know that," said Manning.

Burdin pulled out a pair of binoculars from a case strapped around his neck and began to scan the countryside. The evening was beginning to clear, but any better daylight would not last for long. Night was moving in fast from the east. It did not take Burdin long to fix the binoculars on the Manning house.

"How is your guest?" he said without taking his eyes away.

Manning felt weary. He decided against any further resistance. It always ended the same anyway. MI6 had him by the balls. He knew it. They knew it.

"He seems fine; keeps himself busy taking photos. Why are you interested?"

Burdin lowered his binoculars and smiled.

"Mr. Pender is a man who travels to interesting places. He sees things, hears things. We're always interested in people like that as you well know, Eamonn."

"Well then, as you doubtless know, he's considered to be one of the world's foremost news photographers. What do they call him? Big Shot Pender or something like that."

"Lucky shot actually," said Burdin. "I think he's inspired a lot of envy in his business. He just seems to have the knack of being in the right place at the right time. Right for him, of course. Usually wrong for his photographic subjects."

"Does this mean I've only a short while to live?" asked Manning. His tone was caustic but there was a more probing question attached.

"I said nothing to suggest that Mr. Pender causes people to die, Eamonn. It's merely the case that sudden death and the physical proximity of Mr. Pender have a habit of coinciding."

"There's an undertaker down in the town. His name is O'Connor. Maybe you should check him out as well," said Manning. He was beginning to feel cold. The damp was working deeper into his bones. It was always better to keep moving here than just stand still.

Burdin, sensing his companion's discomfort, reached into a pocket and pulled out a silver flask.

"Not Irish, I'm afraid, but it's rather good Scotch," he said offering Manning the container. It had an etching of a fly fisherman on it and a couple of dents in the metal. It had seen service.

"No thanks," said Manning. "I had better get back. Pender will be expecting to be fed."

"Your man Michael will be seeing to that, won't he?"

Manning fixed his eyes on the Englishman. To look at him he didn't appear to be the kind of man who made his living as an intelligence agent. He might have been on her majesty's secret service, but he was no James Bond. Nevertheless, Manning had long come to know that you did not judge an individual's capabilities purely by mere outward appearance or physique.

"How did you know about Michael? How long have you been watching the house?"

A slight smile crossed Burdin's long and narrow face, even as his eyes remained fixed on the distant house.

"It doesn't really matter what I know, or how I come to know it. What is important for you, Eamonn, is that you help us as we try to find out more about your present and future guest."

Manning frowned. "Future guest? What do you mean?"

"Your ambassador will be asking you to accommodate Mr. Pender for a few days in Washington. She will ask the favor of you when you get back to the embassy. Don't let on you know, of course, because that wouldn't do at all. But you will naturally comply with the request, even as you feign surprise."

"Jesus, Burdin, have you got her office bugged?" said Manning in a tone more resigned than angry.

"Goodness no, well at least not that I'm aware of. But you know your ambassador. Lovely woman, of course, but she likes to talk, and she's rather chummy with our man in Washington. Indeed there's been some gossip."

Manning just about stopped himself from letting loose with a loud guffaw. Here he was half perished on top of an Irish mountain being patched into the diplomatic blather in Washington D.C., three thousand miles and a lot of rain to the west.

"So he ends up staying in my place. I'm sure you people have one or two operatives on punishment duty in Georgetown. You can keep an eye on him yourself."

"Of course we can, Eamonn. But we've long appreciated your very singular skills, and we'll try to make this pill a little easier to swallow. As you will recall, our arrangement does have its little quid pro quos, and I'm going to give you one right now."

Manning turned and faced Burdin. "I'm all ears," he said.

In fact he was anything but. Burdin launched himself into a series of what he presented as revelations about British Embassy tactics in the never-ending game of diplomatic one-upmanship in Washington. Mannings' eyes narrowed, and he stifled a yawn. The air hereabouts, as always, was good for sleeping, even while standing on top of a mountain.

He caught the occasional word and phrase. Burdin interchanged Sinn Féin with the sobriquet "shinners" and sought occasionally to secure common ground with his presumed listener by making jibes at the Americans.

As if sensing that his companion was lost somewhere in the dampness, Burdin brought his lecture to a screeching halt with a firm admonition.

"And be careful of what you say to Fitzhugh."

The Irishman's eyes opened wider again, his eyebrows rising.

"Mortimer Fitzhugh?"

"Yes, your counterpart at our embassy, that Fitzhugh."

"There are no other contenders," said Manning. "But don't tell me he's MI6 too and that I should be careful of what I say to the man. We figured that one out already Roger."

"He's not MI6," Burdin said, slowly and with an emphasis that promised an even more revealing addendum.

"Ah," said Manning, "I am now absolutely all ears."

"Mortimer Fitzhugh is a hybrid," Burdin said. "By that I mean he inhabits a space between us and the Americans."

"He's a double agent?"

"Not quite. After all, we are so very close to our special American friends. But that's exactly the basis for his status and the means of justifying it."

"Go on," said Manning. He was looking at his watch. Daylight was becoming an issue, and Burdin was on his own. There was no way he was getting near the house. His father would rise from his grave if a British agent came within reach of the garden gate.

"Fitzhugh is with the other lot, MI5," he said. "He's also on loan to the CIA. He works both corners and reports to both."

"I thought MI5 were confined to domestic operations," said Manning.

"Come on, Eamonn, you know you don't entirely believe that. And remember what they say about all news being local. Well, it's the same in the intelligence game. There are no barriers or borders anymore. Everybody is everywhere and works all over, tout le monde so to speak."

"So who's your man, or woman, at the embassy, Roger?"

Burdin laughed.

"Now Eamonn, there are things I can say and things I cannot say. But you know that. Suffice it to say Mr. Fitzhugh does nothing for us. Indeed, part of his job is to keep an eye on us. As you know there are times when there is a lot more between us than just a single digit. Cain and Abel and all that."

Manning was turning over and assimilating this information as quickly as he could. Several things came immediately to mind and began to make better sense. Like the time that the British embassy's first secretary had pumped him over lunch for his views on a long list of his colleagues at her majesty's embassy. He was trying to find out the identities of special friends who might be inclined towards talking loosely with "you Irish lot," as he so indelicately put it.

"I always did think that Mortimer was lacking in the kind of subtlety that I have come to expect from your side," said Manning.

Burdin was looking through his binoculars again. He had said all he was going to say about Fitzhugh and his secrets.

"Good lord, but the light is fading fast. Time to be on my way," he said.

THE SOUTH LAWN PLOT

"You had better be quick about it and careful. The ground is wet, and you will have to move fast to get down the side you came up," said Manning, with a measure of genuine concern in his voice.

"Don't worry, Eamonn. I have one of those miner headlamps in my pack, and I once did a survival course. Marooned in the Scottish Highlands for a week. They called it a perk of the job, the buggers. And my car's at the bottom," Burdin replied.

"Let me guess; it's an Aston Martin."

"You've been watching too many films, Eamonn. Remember, we want to know what your friend Pender is up to. We'll be in touch once you are back in the States."

"He's not my friend," said Manning. But Burdin was gone. With a nimble-footedness worthy of a goat he had started back along the scrape that passed for a path down the south side of the mountain. He was already almost out of sight.

Manning took a moment to absorb what Burdin had imparted. Fitzhugh was a bloody spook. That was no surprise. But the identity of his dual employers was interesting news. Manning figured he now might have a bit of fun with the man, send him off on false trails with information that appeared loosely and casually dropped over Cabernet Sauvignon.

But so much of what lay ahead, not to mention in the past, was anything but loose and casual. As he considered all this, Manning began to make his way back down the slope, feeling hungry and in need of shelter and warmth.

As Manning closed in on his objective, Pender took his eye away from the zoom lens. He had been just able to make out the summit from his bedroom window by looking from a sideways angle. Despite the distance and poor light he picked out the two men at the top. One was gone, and the other was now only a few minutes away from the house.

Pender sensed a presence and turned. The old man, Michael, was standing in the bedroom door. Pender smiled.

"Great smell from the kitchen. Dinner must be ready. I'm starving," he said.

"It will be ready when Mr. Manning gets back," the old man said. He lingered in the door for a few seconds.

Pender thought that the old man was trying to read his mind. Certainly, he was no fool.

"I reckon he's no more than two or three minutes away," said Pender, eyes fixed on the old man. "Can I give you a hand serving it up?"

The old man did not reply. He just turned and walked back to the kitchen.

9

Bailey had bottled up his curiosity long enough. Henderson had been in the newsroom for thirty minutes but had still not come over to his desk. Nor had he summoned Bailey to his.

Bailey kept glancing over his shoulder. But all he could discern was Henderson on several phone calls, his head bent low over his desk and occasionally his free hand masking his mouth.

What the hell was he up to, Bailey thought. Normally the first few minutes of a Henderson shift were loud and furious. The man wanted everyone to know that he had arrived, was on the job, and that what he described as the lazy hours of the day were over.

A lot of people found it necessary to rush to the lavs or take smoke breaks during this initial assault. Henderson usually settled down after about twenty minutes, and the evening would fall into its less frenetic routine.

But today is was different. And Bailey wasn't the only newsroom inhabitant to notice.

Still, looking at a gift horse in the mouth and all that, Bailey said to himself. Perhaps Henderson had acquired a new girlfriend, or his first. Few in the newsroom had any appreciable knowledge of the man's private life. Old Percy was the best bet. He seemed to enjoy a charmed existence around Henderson, a bit like a pilot fish with a shark.

Bailey made a mental note to quiz Percy later if nothing made itself plain. He resumed his rummaging through the Internet for information on a story he was half working on, a turgid tale about passport forgeries.

Nick Bailey considered himself to be pretty sharp at his work, if sometimes reluctant. Newspaper reporting had not been his original career plan. It had started almost by accident with a summer job in a small newspaper down on the Kent coast. His father had known someone on the staff. He was the office Jack-of-all-Trades, which meant he made a lot of tea.

But he had watched the handful of reporters at work. He would sit beside them trying not to be noticed. Some of them were rather tetchy, but slowly and surely he began to understand some of the mysteries of how a newspaper worked. It was remarkable how little he knew about how a story reached a page. Nevertheless, in time, he began to notice that he was sometimes several steps ahead of a couple of the reporters in seeing story angles, spotting lead lines and even dreaming up headlines.

Yes, he had looked over a lot of shoulders as he lugged pots of tea. After a bit of pestering he had been given his chance. His first story had been about the mistreatment of a horse, and it had caused an absolute uproar. And here he was now, in one of the world's most famous city tabloids.

Bailey had once fancied the idea of being a stockbroker. Real flash, money, good car and girls galore. The idea still occurred to him from time to time. But something always pulled him back to the news business. He could not quite explain it. Certainly Henderson was not the reason.

Bailey's daydreaming was abruptly ended by a shout from the same man. It took him several seconds to comprehend the fact that he was being summoned the short distance to Henderson's desk.

Henderson did not stay seated, however. He rose and walked towards the small office that was his own private preserve, rarely used, but occasionally pressed into service, usually to threaten an errant reporter's health or marriage prospects.

Bailey allowed anyone who was looking to see his eyes roll to heaven. He was one of the few in the newsroom not intimidated by Henderson. Or so he liked to think. One of the young gossip page reporters was staring at him as if he was walking to the gallows. Bailey gave her a smile, a wink and the once over. She was dating material for sure.

But all thought of such pleasures quickly evaporated when he entered Henderson's keep.

"Sit down, grab that pen and notebook," Henderson barked. "And write me a headline and first line for a story that links the death of two priests in the same order, and at the same time speculates that there might be more bodies littering this blessed isle."

"How many bodies?"

"Pick a number."

"Jesus Christ," said Bailey.

"He's not on the list," Henderson said with a snort. "But he might end up being unique in that respect."

Bailey reached for a blank piece of paper and plucked a pencil from Henderson's pewter beer mug.

He scribbled a headline and began to write the first line of a story that was based on suspicion.

"Let me see," Henderson demanded.

"I haven't bloody finished," Bailey said testily and without looking up. But Henderson grabbed the page anyway.

"Good," he said. "And do you know what's good about it?"

"The alliteration?"

Henderson leaned back in his swivel chair. "No," he said. 'Clergy Killer' is okay, but frankly I prefer to be more specific. Vicar or priest, in this case priest, which is the better of the two anyway. The Catholics are more mysterious to our readers and downright threatening to some of them. 'Priest Killer' would have been better, but that's not it, Nick."

Bailey shrugged.

"It's the question mark, you nitwit," said Henderson.

Bailey looked again at the page. He had indeed finished his headline with the symbol.

"Think about it," said Henderson. "We're still short of most of the facts, but we have a theory. There may be a nut job out there who likes popping off padres. Now there's a line, must remember that."

To Bailey, it seemed that Henderson was reasoning with himself and that he was only filling a seat.

"Yeah, but we only have two of them, time and miles apart and both looking like suicides even if the coppers might be thinking different. Hardly a big line to hang the washing on," Bailey said if for no other reason than to remind Henderson that he was only a few feet away, across a desk piled high with newspaper cuttings. Henderson's cubbyhole was the final nail in the coffin of the theory that computers would eliminate paper in the modern office.

In fact, and as Bailey was taking note of yet again, this hole in the wall that passed for the chief news editor's command bunker didn't even possess a computer. It was rumored that there was manual typewriter buried under papers on the floor somewhere, but nobody had ever tried to find it.

But there was one thing about Henderson, and all in the *Post* acknowledged it: the man had instinct. He was like an animal on the scent of raw meat. And more often than not he found his prize. Henderson, quite simply, was the best that the town had to offer. Even so, Bailey was less than convinced about this one.

And he was suddenly conscious of a role reversal at very close quarters. Henderson was the reporter, and he had become the doubting editor. This odd state of affairs would not last for very much longer. Soon enough, Henderson would issue a specific direction to check this, or find that. And sure enough, it came.

"I want to you call Plaice," he said. "Ask for a meeting. You'll go to see him, not at the station because that will be noticed and who knows how many coppers down there have contacts with the *Sun* or the *Mirror*. He'll agree to meet. Suggest a pub, he doesn't mind a sup. He won't necessarily lay it out for you. You'll have to work for it, tease it out of him. But he's a good sort and really doesn't have hang-ups about the press like some of them."

"And I tease out precisely what?" said Bailey.

"That some lunatic is popping padres."

As Henderson and Bailey were settling in for another evening of edgy proximity, Samantha Walsh was trying not to give into her dizzy spell. She had approached the edge of the bluff cautiously and with more than a little trepidation.

She had never liked heights, nor lonely places. Now she was dealing with both. It was also a place of death, and to make matters worse, the daylight was dwindling. The only comfort was a mildness that bordered on warmth for the time of year and the cell phone she clutched in her right hand.

She had been cautious in her approach to her mission in the village of Little Polden, about a mile away as the gulls flew. Her story for local consumption was that she was checking out property in the area, thinking about a small cottage close to the sea where she might find peace and quiet to write a book. It was perfect cover for asking not just about the area, but also coaxing the more talkative locals into discussing people and events, not just real estate.

The sudden and shocking death of Father Jeffrey Dean had clearly been the biggest thing to happen around these parts in years, certainly the biggest since the German Heinkel had crashed in a field back in 1941. You could still see the rut in the ground that the doomed bomber had left, she was told by at least six villagers.

But there were no Cornish voices now, and even the seabirds had settled in for the night. She had to walk to the edge nevertheless.

10

Pender wiggled his toes, flexed his fingers and tensed his back. The flight was number two for takeoff. The hop from Dublin to London would take about an hour. He thought of trying to sleep, but that would now be impossible. The Irish air had been a relief because Pender usually had difficulty staying more than four or five hours in a bed. He hadn't slept as well in years as he had the past few nights.

But the present atmosphere was not the sharp and saturated stuff he had spent the past few days drawing gratefully into his lungs. This was the aircraft cabin recycled variety. Pender had traveled to every corner of the globe and was a connoisseur of air much in the same way that some were experts on wine. Ireland's air, he decided, was to be highly commended despite the tension evident in it as Manning bade final farewell to his father's lair.

His host's obvious distraction had allowed Pender to observe without drawing too much attention. Manning did not appear to suspect a thing. He had clearly been simply doing his superior, the ambassador's, bidding.

It had been clear that the Irishman was uncomfortable having the Englishman around, but he had done his best to disguise the fact. He would be equally reluctant but ultimately cooperative when Pender turned up in Washington.

The aircraft turned at the end of the taxiway and faced down the runway. Somewhere in the distance there was a roar as the plane ahead lifted off. The pilot told Pender and his fellow passengers that they were now next in line and that the cabin crew should prepare for takeoff.

Pender pressed his eyes shut. This he could never quite fathom. He was as cold as ice when required to assassinate a target. Yet he was a nervous flyer.

The aircraft thundered down the runway and took off into a steep climb. It banked to its port side, and Pender pressed his eyes even more tightly shut. He concentrated his thoughts on Africa and the nights crouched around the rickety table with the hurricane lamp that was just about keeping at bay the pitch darkness inches beyond the rotting verandah.

John, the dissonant priest, and Pender had spent many hours by the lamp discussing all manner of things. Sleep was impossible unaided. The dead air conditioner was a casualty of three civil wars. So they had sipped Johnny Walker from chipped china cups and matched the alcohol intake with an equally significant consumption of nicotine.

John, whose priestly calling had been revealed to Pender after about a week spent at the old mission, had a taste for a strong French brand. He had laid responsibility for his habit on an old Belgian priest, a Father Jules. The man was a seer who had claimed that his chain smoking was merely a last ditch effort to counteract the legions of night insects. After forty years of defending himself, with a fair degree of success, Fr. Jules had succumbed to emphysema.

"It was a fair enough deal," said Father John. "Four decades of not being bitten to death for a few rather uncomfortable months at the end."

Pender, sucking on his American brand, had nodded in agreement at this weighing of relative agony.

"Right now, I'm all for the ciggies," he said and blew a smoke ring in the general direction of the ceiling fan which had quit, again.

Pender had been wary of the priest when he had first answered the question as to his calling in life. Father John, whose surname he had never discovered, had evidently detected this because he had quickly qualified his answer with claims of coercion by his mother. Priests, he acknowledged, were not generally known for stating they had taken Holy Orders simply because they had been betrayed by a lover.

Pender had replied that he had initially thought Father John was a civilian aid worker. He admitted to being unaware that his lodging, set up for him by a contact in the capital, had once been a mission. It bore none of the usual trappings, people being the most noticeable absence. But other things had been missing too: crucifixes, pictures of the pope, a saint or two; even Jesus.

The civil war had been to blame, Father John explained. A priest was precious little protection against an assault rifle, especially an English priest with a less than convincing command of French and absolutely no words in the local tongue.

The school and the clinic had been mothballed after customers had fled to the capital 150 miles away. Lacking any clear instruction from his order in England, Father John had decided to hang on in the hope of better times. An elderly local man, with some unpronounceable biblical name, who had lived at the mission since an orphan childhood, was the only other inhabitant. Pender's arrival, naturally, had been an event.

And so the two men had settled into the routine of staying as cool as possible in the heat of the day and as sane as possible during the heat of the night.

Pender's assignment had been to get to meet and photograph Jonas Sem, a rebel leader who had been steadily gaining ground against government troops. Because of this, he had been arousing a degree of western media interest, not least on the grounds that he had once attended the Sorbonne and had appeared to have a remote idea how a shell-shocked nation such as his might somehow settle down enough to give its children a chance of reaching twenty.

But time had passed, and different stories had started to filter out of the bush where Sem was holed up with an army estimated at five to as many as ten thousand fighters.

Nobody had paid too much attention to the first reports of Sem's praise for some of Africa's more dubious national leaders. Sem was known for having a good sense of humor, so comparing himself to the likes of Idi Amin was taken with a pinch of salt.

But there were soon other stories, reports of torture and of so-called war games in which Sem pitched one unit of his force, often boys not much older than twelve or thirteen, against each other in deadly pursuit of the honor of leading him in triumph into the country's capital.

The stories were never quite confirmed, so his advocates and allies in Paris and London had argued that the reports were lies being spread by the unarguably discredited government in the capital. But smoke begat fire, at least in the news media. So a few journalists had arrived in the supposedly democratic republic in search of the "true Jonas Sem." All had failed to get near to the man, and one reporter had died in a small plane crash, fifty miles downriver from the mission.

As was his habit, Pender had watched and waited for the fuss to die down a bit. He knew that photos of African carnage were dime a dozen. Only the man himself would suffice and that would take some patience and luck. Both had landed him in the mission and at the table with the apologetic priest and a seemingly bottomless bottle of Scotch.

"Where did you get all this?" Pender had asked one evening, nodding towards the half empty bottle. "No, don't say it," he quickly added. "The lord always provides."

"Oh no," the priest had answered. "Jonas Sem is your friend on that account. He keeps me up to my halo in the stuff."

"You know Sem well?"

"Just in a passing sense," the priest replied. "I baptized him."

Pender's crystal clear memory of the absolute indifference on the priest's face as he revealed his formative role in the rebel leader's life was washed away by a sudden shower of steamy rain.

"Would you be able to take me to him?"

The priest fidgeted with his glass.

"Not easy," he said. "You don't make any direct approaches. They would shoot you down before you got within a mile of the man."

"So how does he get the booze to you?" Pender asked.

"It simply arrives," the priest replied.

"And what do you give him in return?"

"Absolution, forgiveness, albeit from a distance. I write down his penance on a piece of paper, leave it under a rock, and one of his boy soldiers takes it to him."

"You're not bloody serious," said Pender.

"If I was not bloody serious, Mr. Pender, I wouldn't be living in a place like this. I take all things seriously because here there is very little room to let emotions other than serious ones in. I may laugh, but I don't enjoy the luxury of easy mirth. You would understand if you lived here for more than a few weeks."

Pender could find no easy reply. He lifted his glass and took a slug of the lukewarm whisky. He savored the liquid as it burned his throat and tumbled into a stomach that was already a tropical cauldron all of its own.

"You could send him a message for me, write one and leave it under the stone," said Pender.

"I suppose I could," replied the priest. "But the message I want to ultimately deliver to Joseph Sem will not rest well on paper. I will have to deliver it myself. Perhaps you could accompany me."

The priest shook his head and as he did so he informed his guest that he would soon be leaving the mission. He had to return to England to address urgent business pertaining to his order.

To this, Pender had frowned, and still had a frown on his face as the flight attendant nudged him on the shoulder. He had snoozed after all. She was pointing at his seat belt which was unbuckled. Pender nodded, forced a smile and looked out the window. The plane was turning and side slipping as it made its descent into Heathrow.

Pender had ignored the woman sitting beside him. She had buried herself in a laptop the moment she had sat down in her seat. The computer was now stowed and she was flicking through the airline's inflight magazine.

Pender turned his head and looked out the cabin window. The sky was clear and the London suburbs stretched away to the horizon. Pender recognized the Twickenham rugby ground as the plane straightened for its final approach. Behind it and beyond it the row of houses signaled the march of the great capital into its hinterland.

He had grown up in one of those houses with its neat garden and potting shed. His father had commuted to his government job on the trains. He had early on picked his soccer team and his chums on the road, and life seemed to be as predictable in its future as the present flight path.

How, he wondered, could something so volatile take form out of something so solid, so stable and seemingly fixed in the heavens?

He was conscious suddenly of the woman speaking.

"Nervous flyer are you?" she asked. By her accent she was English, from somewhere in the London area.

Why the hell she had waited until the end of the flight to ask the obvious was a mystery to Pender.

He folded his arms and smiled at her. "Not in the least," he said.

11

London, 1606

Moving swiftly, Falsham pulled his broad-brimmed hat lower over his forehead. He walked along Watling Street and into Candlewick Street, occasionally making small diversions down alleyways before returning to his intended route.

His progress appeared random, but he maintained an easterly direction towards London Bridge. Every so often he would stop and cast a glance backwards. The London he remembered was a nest of spies. Robert Cecil, the Earl of Salisbury, whose agents provided eyes and ears for the king, was never a man to be underestimated.

But no one was following, as best as Falsham could judge.

Falsham's progress took him past stalls and stables, over puddles of slop, some with straw strewn across to spare the walker sudden calamity. Though it was spring, it was still thankfully cool; the street stench had not yet risen to the height of a tall man's nose.

Falsham walked on, his stride lengthening despite the crowds that made passage through the narrower streets slow and frustrating. The city was more crowded than he remembered. But he had been absent from England for seven years, away in Flanders, France and Spain. And nothing remained the same in a fast changing world. The virgin queen was dead, and the new king very much alive, despite the efforts of good and honorable men.

Falsham reached the bridge without incident. London Bridge was both a bridge and tunnel, a marvel he had always admired despite his preference for open countryside. Its stone road rested on a series of wooden piers atop which lay a run of high houses. Each house had a passageway underneath through which people, carts and animals could move back and forth across the Thames.

Falsham entered through the north gate, his eyes given sudden relief in the dim light under the first house. He walked quickly, into the daylight, out of it again, beneath another arch and onwards until he reached the south gate.

On this day, there was but a pair of severed heads perched above the gate, a damnable construction, he thought, and one that was reserved for those done in for treason, whether real or concocted.

Falsham took comfort. The priest was unlikely to join these unfortunates. Spiking a priest's head would be too much a provocation to those ambassadors in the city who spoke for the Catholic courts of Europe, even those lately eager to soothe England's temper.

When he reached the south bank, Falsham turned westward, past the Bishop of Winchester's palace and the mournful dungeon known as the Clink. He felt no fatigue. Indeed, his stride lengthened as he neared his destination. Falsham was fired by little more than anger. But that was more than enough.

He had not eaten since the previous day, and that had been a fitful meal of barley bread and oysters washed down with a jug of sour ale. His night's rest in Nine Elms had been nothing of the sort. The inn had been astir with all manner of activity and Falsham slept on the floor, certain that his bed was a home to all the fleas in England.

Had passersby come close and listened as Falsham approached his final destination, they would have heard a low, growling, voice muttering words in a foreign tongue. Had they an education to boast of, they might have recognized the tongue as Spanish. "Un Deseo Por Tranquilidad," Falsham said as he turned down an alleyway towards the riverbank. He said it again, a snarling tone rising in his voice. "Un Deseo Por Tranquilidad. All of you to hell."

William Beacon rubbed the grime from the window and stared out into the street. There was not much to be seen between the mullions and thick panes blown into a series of interwoven spirals. Beacon's face betrayed anxiety and impatience. Where was he?

He soon had his answer. The heavy oak door to the Fox and Badger Tavern opened with a creaking sound. The tall figure blocking out the light hesitated for only a second before taking the single step down to the near-black wooden floor.

Beacon stepped away from the window and walked to the corner of the room. It was early in the day and only a few lay-a-bouts were availing of the tavern's reputation for a cup of sac better than most others in this dingy corner of the city, a spit as it was from the Bankside brothels and gathering places just a tad more meritorious, the Globe and the Bear Pit.

The room reeked of ale. It was a stale odor that no amount of scrubbing by the landlord's serving girls would banish. Beacon found it a comforting, uncomplicated smell. Perfume on a man always made him suspicious. Ale, by contrast, had an honest stink. It made a man transparent.

Beacon was his real name though he rarely used it. His life was one of many names, many houses and many journeys, mostly by night and by stealth in the expanses to the north of the city.

Beacon lifted a latch on the corner door and stepped into a passageway. A single candle in a metal holder nailed to the wall provided the only light. He knew Falsham would follow and did not turn back to look. At the end of the passage was another door.

Opening it, Beacon almost tiptoed into a room about twenty feet square. Against one wall was a long bench. A dozen men were sitting on it and in separate chairs drawn up to a rectangular table atop which lay an opened map held down by drinking jugs at each end.

The embers of a fire from the night before glowed faintly in the fireplace, cut into the wall to the right of the entry door. There was one small window at the opposite end of the room through which could be seen an enclosed yard at the rear of the tavern.

Falsham had followed Beacon and now he stood just inside the door. His eyes fell on a stack of swords leaning against one of the walls. An arquebus lay on the floor, nuzzling against the sword tips. Falsham could see that the men in the room were wary, their weapons already drawn and within easy reach. He nodded in silent approval.

Beacon interrupted his thoughts.

"John is here and I fear with news of a great mischief," he announced.

Falsham stared over Beacon to the seated men.

"Yes, my friends, I do bring news of the mischief you so rightly feared. The priest is dead. But death is no longer without purpose. We have much work to do."

Falsham stepped across the room to a chair left vacant in anticipation of his arrival. His movement now was that of a man at the end of a long, arduous journey. He seemed to pause a moment, eyeing the chair with some suspicion, before pulling it back and seating himself. He sagged. The days on horseback, the sea passage, the constant need to be alert and suspicious of all manner of even normal incident had taken its toll. He was exhausted.

His weariness, however, did not impede him for more than a few seconds. Pulling himself upright in the chair, he placed both his gloveless hands upon the table. He said nothing for about a minute then slammed his clenched fists into the wood, stained dark from countless nights of drinking, gambling and plotting.

Falsham spoke softly, but his voice filled the room. He reached inside his clothing and removed his prayer beads. Holding before his eyes the gold crucifix attached to one end of the chain he ran his eyes over and through the seated men before and beside him.

"By this we live, for this we die," he said. The men around the table nodded, some gently, some vigorously. One or two crossed themselves. Beacon, who was still standing, smiled, but said nothing.

This was the right man, he thought.

Beacon, a priest behind his secular garb, spread his arms wide. "Dominus vobiscum," he said. To a man, the gathering felt that God was with them in the room, the newcomer his earthly instrument.

Beyond the closed door, down the dark passage, outside the inn and beyond the reach of its stale odors, London was a city flexing its growing financial and trading muscle. The forty-four year rule of Elizabeth was not yet seen as an era. But there was a widespread sense that England had come of age under her stern gaze.

James, the sixth of Scotland, son of Elizabeth's ill-fated cousin, Mary, Queen of Scots, had inherited a kingdom that had not just survived religious upheaval, an attempted invasion by Spain, and constant threat from Catholic Europe, but more lately a satanic plot to blow up king and parliament.

Now, a few months after the foiled Powder Treason, James the first of England, was leading his kingdom into the new century with élan and enthusiasm, at least during his numerous stag hunts, to which he devoted much of his energy. He would be the first monarch to style himself King of Great Britain. And Britain would indeed be great for more reasons than trade and military prowess.

Culture, too, was flourishing. This very year would see publication of Ben Jonson's *Volpone* while Shakespeare's *Macbeth* would be a worthy distraction

from the shocking, treasonous acts of November 1605. There was, indeed, much
to celebrate in the city that had grown along the banks of the Thames since
Roman times.

Back again down the dingy corridor and into the back room of the Fox
and Badger, celebration of a sort was also taking place. It was a celebration of
survival. Falsham's return from the continent was a boost to both prospects
and hearts.

Sitting at the table were men who viewed the course of recent events with
alarm and disdain. England's ability to trade with the world was contingent on
the ability to protect trading routes and shipping. That ability, they all fervently
believed, would be better served if England was realigned with the Catholic
powers of Europe, most especially Spain.

Such a change in the order of things would require intervention. The
king's mother had died for her Catholic faith but the king himself had long
accepted the teachings of the church sprung from the loins, literally, of Elizabeth's father, Henry.

The conspiracy taking form in the Fox and Badger was a collision of faith
and finance, a potent mix. And now it had its sword arm in John Falsham.

One of the men stood. Sir Robert Cummings was at odds with the room
in one respect. He was not a Catholic, though his wife was of that faith. Cummings considered himself a practical man, not much given to religious fervor
at all. He, too, saw great danger in an isolated England and had designs on
making his second fortune in the New World. Enemies could easily get in the
way of such plans.

"You are welcome among us, John. I know I speak for all. We are truly
comforted by your safe return and feel that our work can only now benefit."

Cummings, as was his habit, chose his words carefully. It was he who had
called together the present company. It was he who now placed a sword on
the table.

"Gentlemen," he said, "a sword is a perfect instrument. It both reminds us
of Christ's cross and strikes down those who would still have him on that cross.
We would do well to swear an oath on this holy instrument because we all carry
one about our persons. It will be a reminder to all that on this day we pledge
our lives to the restoration of England to a single common purpose under one
mother church within which all men can find their individual destinies."

All the men stood, and hands reached across the table. One or two were
amused at how Cummings had managed to insert a reformist idea into his

vision of a single religious body at least nominally under Rome. But they were impressed by his choice of a sword as an instrument of holy oath. Better by far than beads. To a man, they were inclined towards a pragmatic means to an end. Religion had its place, but worldly actions were required to assure its survival and prosperity.

The Powder Treason plotters had been dreamers, and they had paid for their foolishness with their lives. It would not be the fate of the individuals in this room. Their task would take time, perhaps a long time.

"A holy sword." Beacon was smiling. "Clavius Sanctus."

Falsham, who had remained seated, now stood and faced Beacon.

"I must not linger long in London; there is too much danger here," he said.

Beacon nodded. "Yes, of course, you must leave the city, but after you have rested. Ayvebury will be ready for you. Our friend there is expecting your arrival even now."

Falsham's brow furrowed. What would it be like meeting with his old friend, a man who he had thought to be in heaven?

"I sold my horse upon arrival in London. It was broken down," he said to no one in particular.

Cummings put his hand on Falsham's shoulder.

"I have many horses, John, and you will have the pick of them." Falsham smiled. He rarely smiled anymore.

"A holy sword. Yes, by God, that is a worthy idea to march behind," he said.

"March, yes, but first rest," said Beacon. "All depends on you now, John. You are the hunter in our midst, and you must be more than a match for that royal stag of ours."

12

MANNING TOOK A LAST LOOK at the house through the rear view mirror.

His mother would voice no objection to his decision to sell the place, of that he was certain. The only problem was he was not entirely sure that his decision to sell would be final. He had doubts. He was reminded of them by the fact that he had not told Old Michael.

He had informed Pender that he probably would put the place on the market. But that was as much to keep the Englishman at bay. Pender had been curious about the property and its history, asking all sorts of questions.

In response to Manning's concession that a sale was probably on the cards, Pender had replied that after one or two more successful assignments, which Manning had taken to mean lots of photos of dead bodies, he might consider buying the place himself.

The Englishman seemed to be thinking in terms of retirement, a prospect still many years off for Manning, the pensioned but unsettled civil servant.

Manning had attempted to steer Pender away from thoughts of making a bid. Either the place would go very quickly, or not at all, he said.

All this had happened last night. Manning focused his eyes ahead, turned the key in the ignition and steered the car slowly down the hill. The Englishman had departed thirty minutes earlier saying something about Africa as he bade goodbye.

When he reached the paved road Manning hit the pedal and covered the few miles to the town without encountering a single vehicle. It was early in the morning, and the weather was deteriorating again. Manning reckoned the local farmers would be putting the spring's work off for another few days.

The town, by contrast, was showing signs of activity when Manning rolled into the main street. These days, people living in country towns were often commuters who worked in bigger country towns. The days of living above your own shop were fading fast.

Manning, like a commuter, kept driving. Michael had prepared a thermos of coffee and wrapped some toast in aluminum foil. Manning had decided he would leave the house quickly, stop at some point along his initial route and have his breakfast before joining up with the main road to Dublin.

The landscape turned wilder about five miles beyond the town. The road took a more or less straight course through blanket bog. It was other-worldly, the only hint of human existence the stacks of soggy peat rising five or six feet off the ground at irregular intervals.

The sun was hidden by dark gray clouds. There appeared little prospect of it breaking through anytime soon. And soon might be days.

Manning's eyes darted right and left seeking out signs of life, any movement at all. A few unidentifiable birds in the distance were the only creatures moving. Manning reckoned there were fewer and fewer places in Ireland where a person could feel alone in the world. This prairie of peat was one of them.

He glanced at the car clock. It was a little after eight. The lights of an approaching truck came into view, moving fast. Manning slowed a little and pulled in tighter to the road's edge. The truck, which was laden with frozen food according to the lettering on its side, roared by without giving an inch, or a mile an hour.

Manning pulled into a wider stretch of what passed for the grass verge. He opened his flask of coffee and unwrapped his toast. He turned on the radio and picked up an FM station on which an announcer was talking excitedly about a conflict thousands of miles away. The Irish were infuriated by distant wars. The one on the island itself, even the relative peace that had followed, had long inspired mostly indifference.

Manning worked the radio dial until he found classical music. It was Beethoven's something or another. He closed his eyes, took a big gulp of coffee, replaced the cup and lid on his thermos, turned the steering wheel hard to the right, gunned the car and headed back the way he had just come. The toast could wait.

Manning studied the road carefully and was ready for the narrow turnoff he had passed roughly four miles back. There were no road signs. The single lane road, if it even amounted to that, ran in a northerly direction right through the bog. Manning turned, slowed a little, and proceeded into the brown expanse.

His new route had once been a literal bog road, built in famine times between somewhere and nowhere in order to justify the minimal feeding of the starving. Though it was so narrow that two cars could not meet without one pulling off, the surface, as Manning quickly noted, was extraordinary. It was spanking new blacktop, courtesy of the European Union. Somewhere in Brussels, he thought, an official had ticked off this bog highway as a job completed, and completed well. It might see only a handful of cars in a given week, but its existence was enshrined in a computerized list along with the motorways, routes, and autobahns of the new Europe.

"For the love of God," said Manning as the needle on his speedometer approached forty, a rare speed in these parts.

As the miles rolled by, the landscape changed. The bog receded and was replaced by small fields full of thistles and surrounded by stone walls, or ramparts of grass-covered dirt. Here and there small scraggly trees were bent sideways by the wind.

Soon, plantations of conifer trees began appearing and the land started to undulate. It would not be long now. Manning was going miles out of his way but Dublin could wait. He had to see the place. One more time and that would suffice. Perhaps. But just one more time. Then he could return to Washington with his mind set at relative ease.

As if to confirm the correctness of his new course, a burst of sunlight broke through the clouds. Its effect was instant and magical. But it made the clouds look even darker by contrast. It was as if nature itself was offering Eamonn Manning a choice.

Now he could see the bend in the road. He remembered it because of its multitude of direction signs. Most of them were for historic sites. One was for a long neglected holy well.

The lone sign relevant to the purposeful traveler announced the town three miles distant. Manning smiled. He remembered from before another sign, a mile closer to the town. It had listed the distance as four miles. Would it still be there, or had someone spotted the discrepancy?

As it turned out, all the signs had been changed. They now displayed mileage in kilometers, and the second sign accurately noted the distance reduction. The country was changing. Seemingly bigger in metric, it had also become more conscientious with regard to measuring itself.

Manning tried to remain easy in his mind as he knocked off the final couple of miles. His reason for taking the diversion from his planned trip back to Dublin was, he told himself, simple curiosity. Of course, it was, and of course, it wasn't.

The road became dead straight in the final few hundred yards before the first houses. Manning slowed the car until he matched the speed limit.

Would all eyes turn to him as he rolled into town, like some gunfighter riding into Dodge?

He knew his fear was baseless. Nobody would recognize him here because nobody knew him. Besides, he was a high-ranking government employee. As such, he possessed something close to a native version of the diplomatic immunity he enjoyed in the United States.

Manning entered the street leading to the center of the town. As he remembered it, three roads met in the middle of the place. At the end of this one, just at the point where the other two branched off, two banks sat on opposite sides. They were stolid pillars of society, guardians of the community's money. Targets.

There were more cars parked than on that day so many years ago. Other than that, the town appeared to be slumbering much the way it was the last time, that unusually hot summer's day when even the town dogs had given up their wanderings.

Manning barely glanced at the banks. He swung to the right and took the street leading northward and out of the town. A couple of minutes later and Manning was back in the countryside. He arrived at the fork in the road. To the left was the fast route to the next county and beyond it the border, while to the right there was the road that led into the wild heart of the adjoining county's hill country.

Manning turned the car into the right fork and pressed his foot gently on the accelerator. He took a deep breath and let it out slowly. It had been a minimal exorcism, but it would do for now.

After a couple of miles the land began to rise. Cows gave way to sheep and the trees turned to the familiar shrunken and gnarled variety. Several things had become fixed in Manning's mind from that day. The ruined cottage by the roadside, the steep hill and the blind bend just before the large period house with the horse paddock. An Irish ranch.

Manning turned the car sharply onto an unpaved road just wide enough for one-way travel. After about a quarter of a mile he turned left into an abandoned farmyard. It looked even more desolate now. The front of the roofless house was almost covered in ivy. Manning stopped and without hesitation stepped out of the car.

He stood and carefully listened. There was nothing except a couple of singing birds and the wind, which, he reckoned, must blow around these parts 360 days out of 365.

In spite of the apparent solitude, Manning was not entirely sure if he was alone. He walked over to what had once been a shed for animals and peered inside. It reeked of dampness and decay. The yard was about twenty yards wide by thirty long. The farm, in its heyday, had been no larger than twenty acres. And that would have been big for the area.

The front door of the house had long rotted away. Manning stooped slightly as he walked into what had once been the combined parlor and kitchen. When they became accustomed to the limited light, his eyes rested on the weed-infested ground in front of the stone fireplace. He shuddered and fought a rising urge to look over his shoulder. A rustling noise from a corner of the room made Manning turn. Just a rat, he thought.

The house was as he had remembered it; a tomb for the memories of vanished generations. Manning turned and walked back out to the yard. The nearest inhabited home was at least three miles away. That was why this place had been chosen. It was off the beaten track as well as being plain beaten.

Manning closed his eyes. He saw nothing. There were no ghosts here. What fears he would have to face had nothing to do with the dead. They only involved the living.

"Rest in peace, you stupid bastard," he said.

13

FALSHAM HAD STOPPED ON THE ROAD. The house was quiet with no life or movement evident despite the growing daylight. The farm, he had been told in London, was behind the house so any early activity in that quarter would not be visible from here.

He looked at his boots. He had walked for several miles in order to rest the horse that had been given to him by one of Beacon's men. They looked like the shoes of a traveler, well worn and muddy.

Falsham had decided to proceed by night to avoid unwelcome attention, whether from those who enforced the king's law, or those who made a living by breaking it.

Even now, with the end of his journey in sight, Falsham was no less cautious. Eyes fixed on the house, he mounted the horse and steered the animal towards the gate and passage under a portion of the house that opened into the inner courtyard.

This place, he fervently hoped, was one where he could truly rest after his journey from Spain. London had been a furious succession of furtive gatherings and whispered talk. He had been surprised by the large number of men who seemed intent on carrying to the end what earlier plotters had so dramatically failed to accomplish. This had made him nervous. More heads were more mouths. Falsham preferred to work alone, or at most in groups no greater than three or four.

Several men, the same ideal three or four to his tired eye, fussed around Falsham's horse as he dismounted. As the animal was taken away to the stables, a young boy came running from a door at the far end of the courtyard.

"My lord, my master bids that you follow me to his chamber," the boy stammered.

Falsham motioned to the boy who began walking quickly towards the door, despite an obvious limp. Saddle sore and stiff in the joints now that England's cloying dampness was making itself felt again, Falsham followed at his own pace.

The boy entered the house and turned to his left, Falsham following him at a slightly faster clip. The hall in which Falsham found himself moments later was spacious but dim. No sun had yet penetrated the windows, and all the night candles had been snuffed out.

The boy again motioned to Falsham to follow him down the hall where a wide staircase signaled access to the rooms on the upper floor. Falsham's sense of anticipation was heightened. He was nervous, fearful for his friend. The reports in London had not been good.

The boy was waiting at the top of the stairs. Falsham followed him down another hallway. He was keenly aware of the wooden floorboards creaking under his feet. Faces of former Ayvebury Hall inhabitants stared grimly at him from the wood-paneled walls. The boy had stopped at a door. It was slightly open, and he gave it a loud knock.

The door was opened fully by a young woman, wrapped in a blanket. She motioned to the boy who entered the room. The woman acknowledged Falsham with a slight nod of her head before walking past him and down the hall. She might have been a ghost. Falsham stood for a moment. The boy came out of the room with a piss pot.

"Sir, the master bids you enter," he said.

Falsham nodded and took a long stride into the room, which, unlike the corridors of the house, was well lit by the morning sun. He saw the man but did not recognize him as his old friend. Where once there had been a formidable presence there was now a shrunken shadow. Falsham barely caught the cry surging upwards from deep in his throat.

"Richard," was all he could say before embracing his companion. It seemed as if the other man might crumple to dust at the slightest touch.

"Sit down, sit down," Falsham commanded as he ushered the man's bony frame back to the chair by the writing desk.

"As you wish, John," the man said. He managed a smile, but the effort was evident.

Falsham was about to ask the obvious question, but the man motioned it away with a wave of his skeletal hand. Richard Cole was clearly facing his life's end.

Falsham managed to smile, but there was little joy in it.

"So, John, what is the news from Spain?"

"It can wait," Falsham replied as his friend slumped in his writing chair.

"No it cannot," the man retorted. There was a rasping sharpness to his voice.

"As you can see clearly, my friend, there is little time left for me. So what, for the love of our savior, is the news?"

Falsham turned his back, took a couple of steps, paused for a second and turned again to face his impatient interrogator.

"You will have heard that Phillip is anxious to make secure the peace with England."

"Yes."

"Our friends in the Spanish court seem to have little appetite for the plot. All they speak of is a desire for peace and trade. Damnable trade. I fear they have given up."

"Not all."

Falsham folded his arms and stared at his friend. The gesture invited further elaboration.

"There are others who have Phillip's attention and trust and they sing a different tune. One of them has been here, at Ayvebury. This emissary expressed a desire for our forbearance on the grounds that Spanish entreaties for peaceful coexistence with England are but a ploy, a foil. Spain simply needs time to replenish her strength. She will strike when the time is right, and when she does, England will be restored to the faith."

"And who might this charmer be?" Falsham said.

"It is necessary," came the reply, "to keep this person's identity secret. The more who know a name and a message, the greater the chance that it might slip by means of accident, design or torture. But you know that well. I trust you, of course, my friend, even more than I trust myself, but revealing this person's identity would pose a risk to our design, your life and what's left of mine."

"If not who, then what is this emissary?"

"Just that, John. An emissary, a friend, a diplomat."

Falsham almost spat. "A diplomat. I have met some. A treacherous lot."

"Easy, John Falsham, you are tired and must rest and eat. We have much to do. Our treason, so alleged, will require patience this time. Patience, planning and, yes, even a little diplomacy."

Falsham turned and walked over to the window where his host had first seen the morning. His eyes narrowed as they focused on a sparrowhawk weaving in pursuit of its prey.

Falsham could not make up his mind. Was he still the pursuer, or now the pursued?

The sparrowhawk struck a small bird a glancing blow from above, and it fell to earth.

"Death is so easy," Falsham said, as much to himself as his friend, who had again turned to his writing.

"You know, and I know, John, that many men who would agree with such a sentiment, though from their graves. But if our venture is successful there will be little death and great reward for the living; that I can promise.

"The November plotters were brave, yes, but they were like the otter who closed his eyes before snapping at the trout only to open them again once in the fisherman's net into which the trout had unwittingly fled. Above all, we will have our wits as we go about our business. Do you not agree?"

Falsham found himself smiling, broadly this time.

"Always the man for words Richard. You would convince a saint that prayer was sin," he said.

"Quite. But now, John, we must convince others that our sins are as prayers."

Falsham was feeling hungry, and, as if in answer to his body's needs, the door opened to reveal several men carrying a small table, two chairs, bowls, jugs and platters of food.

"Excellent," said Falsham. "You, my friend, understand the weary traveler's greatest needs."

As he said this he suffered a pang, not of hunger but of guilt. Judging by his friend's appearance it was clear that it had been some time since he had enjoyed a hearty appetite and a satisfying repast.

The servants busied themselves setting up the furniture and fare in the center of the room.

"I would have us sit by the window, but I find that strong light is burdensome on my eyes, John."

Of course," said Falsham eagerly. "It is the company I keep and not where I keep it that is my greatest joy. It has been too long. We have much to discuss."

The older man nodded and motioned towards the table laden with meats and fowls, venison, rabbit and gamecock. There was also a large load of bread, vessels for ale and a wooden bowl with a grim looking broth that Falsham took to be medicinal.

Falsham watched Cole as he walked to his chair. One of the servants pulled it back and helped his master sit.

"Take off your sword, John. You have no need of it here."

Falsham looked at his sword, and it occurred to him that he had not unbuckled it since his arrival in England. He had slept with it. Even in the room with Beacon and the others he had kept it as close as it could possibly be.

"Of course," he said as he loosened his belt and handed the weapon to one of the departing servants.

"Perhaps you might make its edges a little keener," he said to the servant who bowed in response as he left the room.

Falsham took his seat. Cole motioned for him to eat, and he did with gusto. When he had finished he emitted a loud belch and leaned back in his chair.

"Who is the woman?"

Cole stared intently at Falsham.

"A divine gift, the vessel in which sails your deliverance, John," he said.

Falsham said nothing in reply. He rubbed his bearded chin with his hand and awaited further explanation.

"As you are aware, John, my beloved Mary died some years ago. In the intervening time I occupied myself with my business ventures. As you are also aware, I have been more than successful. Indeed, they say I might be the richest man in England. Of course, they only mean money. My lack of an heir was a poverty I found too hard to bear."

"Ah," said Falsham.

"No. John, it's not how you think it is. The child is mine, yes. But the child will not be the one who holds all of this when I pass a few days hence. No, the person who will take charge of my fortune and estates is one who I trust with my very own life, and you would hardly count a child in that regard, would you?"

Falsham shrugged his shoulders.

"You don't seem to understand. The person who commands my fortune commands our enterprise for as long as it should take. And believe me, it could take some years, perhaps many years. This time we must be patient and only strike when we are assured of success, and assured again."

"I agree," said Falsham.

"Then, John," said Cole, "you will also agree that there is but one man in all of England who can be trusted with my fortune, this, my lately acquired new and final home and, most importantly, my greatest desire for our mother church. And that man is you. John Falsham. You and you alone."

Falsham felt as if the air had been sucked from his lungs. He reached for a drink and missed. A bowl of something fell to the floor with a clatter.

"Jesus," he said.

"I'm afraid not, John. You will have to do," said the old man, and, amused by his own wit, he succumbed to a fit of coughing.

After a few moments he had recovered sufficiently to speak. He stared intently at his friend.

"Richard Cole will soon pass from this life. And that will leave only John Falsham. In a way, God forgive me, you will be like our lord on earth with the heavenly host up there."

The man motioned his eyes skywards.

"But remember John. There's no going into a tomb for you. You must stay alive at all costs if England is to be redeemed."

14

NICHOLAS JEROME BAILEY was in one key respect a fraud. He had encouraged an image of himself at the *Post*, one of a street wise Londoner with more than a tinge of cockney about his words, his attitude and the way he faced the world.

Bailey's roots were in fact miles away from Bow Bells. He was the product of a distant Surrey suburb. It was a life he had tried to shed from the very first day his parents had allowed him to roam London's streets with a couple of school chums.

In the years that followed, Bailey had been drawn into the city and its ways as if he had been a speck of stardust pulled by the gravity of a giant planet. He rarely left the metropolis now, even when assignments and junkets to exotic global destinations were dangled before his desk.

His attachment to the city had been mostly accepted, though on one or two occasions there had been rows over his unwillingness to travel. A fistfight had erupted over an assignment in Brussels. There was more to it, of course. The news editor that had been on the receiving end of Bailey's right hook, if it could be called that, was known for his drinking binges. Henderson, the newsroom's most senior man, had restored a semblance of peace. Bailey avoided Brussels and the offers of overseas assignments had all but dried up.

Henderson had come to rely on Bailey as a reporter who was always within reach. Even on his holidays, Bailey stayed within the confines of the city, often walking the dodgier streets in search of the unusual or the downright mad. More than once he had forsaken days off to cover for others. The union didn't like it and had warned Bailey of his overly generous behavior towards the company. Bailey had told his union head to go screw himself.

It was night now and the next day's edition would be all but set. Bailey had managed to get through this day off without plunging down obscure alleyways in the East End, or drifting into the newsroom.

The Blackfriars story had been a sensation, but it had since stalled a bit.

There had been a couple of follow-ups, but Henderson had told Bailey to bide his time while he made some phone calls to his police pal.

More would be coming presently, but Bailey was under instructions to take a little rest in the meantime. He had reluctantly agreed and only because he trusted Henderson's instincts. He figured, and his hunch would turn out to be correct, that Henderson was loading up on information before going for broke with a front-page story that would send the rival tabloid news editors into a furious tailspin.

A real scoop, according to Henderson, was very different to an exclusive. It was a front-page lead story that all the other papers would have had to run on their covers if they had it. As he had said more than once, a true scoop was a very rare thing indeed.

Bailey plunged his hand into the open tin and was disappointed to discover that he had eaten all his mixed nuts. It was the consequence of a day spent almost entirely in front of the television in his flat. And that day was fading fast. It was nine o'clock. The familiar musical introduction to the BBC news filled the room. A news junkie, Bailey warmed to the sound. He sat up and forgot about his nut crisis.

The top story was the culmination of several days of reports that had even grabbed the imagination of the insular tabs. Tensions were rising in the Taiwan Strait as the United States signaled that its backing for Taiwan's independence bid might not be absolute.

The news anchor, a woman with a South Asian face and untraceable BBC accent, spoke of mainland Chinese sea, land and air forces being mobilized as Beijing warned it would not stand idly by and see Taiwan fall prey to what it described as renegade forces.

Mainland, Bailey thought. Why they didn't call them bloody commies anymore was a mystery. He leaned forward in his chair. It would be just his luck to have world war bloody three erupt just as he was about to break the Blackfriars affair wide open.

"Bugger," Bailey said staring at the news anchor, putting on her most concerned face for the camera.

Bailey got up from his chair and walked into the tiny kitchen. The news from China, dramatic though it was, was of little immediate consequence. Besides, it seemed crazy beyond belief that war would actually happen. Bailey reached for the kettle.

He liked his tea. It slaked his thirst better than coffee and seemed to temper the nicotine buzz that was now just about constant. Bailey fancied himself as something of a tea aficionado. And a cuppa was still an uncontested English thing in an increasingly jumbled up world.

The world's best teas still came from places once colored red on the world map. Not Chinese red. So he had his packets and little replica tea chests stacked neatly on a cheap tin tray that displayed images of London: Buckingham Palace, Tower Bridge, the Houses of Parliament, Kensington Palace and his favorite, the Tower of London.

He wondered if there were trays with just bridges on them. He would keep his eye out for one with Blackfriars and serve Henderson his coffee on it.

The neatness of Bailey's tea pile was the extent of his domesticity. His was a bachelor flat complete with standard furniture, television, stereo, a futon bed and a stack of murder mysteries on the floor of the small bedroom. What passed as art were a few prints brought in by former girlfriends. There was a lone reproduction impressionist and a mish mash of 70s rock and 80s club band posters. Bailey's pride and joy was a signed poster of David Bowie. People once told him that he looked a bit like the singer. But that was years and pounds ago.

There were a couple of family photos on a bedside desk. These gave a clue to a childhood that was rather different from its adult outcome. The largest photo was of Bailey, his doting mother, stern faced father and an older brother who was a moderately successful barrister.

Bailey's father had died before he had escaped grammar school. His mother had moved to a flat on the south coast overlooking the channel, but not, as some of the real estate brochures trumpeted, with a clear day view of the French coast. He visited his mum three or four times a year. She called him once a week, always on Sunday.

The kettle whistled and Bailey went about his tea business. He warmed the small teapot, dropped in two and a bit teaspoons of tea leaves, twirled the liquid in the small pot and poured, tea first and then a little milk. He didn't fancy anything too strong. He tried to concentrate on the brew but his thoughts shot back and forth between Blackfriars Bridge and the Taiwan Strait. He was excited at the thought of what might happen next, both in the home story and in the Far East.

War between the Chinese and the Taiwanese would be a real stretch. Then again, there had been off-the-wall wars in the not too distant past. The Falklands for one.

Bailey took a sip of his tea and made his way back to the safety of his couch and television. It had taken all day, but he was finally at ease. He stared at the screen, the memory of his last visit to his mother barely intruding on his thoughts. She had made another pitch on behalf of marriage. He was not getting any younger, there were nice girls down at the bowling club; she could arrange a couple of introductions.

This was normal fare for a visit to mum. But last time she had scored once or twice. He was, it had to be acknowledged, getting older, and he felt the burden of a decision, one way or another. It was lately pressing in more than usual. And it would be a decision. Simply falling in love was out of the question.

His mind drifted through a sea of old girlfriends. The television was doing a follow-up special on the looming battle for Taiwan. That war might have been over when Bailey opened his eyes. For ten seconds or more he stared at the screen. It was late, very late. He knew because there was a thirties black and white gangster movie on. He had seen it before. Rico was getting his, but it was the thumping on the apartment door that brought Bailey to his senses. Christ, it must be two in the morning, he thought.

Bailey's hand instinctively moved to his tea mug. It was cold. There was a clock in the kitchen, but it seemed of little importance when compared to the ruckus coming from the hallway.

Bailey did not have a spy hole in his door, nor a chain that allowed a look out while the door was still secure. So he grabbed the first weapon within reach, the mug and its stewed contents.

"Who is it?" he roared at the door. The response was muffled, but he recognized the voice.

"Bloody hell," said Bailey as he opened the door. Bailey stared beyond Henderson just as Henderson stared past Bailey. The hallway was otherwise empty. Its dim yellow light was relieved not by the ceiling, or walls, but by the Polish landlady's portrait of the Black Madonna on the wall across the hall from Bailey's door. It seemed to shimmer, all day and all night. There were no exterior windows. Having seen that Henderson was on his own, Bailey turned and stood facing into the room. Henderson was checking out the place.

"There's nobody here, no women, nobody," Bailey said. Henderson stopped in the center of the room.

"Christ," said Bailey, "You look like hell. What happened? Editor fire you or what?"

"No such luck," Henderson retorted. "Have you got your press card?"

Bailey nodded in the affirmative. "It's in the drawer beside my bed." His look asked the next question.

"We're going out," said Henderson.

"Bit late for a drink," Bailey replied, a half smile creeping across his face. "Then maybe not."

"You've a cell phone," Henderson said, ignoring Bailey's attempt at humor.

"Press card, phone, notebook, pencil and one of the old hats with a card saying press sticking out the side. What the hell is going on, somebody shoot the prime minister?"

"Not quite," said Henderson. The man's eyes were bulging, and he seemed to be staring straight through Bailey who was beginning to find the entire scene a bit unnerving. Henderson had never been to the flat, morning, noon or night. All of a sudden he had mounted a home invasion.

"It's the cardinal," Henderson said.

"Who?"

"The cardinal, the Catholic archbishop of Westminster."

Henderson allowed his words land for a moment. Bailey figured what was coming next.

"How? He said.

"I don't know," said Henderson. "But I have a taxi downstairs. We're going to meet Plaice."

"At the station or Blackfriars?" said Bailey. He was awake now, the first trickle of a newsroom's very particular adrenaline beginning to take effect in his veins.

"Downing Street," said Henderson.

"Then I had better grab a tie," said Bailey.

"Does the PM know we're on the way? Will he make us tea?" Bailey's cheek was wasted. Henderson was already out the door and heading for the stairs.

Bailey sensed his world tilting away. A Chinese war was one thing. But somebody was murdering priests and princes of the Catholic Church in his own backyard. This was becoming more than just a story, more than even a *bona fide* Henderson scoop.

15

It was close to noon. The sun had vanished behind clouds and there was the scent of impending rain in the air. A gathering breeze rustled the branches of the great chestnut tree, still a few days away from full leaf.

Falsham was intent on what sounded like a cuckoo's call in the nearby wood and was about to relay his observation when Richard Cole let out a long sigh, one that made plain his ailments.

"It might be spring, my friend," said the older man to Falsham. "But this wretched body of mine is in full winter. And so it shall remain until the end."

"Oh, be still," replied Falsham. "I shall hear nothing of death. There has been too much of it and it must take pause, if only for a short time."

Falsham turned his eyes again to the trees. He scanned their bases but detected no movement. The only sound was the parasitic bird and a lone blackbird. The two were engaged in an unintended duet that Falsham was about to remark upon when the man spoke again.

"Take me to the chapel, John. There is little weight in my bones to discomfort you."

"Where is this chapel? I did not see one upon my arrival this morning."

"And that is good, my friend. A steeple tipped with the cross of Christ is not something to lord over the countryside in these times. No, this is a humble place of prayer. Better still, a hidden one. In your earlier ramblings you might have seem the worn path that leads into the copse to the side of the house. It is there."

Falsham awaited further instruction, but when no word was forthcoming he stepped towards the chair in which his friend was sitting, his upper body stooping towards the earth. Falsham pushed his sword scabbard backwards with a flick of his hand and, bending on one knee, slid his left arm under the man's near useless legs.

The old man leaned with the chair and Falsham, with little effort, scooped him upwards and out of his seat. Cole's face betrayed his discomfort.

"Thank you, John. Now if we could proceed to the chapel. It is time for my *psalterium beatae virginis*. You can join me if you wish. You will need our holy mother on your side if you agree to undertake the task I am about to set out before you."

Falsham began to speak but was interrupted.

"Ask no questions yet," the old man said firmly. "What I must say I will say in God's presence. Now hurry. I feel rain on my face, and I have no wish to be wet besides all else that troubles me."

Slowly at first, but then with longer strides, Falsham covered the ground from the tree to the path. Skirting the old moat, he carried Cole to the trees that stood like sentinels on one side of the great house.

"Keep on this path," the old man said, breathing hard despite being carried.

Before long the two reached a clearing.

Falsham looked around. "I see nothing of this chapel," he said.

"My retreat, John. Perhaps I shall rest here for all eternity. I could imagine no better place. Cathedrals are too noisy, don't you think?"

Falsham laughed. "Trees and a leafy floor into which you have placed your chancel and knave. There was a time when you were a man of grand style, Richard Cole. You have evidently trimmed more than that beard of yours. What little ambition you have. Why, I seem to recall we once planned a mighty monument to you in Seville, or was it Granada?"

"Cadiz. And that was the wine, John."

Falsham scanned the open space which appeared to his eyes as bell-shaped. At the narrower end he saw a low cut table covered in a lace cloth. There was a book and other objects. Beside the table was a kneeling stool.

"Your cathedral is a most sensible affair. It even affords a view of the heavens," Falsham said.

"All a wise precaution," said the old man. "From time to time we have visits from the king's men, and they are alert for all trappings of popery.

"I am impressed, as I am sure is the son of our heavenly father. He would feel quite at home here," said Falsham.

"Yes," said Cole. "Now if you would be so kind, please carry me to my sanctuary."

The altar, with its lace triptych, was adorned with two candles already lit. They were protected from any wind by two hollowed pieces of wood that served as screens.

"The stable boy," said Cole in answer to his friend before he could ask the question.

"Can he be trusted?" said Falsham.

"Can anyone?" Falsham shrugged and turned his attention to the table.

A small wooden carving of the virgin occupied a corner. There was also a jug of water, two small goblets and an apothecary pot.

"A simple holy place, John," said Cole.

Slowly, Falsham eased the old man into a kneeling position. With great effort Cole straightened his back and placed his gnarled and broken hands together in supplication.

"Is there a priest hereabouts?" Falsham looked around the clearing as if he might encounter a robed monk saying daily office in a shadowed corner.

"Yes, indeed, there is. He is in the house. But you'll not find him. He has a hidden room and there he will remain for a few days yet. We are soon to have visitors other than our Spanish friend. They will not be of the sort that takes kindly to a servant of Rome."

"Visitors? You are well informed," said Falsham.

Cole did not reply. Instead he appeared to enter a trance, one that lasted for several minutes as he gazed at the flickering candles. He broke his silence with a long sigh.

"Do you remember that time, John, when we met in the mountains north of Madrid? I was returning to England, you were just stepping a first foot in King Phillip's sunny garden."

"Yes, I well recall it. We discussed vigorously the heavens and the order of the spheres. You worked hard to convince me of the truth of what that Pole, his name I forget..."

"Copernicus."

"Yes, precisely. Copernicus. You agreed with his view that our world went around the sun. I challenged this though you must understand that I merely did so for sport. I believe I did agree with the concept. I recall suggesting that it was we who did the moving by virtue of God being wise enough not to throw fire all about the sky lest it fall from its heavenly path and set the world aflame."

"A most sagacious assumption; or perhaps blasphemy. Perhaps you should be an astronomer. You could dance around all the mathematics such men employ and merely order out the universe by means of a little faith and sense."

"I believe mathematics to be sensible," replied Falsham.

Cole smiled and returned to his silence.

Falsham, not so patient the second time, interrupted. "How is that you own this house? I was unaware of such wealth and substance in your family. You did not display the like of it in Spain."

"Why display wealth? It merely turns minds the wrong way. This is my family seat. The woman with whom I now share a bed is my wife, and, by some miracle, she carries our child. It will be born about two months hence."

"Ah." It was now Falsham who chose silence, if only for a few moments. "But," he said.

Cole waved his hand. "Yes, John, I can sense your thoughts. Soon, she will be a widow with child. But ease yourself. I have been preparing busily for the day, the end. In order to keep it out of the king's reach I have sent much of my money to trusted friends in Antwerp, Amsterdam and Delft, where I procured this apothecary pot. The Dutch are a pragmatic people. They care little who they do business with, so long as it profits them.

"So now I have just this one substantial property left on English ground, at least that part of it that is Essex. Should the enemies of our mother church come for me they will find little to take. I do own a house in London and for a time it allowed me to be to be close to the finest learned men of the healing arts. But that is no longer important.

"My wife is a wonderful woman and has cared for me well. We were married in secret so she is not known publicly as the wife of Richard Cole. And that, of course, will mean that when I am gone she can just as easily be another man's wife."

Falsham stared at his friend, a thought forming in his mind, a question on his lips.

Cole, however, had turned his face away. Words tumbled forth from his mouth.

"Pater noster, qui es in caelis, sanctificetur nomen tuum."

Falsham was staring at a rabbit that had emerged from the undergrowth into the clearing just a few feet away. The animal seemed unconcerned with the two men.

"Adveniat regnum tuum. Fiat voluntas tua, sicut in caelo et in terra."

Falsham looked to the sky. The sun was breaking through the clouds. A dart of light made him blink. The rabbit, he knew, did not have the means to shut out what he did not want to see.

"Panem nostrum quotidianum da nobis hodie, et dimitte nobis debita nostra sicut et nos dimittimus debitoribus nostris."

Falsham rose to his feet and walked toward the tiny animal. He wanted to give comfort, but the rabbit turned and fled back into the cover of the trees.

"Et ne nos inducas in tentationem, sed libera nos a malo."

For the first time since he had set foot back in England, Falsham recognized the nagging thought that had been kept at bay only by constant, secretive travel. It was not quite fear, but rather an overwhelming sense of not knowing while at the same time suspecting.

Others had plans that would involve his active participation. He was just beginning to understand what they would entail. He shook his head, bowed his head and put his hands over his eyes.

"Amen," he said in response to his companion's beseeching.

16

THE TAXI HAD BEEN RATTLING its way across London for twenty minutes before Henderson said a word.

"Needs new shocks."

The reference to the vehicle's sorry state was not directed at Bailey. Henderson was merely thinking aloud. He continued to look out the window. Occasionally, he would name a street. At one intersection he relayed a grim history. Just down the lane to the right was the scene of a stabbing murder. He mentioned a name. It didn't ring a bell with Bailey. Probably years ago, he thought. But Henderson sure knew his London.

The city had fallen into a fallow period between the time that night revelers finally headed home and the first business of the new day started up. It was a diminishing span, but London was not quite yet Bangkok.

The relative calm allowed the taxi to cover the distance from Bailey's flat to Downing Street in short order, despite its condition. The driver said nothing. He too sensed that the heavy-set man who occasionally talked to himself wasn't up for chit-chat.

The driver had reggae music playing at low volume on his radio and from time to time he barked something to his dispatcher. Each man was working his own patch. Bailey knew what his was, and what the driver's was. Henderson right now was a complete mystery.

"We're nearly there," Henderson said, this time clearly directing his words at Bailey.

"Yeah, things have been getting familiar the last mile," Bailey replied.

He wanted to go on, ask Henderson what the hell they were doing out in the wee hours. But he opted for a less direct approach.

"I take it the paper was gone by the time you got the news."

Henderson said nothing for a moment. "No, it wasn't," he replied.

Bailey, who had been slouched in his seat, pulled himself up. He waited.

"I got the call, but the deal was I couldn't run with the story. Nobody else will have it in this morning's editions. Television and radio will get it later and so will the *Evening Standard*."

"But we'll get something extra," Bailey said.

"We'll see in just a few moments, won't we?" said Henderson. "Just in here, pull in behind that parked car across the street if you can."

The driver appeared to jump slightly in his seat. He pulled his cab across the opposite lane which was free of traffic, and in behind a dark colored car. The Downing Street security gate was visible just a few yards farther on.

Henderson paid the driver and by the reaction from the man Bailey reckoned that a generous tip had been proffered.

Bailey moved to get out of the cab but a strong hand grabbed him by the arm.

"Wait a minute," Henderson said. He pulled a cell phone from his pocket and began hitting numbers. Somebody answered, and Henderson began to speak. After identifying himself he said "yes," "okay" and "yeah" for about thirty seconds before turning off his phone.

"Sit tight for another minute," he said.

The driver said nothing, evidently happy to absorb the extent of Henderson's largesse.

Henderson said nothing, and Bailey tried to restrain himself. His self-discipline didn't last.

"Eh, I don't suppose there's any place around here where a working man can get curried chips?"

Henderson was silent.

The driver wasn't. "Maybe we can order some by phone and charge it to the prime minister," he said.

"Now, there's an idea. A kind of tax rebate," Bailey said.

Henderson turned his eyes towards Bailey and glared. "Put a sock in it. I'm working on something."

Bailey shrugged, and the driver shifted again in his seat. The tip was beginning to wear off. Before it finally expired, Henderson opened the door and stepped onto the pavement. Bailey didn't need an order, or an invitation. With a quick good night to the driver he was standing on the street.

Henderson was already half way to the parked car. Bailey set out in his wake. He had figured out that the occupants of the car were coppers. It was Henderson's exact role in whatever all this was about that he couldn't put a precise finger on.

Bailey shivered. He remembered some line about the coldest hour being just before the dawn. It clearly also applied to the second, third or whatever it was.

He hesitated for a moment, not quite certain what to do. Henderson had slipped into the parked car. The taxi pulled past him and headed down past the Downing Street entrance and into the night. There was only one place to go. Bailey covered the last few steps to the car and opened the rear passenger door.

He caught the whiff of perfume as he sat inside.

Henderson, his head leaning back on the seat, had his eyes closed. He appeared to be sleeping, though Bailey knew that to be impossible. Henderson, so far as he could tell, didn't need sleep like other mortals and probably managed with less than the reputed three hours, give or take, that sufficed for Margaret Thatcher and Winston Churchill.

Bailey recognized Plaice at once even though the detective superintendent was only showing the back of his head. The car's driver was the source of the perfume, but he could only make out the back of a head adorned with short hair that appeared fair, though not blonde. The car was turned off, and there was not even a glow from the dashboard.

"Good morning, Mr. Bailey," said Plaice. "Sorry to have you up and out at such an ungodly hour, but you can thank Bob for that."

Henderson did not respond.

"No bother at all," said Bailey. "In my next life I'm going to be a night watchman. Nice and peaceful job."

"Well," said Plaice, "you could be a policeman. That's how we started out you know, being the night watch."

Henderson stirred and coughed. "Nick isn't interested in history, just the next story," he said.

It was actually an attempt at humor, but it missed the mark.

"Then we should move on," said Plaice sternly. "Oh, excuse me, Mr. Bailey, this is Detective Sergeant Samantha Walsh."

"Top of the mornin'," said Bailey in a bad imitation of an Irish accent.

"Nice to meet you, Mr. Bailey," said Walsh in an accent that was as London as his own. She half turned, and Bailey could make out the face of a woman of about thirty, attractive though no bombshell, with a strong chin and slightly coquettish, perked up nose.

Not bad for the plod, Bailey thought.

Henderson shattered the moment.

"We definitely have something. But just what is it?"

He was throwing the question out generally. Bailey shrugged, Walsh looked at her superior.

"What we have," Plaice said slowly and deliberately, "is a series of unusual deaths with a common, though as yet unpublicized thread that is seemingly linking them together."

Plaice paused for a moment. He was, Bailey thought, assembling a jumble of half-baked theories and ideas into a sequence, of sorts at any rate.

"First of all we have a priest dangling from Blackfriars in an apparent suicide. No matter what the truth of the matter, that will likely be the view of the coroner's hearing. Second, we have another priest from the same obscure order who apparently tumbled over a cliff to his untimely demise. That will likely result in an official verdict of accidental death."

"We have two deaths. The first seems highly suspicious for the simple reason that instances of clergy killing themselves are extremely rare. The second, well, I'll allow DS Walsh to throw in her sixpence worth on that one."

Walsh turned around almost completely, and Bailey could make just about out her full face by the glow of a nearby streetlight. She was better looking full frontal, Bailey thought. He smiled, but it was a wasted effort. Walsh was working.

"The spot where the priest went over the cliff is only yards from another part of the cliff walk where anyone intent on suicide would more likely choose. It's a sheer drop from there almost a hundred feet to a cluster of jagged rocks."

"But of course the local police are not thinking in terms of suicide. They have been working on the basis of an accident given that there were no signs of foul play, the priest had no known enemies, had lived in the area for several years without incident, and appeared completely happy in his life and work. In addition, there hasn't been a murder in the area since the 1950s. The local constabulary has only had to deal with accidents so far as anyone can remember."

Walsh paused, allowing the three men to absorb to ponder the conclusions of their faraway colleagues. She didn't buy them, and she was certain that she would not be alone long in the view that the locals had got it all wrong.

"By the way," she said, this time directly to Bailey, "I'm talking about a place in Cornwall called Little Polden. The dead priest's name was Father Jeffrey Dean."

Bailey had a vague recollection, a couple of paragraphs in one of the other papers.

"Sure, okay," he said.

"Well," Walsh continued, "Father Dean knew the area well. He would have known the ideal lover's leap, and he would have known the place where he fell over the edge was not particularly dangerous."

"But he fell over anyway," said Bailey.

"Had he just stumbled over while standing or walking by, he would not have come to any harm," said Walsh.

"The rocks below the cliff at that point are even more deadly looking than the lover's leap ones, but there's a grassy ledge just out of sight of the cliff's edge."

"Ah," said Bailey.

"Father Dean, being familiar with the area, would have known about it. Of course, if he was intent on killing himself he could simply have stepped onto the ledge and then off it. The end result would have been the same as at lover's leap."

"But you don't buy two priestly suicides," said Bailey. He was conscious of Henderson's eyes boring into him.

"We're not convinced there was even one," said Plaice, "but please continue, Sam."

Sam, Bailey thought; very cute.

"What I, we, believe might have happened is that Father Dean was not alone. That he might have been helped on his way, but by someone who might not have been so familiar with the locality. To fall over where Father Dean went over, you would have to jump twice. Or be pushed very strongly once."

"That's okay as a theory goes, but that's all it is. The best you can expect with that is an open verdict."

Walsh looked at Plaice. Bailey noticed the nod from the detective superintendent.

"There was someone in the area about a week before the, well, incident, who visited Father Dean at his rectory. Dean was attached to a small parish about two miles outside Little Polden and used to ride a bike to church services."

"He was a fit enough man then," said Bailey.

"Yes," he was, quite the fitness fanatic in fact," Walsh replied.

"We went through all his stuff, his books, family knick knacks and his wardrobe."

"As you would do," said Bailey.

"Funny thing was, he had no coats with any buttons in them. In addition to his working outfits he had lots of wooly sweaters, a couple of windbreakers and tracksuits. He did not have any coats with buttons, not even a long black one, the kind that priests use."

"Hardly reason for excommunicating the man," said Bailey.

He was conscious all of a sudden that he and Walsh were dealing back and forth between themselves. Their superiors were just listening, letting the two of them work through the muddle of supposition and conjecture to some, as yet undisclosed, final conclusion.

"No," said Walsh. "But when I looked around the spot where he went over the edge I found this."

Walsh had reached into her pocket and had pulled out a plastic baggie.

Bailey couldn't quite make out the small object inside.

"What is it?"

"It's a button," she said. "A button with a piece of thread still attached and also a tiny swatch of material. It was well down in a tussock of grass on the ledge, very easy to miss."

"Unless you were down on your hands and knees feeling every inch of the ledge," said Bailey.

"Precisely," Walsh replied with some emphasis.

"Somebody, or more than one other body, helped our poor priest over the edge," said Bailey. "The good father, fit as he was, put up a bit of a fight and managed to get his hand around a button and rip it off the killer's coat."

"That is exactly what I think happened, Mr. Bailey," said Walsh. "But as you know, it's a long way from thinking something to proving it."

"Not if you write for a tabloid, Detective Sergeant," Bailey replied.

He wondered if she had noticed his wink.

But she had turned around and had started the car.

"Which one of you gentlemen lives closest? Number Ten is booked for the night so it will have to be home sweet home."

Bailey stared at Walsh's illuminated frame. He didn't want the moment to end too soon.

"He does," he said pointing at Henderson, who, by his silence, allowed his subordinate's little lie to pass.

17

"Does the priest say his mass here?"

"No, it is not safe to do so. It is offered in the house. Perhaps you would like to attend during your stay."

"Perhaps."

"I detect a little uncertainty, John. Are you unsure of our faith, our principles and our designs?"

"No," Falsham replied with emphasis. "But I am unsure of priests. They are hunted and though some might possess a strength that is divine, I find most of them all too human and inclined to babbling beyond what is their preserve."

"Let me tell you of a priest, John. He was once inclined to great conversation, and his faith was matched only by his wit in all manner of things. He was also given to being outspoken, and some would say to a fault; but he was fearless in defense of our faith, and similarly erudite in condemning the heresy that is a sad fact of our modern times."

Cole, as if in sympathy with his subject, let out a long, rasping cough.

"As you know, our plot to see off this king and his fellow usurpers at Westminster was thwarted. I had this friend who was taken to the tower for what, happily, was just a brief interlude. In time, it became known to me that he would face what the king apparently believed to be the gentler tortures. He was ready to make his peace with God and, pray heaven, be borne to him on the wings of whatever angel might still be watching over him."

Cole seemed to smile and for a moment is seemed to Falsham that his friend was in ascendance over his body's pain.

"Well, there my friend sat in his cold dungeon awaiting his fate. But God's hand was at work beyond his door. One of the jailers, a large fellow with few teeth, seemed to take pity on him.

"And it was more than that. It was the case that his wife was of our faith and about to deliver another in a long line of very hungry children. This jailer, though by no means entirely supportive of our cause, had spoken to someone else about my friend's situation, at the urging of his good woman. In turn, he began to speak to my friend of a man who desired to see his plight reduced. He merely hinted at first; or tried to. He was rather a simple soul, and clearly not given to great deceit.

"The jailed man, my friend, had suffered through some of those preliminary gentler tortures, which, John, I can assure you were anything but gentle. At this time, and it was timely for sure, mere speech from the jailer began to take the form of action.

"The jailer told my friend of a man who had come to him, a man of some wealth, it seemed. This mysterious person had offered a mad, yet compelling proposal. For a sum of money, one apparently large enough to feed all the jailer's children until they were as fat and grown as he, the man would take my friend's place in the tower and submit himself to the fate that had been so cruelly prescribed for him."

Falsham's brows were furrowed and he began to kick the ground with the toe of a boot. Cole sensed that Falsham was both impatient and having difficulty in believing his story.

"Before I go any further, John, look at me. I am here, not in another place of God's choosing, and there is a reason for this." Cole waited a few moments until he was sure he not only had Falsham's full attention, but that his friend appreciated the importance of his account.

"The money, or part of it," said Cole, "was quickly handed over. My friend's as yet unknown benefactor was quick enough in the head to draw the jailer into his little plot before he could take flight from it. Once money had been exchanged he was like a fish in this mysterious stranger's net.

"The jailer came to my friend late one night and explained how it would all transpire. Unluckily for my friend, the jailer also explained, he would have to suffer the evils of the rack and other instruments up to the eve of his anticipated execution. This was unavoidable and necessary and indeed he did suffer these things, and the evidence will be with him until the end of his days.

"The night before the man was to be roped, drawn and quartered, the jailer came to his cell. It was late. He told the man that he was going to beat him about the face to the point where he would be all bloodied and bruised.

"He would explain later to the warden of the tower that the man had attempted to attack him and had denounced his majesty with such low words that he could not hold back. What the man was unaware of was that his benefactor had already suffered at the hands of this seemingly brutish jailer, though as part of the plan."

"So what happened next?" said Falsham.

Cole took a breath, one as deep as his body would allow.

"The jailer carried my friend to another, empty cell where his benefactor was waiting in an equally sorry state. They exchanged no words, John. My friend could barely move his lips anyway, but he later told me that he would never forget the look in the other man's eyes. It was not love, John. It was something far beyond that, something he had never seen before except in his imaginings of our savior Jesus. The man had the look of Jesus in his eyes, John; this I swear to you on what remains of my life." Cole took another breath.

"What happened next?" said Falsham once more. He was leaning closer to his friend, not wanting to miss a single detail.

"As it was told to me the mysterious man was put in my friend's clothes and moved to his cell."

"Did he resemble your friend in any physical way?"

"After that ham-fist of a jailer had done his worst John, neither man resembled any person. Only the benefactor's eyes seemed to have survived the beating, and even then my friend could see they were swollen. His beard was identical to my friend's, and his hair of similar hue.

"In total length and circumference both men were the same, and I suppose in similar clothes they could have passed for each other, unless a careful study was made."

"And it was he who was executed the following day?" said Falsham

"Yes. The jailer took my friend through the more foul and stench-ridden passages in the tower and to a door leading into a street. His wife was waiting. My friend was told to behave as if he had too much ale, as if he had spent the night in some Southwark brothel. He managed with little effort because he was drunk with pain. The woman was almost as strong as her husband, but she had a virtuous voice. She prayed quietly as they made their way to a safe house, not hers and her husband's as it turned out, but of an accomplice to the man now spending his last night alive in my friend's cell."

"He was not recognized the following morning?"

"He was not. The jailer made sure he was assigned to lead the escort party. My friend's original inquisitors were not present as much of the torture had been carried out at night, and this was now dawn. They were in their beds, warm and undisturbed by thoughts of execution. Their damnable work was done.

"I have no doubt that some eyes closely regarded the man being taken to his death, but to those eyes there was nothing strange in the sight of a broken and mutilated body, especially when that of a condemned man."

"And this savior. His identity?"

"My friend, now blessedly free, had been instructed not to ask too many questions. But, and as you might now suspect, he was a brave and holy man. He was smitten with the deepest consumption and an even deeper rooted desire to be a martyr for God, our blessed mother and our church."

"He died on the scaffold? By rope or by the axe?"

"I do not know for sure. But he did not take his own life. Others did. He is in heaven, John, where soon, I hope, I will get to know him better. He might well be a saint by now. I shall look out for his halo."

Falsham smiled. Humor yet lived in his friend though his better humors had deserted him.

"An extraordinary tale," he said. And if I'm not mistaken the friend who was freed in such unlikely circumstances is not too far distant. He is that priest perhaps, the one so outspoken and the one now hidden in a cavity in your house?"

"It is an extraordinary tale, one of such luck," replied Cole. "If it had been me in that dungeon, I am certain I would have died without a saint so much as sparing me a *pater noster*.

"But you are correct in your assumption. My friend is close, and, indeed, he is that priest. But the point of my story was not so much to inspire as to impress that, if we are to carry out our task, we will be required to display a selfless devotion to match both this priest and the man who martyred himself for him. Any life can be forfeit, and my life will soon end, and possibly even before God intends. But there can be a purpose in death than can change the course of events. It was so with my friend the priest and his God-sent benefactor, and it will be so with me, and you, my God-sent benefactor.

"We struck at the king, John, and we failed. I have considered the reasons for that failure very closely and know now how me must, and will, succeed in our next attempt."

"And who exactly are we?" replied Falsham.

"Fewer in number than before, but we will match numbers with cunning," said Cole.

"What is fewer?"

"Fewer, for the present, John, is but two. You and me."

"But what of our friends in London?" Falsham said, the tone of his voice rising.

"Perhaps they explained to you, John, that they have a plan to kidnap the king and replace him on the throne with some relative. It is a foolish and capricious scheme, one I believe is doomed before it unfolds. Our friends mean well, but they will miss their mark. Besides, London is awash with spies. I would be surprised if even now they are not compromised. I assume that they merely know you as John?"

Falsham, nodding, said nothing.

Cole was staring intently at him. Falsham closed his eyes and drew in the sweet smell of the forest and the new growth of spring. Somewhere, from the direction of the great house, a jackdaw cackled.

The rain, which had been light, was steadier now and Falsham stretched his right hand with open palm to catch drops. After a minute he drew his hand back and rubbed the rainwater into his eyes. He had forgotten how restorative English rain could be.

"How do we kill a king?"

Cole did not immediately reply, not until Falsham noticed a faint smile taking hold of his friend's otherwise pained countenance.

"To kill a king, we must first save him," he said.

18

Bailey silently swore.

He had only closed his eyes for a moment but he had fallen asleep in the back seat of the car. His first thought was simple. If he had snored it would be all over before it started. He didn't move for several minutes and made rustling noises as if he was turning in his sleep, and not snoring.

Henderson and Plaice had gone. He remembered Plaice talking about checking something out at the yard. It was just a few minutes' drive from his office, and he had another car available nearby. Henderson had evidently departed with his pal. And now there was just Bailey and Samantha Walsh.

Bailey stole a glance. Walsh was sitting upright and was clearly awake. There was more light in the sky and less sporadic traffic. The new London day was starting.

Bailey wanted to say something but kept his peace for a few more moments. Whatever his first words of the new day he wanted them to sound good, appropriate, smart, witty. He managed to choke back a "top-of-the-morning" and settled for "hi." Walsh, however, was ahead of his game.

"Good morning, Mr. Bailey. Sleep all right?"

There was no point in pretending.

"Yeah," he said, "always loved kipping in cars. Must be something to do with always being ready to roll. Looks like London's getting up. How long have the big boys been gone then?"

"Oh, a little over an hour. They went to New Scotland Yard," Walsh replied. She was so precise, Bailey thought. New Scotland bloody Yard.

He rubbed his eyes and promised himself an early night. But thirst and hunger would have to be dealt with first. Walsh seemed to read his mind.

"Cup of tea," she said and without waiting for an answer reached into a cloth bag jammed between the two front seats of the car. She pulled out a flask and unscrewed the top. Reaching into the bag again she pulled out a gray mug with the letters NYPD on it.

"Were you in New York?" Bailey asked.

"Yes, last year, an exchange with the New York Police Department. We were comparing notes on how to deal with terrorist threats."

"No doubt," said Bailey.

He was sitting up straight now, and his back hurt. Walsh poured some of the milky brew and offered the mug. Bailey reached for it with both hands, grateful for a little warmth. The air outside was chilly as was the inside of the car. Walsh had not switched on the engine.

Walsh poured some tea into the flask's plastic cup and took a sip. Bailey eyed her through a faint wisp of steam. She wasn't bad at all, he thought. And there was something else though he couldn't quite put a word on it. Not sexy. Confident maybe. Came with the warrant card and the job. She was nobody's fool.

"So the boys went for a big breakfast in the Yard canteen," Bailey ventured.

"I couldn't say," said Walsh. "But they did say they wouldn't be back."

"I don't remember that," said Bailey.

"DS Plaice called me. You were asleep," said Walsh, laying clear emphasis on the final word.

"Did he, now? Those two have me wondering. Thick as thieves, the pair of them," Bailey said, ignoring the jibe.

Walsh did not reply. An early bus rumbled by and somewhere a siren announced a fast moving ambulance. Somebody was having a lousy start to the new day, Bailey thought.

"What time is it, anyway? Must be time for breakfast," he said.

Bailey was hungry. He was also desperate for a cigarette. But hunger, he had concluded, was the more socially acceptable craving. Before he could check his watch Walsh had informed him that it was just after six.

"Don't worry about breakfast," she said. "I'm supposed to stay here with you, but I called a mate a while back, while you were asleep, and he's going to drop by with something. Should be here anytime."

Bailey warmed to the prospect. Breakfast with Samantha, he thought. Not too shabby. But who was she? No ring and probably close to thirty, a lesbian maybe. No, not that. More of a career copper, pushing hard to make higher rank by the big three-o. A few boyfriends, but no all out heart throb. Bailey decided to fish.

"Your boyfriend mind you working all these nights?"

"I rather like working nights. Feels like the time for real police work," Walsh replied. She was not taking the bait.

"But you do get a couple off each week," said Bailey. He was pushing it but something, he felt, was spurring him on, though exactly what he could not fathom this side of a brew stronger than Walsh's tea.

Walsh was paying no attention. She was looking in the rear view mirror. She turned her body fully around to look past Bailey and out the back window.

"Breakfast's up," she said smiling. It was the smile that did it. Bailey knew he would have to ask her out. Police and press liaison duty had its limits.

Breakfast was delivered courtesy of a detective constable who looked like he had wandered out of the English rugby team's scrum.

"Morning Leo," Walsh said with more enthusiasm than even the arrival of what turned out to be hot croissants and coffee deserved.

"King of beasts, indeed," said Bailey, only half under his breath. Walsh heard him and gave him a reproachful look. Bailey's wit evidently did not reach beyond the car's interior, because Leo simply gave the back seat passenger a cheery nod.

"Fresh out of the oven. London's best of French. Do you ever sleep?"

Leo's concern for his superior carried a familiar tone, and Bailey was worried for a moment. Then he noticed the knuckle-duster wedding ring. Leo had his lioness all right, but Samantha Walsh wasn't in the pride.

"I have the weekend off, so I'll catch up then," Walsh said.

"Righty-ho," said Leo before turning back to his car. Righty-ho, Bailey thought. Christ.

"Here," said Walsh, offering Bailey the bag and a tall paper cup that promised wakefulness.

Bailey took the offering slowly, didn't want to appear greedy. He removed one croissant and returned the bag.

"The policeman's lot is not a happy one. But with Leo around I'm sure it can be tolerable enough," Bailey ventured.

"Leo's a good sort," said Walsh. "Gentle as a lamb. Doesn't have to be anything else. Most of the yobos take one look at him and throw their hands up in the air."

"I'll bet," said Bailey chewing his croissant. He took a mouthful of coffee. It was hot, black and very strong. Perfect.

"I do have a little container of milk if you'd like some," said Walsh.

"No thanks," said Bailey. "This is how I like it."

We're getting all domestic, he thought.

"In case you were wondering," said Walsh, "my job is to keep you off the streets until a little before eight. The Prime Minister will be speaking to the press from the doorstep of Number Ten about nine.

"I know you have a press card, but the officers at the security gate tend to look for parliamentary identification on top of the regular card. And no matter how many cards you have they will only let in fixed camera position people at that hour. The rest of the press will be cleared in at about a quarter to nine."

"But I'll be ahead of the posse," said Bailey.

"Precisely," Walsh replied. "My job is to get you in early so that you can get a front row spot behind the crash barrier in the middle of the street, just opposite the point where the PM will stand."

"I'll be in pole position," said Bailey.

"That would be correct, Mr. Bailey. At about seven thirty, Mr. Henderson is going to call you on my personal mobile. It's a restricted number. I believe he will then tell you what he wants you to ask the PM."

"How's his missus? And please call me Nick. Can I call you Samantha, or Sam?"

"You can call me Detective Sergeant," said Walsh. "But if you're going to ask me out on a date for God's sake get it over with. I haven't got all morning."

Bailey almost choked on his coffee and did burn the roof of his mouth.

"Wherever did you get such an idea from?" he said. Despite the pain in his mouth he was smiling.

"Interrogation technique. I can read minds, body language," said Walsh.

"What sort of body language can a bloke give off slumped in the back seat of a car and snoring?"

"You weren't snoring. At least not much," said Walsh.

"You're too kind. How about Friday night?"

"Sorry, working," said Walsh. "I'm okay for next Tuesday."

Bailey's mind tried to imagine Tuesday. He was down for a late shift but could swop with someone for an earlier one. And, as luck would have it, he had Wednesday off.

"Tuesday's good," he said. "Fancy dinner?"

Walsh nodded. "We'll work out the restaurant later but first up, I'm curious. What kind of story do you expect to come out of all this?"

"I don't really know," said Bailey. And he was speaking truthfully.

"What do we have?" he said. "A couple of dead priests, maybe some more deaths linked to them, who knows? Now there's a dead archbishop, cardinal or whatever. Are they in any way linked? Is there a nutter out there who's knocking off men of the cloth? Honestly, I'm not sure where this thing is going, or if it's a thing at all. And why are you asking me? You lot have the inside track when it comes to getting to the bottom of this kind of thing. We feed off you, not the other way around."

"Yes," said Walsh. "But we follow set procedures. It's you lot in the press who can leap ahead and speculate. And if you were speculating, Mr. Bailey, what would you be writing?"

"Call me Nick," said Bailey trying to match Walsh's slightly mocking tone. "Okay, if I was speculating I could easily join a few dots, find a few common threads and point to the mysterious deaths of these guys. But in the case of the archbishop, what's his name, Murray, as far as I know he popped off in his sleep after hearing the angels call."

"Yes, Nick," said Walsh. "But if that was the case would you be sitting here in this car waiting for Henderson to call with a question that is obviously going to be based on the belief that the angels were a little surprised to make the acquaintance of Cardinal Murray at the religiously tender age of 58?"

Bailey said nothing, took another bite of his croissant and a mouthful of coffee. He was staring out of the car window at a street sweeping truck on the far side of Whitehall.

"I do believe you are on to something there, Detective Sergeant, ah, Samantha. We'll have a better idea in a few minutes when Henderson calls. Perhaps you should hang around. I might need a getaway car when I throw his whopper at the PM."

"I'll keep my engine running," said Walsh.

"I'm betting on it," Bailey replied.

19

Leonard spencer was paying attention to detail. And he was delaying the inevitable. He had pulled the zipper up on his rainproof coat but not so far as to obscure his old school tie. Behind him, several people were fussing with umbrellas. Spencer felt tired. It had been a long night, but if nothing else the rain would dampen the ardor of the braying pack of reporters outside the front door.

Spencer looked behind him. Peter Golding was standing at the bottom of the grand staircase, beside the portrait of Walpole, the first occupant of the house and, in the eyes of not a few, one of the wisest as a result of his acerbic assessment of his fellow parliamentarians.

"Peter, what was it again that Walpole said of other politicians?"

Golding's face betrayed just a hint of annoyance, but it vanished when he matched the question with the questioner.

"All those men have their price," he replied.

He had, of course, been asked the question before. Many times. It was a bit of a joke between two men who had little time for light humor.

Golding's eyes returned to a sheet of paper, one of a thick wad he was holding so tightly that his knuckles were red. Spencer and Golding had been in the trenches together for some years. Golding, now a minister without portfolio in the Spencer cabinet, was the Prime Minister's must trusted confidante. The two men could just about read each other's mind or so it was being said by the more astute political columnists. Spencer sensed that Golding was not so much tense over the contents of the briefing papers as he was alert to the possibility of the wind, now blowing almost horizontally through Downing Street, spiriting his sheaf of confidential cabinet briefing papers into the snatching hands of the press. Spencer allowed himself a momentary smile.

"Come along, Peter, for God's sake. The hyenas are hungry. Let's be done with it. My God, it was fine a few minutes ago and now look at it."

Golding raised his head. "Yes, Prime Minister," he replied with little apparent enthusiasm.

"You know that they will be looking for even the slightest hint of divergence between ourselves and the Americans on this one."

"Yes, Peter, and do stop repeating yourself. You made that point five bloody minutes ago."

"Ah, yes, um, right."

Spencer nodded and a hand reached for the inside handle of the front door of Number 10. In contrast to the black-painted exterior, the inside panels were painted white. But coloring was only part of the story. The door's interior had been bomb-proofed following the IRA mortar attack on the residence in February 1991. The terrorists had managed to lob a mortar into the back garden. It tore a chunk out of the garden wall as the cabinet was meeting to discuss military action against Saddam Hussein. War had come a lot closer to Britain's leaders than the far off Persian Gulf that day, and the outrage had neither been ignored, nor forgotten. Not only had the front door been reinforced, but other parts of the building, too. The glass in the windows of the Cabinet Room was now three inches thick. "Outside this space," a minister in a previous government had famously remarked, "nobody can hear you scream."

A blast of cool air invaded the hall as the door was pulled open. Spencer stood back as a couple of his police bodyguards moved out first followed by Golding and several other members of his personal staff. Drawing in a deep breath, Spencer stepped through the doorway into the gathering storms of a new day.

The camera flashes were all the more intense in the gloom, and he looked to the ground as he walked to the podium, sheltered to a tolerable degree under competing umbrellas offered by eager acolytes.

"The prime minister will take a few questions, but you will understand that we are on a very tight schedule today, so time, ladies and gentlemen, is somewhat limited," Golding said.

And thank God for that, Spencer thought as he flashed a wave and a smile in the direction of the journalists huddling behind a metal crash barrier. "Good morning, good morning. I expect you have a few questions, but first I just want to convey my own and my government's deepest sympathies to the family of Cardinal Murray and indeed the entire Roman Catholic community. I will issue a fuller statement later in the Commons. So, any questions?" He needn't have asked. "Prime Minister, how close are we to an armed confrontation with China?" "Prime Minister, have you talked to the Americans and what did President Packer say?"

"Thank you again. I'll take them one at a time if you don't mind. Firstly, I don't believe there is any likelihood in the world of an armed confrontation, never mind a war, with China over Taiwan. All the parties concerned have been, as you will fully appreciate, working around the clock to ensure that this matter can be sorted out peacefully, amicably and in the best interests of people, both in the region and beyond.

"As for the second question. Yes, I have been in constant touch with Washington. President Packer and I spoke last night. As you know, they are five hours behind us, so the White House is not as well advanced in its day as we are. The president assured me however that every effort was being made to, shall we say, lower the temperature, and I believe the United States is in a particularly good position to do just that."

"Prime Minister, Trevor Mitchell from *The Guardian*. What exactly are we saying to Beijing, and what have they been saying to us?'

"Well, obviously, very obviously, we have been in contact with the Chinese authorities, both through our ambassador in Beijing, with their ambassador here in London and also at the United Nations in New York. We have sought to assure the Chinese leadership of our good offices and our intention to work strenuously towards a peaceful and satisfactory resolution."

"Prime Minister...'

"And might I say, we fully appreciate the concern of the Chinese government in the matter. Of course, as you all know, we do have some experience in this area in the context of our negotiations over many years before the transfer of sovereign power in Hong Kong back in 1997."

"Prime Minister, what are we saying to the Taiwanese? After all, they seem to have started the whole thing up with their pledge to declare themselves independent a year from now."

"Well, I am not quite sure it was a pledge in the generally accepted meaning of the term. As I recall, the Taiwanese president ordered a plan to be set in train for a referendum on the matter of independence next year, and, yes, early polls seem to indicate a strong public current in favor of independence from the Chinese mainland. But I should remind you that nothing is set in stone yet."

"But the Chinese seem to be seeing stone."

"Is that a statement or a question? Of course there are varying interpretations of what was said, or meant, but let's leave it to the diplomats to work that one out, shall we?"

"Ladies and gentlemen."

It was Golding, now sidling in front of Spencer and making noises as if he was trying to clear his throat.

"As I said, the prime minister is pressed for time, and, as you know, we are meeting with Her Majesty a day earlier than is customary because of the cabinet meeting that has been moved up to tomorrow. So, if that will be all. . ."

"Just one more question, Prime Minister. Nick Bailey of the *Post*. Are the authorities satisfied that Cardinal Murray died of natural causes?"

Only the most careful of observers would have seen it. And one would have had to be standing just a few feet from Leonard Spencer's face. A barely perceptible narrowing of the eyes, a slight, almost invisible sucking in of the cheeks as Spencer took in a breath.

"I'm sorry, ladies and gentlemen, but the prime minister has to go." Golding was doing his best impersonation of a clucking mother hen.

"No, Peter, we shouldn't leave something like that hanging in the air. Not that it would hang for long in this wind."

One or two reporters let out awkward laughs. Spencer paused for a moment. He knew the kind of question. It was open-ended, and if the questioner had additional knowledge, his brevity did not reveal his hand.

"As you all know, Cardinal Murray, a most beloved figure in the eyes of every Briton regardless of religious affiliation, died of a heart attack."

"Stroke, sir." "Thank you, Peter. Sorry, a stroke. I was in contact with Westminster Cathedral as soon as I heard the news. I only know what I was told, and I have no reason to doubt the veracity of the Catholic Church authorities, and I am sure neither do you, Mister, ah, Bailey. I can say no more at this time. I understand funeral arrangements are well in train, and I will, of course, attend. Anyway, if that will be all, thank you all again for coming today, in the rain."

Another concentrated barrage of camera flashes erupted as Spencer covered the handful of strides to his waiting car. He almost charged through the open door, Golding following right behind. The driver gunned the engine, and the car made for the open security gates at the end of the street. From there it turned into Whitehall for the short drive to Buckingham Palace.

"Jesus Christ, Peter, where did that come from?" said Spencer.

"I don't know, Prime Minister."

"Check it out later. We have other things to worry about right now such as how to get through this meeting for starters. Her Majesty has been cranky lately. I'm not sure she particularly likes me."

Back on Downing Street the press crowd was breaking up. One or two reporters had quizzed Bailey over his question, but, as instructed, he informed his colleagues that he had been merely fishing. After all, there were all those questions about the first Pope John Paul and his untimely demise. "Besides," he said with a half smile, "I am from the *Post*.

"We are fishers of weird and wonderful stories."

His pun was lost on the throng, now scattering fast as the rain had turned into a drencher.

Bailey punched in numbers in the cell phone he had borrowed from Walsh. Must remember to add mine to her list, he thought. His vision of Samantha Walsh evaporated when the voice came on the other end.

"You were right," said Bailey. "I think the PM knows more than he was letting on. Bloody hell, we may be on to something."

20

"I'M SURE SHE DOESN'T LET HER PERSONAL FEELINGS get in the way," said Golding. He was rapidly pressing buttons on his personal organizer as he spoke.

It was a measure of how close the two men had grown over the years. Formality could be dispensed in private moments.

"I mean it's not exactly a case of off with the prime minister's head."

"Are you saying then, Peter, that Her Majesty indeed doesn't like me and is merely content to spare me?"

"Not at all, Leonard. I'm merely reminding you that business is business and that you sometimes take things wrong if people are not falling all over you and licking your arse."

"If anybody else said that to me I would throw him out on the street."

Golding pushed himself deeper into the welcoming embrace of the leather seat and stared out the car window. It afforded a clear view from inside but was smoked on the outside for security reasons.

"This rain might be down for the day," he said, as much to himself as Spencer.

"There might be more than rain falling from the sky if we don't rein in the bloody Chinese, the whole bloody lot of them," Spencer said.

"That would be one point three billion, give or take. Should we send one gunboat or two?" taunted Golding.

"Don't be so bloody smart. God, I need another breakfast. Let's be quick about this.

Golding nodded. "Step on it," he said to the driver, who was following close behind the lead police escort car.

Golding, too, was feeling the need to give orders. And that, he thought, was the way it should be whenever disorder threatened. Just give the necessary orders and all would be well again.

He glanced over at the man beside him, Leonard Gregory Spencer, Prime Minister of Great Britain, Northern Ireland and the few scattered islands around the globe that were the final remains of a once boundless empire. Spencer had closed his eyes, seemed to be far away. Probably winning Wimbledon, Golding thought, yet again.

Golding's gaze returned to the passing city. They were on Horse Guards Road, cleared of traffic by the Metropolitan Police. There were only a couple of logical routes to Buckingham Palace from Downing Street, but in these troubled times the actual route taken on any given visit to the queen by her prime minister was always varied, thus sometimes making the drive longer. It was either one of the straight and obvious ones, or one of several alternatives, but rather more circuitous routes. It all depended on the security considerations of the day. On this one, time being of particular essence, the convoy was taking a fast track along Horse Guards and Birdcage Walk.

"*Salus Populi Suprema Lex.*"

"The safety of the state is paramount."

"Excellent, Peter. Up on your Latin, I see."

Golding kept his counsel. It was he who had first uttered the phrase in the context of, well, he could not quite recall.

"Are we going to have a problem with the Chinese?"

Spencer straightened himself and made the face he liked to direct at television cameras when it was time to act tough. It was, as he liked to call it, his Battle of Britain look.

"Honestly, Peter, I couldn't say. You know how hard it is to read Beijing's mind on things. And that's really the problem, isn't it? So many bloody minds in the place. A bunch of bloody warlords. Christ, but I would love to give them a bloody nose. A bit of payback for Hong Kong would be just what the doctor ordered. A new bloody opium war and the whole lot of them staggering around their Peking compound high as bloody kites."

"It could get very messy," said Golding.

Spencer nodded in agreement. "The world is a messy place, Peter. Quite frankly it all ran itself a bit better when we had our empire."

"Ah yes, the empire. Your trouble is that you're the right man for the wrong time. You really envy Walpole."

"And a few more besides. But Walpole, yes, lucky man. It was all ahead of him, wasn't it? But I'm not quite sure about this being entirely the wrong time. We may have lost our empire, but we still have our united kingdom, our realm, despite all the devolution drivel. And if any jackass thinks he can take that away from us he had better watch his back."

Golding was studying his boss. Another look had come over the prime minister's face. Golding had seen that look only a handful of times in the past. And it had rather unnerved him because it never seemed put on.

He glanced at his watch and out of the car window again. In a few moments they would be in the presence of Her Majesty. The aging queen, Golding thought, was perhaps the only soul in the kingdom who was truly safe from Leonard Spencer with his rear end up.

The queen, at least, Golding thought, would be spared any impending outburst.

"Slow down a little please." Golding was taken aback. Spencer did not usually dispense instructions about the car. He preferred to be driven at quite high speed, and moments before he had been very much a man in a hurry.

"Before we go in," he said, "I want you to look into that question regarding the cardinal. What the bloody hell was that reporter doing asking it?"

"I don't quite understand," said Golding.

"You should, Peter," Spencer replied. "Think of it man! A rag like the *Post* is not going to drop a lead into a possible exclusive story all over a street full of rivals in the way that what's-his-name did."

"Bailey."

"And it was the *Post* that scooped the rest of the buggers with the Blackfriars Bridge business. That priest, the suicide."

"Yes, it was."

"Well, they must be on to something. Joining dots. Looking for links. I want to know what I'm going to be reading tomorrow, Peter. And I want you to find out. You have friends in the press."

"Good God, Prime Minister. You're not suggesting there's some lunatic out there seeing church clerics off to their eternal reward. A bit sixteenth century I should think," said Golding, a half smile on his face.

"But you said it yourself, or at least didn't deny it. The cardinal popped off in his sleep, called by the angels to his heavenly home and no more than that."

"That, of course, Peter, is how we should all understand it. How the government understands it. But I don't have to tell you that these Fleet Street people, or wherever it is they hang their hats these days, are quite capable of turning a misplaced parking ticket into a massive bloody conspiracy."

"Quite," said Golding. "I'll find out what I can, although I'll have to be careful. If the papers hear of us coming back to them on this one they are going to really think that something funny is going on. But you're right, I do know one or two people in the business that can be trusted, who will answer questions and ask none."

"Tweedledum and Tweedledee?" said Spencer.

"A little better than that. I'll get on it while you're meeting Her Majesty."

"Good man," said Spencer.

The car had almost reached the palace, and the two men lapsed into silence. This was typical. Before a meeting Spencer liked to mentally rehearse how he would brief the queen, what he would emphasize, and what he would play down. She would sometimes catch him out, ask questions about issues that he was less than fully inclined to go on about. But he had to oblige her, humor her, and, though rarely, indulge in a little flattery.

The relationship between prime minister and queen was invariably cautious, rather extremely so at the beginning. Her Majesty had the upper hand, of course. She had dealt with and seen off a lot of prime ministers. She clearly had favorites down the years during her epic reign. It was easy to discern which of Spencer's predecessors had found particular royal approval. She would mention meetings with them, crises mulled over long ago, and still cherished moments of levity.

Spencer didn't figure himself to be at the top end of the favorites list, but neither, he believed, was he at the bottom of it. He was hovering somewhere in the middle, a locality that, he was certain, would not have suited his hero Walpole.

Spencer was not conscious of the fact that his hands were clasped together firmly. Neither was he aware of the fact that he was breathing rather rapidly. But Golding was taking note. The prime minister's man paid close attention to his superior's moods, habits and nervous ticks. And this pre-meeting assortment was typical and right on cue.

Despite his bluster, his sometimes blasé remarks about the queen, Golding knew what many failed to appreciate. Leonard Spencer was passionate about the monarchy and to a degree that seemed at complete odds with the times. And now, though this meeting was a weekly event, he was preparing himself for something that he had dreamed off as a boy, a young man in the service and a callow MP with an eye for the main chance. It was the privilege of sitting in the presence of a woman who had inherited the mantle, and the burden, of a thousand years of glorious history.

Leonard Spencer was now only moments away from bowing to his sovereign and remembering afresh that order in the world did not rise from the bottom of society, but was bestowed from its heights. If he had one regret in life it was that he himself had not been born a king in an earlier time, one when earthly rulers did not have to take direction from the emissaries of the common people.

Leonard Spencer, in truth, was a most unusual prime minister. Some who had held his office had been closet republicans, closet fascists, and for all he knew, closet bloody Stalinists. But Leonard Spencer was something entirely different. He was a closet absolute monarchist, hemmed in by 21st century constitutional norms. And he was being driven to meet a woman whose reign was but a pale shadow of this deep and abiding belief in a monarchy more suited to times long past.

"We're here."

Golding's words dragged Spencer back to the present and the sight of the palace gates.

"Good, yes," he said. "Are we on time, Peter?"

"As always, Prime Minister."

21

Pender had given up his battle for sleep. But he had dreamed nevertheless.

Just one more job, and he would be packing his bags for a new life. There would be marriage, perhaps, barefoot children and a hammock. Occasional forays to exotic parts of the world for photo shoots. Yes, one more job and all this would be his for the taking.

And with a clear conscience, because his one unflinching condition with all clients was that his targets had to be bad guys, the badder, the better.

Dawn was still a couple of hours away. The city's hum was at its lowest ebb but the relative silence made no difference whatsoever.

For a time he had read *Revolt In The Desert* by T.E. Lawrence, and flicking on the bedside light he took another stab at it.

"At dawn on the sixteenth of September 1917 Lawrence rode out from Rumm. Aid, the blind Sherif, he wrote, had insisted on coming, despite his lost sight, saying he could ride, if he could not shoot, and that if God wished it, he would take leave from Feisal in the flush of success and go home, not too sorry, to the blank life which would be left."

A blank life, if God prospered us. How simple. Lawrence of Arabia, a war and a simple mission: kill as many Turks as possible, win a vastness of sand for dear old England.

Pender envied Lawrence. He envied all men who could refer to themselves as being of somewhere. Pender of Clapham, he thought. Who would write the book, produce the film? Who would play him when all this was done? Would anybody ever know?

He put down the book and got out of the bed. A few steps across the bedroom and he stood before the mirror, the little light above it flickering because of a loose electrical connection. The time for a planned repair job was almost over, he thought. Leave it.

Pender splashed his face with cold water and stared at his reflection. Not bad, he thought. Still on the young side of middle age and a visage that was of the sort that seemingly gave comfort to others. He certainly did not present to the world the kind of countenance that hinted at threat, or ill intent, quite the contrary. He might, indeed, have been a country parson, all tea and sympathy. Satisfied that his mask of innocence had made it to one more day, Pender returned to his bed and stretched out. He had a few hours before he was expected to show up for the rendezvous.

It was a good thing indeed that he had set his alarm clock or otherwise he would not have been standing at the edge of Clapham Common at the appointed time which, as it happened, was the same moment that Bailey was lobbing his question at the prime minister on the other side of the Thames.

Pender shuffled and pulled up his coat collar. It had started to rain. But the man he was meeting was punctual. Better than that, he was carrying a large red golf umbrella.

"Good morning, Stephen," the man he knew only as Father John said while walking right by. "Start walking with me. Here, there's plenty of room under my roof."

The old priest's cheerful greeting defied both the purpose of their meeting and the elements.

"Sorry to have kept you waiting."

"Not at all," Pender replied. "You were not late at all."

"I was, by three minutes."

Pender shrugged his shoulders.

"Let's take this path across the common," the priest said.

For his age, Father John could keep up a lively pace, and at first the considerably younger Pender, still stiff from his half sleep, had a little trouble keeping up.

The old man had not moved much in Africa. Nobody did. Pender noted that the priest's face was still tanned and lined. The equatorial sun had left its mark and no amount of English rain was going to wash it away.

The common, a 220 acre green lung for the great city, was almost deserted, the inclement weather imposing its own curfew. A few hardy dog walkers were about, but the hour for their meeting had been well chosen. The early morning joggers had departed and the lunchtime strollers were hours away.

"So, how are things in the photo business Stephen?"

"It's paying the bills," Pender replied. "I recently got back from Ireland, managed to put together a coffee table book, rather a fine one if I say so myself."

"Ah, Ireland," said the priest, his voice momentarily trailing away. "I was there once, many years ago, on a retreat. Best poker game of my life."

"Ireland's always a good bet for a relaxed time," said Pender.

Father John ignored Pender's little pun. He had stopped walking and had turned to face his companion, the umbrella now pulled down low over their heads.

"One last time then," said the priest. "Are you up for it?"

He was looking straight at Pender, eyes boring into the younger man's face, seeking out the slightest hint of self-doubt, reluctance, fear, ennui.

Pender returned the stare. "I still don't know yet what the job is exactly," he said. "I have killed before and I presume I will have to do so again in the near future. You, both of us, are long past having any qualms when someone deserves to peg it."

A hint of a smile crossed the priest's face.

"Of course," he replied. "But I rather suspect that this job is going to give you cause for a little consideration, perhaps even a change of mind. Put any thoughts out of your head, Stephen, that this mission will be as easy as the African affair, or others before it. Anything you have done for us up until now has been puff pastry, sinecure stuff, compared to what follows from this minute onwards."

"As I said, Pender replied, "I will do what is required, so long as I have the time and resources. Given that this is my last outing, I have been readying myself for something big, very big. Are you going to let me in on the secret here and now? I'm sure we're in the clear here."

It was not unknown for her majesty's secret services to lace even corners of public parks with high-powered listening devices. The two men were standing on a swathe of the common that, in the rain and a wind that had steadily increased in force all morning, had all the charm of a storm over the Siberian tundra.

"It's clean and clear," said the priest. "We have a few favorite spots, and we check them regularly. Besides, what I'm going to say here is not going to mean much to anyone, including you."

Pender was not in the least bit surprised that his companion was only prepared to divulge the initial stages of the task ahead.

"I can't reveal everything to you now, Stephen. However, I will say that it means traveling to the United States."

Pender's eyes narrowed, though due to a sudden gust of moisture-laden wind as much as surprise over his destination.

"My favorite place in all the world," he said, smiling.

"That might be, Stephen," the priest responded, "but also one of the more difficult places to operate given the level of security, especially since September 11. And, not, I should add, not only security enforced by the Americans. We have to consider our people, too."

"MI6," said Pender.

"Not them alone," Father John replied. "MI5 as well. They work off a pretty broad definition of their domestic security remit."

"But right now there is no mission, no plot, no suspect, just two men talking in the rain on a patch of soggy England," Pender said.

The old priest said nothing for a moment. He seemed to shrink into his raincoat.

"This mission will take you into their realm, Stephen. There's no way to avoid them, and the Americans and their myriad of security agencies. This is going to be like swimming in a shark tank."

"The more, the merrier. I'll spot them a mile off." Bravado was cheap, and he well knew it. But why not, he thought. It would warm him up a bit.

"Will you then?" the old man responded, a sharper tone to his voice.

Both men, their backs now to the wind, had noticed a homeless man about thirty yards away rummaging in a litter bin.

"Supposing, Stephen, that man was an agent. How would you rumble him? What might you look for?"

Pender stared at the man.

"Let's try him out," he said, grinning.

They began walking towards the man, who was paying them no heed. Within seconds they had passed him by.

"Stop here," Pender said.

The homeless man was still rifling through the bin, with some success. He had plucked a newspaper and the better part of an apple. Pender walked right up to him and reached into his pocket.

"Here you go, old chap," he said, offering the man a pound coin.

The man lifted his head, looked sideways and away from his benefactor and extended an open palm. He nodded, but said nothing. Pender gave him the coin and at once turned on his heel and walked back to the priest. "Walk," he commanded the older man.

They strode towards a grove of wind-blown trees, the sole inhabitant of which was a huddled gray squirrel.

"I don't reckon he was a spy," said Pender.

"And how would you reach that conclusion?"

"His hands," Pender replied. "They were all dirty, hard and cut. If he ever worked in an office, it was when dinosaurs roamed this place."

"Not bad, Stephen," Father John said. "You might make a spook someday but for now we only desire your services as…"

"An assassin," Pender interjected.

"We would use a very different word, Stephen. You are, for us, simply a deliverer."

Before Pender could respond, the priest was stabbing his finger into the saturated air.

"Did you know that a Luftwaffe bomber crashed over there during the war? They say the pilot was heroic in keeping his plane up long enough to avoid Clapham High Street. It's a funny thing, war, when you consider it. One minute you're killing people by the thousand and the next you're doing all in your power to avoid killing people you wouldn't think twice about annihilating from twenty thousand feet."

"Fancy a tea or coffee? There are some pretty decent cafés just off the common," said Pender.

"No thank you, Stephen. If it's all the same, I'll be on my way. And so will you, back to your flat. The first part of what you need to be aware of has been deposited there while we've been talking here. Don't worry, no damage done. Our man could pick the lock of the Bank of England and they wouldn't notice."

"So that's where you get all your money," said Pender.

The old priest did not respond. Instead he simply stood and smiled.

"I'll be off then," said Pender. "And you'll be in touch."

The priest nodded. Pender began walking briskly, giving silent thanks for the fact that the rain was easing a bit.

The homeless man, now far in their wake, lifted his head from the remains of a discarded fish and chip meal. It had been wrapped in a tabloid newspaper adorned with the headline "Loony Bus Driver Bit My Bum."

The man stared hard after the figure now fading into the misty distance and then looked downwards at his open palm. It contained not just the coin, but also a bronze colored medal in the shape of a cross.

He stood up. He had long given up hoping for relief from the pain in his bones and took what comfort he could from spiritual balm. His eyes now focused on the old man, who had turned and was walking back in his direction.

Good, the man in rags thought. If the pain of the body had to be suffered it was always more bearable in the company of one's confessor.

22

THE SKY WAS THROBBING. It flickered on and off as the storm rumbled over the East China Sea. A particularly strong flash made Henry Lau's eyes blink. This storm had its eye on the city. It was, he thought, at least an appropriate metaphor, if not an outright omen.

Darkness had fallen over the towers of Taipei, and most of its inhabitants were bedding down for an anxious night.

The city's frenetic routine, though unchanged at a casual glance, had been turned on its head by the government's decision to hold a referendum on Taiwanese independence. The natural storm that would strike within the hour paled against the political maelstrom that had followed the announcement. The island was feverish with rumor and speculation, much of it directed at its giant neighbor just across the Formosa Strait.

Beijing's verbal fury had been unrestrained. The military equivalent, for years made plain in excruciating detail by the mainlanders, left little to the imagination.

The Taiwanese leadership, in turn, had left no doubt that it wanted the roughly twenty-four million inhabitants of the island to back a proposal that would put more than the strait between them and the mainland.

Henry Lau supported the idea of independence, but for the moment he was not especially concerned with the reaction of the hated Beijing Communists, or whatever they lately called themselves. His mind was mostly focused on the pulsating pain in his head.

Still, he knew a vote for independence could mean war. Indeed, many felt that even an inkling that the vote would go that way could trigger an invasion well before the plebiscite itself. Perhaps, Lau thought, an invasion would offer an opportunity for an alternative form of death, and a far more glorious one at that.

Beyond the office window, the storm unleashed the first drops of rain. Taiwanese people were used to tropical downpours. If nothing else it would churn up the waters out at sea and make the night uncomfortable for the Chinese navy ships.

Taiwanese people, Lau thought. Not Chinese, but Taiwanese.

Henry Lau was one of the richest men on the island, yet he still considered himself an ordinary man, a man of the people. He had been born on the mainland in the industrial city of Chongqing during the height of the war against the Japanese. In those days, the city was known as Chungking, and for a few years, and for all of World War Two, it had been designated the capital of free China.

His father, a devoted nationalist and follower of Chiang Kai-Shek, had worked himself to an early death in a coal mine. But that same mine had saved his son during one of the heaviest Japanese air raids on the city.

Chungking was a river city, its heart on an island split by the Chang Jiang River, better known in the West as the Yangtze. This had proved unfortunate for Lau's hometown. On moonlit nights the Japanese had merely to drop their bombs on the blacked out space between the diverging river channels to hit their target.

During one such raid, Henry had arrived into the world, not just on the edge of town, but also deep beneath its surface. The thought of it still gave him nightmares despite the passing of decades since his first cries in a coal pit.

As a little boy, he had been nicknamed Coal Lump. He had taken the name of Henry Lau many years later in Hong Kong. But he would always be Coal Lump to his family.

Henry Lau was a vigorous man and looked years younger than his age. His story was a classic rags-to-riches tale, but by no means an uncommon one in the Hong Kong of the 1960s and 70s. After Mao's Communists had vanquished Chiang's nationalists in 1949, Henry's mother, with a degree of insight fueled by years of her husband's anti-Communist tirades, had decided to move her family to Canton, ostensibly to be closer to her sister.

The move was accomplished before the new rulers in Peking began to exert control over internal migration. Canton, however, could not long compete with the allure of the down-river British colony of Hong Kong. Henry's family had duly crossed into British territory. They did so in the dead of night, and, to the young Henry, it seemed as if all the decisive moments of his life would take place in darkness.

Lau had his eyes fixed on a blinking neon sign in the street far below his suite of offices and his own private retreat, the inner sanctum of Lau Industries Incorporated, manufacturers of, well, just about everything.

The girl had departed half an hour before. She was one of his favorites. Part Japanese according to her story. To remain vigorous, Lau believed, one's vigor had to be tested on a regular basis, at least every forty-eight hours or so, preferably after ingesting some of his favorite traditional Chinese herbal concoctions.

He prided himself on the breadth and depth of his taste in all things, not least women. He insisted on treating his dates, as he liked to call them, with respect. Still, they were required to work hard, usually for an hour at a time. Henry paid them well and swore to his handful of cronies that they were wasting a lot more than mere time by working out in gyms, crashing around in squash courts, or getting lost in the rough of golf courses.

Sex, Henry would proclaim after a few slugs of sake, or just about any Château, was the secret of a long life.

That was until he had been diagnosed with an inoperable brain tumor.

Rain began to splatter against the window. Lau retreated to his desk. It was bare apart from a laptop computer and a blank writing pad with an expensive pen awaiting its master's hand.

Lau was left-handed and addicted to writing things down on paper. He was also neat. Behind the desk, a table made of rare wood from Thailand was covered with framed photographs.

There were the usual family snapshots of Henry's French-born wife and the couple's four children at varying ages, up to, and including adulthood. There were also two dozen photos of Henry with world leaders. Henry smiled alongside the British prime minister, the French president, the Dalai Lama and the last pope.

There were others too, a couple with some of the more prominent Kennedys and a smattering of Saudi princes. Lau rotated his photo collection, showing only a fraction of it at any one time. There were many more stored in a closet in the corner of the room.

As he sat down at his desk, Lau made a mental note to change half a dozen of the photos in the next few days. He would also count, for the umpteenth time, his world-class collection of autographs, the scrawls and monikers of countless statesmen, the occasional female head of state, several despots and dictators and at least one former central African leader considered off his rocker by the rest of the world and rumored to be a cannibal.

Henry was particularly proud of his Saddam Hussein and Colonel Qaddafi pairing on the same page of his leather bound book. He also had a Stalin and a Hitler bought on the autograph market, but didn't show them around too much. People could get very funny about it when those two were produced, particularly Hitler.

He stared at the laptop, the e-mail still up on the screen. "Hooray, Henry."

Sir Percival Bertram's calling card had never varied. They had spent much of the afternoon in the office together, discussing the old days in Hong Kong. Percy had been sent by Spencer with a very special favor to ask of a very dear friend of Great Britain. Henry Lau had listened intently at first, nodding occasionally and refilling his friend's cup with tea. Percy was off alcohol, a wise move considering the years he had spent knocking back a frightening proportion of Hong Kong's stock of gin.

Lau smiled, recalling the meeting.

"You know, Henry," Sir Percival had said in opening their talk, "that we are very worried about the situation with the Chinese, the mainland lot."

"Yes, I can see that," Lau had replied. "I read the *Times* and *Telegraph* on the web every day. What do you think is going to happen?"

"Well, you remember back in the Cold War, those halcyon days, they had this clock, five minutes to midnight, a nuclear war and the end of the world and all that rot. Never happened of course, but in the end everybody turned out to be really rather sensible about it all. Even the Russians."

"But now, it's the mad Chinese."

"Yes, well, nobody is suggesting that Beijing is going to start flinging nuclear missiles about, but the feeling is, and I am reflecting the views of some of our top intelligence people, that they might be on the verge of deciding that a couple of hundred thousand dead soldiers might be an acceptable price to pay to reconcile your renegade province with the motherland."

"And why so? Why now?"

Sir Percival had an idea that his friend knew the answer to his own question but wanted to hear it stated out loud nevertheless.

"Well, you've heard the rumors about virtual rebellion in parts of the Chinese countryside and some pretty vicious fighting between the People's Liberation Army and what is beginning to look very like a viable resistance to the Beijing leadership in several provinces."

"Rumors yes. Always there are rumors, rumors, rumors."

"Seems they are substantially true this time. Large parts of the mainland are in a state of virtual civil war, although it has been hard to confirm with all the new restrictions on press movement and the official media prattling on and on about China's relentless economic growth."

"So why risk even more bloodshed by invading Taiwan?"

"Same old story, Henry, the need for a distraction, an overriding common cause if not exactly an outright enemy. The Beijing comrades can't label their Taiwanese brothers and sisters enemies, although I wouldn't bet too heavily on the prospects of your president and a few others when the PLA march into Taipei."

"And me, Percy?"

"If I remember it correctly, your British passport is about up for renewal, Henry. I can, of course, speed things up with our consular people."

"And beyond that, Percy?" Henry Lau was smiling at his friend who blinked back through his bifocals.

"We want to you to divest. Move everything out of here to Britain or a British territory, Bermuda perhaps. Every facility would be put at your disposal."

"I wouldn't know where to start, Percy. I am a man devoted to detail, but even I can't give you an exact figure for my assets. I have a rough idea, of course."

"You're worth just over thirty-two billion dollars. American. Trust me on that," Sir Percival had immediately replied.

"My, you have been a busy bee," Lau retorted, still smiling. "Should I assume that was this morning's estimate? What's happened since then? Another few million in interest in the family vault?"

"Very funny, Henry. But seriously, my good man, you have to see that the writing is on the wall. And it isn't a democracy wall. The Americans are going to cut and run this time, and there will be nobody left in the region capable of dealing anything like an effective blow to the PLA. It's been coming for years now. Taiwan, God bless it, is a democratic sacrificial lamb. There's simply too much at stake. Beijing has to be accommodated in the world, and that's that."

"Yes, I know." Henry Lau was no longer smiling. "What would you like me to do?"

"Come to London. I'll set up a meeting with the PM. We have a bloody marvelous plan that will secure your future, that of your company and family and not a few Taiwanese who you might decide are essential for the smooth transfer of Lau Industries to parts of the world where invasions are as likely as orgies in a convent."

"I know one." The tension was broken, and both men laughed heartily.

"Okay, Percy, I'll come to London to meet Spencer, and perhaps the queen, too. By the way, what is this great project you're thinking about? What is the plan?"

"Oh, did I not mention it? You're going to save Belfast and Northern Ireland. Maybe even the entire United Kingdom."

"Oh, really? Another cup of tea?"

"One more for the road, Henry, and then I had better be off. I have to meet someone in Tokyo."

"Dear me, I hope you have shares in British Airways. You're a one man profit margin."

"You should know, Henry. Anyway, we expect the announcement of your big move to set off quite a stir. I think we may already have announced a trade conference in Washington, a match for that last one way back in '95. And we are hoping that your intended arrival in Northern Ireland will be the main headline at the damn thing. Might even mean a visit to the White House and a chat with President Packer. I don't see his photograph over there."

"No, Percy, you don't." Henry Lau had leaned back into his high-backed chair and was staring at a point in the ceiling. "I've long looked forward to meeting with the leader of our wonderful free world."

A great flash lit up the room for an instant. Lau glanced at his watch. His second visitor of the day was due. As he considered this prospect his cell phone jangled with a ring tone version of the "The East Is Red."

The watch, custom made, had been a gift from an acquaintance with an edgy sense of humor. And this was an edgy moment.

Lau lifted the phone. "Come right on up," he said. "I've been waiting for you."

23

THERE HAD BEEN REPORTS of his proximity but as yet no sign of the king and his hunting party. Richard Cole had remained in the house since Falsham's arrival while Falsham had set about exploring the Ayvebury estate, both on foot and on his rested horse.

The weather was warming with the advance of spring and Falsham felt good to be outside and away from sickness and the incessant praying that occupied most of his friend's waking hours.

The farm and the surrounding lands had impressed Falsham. Ayvebury was by no means the most extensive estate in this part of Essex, but it displayed clear signs of sound management over many years. Still, the suggestion by Cole that the house and lands would somehow provide the foundation for a renewed plot against the king's power seemed beyond understanding.

The estate sustained itself and gave work, directly or indirectly, to several dozen people, but it was no empire. There had to be more but Cole had not hinted at anything beyond what Falsham's eyes had seen.

What they had seen was a farm that had long been broken up into enclosed fields. Some of them were behind hedgerows now centuries old, one or two surrounded by ditches that were dug by Romans. Roughly half the land was devoted to the raising of sheep, the rest to various root crops. The land was again divided between that part devoted to the house, and the fields that were rented to tenant farmers.

Swine, fowl and some milk cows provided for much of the daily needs of the house. The sheep provided for most of the farm's monetary requirements. Lambing season had passed. Every man that Falsham had spoken to during his explorations had told him, through often toothless smiles, that it had been a good year for lambs and that there had been much celebrating on Lady Day, March 25th, to mark the season and new year.

Though no farmer himself, Falsham had a keen appreciation of order and efficiency. Ayvebury enjoyed both. Living here, he had concluded, was not only possible but was indeed a prospect replete with the promise of many comforts.

Life's comforts, though, were not foremost on his dying friend's mind, and Falsham tried putting all such thoughts to one side as he contemplated what soon would be the most critical act of his life, a task far more dangerous than the raids on the Moorish coast he had undertaken with the Spaniards, the ones who had called themselves crusaders but who, if truth was told, were little more than pirates.

Cole's plan, what he had revealed thus far, did not impress Falsham. The physical part of it was easy enough to grasp, and could, he believed, be executed with proper planning, and not a little serendipity.

It was what would follow that seemed to be little more than in the lap of fate and happenstance. The king's reaction would decide the issue but just who, he kept thinking, could read the mind of a king? Certainly not himself, nor the ailing Cole.

A frightened and infuriated James might put the household to the torch and all its occupants to the sword, or the gallows. Any hint of papist plotting and all would be forfeit without question, perhaps even without a trial. And if the king's fury were thus aroused, the popish element would reveal itself to whatever degree the king and his less scrupulous agents required. Threaten to lop off a finger and it was easy to persuade its owner to point and accuse. Truth or falsehood would be of little consequence.

Falsham was puzzled, and he was impatient. But Cole had merely turned to his books and writings when pressed on the matter.

How, Falsham kept asking himself, could the king's mind be turned one way as opposed to the other? How could it be guaranteed that Falsham would find himself lord of these lands, so in a position to use his new status as a means to hatch a fresh plot against the king, a plot that would, God willing, enjoy the kind of success that that had so cruelly eluded the others in London? There had been no answers to these questions, not from within Falsham's own mind, and not from Cole's.

It was on the sixth day that Falsham took rest from his inspection of every nook and cranny that Ayvebury had to offer. A heavy rain had arrived in the night and staying indoors, close beside a large fire, was deemed the wisest course by all in the household.

Falsham had obeyed the older women of the kitchen and had placed himself beside a blaze, boots off, in the dining hall. A little before the noonday hour,

Cole had descended from his room, aided by a boy and followed by another carrying papers.

Richard Cole measured his day in canonical hours. Falsham was more elemental, preferring to mark its passing in degrees of light and temperature, and both the proximity or distance of meal times.

Cole, by this time, had done with his Matins, Lauds, Prime and Terce. His appearance coincided with Sext, the sixth hour since Prime at 6 a.m. Falsham braced himself for an earful of prayer but, surprisingly, his friend had other matters on his mind.

"Join me by the fire," Falsham said. There was no need to make the request. Cole covered the distance from the base of the stairs to the fire with surprising speed.

"You are recovered a little, Richard. That was quite a display of youthful spleen and vigor."

Cole sat in the other of the two high backed chairs that flanked the large fireplace. A momentary smile crossed the older man's face but just as quickly vanished as a result of a bout of coughing. One of the boys walked quickly to the kitchen for a draught. He returned moments later with an apothecary pot.

"One of my favorites," said Cole. "From Delft, you know."

Falsham nodded. The pot was to be admired, if not its contents. Cole passed this concoction between his lips several times a day. It was composed of a foul smelling liquid mixed with an egg yolk. Falsham had refrained from inquiring as to its precise composition but had heard kitchen whispers that hinted of a purgative composed in part of castor oil, rue, henbane and the juice of nightshade.

Cole said nothing for a few minutes. He sat rigid and gazed at the flames.

Falsham, though worried that the liquid was drawing his friend's last breath, was reluctant to break the silence. He did not have to.

"When you are a young man it is hard to imagine hell, though there are many types of heaven," Cole said. "And when you are a young man a sword seems eminently more dependable than the will of God."

Falsham said nothing, but he was staring intently at his friend.

"When you are a young man," Cole continued, "all in life seems possible."

Falsham made a noise in his throat that signaled agreement.

"I well remember myself," Cole continued. "But of course the passing of time trims the possible. Sometimes this is a matter of a man's choosing, but more often than not it is the actions of other men that determine the course of one's own life and the fate of one's own country."

Cole raised himself slightly in his chair and stretched his stocking feet towards the flames. Falsham sensed that a proposal was only a few words away.

"But above all this," Cole said, "there is no greater possibility in all of worldly life than the meeting of a man and a good woman."

Ah, Falsham thought, I was correct.

More than once in the days since his arrival at Ayvebury, Cole had spoken of the many virtues possessed by the woman who shared his bed. Her name was Ann Rook and though Falsham had at first suspected a mere dalliance, Cole had revealed that the young woman was in fact his wife. She was a cousin of one of the London plotters and, for all the rest of the world, a passionate devotee of the new faith. She was, of course, a most ardent recusant, a devotee of the virgin mother, Saint Ann and, for good measure, the late Pope Clement.

Cole smiled. "You have guessed John."

"You are a sly old fox," Falsham said. It was one of the few moments of mirth that the two men had shared.

"Yes, I have seen you cast your eye over Ann. And I take no offense. She is my wife now and for what time I have left. But that time is short. I must be assured that she and the child will be cared for after I am gone to God. Can you thus assure me, John Falsham?"

Falsham waited a few moments before replying. He knew what his answer would be, but he wanted to accord Cole's proposal the full measure of respect it deserved.

"It would be my honor," he said simply.

"Then it is settled," replied Cole, his voice cracking slightly. But there was no mistaking his pleasure.

Falsham said nothing. He knew there was more.

"Of course," said Cole, "it would do the honorable woman little good to be known as my wife. That is something that must remain secret between us."

Falsham glanced around the room and towards the various exits.

"You fear the servants, John," said Cole. "You need not. They are all of the faith, and their fate is bound with ours. Besides, they love their mistress greatly. She is nothing but kind."

"Nevertheless," said Falsham. But Cole waved his hand dismissively.

"Your marriage will be no secret. It is Ann's widowhood that must never be spoken of."

"So the child is mine, ours," said Falsham.

"A gift to both of you from God."

Forgive me," said Falsham, "but this blissful vision does not, to my eyes, entirely match our other, greater purpose."

"No, not as you are imagining events, John. But trust me when I say that I have considered our every move. When the moment comes I will merely be a papist zealot, a madman foaming at his mouth. You, by contrast, will be an upstanding husband and loyal subject. All eyes will see what all eyes will be made to see.

"And when it is done there will be mouths to speak, whisper and persuade. All will be well and our designs can follow at the speed of your choosing. I, God willing, will survey their execution from our savior's realm."

Falsham's eyes were fixed on his friend. Cole's precise plan was still a mystery, but that it would lead to at least one death and two new lives was plainly part of his intent.

"I pray to God that you are right in all this," he said.

24

THE HOUSE WAS QUIET. Pender stopped for a moment as he stood between what passed for the twin sentinels just inside the front door. The ancient Egyptians had used statues of their gods to ward off evil. Mrs. Leslie, the landlady, had opted for an umbrella stand topped by a framed photo of Princess Diana. On the other side was the potted aspidistra.

Pender eyed the door leading into the ground floor flat. No sound from Mrs. Leslie or her yapping Yorkies. Blessedly, Pender thought, the Scottish scourge and her mutts were out.

He took the stairs in a few quick strides, his hand gliding along the polished banisters. All seemed absolutely as it when he left for his meeting on Clapham Common. But of course it wasn't. Someone had been here.

Perhaps, he thought, the visitor had been rumbled by Mrs. Leslie and had delivered the kind of *coup de grâce* that he conjured up in his imagination every time she complained to him about leaking pipes, hissing gas stoves or dripping toilets.

The front door of Pender's flat was at the end of the hallway, far from the other tenant, a taciturn middle-aged man named Poole who worked in an insurance office and received no visitors. The two men confined themselves to exchanging nods whenever their paths crossed.

Pender's flat was at the front of the house, Poole's at the rear. It was an unremarkable hallway in an unremarkable row house. And that's how Pender liked it. The less attention he attracted the better. It was bad enough being one of the world's most famous news photographers. All else, he felt, had to be below the radar as best as possible, hence the bachelor pad in a street that looked like it was part of a studio lot version of London.

Pender, in both of his occupations, had a habit of dwelling on contrast; contrast between light and shade when his eye was behind the shutter; contrast between life and death when it was a sniper scope, though that had been a one off.

He had been standing at his front door for almost a minute, listening. Whoever had been in the flat was, he knew, long gone. There was no sign that force had been applied to the keyhole, no scratches on the wood. Pender inserted his key and turned it slowly. No friction, no resistance. The lock had been expertly picked.

Pender sniffed when he entered the room. No telltale cologne or after-shave. No perfume for that matter. Good attention to detail, he thought. And as he did so he smiled. He had caught the whiff of another's presence in the hallway, and while it was less evident in his castle keep, he could just about smell it. He had left the windows closed with precisely such circumstances in mind.

Just inside the door was a little alcove with hangars on the wall for hats and coats. Beyond this was the combined living and dining room, the table nestled against two windows that gave a view of the street below. Pender saw the brown envelope at once but made no move towards the table. Instead he walked the few paces to his favorite chair, a stuffed cloth affair with iffy springs. Pender sat and stared at the table and its addition. In it, he knew, would be the target, or targets, for his final operation.

Pender closed his eyes and allowed himself to doze. He needed a few more minutes of blissful ignorance.

And so it was that he found himself back on Beresford Close at teatime on a late summer's day in the 1970s. The whir of hand-pushed lawnmowers and the chorus of protesting dogs could scarcely drown out the din of the pack of boys kicking a scuffed soccer ball up and down the street.

Occasionally, the ball would hit a parked car with a thud and the posse would break for the other end of its world. When no irate owner emerged it would surge back down the street, its members pushing and shoving one another as they attempted to lay claim, if only for a few seconds, to the orange colored Wembley Special.

Beresford Close was made up of two distinct categories of house. Though they looked exactly the same, each with a prominent bay window, more often than not protected from stray balls with a large bush, the street was split into old and new. Half the street had been flattened by a bomb that had fallen just to the rear of Number Fourteen during the blitz. But it had been restored after the war with an attention to detail that was more pedantic than loving. There was a subtle divide on the street between those who claimed to have shaken a defiant British fist at Hitler and his Luftwaffe, and the blow-ins who had shown up when the scrap was over.

The Penders had been listed among the fist shakers, but the years having advanced, they were now part of a shrinking minority. Most of the neighbors now thought of war in terms of first division soccer teams. One or two, the more seriously minded, occasionally argued over the Middle East or a place called Vietnam.

Pender's father, a career civil servant who had spent his working life wrestling with the intricacies of Britain's overburdened transport system, had died from a stroke shortly after retirement. There had been suggestions during his last days at the office of some honor from the palace. But it had never materialized. The failure to reward a lifetime's service had fallen heavily on Pender's mother, the former Dorothy Hollings. She had been quite giddy for a while at the thought of being married to R.A. Pender, CBE, or letters along those lines.

Dorothy was an energetic woman, but one who devoted herself to husband, son, home and little else. The failure to honor her husband had been a blow, and the hurt had festered through the years following his death. Once or twice, Pender heard his mother muttering to herself that her husband had been ignored because of his Catholicism. He had paid little attention.

Dorothy's heart had given out as much from the perceived social slap as it had from corroded arteries. Her death certificate did not state it, but she had died from anonymity, hers and her husband's, as much as a blocked cardiovascular system.

Shortly before her death, Dorothy had made her son promise to work hard, do his best but not to expect too much in life. She had made it as plain as she could that she did not think photography, or the news business, to be entirely respectable.

Perhaps, she said, he might make a late run at a civil service posting. The Foreign and Commonwealth Office would be perfect. She had a cousin who knew someone at King Charles Street.

In the final days, she had pulled her lines in tighter, closer to home. Look after the garden and potting shed she had instructed Pender the day before she finally gave up.

After her death, Pender sold the house on Beresford Close and stashed most of the money in a bank. He wanted to travel and take pictures. One or two friends from university had managed to land themselves in respectable

Fleet Street dailies. One had even ended up in a tabloid but claimed he was having such a bloody marvelous time he wouldn't think for a minute of graduating to one of "those snotty broadsheets," as he put it.

Pender avoided the London papers in their entirety and headed first for India. His father had never been, but a small collection of books on the Indian railway system had been his pride and joy. Pender Senior had dreams that had never come to pass. The son decided he would live some of the dreams for the old man.

Pender Senior had been a man who gave off an air of holding great secrets. He had been quite talkative when he had wanted to be, or when the subject was to his liking. But there had also been long periods of brooding. Occasionally, other broody-looking types would turn up at the house, and his father would close the living room door.

From the age of thirteen or so, Pender, with the raised consciousness that sometimes comes with being an only child, had an inkling that unseen hands were at work in his life. His father's apparent income never seemed up to the level of his son's education that, by the time he was fifteen, had taken something of a leap from a local secondary modern to a fairly posh Catholic boarding school. Pender managed to do well in his final exams and found himself on his way to Cambridge.

He didn't give his good fortune too much thought. His father had vaguely alluded once to some kind of church-based group that helped out the parents of bright young Catholic men. Stephen had never been able to squeeze out the full story. "Kind of Masons, only Catholic," the older Pender had said in the shed one Saturday afternoon as he shuffled his pots of geraniums. Pender had half-heartedly pressed his father for more details, but he had merely grunted in reply and followed up with a sharp instruction to find the trowel.

His father's death had occurred in the second term of Pender's year at Cambridge.

Disaster seemingly loomed, but his mother had contacted him quickly to say that he need not worry about money matters. Things were being taken care of by friends, she had assured him. He had never discovered who the mysterious benefactors were. He graduated with his bachelor's degree and proceeded to make travel plans. First, however, he had to make funeral plans for his mother who gave up the ghost as soon as he was conferred with his parchment.

The day after Dorothy was laid to rest with the old man, Pender spun a globe to pick a destination but deliberately stopped it with his forefinger poised over India. Madhya Pradesh to be precise. He was on a British Airways flight to New Delhi within a fortnight.

Pender's eyes were open, all memories of Beresford Close banished. He stood up and walked to the table, pulled out a dining chair and sat down. He looked at the envelope for a few seconds, picked it up and sensed its weight. He gently opened the sealed flap and tipped out the contents. Inside were two popular news magazines. He didn't flip through the pages looking for notes or photographs. He knew he didn't have to.

One of the magazines had landed cover up. The photo was of a grim faced Leonard Spencer.

"Well you can't kill the bugger twice," Pender said softly.

He was impressed with his absolute lack of either excitement or emotion. His clients had only ever sent him after totally evil bastards. Spencer wasn't quite up there with some of the nastier dictators and warlords that he had seen off but there were rumors about the man. Pender had always thought the prime minister to be a nasty piece of work. Presumably, he was even worse than he had imagined. Bumping the prime minister off would be difficult, but not impossible. Much depended on his paymasters and whether or not they wanted it to look like a natural death.

Pender's hand slowly turned over the second magazine. He was smiling because the rear cover had an ad for a well-known brand of digital camera.

But the smile vanished when he saw the beaming face on the magazine's cover.

"Jesus," Pender hissed.

He was looking straight into the eyes of Billy 'Bud' Packer, the President of the United States.

25

THE DREAM NEVER VARIED and was as precise in its detail as the event that inspired it. Still, Manning had made it through his entire Irish sojourn without a recurrence. Georgetown, however, was another matter. It had come to him on his first night back at the house.

He was, as usual, in the driver's seat of the car. Dinny sat in the passenger seat and Rob was in the back, biting his fingernails. The three combined to make up all but one of the Irish Freedom Force's top four-man active service unit.

The other car was just in front. It, too, had three in it though not all of them were men. The woman in the passenger seat was Maeve. She was twenty-four, pretty and a knockout in tight jeans. She would be first into the bank on the west side of the street.

The three-member units were each to be joined by a fourth volunteer once the two trucks had been placed in position.

Group One, Maeve in command, would take out the west side bank while the other bank, right across on the east side of the street, was the responsibility of Group Two, Manning's unit.

The cars were to be parked at the end of the street, just as it began to give way to the farming country that provided most of the town's income. It was the end of the week, and banks were flush with money to cash the checks for the county's agricultural workers.

As cover, in case a Garda officer came walking by, both units had maps and brochures detailing the area's better trout fishing spots. But there had been no sign of any police, no sign of anybody in fact. It was an unusually warm day, and locals were staying indoors.

The scene reminded Manning of a spaghetti western in which a sleepy Mexican town was about to be hit by a band of gringos from north of the border. This was not an entirely far-fetched analogy. Rob was from Belfast, and Joe, in the front car, hailed from Tyrone.

Most of the group was, however, from south of the border. They represented just about all of the fighting power of the Irish Freedom Force, a hitherto unheard of republican paramilitary group, but one that was now poised to make its entry into the world with a big bang, indeed two.

Manning glanced at his watch. He looked at Dinny and nodded. Dinny said nothing, just leaned slightly forward in his seat belt. They were not going to be stopped for something trivial, and Dinny, who did not like wearing a safety belt, had been warned that this was one time that he would, at least until the two units were making their getaway.

"Then you can fly through the windscreen and get there before us," was how Rob had put it.

Dinny had said nothing in response. Indeed, he said very little as a rule and that made some of the IFF's people nervous. There were stories about Dinny, rumors, they had hoped.

It was said that he had been rejected by the Provos because he was seen as being too much of a headbanger, too violent for even their hard men. Dinny had denied any involvement at any point with the IRA. His word had been accepted. But Manning wasn't the only one who kept a wary eye on their newest recruit.

The order for the job had been simple. Speed and coordination would preclude the need for any violence. The money would not be in any locked safe when the units hit the banks. If all went to plan, the active service members would be miles clear of the town before the police could mount a pursuit.

That would be because of the trucks. But where were they?

Manning glanced at his watch again. He was almost willing the big hand backwards. Liam was late with the truck. Liam the Loser, Dinny called him. Perhaps he was right.

The safety and success of the operation depended on the synchronized arrival in town of both trucks, one of them, with Liam behind the wheel, piled high with bales of hay, the other an empty cattle transporter driven by a man named Dermot who had been assigned to the operation at the last minute by the IFF's central leadership.

At least, Manning thought, Liam and Dermot were in radio communication. If they were late by just a few minutes it would be okay, so long as they were tardy in tandem.

His anxiety was relieved just a fraction when the side mirror was filled with the hay truck.

"Let's go," he said even as his foot eased gently onto the gas pedal. The car ahead had seen the truck also and was already pulling into the street, its signal light flashing pedantically. The two cars drove slowly, the truck just behind Manning's vehicle. Rob was humming a tune to himself, some patriotic ditty.

The town had a simple layout. There were three roads leading into a square that was adorned at its center by a statue of a pike-wielding rebel from the rebellion of 1798. The banks faced each other across the square. It was well known that the customers of each were split along political party lines.

Manning's team was to hit the government bank, the other team, with Maeve in command, was responsible for rifling the contents of the opposition bank.

The role of the trucks was simple. At appointed positions on their respective entry routes they would be turned sideways, rammed into parked cars and abandoned. The drivers would take the keys, and the front driver's side tire would be deflated by means of a hunting knife. This was all to be accomplished in a matter of seconds. With the trucks blocking two streets, there was just the lone remaining street that offered an escape route.

The Garda station would be left in temporary isolation on the wrong side of Dermot's truck. Liam's truck would keep other unwanted traffic at bay for the time the two teams needed to make their escape.

It was a simple plan. It had just a few minutes to succeed or fail. Precision and speed were central to the desired outcome.

Manning was still looking in the side mirror when Liam's truck suddenly swerved to its left. It slammed into a parked car and stopped. Manning didn't bother to watch the rest. The car ahead was now speeding to its target, and he pressed his foot hard against the pedal.

"El Fucking Paso," said Dinny to no one in particular.

As they had anticipated, the town was in its high noon torpor. The planning team had predicted that weather would play a crucial part in the operation. Rain would keep people indoors, but high speed driving would be riskier. Also, traffic tended to slow down and condense in wet conditions. The last thing they needed was a traffic jam.

The better option was exceptionally warm weather. The day of the week when the money was in the banks was a constant. But Irish weather was a crapshoot.

The operation was fixed for a week in August, weather permitting. And today it was doing just that. The temperature was nuzzling above eighty degrees for the third day in a row. The locals, Manning well knew, would be complaining bitterly about the heat after months of complaining bitterly about the damp and the chill. It was the Irish way.

The IFF planners had been right. The square was deserted bar a sheepdog relieving itself against a parked bicycle. The first car pulled into a "no parking" spot just outside the west bank. Manning pulled into a space across the street from the east bank at an angle that allowed for a quick exit to the escape route.

The first car would have to round the square so its team was given a thirty-second start. Manning watched as Joe approached the first car and opened the trunk. The team members, their faces hidden by balaclavas, emerged from the car. Joe was pulling weapons from the trunk. They were inside the bank a few seconds later.

"Masks and gloves," Rob said. "Give them thirty seconds."

It was an age. Manning pulled on his balaclava and gloves. There was a slight bump to the rear of the car as Liam arrived and popped the trunk.

"Let's go," Manning shouted.

They were in the bank. The west bank had plexiglass security screens, and that called for either a hostage to be taken or a bullet into the lock leading to the inside area where the bank tellers worked.

The east bank was an old fashioned affair, one of the few banks in the country that still lacked security screens. It would be a straightforward stickup.

Liam and Rob were in front. Both were carrying automatic pistols and large canvas bags. As soon as they were in the main public area, they fanned out, Liam to his left. Rob to the right. Manning, with an AK47, and Dinny, with a pump action shotgun, went straight for the middle teller points.

"The fucking money. All of it," Dinny roared as they crashed against the counter. Liam and Rob had turned inwards and simultaneously tossed the bags across the counter.

There were two customers, both women, one elderly the other about thirty.

"Down, on your faces," Dinny shouted. Both went to the floor. The old woman seemed to crumple. The bank staff pulled handfuls of bills from their cash drawers.

Dinny raised his shotgun and pointed it straight at the face of a young teller. She appeared surprisingly calm. Manning moved the barrel of his assault rifle from side to side in order to keep the four bank officials behind the counter from making a break for the rear office.

"Not just this rubbish," Dinny shouted. "Get the big stuff." The woman looked at a man beside her. He was evidently in charge.

"Get it," he said. Two of the tellers stepped back a few paces and pulled open a large floor level filing cabinet shelf. They each pulled out square packages wrapped in brown wrapping paper. These were the high denomination notes.

"Here, in the bag," Dinny commanded. One of the bank officials rammed the package into a canvas bag but the second, a young woman, hesitated.

"Now!" Dinny screamed. Manning turned to tell him to cool it. Rob was already heading to the door with one full bag, Liam just behind him.

The young woman said something, but Manning did not hear the words. They were drowned by the thunderous blasts of two shotgun barrels.

Manning froze. The woman stood for a split second and stared at him. He shook his head. "No, it wasn't me," he shouted.

She tried to speak. Dinny was reaching over the counter waving his gun at another young woman who quickly stuffed the package in the canvas bag and hoisted it over the counter.

Manning didn't pay heed. His eyes were fixed on the woman who had been shot. Her white blouse had turned crimson, and she had stumbled backwards against a table, trying to speak but with no words coming out.

"Dinny," Manning shouted, but Dinny didn't pay attention. He was shouting louder.

"You don't fuck with me!" he was screaming.

Manning's hand reached for the clock, and it fell off the bedside table. It was still dark outside the house, but Rebecca had an early meeting.

"Just ten minutes more," she said, sounding fully awake.

"You were having a bad dream. You almost drop kicked me out of the bed."

Manning said nothing. He was thankful that in the pre-dawn darkness his wife could not see the tears flowing from his eyes.

26

HER BODY TENSED, and without opening her eyes, she clenched her right fist. Then she remembered. She was in her own bed and the snoring corpus beside her belonged to Nick Bailey.

Samantha Walsh wasn't quite sure how she felt about her night out, the dinner at the Thai restaurant and the invitation from a man she barely knew. Mostly, however, it was occurring to her that she might have to make a whopping breakfast, bacon, oozing eggs and all the rest.

Then she remembered, and it prompted some relief, that despite it being Saturday morning she was expected in the office first thing. Bailey would have to look after himself. He had muttered something about a shift of his own beginning in the late afternoon. That he was still sleeping soundly was, then, no surprise.

The alarm was ten minutes from going off and with a flick of a finger Walsh made sure it would keep its peace.

Bailey was lying on his back. Walsh lifted the covers a bit and inspected the man. A bit skinny and a bit pale perhaps, but overall not too bad. And he had been unexpectedly romantic and attentive over dinner, not at all what she had expected from a jaded hack from the likes of the *Post*.

Whatever his work habits, Bailey had been anything but jaded a few hours previously when they had returned to Walsh's pin neat flat.

"Rise and shine, sunshine. I don't suppose so," she said in a whisper. Walsh didn't want to awaken him just yet. She needed a few minutes to get her thoughts in order.

At the beginning of the week she had been due Saturday off. But that had changed by Friday evening. The phone message from Plaice had not supplied any details, but the urgency in his tone was clear. A break in the case of the dead priests was a possibility, but at the end of the message Plaice had hinted at something more personal.

"A bit of an opportunity for you," is how he put it, without elaboration.

Walsh, now sitting upright, regarded her own body. She stretched to a respectable five feet seven inches. Not bad for her age, she thought, not bad at all. But of course she was a copper, and one who had taken every opportunity for physical fitness that the job allowed. Nevertheless, she felt more than a little self-conscious. Whatever about the throes of passion in the darkness of night, she was not quite ready to present herself full frontal to Bailey in the light of day, or what would be the light of day when she pulled back the heavy drapes.

She reached over to the bedside chair and grabbed the extra large tee shirt with San Francisco inscribed in beg red letters on the front. She pulled the garment over her head and yawned. There was still no movement from Bailey, so she swung out of the bed and tiptoed towards the bathroom.

She only got half way.

"Morning, all," said Bailey, his voice giving no hint of a man emerging from deep slumber.

"You were awake," said Walsh, sounding not exactly unpleased. "You sneak."

"I was daydreaming," Bailey replied. "Nice one, too. All about how I got arrested and dragged into the scratcher by this super sleuth with a sexy voice."

"Stoppit," Walsh said. She turned her head away to hide the smile.

"I'm sorry but you're going to have to get your own breakfast. I have to go into the office. I'll manage a quick shower and that's about it."

"Room for two?" Bailey said.

"You stay where you are or I will indeed arrest you."

But of course he didn't.

Walsh was still trying to figure out why she found Bailey so attractive when she knocked on Plaice's door. She had a foot in before Plaice had time to say anything.

"Come in. Good morning," said Plaice. "Thanks for being so punctual, not that I would have expected anything less from you."

"Morning, guv," Walsh replied.

"Take a seat," said Plaice. "Tea? Coffee?"

Walsh shook her head. She went straight at it. "News about the priests?"

"Well, some but not much. I think the inquest on Blackfriars is heading towards a suicide after all. Your Cornwall business is as was. We've asked the locals to ask a few more questions, but I wouldn't bet my last pound on a result. The other couple, well..." Plaice allowed his voice to trail away.

"That said," he quickly added, "I am still not fully convinced that the Blackfriars death was self administered. I have been looking into the man a little more. From what we have uncovered he just seems too private an individual for such a...," Plaice paused for a moment, "display."

Walsh felt a little frustration creeping in but it was just as quickly pushed aside by fresh thoughts of Nick Bailey. Her parents would never approve. A journalist was bad enough, but a reporter for a paper like the *Post* would be met with scornful dismissal.

She was conscious of Plaice talking, and then conscious of his silence.

"Sorry, guv. I've been a bit distracted. A family matter."

"Nothing serious I hope," said Plaice.

"No, not really. But, guv, I was sure that there was something really odd about the Cornwall business. Shouldn't we have a longer look ourselves before turning it back to the locals?"

"Of course, Sam," Plaice replied, leaning over his desk and clasping his hands in that 'I want to be perfectly frank with you' pose that Walsh well knew was a precursor to an entirely different tack.

"But there are other matters to attend to. Matters that concern your career and advancement."

Walsh sat back in her chair and stared at Plaice. That she had done something wrong was her first thought, but Plaice did not appear to be heading in that direction. He seemed too relaxed for that.

"You have been a terrific asset to this team, Sam," Plaice said.

Walsh started at Plaice and slightly beyond him. Plaice had pulled a file from the side of his desk and had opened it. Walsh assumed it was hers.

"You have been very diligent, Sam, when it comes to taking courses and adding to your *curriculum vitae*. Most laudable."

Plaice paused and shuffled a few papers.

"Most particularly," he said, "that stint up in Milton with SO19," he said referring to the Metropolitan Police firearms training facility. "Turns out you're a crack shot, one of the best they have ever seen. A right Annie Oakley."

"It was very enjoyable and interesting," Walsh replied allowing herself to inject a little more enthusiasm into her words.

"Well, also revealing," said Plaice. "You came out tops in the all the psychological testing, and I see here that you are more than proficient with several weapons."

Plaice looked at Walsh. He was inviting a further response to what was now a well and truly changed subject

"Yes, guv," she said. "Glock 17 and Heckler and Koch MP5 carbine."

"Precisely," said Plaice. "The only problem is that you didn't complete the course."

"There was a family matter. You probably remember that my mum wasn't too well."

"Ah yes," said Plaice. "I understand. But have you thought about finishing what you started? You are most of the way there as it is and there would be no problem in facilitating the necessary time."

"Are you trying to get rid of me?" said Walsh, her smile a cover for her rising puzzlement, and the first atoms of annoyance.

"Let me be frank with you," said Plaice. "The most exciting future in this force, sadly perhaps, is for those officers proficient with firearms. To the public eye we are still an unarmed force. But you know that the number of officers carrying firearms is rising all the time. There will come a day, and it isn't all that far off, when the unarmed bobby is going to go the way of the police whistle."

Plaice paused to let his words sink in.

"You have a chance to get in ahead of the rush. Most armed officers are still men. You can handle a gun better than most of them according to this file. And I don't have to tell you that this is the sort of orientation and proficiency that will propel you into even higher ranks. And you do want to advance in the ranks?"

"Absolutely, of course, yes," said Walsh nodding her head. "I wouldn't mind being chief constable for that matter."

She immediately regretted this, but Plaice didn't seem to take it as facetiousness, or cheek.

"I know you're interested in travel, Sam," said Plaice. "That time we were doing a course exchange with the Germans you almost took a flying leap into the plane."

Walsh smiled, this time prompted by memories of going on night patrol with the Frankfurt Polizei, not to mention a little after-hours activity, much of it involving beer and singing.

"Now there's the Special Branch, the various anti-terror units and the royal and diplomatic protection units. All of them work on a have-gun-will-travel basis," said Plaice.

"I know your family roots are in Ireland and a Special Branch posting, for example, would have a nice twist to it."

"How so?" Walsh responded.

"Well, you may or may not know that the branch was formed back in the 1880s to specifically combat your Fenians when they were trying to blow up buildings around here with politicians in them. They called it the Special Irish Branch at the time. It evolved from there, although I dare say the middle name in the title was never too far in the background in the bad days of the troubles in Northern Ireland."

"That's fascinating, sir, but what guarantees do I have that I could make the transfer to any one of these units. I could apply, yes, but I'm sure there's quite a queue for all of them."

"Sam, you underestimate yourself. You're top of the line, and I have that from above. I know that you made an inquiry last year about diplomatic protection work. I think that would be an ideal start. You get to be seen, and you meet all sorts of interesting people."

Before Walsh could reply, Plaice closed her file and stood up.

"What I'm saying is that I know there is a vacancy coming up in the prime minister's protection team. And they want a woman. Not a token woman, but an officer who really could save the man's life."

The day was not panning out quite as Walsh expected. She stared at her closed file and did not immediately reply.

"Sounds very interesting," she said after a few moments.

"Listen, Sam," said Plaice, "I don't want you to rush into a decision, but all I can say is that another visit to Milton will do you a lot of good. Trust me."

"I do," Walsh said, rising from her seat.

"I'll let you know by Monday. By the way, am I working on cases today?"

"No," said Plaice. "The day's all yours, and I hope it wasn't inconvenient that you had to rush in this morning."

"Not at all," said Walsh, turning towards the door. "All that you said was very interesting. And I appreciate it. It sounds like you put in a good word for me."

"Don't mention it. On your way out please tell Detective Sergeant Smith that I want to see him for a minute."

Walsh nodded and stepped into the corridor. She punched the air with delight and just as quickly folded her arms. It was flattering to be presented with such opportunity. But something was nagging her.

She couldn't quite let go of the idea that the higher ups that Plaice had been speaking with were less interested in her progress through the ranks as they were in diverting her from the Blackfriars case and the other, quite possibly connected, cases involving dead Roman Catholic priests.

Something was up, she thought as she went in search of Tony Smith.

27

THE STORM WAS VENTING its full fury over Taipei, the flashes lighting up Henry Lau's office almost overlapping.

More than one bolt had struck the antennae atop the Taipei 101 building, which, for a brief time, had been the world's tallest structure.

Lau preferred low light in his office so the contrast between the dim glow and the flashes was both startling and stimulating. The light within came from five lamps distributed around his sanctum, each with a shade illustrating a scene from imperial Chinese history. There were, additionally, inset lights in the ceiling in one corner of the room, but they were switched off. In the relative darkness, the effect of each lightning bolt was all the more dramatic.

Lau covered the few strides to a drinks cabinet big enough to entertain half the town. He opened the doors and lifted a tray already laden with a bottle of wine and two glasses and made his way cautiously back to the desk.

Another flash and a bang, but it didn't entirely drown out the firm tapping on the office door.

"Come right on in, Roger," Lau said into an intercom speaker that relayed his command to the hallway outside the office.

The door opened to reveal a man who was clearly a little worse for the weather. In his right hand he was holding a leather briefcase.

"Quite a show. Far more exhilarating than what we are used to in England, even with global warming," Roger Burdin said with mock cheeriness.

"I grew up with loud bangs and explosions," Lau replied. "You get used to them. Step in, Roger, take your coat off and sit down. A glass of wine perhaps."

"Delighted," said Burdin.

The man who enjoyed mountain walks stepped firmly across the carpeted floor and sat down heavily in a swivel chair on the far side of the desk from his host.

"Not English rain at all. I was only in the open for a few seconds, but that's all it took. Cats and dogs has nothing on it. I'm drenched," Burdin said.

"Yes, I imagine you come from a corner of the world where it rains frequently, but never with such ferocity. You never have told me exactly where you hail from, Roger," Lau said.

Burdin was staring intently at the label on the wine bottle. It was, astonishingly, a Chateau Lafitte '61.

"Kent. By the sea," he said, still mesmerized by his host's offering.

"I have never been to Kent. Never have been outside London on my visits to your country. It's nice there, in Kent, I mean?" Lau said.

"Oh splendid," said Burdin. "But I didn't dally, as you are aware. It must have been growing up by the sea, but I always wanted to travel the world. So the Foreign and Commonwealth Office seemed the cheapest and most sensible way of doing it."

"You English are so sensible," Lau said. He smiled as he expertly attacked the bottle with a corkscrew topped with a dragon's head.

"So," Lau continued, "Sir Percy was here earlier this afternoon. It was straightforward FCO business. Not with the MI6 twist that you bring to the table, Roger."

Burdin did not immediately reply. Instead, and by long habit, he half glanced over his shoulder.

"Don't worry, Roger. First of all I know you were not followed here tonight. I made sure of it, just as I'm sure you did. And this office, indeed this entire floor, is completely bug proof. Nothing is recorded, unless I desire it."

"I never doubted," Burdin replied. He had folded one leg over the other and his foot had been tapping at the air in an agitated fashion. Now, Lau noticed, it had stopped.

"You have the documentation, Roger?"

Burdin nodded towards the briefcase. He had set it down on the floor beside his chair.

"Excellent," said Lau. "But before business we should relax a little over a glass. It probably should breathe a little longer, but life is too short, and we have work to do."

"I agree," said Burdin.

Lau poured a glass of the vintage for his guest and then one for himself. It had noticeably less wine in it. Henry Lau had a high tolerance for pain but a low one for alcohol, so although his wine collection was one of the best in the world, it was mostly enjoyed by others.

"What do you think I'll have to do and how much will I have to spend to drum up interest in this Northern Ireland trade conference?" he asked his guest.

And without waiting for a reply, "It hardly seems to be that important with Taiwan about to go down faster than the Titanic, but Percy is most enthusiastic about it," Lau said as he raised his glass.

"Well, actually, that might help you a bit," Burdin replied, raising his drink in return.

"The Americans are clearly going to be embarrassed by what's going to happen next no matter what way they try to explain it. All those years of standing by Taipei and, poof, they cut and run as soon as the Chinese threaten to take to their landing craft."

"But why, Roger? Why after all these years? How could the Americans betray us?"

Burdin shifted in his chair.

"No mystery, really. Not in my trade anyway. After the Islamic fundamentalist attacks a few years back, Washington cut a secret deal with Beijing, or perhaps it might be more accurate to say that Beijing cut the deal and Washington acquiesced.

"In return for Chinese support, or more to the point, little or no Chinese opposition at the United Nations or anywhere else, Washington would attempt to persuade Taipei to move towards integration with the mainland. China, in turn, would use its influence with South Asia to help pave the way into Afghanistan, allow over-flights by U.S. aircraft and so forth. There was also a fair bit of intelligence swapping on Muslim radicals in Malaya, Indonesia and the Philippines, that sort of thing. The Chinese have their tentacles out a long way these days, you know."

"And, of course, there's North Korea and Korean unification," Lau interjected.

"Correct," Burdin replied. "And there are other factors as well. I don't have to tell you that the differences between Beijing and Taipei on the matter of capitalism versus communism have dwindled to almost nothing. It's old enmities versus global power politics, Henry. The Chinese are too important to piss off indefinitely, so Taiwan is toast, at least in the way we have known it.

"The rich on both sides of the strait will make as much money as they ever did, even more in some cases, although I suppose there are one or two who feel betrayed on a more principled level. You being one of them."

"The world if full of deceit," said Lau as he took a sip from his glass.

Lau appeared to be talking to himself, and Burdin was looking at him with a quizzical expression on his face.

"Bet your life on it, Henry," he said.

"But as I was saying," Burdin continued, "the Americans are eager for any distraction. They want to give Northern Ireland's economy one more roll of the dice and will likely make a big fuss about the conference. It's all a smoke screen, of course. All part of merely throwing up legitimate escape routes for those in Taipei who want nothing to do with Beijing. In this case it will be your opportunity.

"There will be other such outlets, for you and for others: trade and tax deals, incentives to move assets, all that sort of thing. And Beijing will not complain too loudly. After all, they are about to claim the biggest prize of all."

Lau held up his glass and stared at it. "The biggest prize of all," he said softly.

There was a flash and a bang. The storm was right overhead.

"Good heavens," said Burdin. "It's like something straight out of Shakespeare; storms and stormy intrigue. But before we continue, Henry, I do have to ask you something. You don't have to answer, but you do know that I am nothing if not discreet."

"By all means, ask," Lau replied.

"I'm curious as to who found whom. Did we find you, or was it the other way around?"

Lau said nothing for a moment. He clasped his hands together and brought them to his face, seemingly hesitating.

"It was quite simple, really," he said. "My family escaped the mainland with the help of an English missionary priest. He belonged to a small order that even some of the Catholics in our city had never heard of. I am not a Catholic, not much of anything really, though I do veer towards the Asian idea of venerating one's ancestors. And repaying one's friends and benefactors."

Lau allowed a moment for his guest to digest his words.

"Over time, I began to make money, a lot of money. I sought out the order that the old priest belonged to. Funny, I can't even remember his name or the order. Saint something. Anyway, to cut a tedious story short I gave them some money, quite a lot of money in fact. In repayment you see. And there it rested for a time. Indeed years."

Lau went silent.

"But it didn't finally rest there," Burdin said by way of prompting more.

"No, it did not," Lau replied.

"A few years ago, a priest from that same order, a Father John, came to visit me. A quite extraordinary man. I entertained him, of course. He was able to tell me things about my family, my parents. It was information that I did not possess. I was only a boy when much of all this had taken place, you understand.

"He was privy to a great deal of additional information that could never be described as spiritual. I have my connections around the world, some in very high and influential places, but what this man told me was extraordinarily revealing, indeed shocking to a degree I did not think possible. He changed my view of a world I thought I knew, as you say, inside out and upside down.

"It was evident to me, as I am sure it has been to you, that this man of God did not inhabit either a worldly or a spiritual realm. Rather he seemed to hover between both, in this time, in the past and, by virtue of the information at his fingertips, the future.

"Much of what he predicted came to pass in the months that followed our first meeting. And I have no reason to believe that more of what he foretold will not soon come to pass."

"Like the fall of an independent Taiwan," said Burdin.

"That and more," said Lau.

"Yes," Burdin continued, "our Father John is a singular individual. I concur with everything you have just said. But there is more as you might rightly suspect. Knowledge has its price, and he gives nothing for free."

"Nothing is for free," Lau quickly agreed. "I have made a decision as to how I will pay for the information that Father John, you, and your organization, whatever it is, will supply next. Obviously I know the kernel of it but lack a proper understanding of the surrounding shell. It is all contained in your briefcase, yes?"

"As much as we know thus far, Henry," Burdin replied.

"Then let's have a look at it. Let me see what kind of treachery demands the end of a president's life."

28

THE CAT WAS TURNING IN CIRCLES, pursuing its own tail. Falsham, hunched in a chair with a great wool blanket covering most of his burly frame, watched the animal intently.

The cat's role in the household was to catch mice. Either, Falsham thought with what amusement he could muster, there were no mice in the house (an unlikely state of affairs for sure) or the beast had long since divined that food would arrive by other means, which was no doubt the truth. The cat was far too rotund for an animal supposedly dependent entirely on hunting tiny creatures.

Falsham had been unable to sleep and had come down from his room to await the dawn. The first slivers of sunlight were evident in the windows at the front of the house, and the cat was twirling in the light of a beam through which countless specks of dust were floating up and down, as if on strings.

Falsham, alert despite his sleeplessness, lifted his head and cocked it to one side. He could hear the first stirrings of the household. One soul, at least, was afoot.

He shivered and pulled the blanket tighter around himself. The cat stopped its circling and regarded him. Lazily, it lifted itself and walked slowly towards the remains of the fire that had blazed well into the previous night. It seemed to understand that someone would come to revive this and other dormant blazes, thus making it possible for others to rise from their beds without fear of instant paralysis in the morning chill.

Falsham observed the cat with no small degree of envy. It was required to care for nothing other than its own comfort. None among the household ever counted the dead mice in the morning for the simple reason that they were so rarely to be found.

The cat, it seemed, was only accountable to an unseen deity, a feline lord. Imperator Felix. It had no reason to concern itself with the death of other kings.

Falsham rose from the chair and stretched in an effort to rid himself of the stiffness in his body. He longed for Spain, but England was now his lot, England and a woman who might be his wife, and a child whose birth was only days hence.

He blinked, his eyes irritated by the dust being blown about by some invisible draft. Perhaps, he thought, a walk outside would clear his eyes and his mind. But he did not dwell on the idea for more than a few seconds. One of the servants walked in purposely from the far end of the great room with a pail in one hand, a wooden spoon in the other. He nodded at Falsham and muttered a low salutation as he began to tend to the slumbering fire.

Falsham watched as the man stirred the contents of the pail and applied dollops of what appeared to be animal fat to the embers. There was a crackling sound and some flickers amid the wood that had not fully burned. The man added sticks and then larger pieces of wood. Within seconds the fire was renewed. The servant rose, bowed slightly, and hurried out a door at the opposite end of the room.

All thoughts of venturing outside now vanquished, Falsham crouched in front of the spitting flames. The heat worked its magical powers, and, for the first time in many hours, he began to feel as if his limbs and extremities had not died of their individual accord.

"A fair morning, John."

Falsham turned his eyes to see Cole standing in the middle of the room, a cloth cap with ear coverings clamped firmly atop his head.

"That it is," Falsham replied, standing up as he did so.

"Come to the fire and be warm," he instructed his friend. "The flames are a tonic for body and soul."

Cole shuffled across the flagstones and slumped into another of the fireside chairs.

"At least on this earth. Hades is quite another story," Cole said.

Falsham noticed that the old man, who was rarely to be seen without bundles of papers under his arm, was carrying only a small document. As if he sensed an inquiry, Cole held up a printed packet.

"The latest from London," he said. "It arrived late last night by messenger. Our friends in the city are at the very least attentive. I think this reflects the temper of our times well enough. And it is not good, John."

Cole reached into the folds of his clothing, pulled out a pair of reading glasses and began to read aloud.

" 'The anti-Roman packet or memoirs of popes and popery.' 'For the conviction of papists and the confirmation of Protestants.' "

Cole looked up as if to ensure that he had his friend's full attention.

"I am listening," said Falsham. "Please continue."

Cole cleared his throat. "What this is my friend is a blasphemous reworking of the lives of our beloved successors of Saint Peter. Yes, some have had their faults, I have no doubt, but they are mere human flesh burdened with a heavenly mission. Blasphemy indeed. Listen!"

And so he continued. "I will pass over the words in Latin. The story is a continuance of the sordid falsehoods contained in its predecessor. Hear me now. Of Pope Gelasius, Pope Calixtus."

Cole began to mutter words. He was hastening to the most insulting lines.

"Ah, here, yes," he said. "A legate in England rails against the marriage of priests and is himself caught in bed with a whore. And here, John, our holy pope is dubbed the grand Lucifer at Rome, and we here in England, who have struggled for our faith, are his little pugs. There has not been such insult paid since the days of Reginald Pole.

"I will say this for the virgin queen, she was no friend of our faith but she knew well enough to put a stay on such gross public opprobrium. If I found the printer of this blasphemy, I would duck him in his own ink vat."

"Reginald Pole. I know that name," Falsham said.

"He was the last of our faith to sit on the bishop's seat at Canterbury. He passed in the year '57, or perhaps it was '58," Cole replied.

"Ah," said Falsham, nodding slowly. "It concerns me that you find this screed so vexing. Perhaps you should cast it into the flames and be done with it."

Falsham waved a hand towards the fire, by now a considerable blaze.

But Cole ignored him and continued to read, though now in more subdued tones. He only stopped when seized by a violent fit of coughing. Falsham, alarmed by his friend's discomfort, stood up but was entirely uncertain as to what he should do. His anxiety was eased by the return of the same man who had rekindled the fire. He was holding a phial that was full to the brim with a dark liquid.

"Thank you, Tom," said Cole before placing the phial to his lips and sucking down the entire contents in one gulp.

"What is it? Falsham said.

"It is better not to ask," Cole replied. "Some might accuse the maker of witchcraft." His coughing had stopped, however. Cole forced a smile, but it did little to hide his evident pain. He placed the packet on his lap and sat back in the chair, his eyes closed and breathing shallow.

"Death is not far away, John, but before he strikes I have my own answer," he said.

Falsham, still standing, his arms folded as he stared intently at the old man, said nothing.

"Help me up, John, there is something I must show you."

Falsham did not argue. Gently he lifted Cole to his feet and held him steady by grasping his upper arms in a firm grip. He was shocked at how thin the old man had become. Whatever the consumption, he thought, it was as ravenous as it was malign.

Cole pulled his arms free and drew in his breath as deeply as he could. It seemed to Falsham that his friend rattled as he inhaled and exhaled.

Cole, without saying a word, began to shuffle towards a door at the far end of the room.

"Follow me," he instructed, his voice drawing on what seemed to be a renewed and purposeful inner strength.

And so Falsham walked slowly behind his mentor. At first the halls, the doorways, alcoves and nooks were familiar. Ayvebury, however, was a large and rambling house, both wide and deep, and Falsham had devoted most of his time so far to the exploration of the estate. Much of the house was still unknown to him.

Cole led him to a long corridor in the rear of the house at the end of which were stairs to an upper floor. The wood lacked the polished finish of the broader staircases in the more traveled part of the house, and at each step the wood gave off a groan as if it, too, was suffering from some wasting ailment.

Cole said nothing, and Falsham judged it better to remain silent. He had a sense that Cole was so deep in thought that words would be ignored anyway. As they climbed upwards Cole began to speak to himself, though very softly. His words rose slightly, and Falsham heard the words of prayer.

At the top, there was a way to the right and one to the left. Cole turned left and advanced on a heavy door that blocked any further progress about twenty steps from the top of the stairs. He turned the handle and walked into a room that was, to Falsham's surprise, the most lavishly furnished that he had seen in the entire house. A great pile of kindling and firewood stood in the grate. The room, however, was cold and there was no evidence or indication of recent occupation.

Cole walked slowly to the great fireplace and upon reaching it placed a hand on the stone mantle. He was having obvious difficulty in breathing but he turned to Falsham and smiled.

"I have enjoyed the fruits of this life in this room on occasion, John. It is full of memories."

Falsham nodded. No matter its cushioned luxuriance, he thought, there was little for Cole to do here now other than dwell on past glories.

"I am sure with the fire ablaze there was warmth enough to match any desires," he said.

Cole, however, had partly entered the fireplace.

"Come here, John," he commanded.

"There was a time when the queen's men were very energetic in these parts, seeking out priests, so whenever we had unwelcome or unexpected visitors we would set this wood ablaze and engage in a game of chess. After they had gone and after the fire had eased we would..."

At this point Cole strained. His two hands were stretched upwards into the sooty darkness, and he was pushing against the inside of the mantle.

Falsham could not easily see the stone backing of the fireplace, but he was conscious of a grinding and rumbling sound. And then he could see flames and with some alarm took several quick steps towards Cole, his hand extended to pull him out.

"No, John," said Cole, with some alacrity. "They are only faggots burning to light our descent into the hidden room. I had Tom light them. As you can see there is a system of levers and pulleys that are activated by hands placed against precise spots in the stone. Your fingers will not detect any grooves or indentations. It is by practice that you will learn the pressure points."

"I am impressed," said Falsham. "I have of course seen priests' hidden quarters before, but they were invariably hidden behind wood panels. Stone is God's own work."

Cole was already through the portal and descending what seemed to be a curved stairway.

"Time is short," he said without turning. Falsham followed.

"What I did not tell you is that the messenger who brought that damnable packet also brought word that the king and his party will be here at Ayvebury by tomorrow. Clearly we must advance our plan."

Cole stopped and turned his head. The shadows from the flames flickered across his pained face, but again he managed to smile.

"I have all my life longed to gaze into the face of my savior, John. My time has finally come, and you will be my instrument."

29

What had changed the game as far as Beijing was concerned was Taipei's constitutional referendum, and its anticipated result.

No matter all the reassuring words from the advocates of independence, it was seen in Beijing as the end of a manageable standoff. For decades, the two Chinas had been locked in an embrace of sorts. Each claimed ownership of the other. Thus, the Republic of China and the People's Republic, had been able to live with a stalemate. Now it was different. Taiwan had taken a step too far for the rulers on the mainland to bear.

And so they resolved to bear it no more.

Three files were spread across Henry Lau's desk, all of them opened but the pages still untouched and in order. Lau had stared at the documents for what to Burdin had seemed an age. But he had said nothing.

Eventually, however, Burdin felt it necessary to speak, though on a less weightier matter than the secrets of a superpower.

"Any chance of a tipple? Something a little stronger than this admittedly excellent vintage?"

For a couple of seconds there was no response but Lau was not entirely absent from the moment.

"Forgive me, Roger. I am a horrible host; anything of course. Please, step over here and take your pick."

Lau motioned towards his exquisite collection of booze but made no attempt to rise from his seat. The tension, though not broken, had been eased. Burdin stood up and briskly walked over to an array of bottles and decanters worthy of a man as wealthy as Henry Lau, a man, of course, who did not touch alcohol very much at all himself, except for the occasional sip of a top class wine.

Burdin allowed himself a small Scotch and stood for a moment staring through the windows and into the night sky. The storm had done it worst and all that remained was the occasional flicker of lightning, now some miles distant.

"You know, Roger," said Lau, "I have dealt with the lies and chicanery of business rivals and friends for all of my life. Deceit has never surprised or shocked me. It is what I expect. Each and every day I expect to be cheated, laid waste by those who publicly toast my health."

Burdin, sensing a summons, returned to his chair.

"So why should I be surprised if the affairs of nations night be any different? Of course, I am not. Betrayal of one nation by another, even a friend or an ally, is as old as nations themselves. Perhaps we Chinese invented betrayal. After all, we invented just about everything else."

Lau folded his arms and smiled.

"The difference is, of course, is that I am not helpless before my business enemies and rivals. Quite the contrary, and I have been lucky over the years in that I have been able to smite most of them. I have suffered some wounds, I have lost out on some deals, but nothing has been fatal. So here I am, one of the richest men in the world and yet helpless in the face of treachery and betrayal that is continental in scope and will likely decide the future course, not just of Taiwan, but all of Asia and beyond."

Burdin nodded and took another sip of his drink.

"Most of humanity, Lau continued, "is born helpless and dies helpless. It is the natural course of things. So you can understand the even greater sense of helplessness that a powerful man feels when that power is suddenly like a water vessel with a vast hole in its side. The pain, the frustration, is beyond normal appreciation and understanding. I might as well be some dirt-digging peasant in a remote province that Beijing still considers Maoist."

Burdin nodded again and took another drop. He wished he had poured more of the elixir into his glass. He was familiar with Henry Lau's tendency towards homilies though this was a sermon rooted in genuine angst and justifiable anger. It was, in his own world, as if the Americans had abandoned Britain to the old Soviets.

"I am a dead man, as you know," Lau said, taking Burdin a little by surprise with his change of tack. "My cancer is inoperable. I might live a year, a little more or a little less. Time is not my friend, and history is rushing past me like a stream of melted mountain snow. A month seems like a minute, a week like a split second.

"A thousand years of history is about to be written, and I have but a few moments to stake my claim on posterity. So rather than me languishing over these documents, Roger, why don't you summarize them for me? I already have an inkling but I must hear treachery's name spoken by someone I trust. And that is you, my friend. This first file, it is in Mandarin, I see. Do you speak it?"

"Not beyond a greeting and a farewell I'm afraid," said Burdin with a look of mock seriousness on his face. He put down his drink and lifted the file from the table, holding it with the cover facing its host.

"But I do know what it contains in a general sense. What we have here is Beijing's wish list as communicated to the Americans.

"As you can imagine, it is not exactly a 'Dear Santa' letter. It is rather rude and hectoring, full of self-justification and historical claptrap. You really don't need to read it at all because you well know the form. The end of it, however, is of greater interest. This is the carrot where much that has gone before has been the stick. It offers all manner of deals and tradeoffs if the United States looks the other way. These are offers that would be very hard to refuse if you're thinking strictly about jobs and the future of your nation's rather battered economy."

Burdin paused for a few seconds before opening the second file.

"This one, in English, of course, deals with scenarios. It is a combination of assessments from the CIA, the Pentagon, NSA, DIA and a couple of others. The documents, all copied from the originals as you would expect, are variously marked 'restricted,' 'classified' and 'top secret.'

"What they mostly do is to sketch out the likely build-up to an attack. They accurately predict unrest on the mainland as a primary precursor to invasion of this island. We are already witnessing such scenes, or at least we have become aware of them."

"Yes," Lau interjected. "And I have in my possession a number of firsthand accounts from friends on the mainland, and in one case, a cousin. Armed resistance to the so-called People's Liberation Army has been growing in several districts, and so too has the PLA's retaliatory repression. There have been hundreds of deaths, and many other have disappeared, but the fires of rebellion, if anything, are spreading."

"Quite so," said Burdin. "I am separately aware of a British plan for the evacuation of United Kingdom nationals from at least one large southern city. The expectation clearly is that the unrest, though mainly rural at this moment in time, will eventually spread to the cities."

Burdin pushed the folder across the desk.

"As you read this, in your own time of course, it will become increasingly clear to you that those making these assessments consider the defense of

Taiwan an ultimately futile venture, one that would lead to enormous losses for the US. and possibly even result in a world war.

"One of the files, the one merely marked 'restricted,' outlines the fig leaves that Beijing will use in advance of an actual invasion. As you will see there are fifth column units allied with Beijing already in place on the island. The author refers, without a hint of irony I might add, to a Gulf of Tonkin-type incident off the coast that could also be used as an excuse for retaliation by sea, air and land.

"The assessments predict stiff resistance by your own armed forces and pleas from your government for international help. It outlines the likely effects of missile strikes from the mainland and even allows for the use of tactical nuclear weapons by the PLA. They would not be directed at Taipei but at some of your military units at the other end of the island. They want your capital intact, if possible."

"Of course they do," Lau said, sitting straighter in his chair. "Please continue."

"There is a file marked 'top secret,' this one, that warns of a possible attack by North Korea on the South as the Chinese attack on Taiwan gathers momentum. Beijing, of course, turns a blind eye and all of a sudden Washington is facing twin Asian wars simultaneously."

"Ah," said Lau, "that's how they get out of it. Washington's greatest nightmare. So they choose to see it all as a choice, Taiwan or South Korea, and, of course, it will be Seoul, not Taipei. Clever, I suppose."

"Yes," Burdin replied, "such a predicament would force the hawks on Capitol Hill to back away from Taiwan even as they are seen rushing to the defense of South Korea. This occurs even if Pyongyang does not attack. There only has to be authentic sounding reports of preparations for an attack from north of the 38th parallel. And who, in a crisis as great as this, is going to pay any heed to a North Korean denial? Nobody."

"Precisely," said Lau, clapping his hands in agreement.

"A central part of the plan, said Burdin, "is that US naval forces are as far from Taiwan as they can legitimately be when the initial, supposedly surprise, Chinese landings take place. Perhaps they will be holding exercises with the Japanese or the Australians. There will be protests, uproar and a lot of saber-rattling, but within forty-eight hours the American public will be presented with a sad but unavoidable *fait accompli*.

"And, of course, it isn't all that bad, really. The Chinese are not really Reds anymore, and Chinese unity is not entirely an undesirable thing, indeed good for trade relations in the long run. Beijing will be slapped with some short term sanctions, the ambassador in Beijing might be summoned back to Washington for a while, that sort of thing. But not much more than that."

"You forgot one thing, Roger."

"And what might that be?"

"What if we Taiwanese begin to kick mainland ass, as the Americans might say?"

Lau almost spat out the words and smiled broadly as he did so.

"Won't happen, Henry, I'm afraid," Burdin quickly replied. "And this is something I have separately from the American files. Apart from the sheer number of men that the mainlanders are going to throw at you there are several of your generals who have been compromised. They will either surrender, sit on their hands or join with the attackers, all in the interest of saving lives and ensuring a new national harmony of course."

"And if we had nuclear weapons of our own?"

"Do you?"

Lau grimaced. "We would if the fools in government had listened to me twenty years ago. What's in that third folder?"

"It's the recommendation to President Packer from his military brass, advisers and cabinet members. It sort of gets him off the hook."

"It advises him to turn his back on Taiwan and leave us to the mercy of the Communists," said Lau.

"More or less."

"And Packer's response?"

Burdin pulled a single sheet of paper from the file, and although it was a copy, the seal was clear. He handed it to Lau.

"From the desk of the president," said Lau, scanning the sheet.

There was no date on it but Lau recognized the signature because he possessed a personally signed letter from the president. But it was not the name that held his gaze, rather two simple words above it.

"I concur," Lau said, almost in a whisper. "I concur." Then, more loudly, "To whom?

"It was written to a member of the president's inner circle, but precisely which one I am not sure," said Burdin.

"If there are other such notes, they expressed the same agreement with the general consensus."

"How did you come by these documents, Roger?"

Burdin tilted back in his chair and stared momentarily at the tiny pin-prick lights in the office ceiling. He tilted forward again and looked at his companion directly.

"I don't know which individual provided this information, only to which individual it was provided. They say that the Lord provides, Henry. In this case, however, it was more a case of someone providing on his behalf."

"These documents," said Lau, his hand passing over the files in a sweeping motion, "amount to a death warrant for my country."

"That they do, Henry," Burdin said. "And there's a little more, again not in these files. A considerable flow of Chinese money is finding itself into the concentric circles of the Packer reelection campaign. It's all disguised and well hidden, of course, and none will show up in a Packer PAC, but there's millions being funneled to specific individuals and organizations."

"With layers of plausible denial for Packer of course," said Lau.

"Absolutely," Burdin replied. "I think you can see why we came to you, Henry. A murder squad officer might say you have always had the means. Now you have the motive."

"And the opportunity?"

"Leave that to us," Burdin said, draining his glass.

Lau inhaled deeply. The pain in his head had returned, now worse than before.

"So you want me to assassinate the president of the United States. I will await with interest your advice as to how I should go about it."

30

Two men were standing in a room that was approximately twelve paces by that same number. Before them was a low table adorned with lighted candles, a crucifix, chalice and several other vessels.

"Is there a priest hereabouts?" Falsham asked his companion.

"Oh there is and very close by, John," Cole replied. "Help me kneel. I have taken the liberty of placing a pair of cushions on the floor. We deserve a little comfort."

Falsham helped his friend to his knees before the table. He looked about for a figure to emerge from the shadows, perhaps even the walls. But there was no sign or sound. There was no one else in the dungeon-like room.

Possessed of keen senses in the matter of detection, Falsham closed his eyes for a moment and sniffed. He could detect no recent, unfamiliar human odor. Yes, he thought, they were indeed alone.

"So we just pray," he said to Cole, whose head was now bowed, hands joined in supplication.

"*In nomine Patris,*" Cole said.

Falsham chimed in. "*Et Filii, et Spiritus Sancti*"

Before he could say amen, Cole raised his right hand. There was no mistaking the older man's intention. He was instructing Falsham to be silent.

Cole continued to speak. "*Introibo ad altare dei.*"

Falsham felt surprise and then astonishment take hold. Cole was speaking the opening words of Mass.

"My friend, what is this? You cannot, it is blasphemy," he said, almost in a whisper, as if God would be deceived by a plea uttered under breath.

But Cole simply raised his hand.

"Be at ease, John, trust me. I will explain when I am finished. Please content yourself for now with delivering the responses."

Falsham was silent, but Cole, his red-rimmed eyes now fixed sternly on the younger man, succeeded in eliciting the appropriate line.

"*Ad deum qui laetificat,*" Falsham said hesitatingly. "*Juventutem meam.*"

"Very good," said Cole. "Even after all your soldiering you still remember the discipline that truly matters the most."

Before Falsham could reply, Cole was proceeding with more incantations.

"*Causam meam de gente non sancta. Ab homine inique et doloso erue me.* And now join with me in confessing your sins. You might want to include doubt, and being of little faith."

Falsham, feeling cowed, did not argue. Instead, he dutifully complied and responded to the priestly prayers when required and after some minutes took bread and wine over which the hands of Richard Cole had passed.

After the benediction, Falsham stood and helped Cole to his feet.

"I know, I know, John, a full explanation is warranted. But let us return to the room above. I am in need of a stout chair. Help me up the stairs, and I will answer all, or certainly most, of your questions."

Slowly, the two men ascended the stairs and reentered the upper room. It took Falsham's eyes some moments to readjust to the light. By the time his sight was restored, Cole had settled into his firm chair.

Cole motioned to Falsham to sit in another chair opposite his. Saying nothing, and still feeling confused over the events below, Falsham sat and awaited his enlightenment. Cole, his hands joined again, bowed his head momentarily, then faced his friend.

"I have not been entirely honest with you, John. I was once married to a woman who was truly a gift from God. She took sick and the Lord took her back from me. But this you know. You believe that the woman with child now with me in this house is my new wife. But that is not so. She is a cousin of one of the November plotters, Catesby. The father of the child has long vanished, the dog. I have been her protector even to the point of feigning a marriage, even to the point of sharing a bed.

"This, I admit, has been to my advantage, our advantage. But I could never love another woman, John. That I knew from the first moment of my solitude."

Falsham shifted in his chair. He had a feeling as to what was about to be said, but yet found it hard to believe.

"Are you going to tell me that you took Holy Orders?"

"That is precisely what I did," said Cole. "For some considerable time, notwithstanding frequent interruption, I studied under the tutelage of a French bishop, Jules Thibaud. He has been traveling through England in secret since the last days of Elizabeth's reign. He has ordained many, perhaps three dozen men, all in secret, of course, and in all cases the ordained must preserve their hidden identities. You yourself have seen the consequences of one of us being identified."

"All too vividly," said Falsham.

Cole lapsed into silence for a moment. Somewhere in the distance a bell was struck and he said "Terce," a reference to the canonical prayers that fell at the ninth hour. He began to pray again, his words uttered in barely more than a whisper.

Falsham studied the room in closer detail. It was indeed more lavishly furnished than any other in the house. Then again, he thought, Ayvebury was more than a little Spartan in most of its corners. By contrast to the wood-paneled rooms and hallways adorned with grim portraits, the walls in this room were lined on three of the four sides with shelves overflowing with books and codices. The fourth side had three stained-glass windows, each about the height of a man by an arm's length.

It occurred to Falsham that the room might once have served as a chapel or spiritual study, that function having been now passed to the secret chamber below. The decorated glass panes, however, appeared new. They did not depict religious scenes but distinctly worldly themes: a harvest, a feast at a long dining table, and a deer hunting party. Appropriate, Falsham thought, given the reason for the king now being in the vicinity of Ayvebury.

Falsham, somewhat lost in the exercise of divining the room's former role, had failed to notice that Cole had made his way to one of the shelves and was even now running a bony finger along a row of codices, all of them bound in leather, all devoid of any identifying inscription on their spines.

Cole was clearly counting. When he had reached his finger's intended target he pulled the volume from the rest and uttered a mild exclamation of triumph.

"Stay seated, John, if you please. I have something to show you."

Clasping the volume close to his bosom, Cole returned to his chair. He sat down and laid it on his lap.

"I enjoy my humble collection," he said, his mouth forming what might have been a smile, or an expression of sorrowful regret; Falsham could not decide.

"I possess a Master Caxton, you know. *Confessio Amantis*. It is on the wall behind you. When I have gone, you should seek it and other notable works out and read them, though not at your leisure. There will be little time for leisure given the task that will spread out before you."

"Oh, but just a small dose of leisure," Falsham mildly protested. His attempt at humor, however, fell flat.

"Reading is serious work, John. And reading this even more than most."

As he spoke, Cole tapped the cover of the codex vigorously with the fingers of his right hand. His emphasis had the desired effect.

"That which you hold so closely. What knowledge or secrets does it hold?"

"No secrets at all, John, merely the plain truth of history over the course of my life, from before it began. This is a record, a perspicuous record, if I may say, of treachery and treason, the betrayal of all that was right and just by the king, Henry, a man more concerned with the content of his bed than with the natural order of God's temporal world."

"You are the author," said Falsham.

"Yes, Cole replied. "As you will see, it is written in Latin and amounts to a precise recording of the malodorous stench of these past four score years. I pay particular attention to the dissolution of the monasteries and the many falsehoods, desecrations and persecutions that have continued up to our modern time."

Cole raised the volume and opened it. "Here, you see, some empty pages yet to be filled,"

"Yes, I see," Falsham replied. But his tone carried in it another question.

"That will be for you, John. When I am gone the end of this account will be as your hand, and your hand alone, describes it. Use English if you will. Latin, I suspect, is not your particular *forte*."

"No, it is not. I do better at the Spanish. But I will gladly do as you ask, though I suspect that the conclusion of your epistle will be a bitter affair in spite of my desire for it to be otherwise."

Cole did not immediately reply. He stared at the words on an open page for a moment.

"Number sixteen," he said. "If you look at the point where I pulled this from the others you will see that it is number sixteen on the shelf after you begin from the left side."

"And the others? What do they hold?"

"Oh, just musings, records of the farm's work and so forth," said Cole. "But that one at the very end, perhaps you can bring it to me."

Falsham was on his feet in an instant. He retrieved the end volume from the row of its companions and handed it to the old man.

What occupied the next hour was the old man's detailed explanation of a series of lines, shapes and diagrams. To the uninitiated eye, they did not appear of to be of any particular place or thing. But between a jumble of words and numbers added for the purposes of distraction and deceit, the diagrams were in fact maps and locations of hidden money and valuables in the house. Enough, Cole assured Falsham, to ensure that the estate would both flourish in its visible business, but also in its secret purpose as a sanctuary for the blessed fathers ordained by the Frenchman Thibaud.

Ayvebury, Cole proclaimed, would become a new Canterbury pledged to Mother Church, but for the eyes of the world it would merely be the country estate of a fortunate and most loyal gentleman by the name of John Falsham.

"All that remains," Cole said at the end of his instruction, "is for King James to unwittingly bless our most noble plot."

"Long live the king," said Falsham.

Richard Cole, with a goodly portion of his remaining strength, threw his head back and clapped his hands. He concluded his enunciation of pleasure with a wheezing laugh that quickly turned into a spasm of coughing.

31

In the evening of the fourth day, she stood in the open doorway of the cabin, daring herself to face down the shadowy reach of the great forest. Once the last light had faded, the darkness would be absolute. She had not turned on any of the inside lights, nor had she lit a candle.

Cleo Conway could not remember ever being so alone in her life.

Even on childhood camping trips with her parents the solitude had been illusory. Beyond each line of trees there had always been another tent, filled with moms, dads and babbling kids too excited to sleep.

In this place, beyond the trees, there were more trees. And in those trees were sounds and mysteries and hidden movements.

"Lions and tigers and bears," Conway said softly, daring the forest creatures to show themselves.

Certainly bears were a possibility.

After nothing less than bright and clear conditions, a cold rain had settled over the island. It had come down for most of the day, and it had been a blessing of sorts. Conway had been hoping for an excuse to stay in the cabin. For three days, she had walked between the shore and the fringes of the Tongass National Forest. The only bears she had seen had been on the far side of the river, which, at this point on its journey, was more akin to an estuary. None of the great animals had come close and, mercifully, none had jumped out from behind a tree trunk. But Conway could not escape from the odd tingly feeling that comes from realizing that, for the first time in her life, she was in a place where she was not top of the natural food chain.

It was with this in mind that she had decided that the odds of a close encounter would rise to something approaching certainty on the fourth day. Cleo Conway was inclined to dwell on odds, so much so that she had avoided all forms of gambling. Her father had gambled, a lot. His daughter was afraid of what might be in her blood. She was now also afraid of losing her blood in a lonely place. So she had stayed indoors for the daylight hours and had tried to read her book, a well-thumbed history of Alaska taken from a shelf crammed with damp paperbacks.

Not surprisingly, Alaska in print had been less of a lure than the real thing just outside the door. She took the book up, and put it down, took it up, and put it down. In between, she walked into the tiny kitchen to pour another cup of coffee. She didn't want to walk in the rain, but equally felt like she wanted to run a marathon. She wondered how people coped with cabin fever that lasted for months in some northern parts.

By late afternoon on that fourth day, Conway had felt the first pangs of regret, not just over her choice of destination, but because she had opted to spend her precious vacation days alone. At the same time, she reminded herself, this was not a vacation in the normal sense. It was more a pause, an opportunity for renewal, part embraced and part suggested by her superiors.

Divorce, they had told her, with more than a little experience of their own to back up the assertion, was no easy matter, even if commonplace. So any distraction from the job had to be addressed. She had a few days coming, so why not, they had suggested, just take them and flee to a faraway place. Their arguments had ultimately persuaded. You didn't take too much issue with the United States Secret Service, even when you were counted among its number.

Conway had considered drumming up a few of her single, free and divorced friends for a sun holiday. The Virgin Islands would have been easy and welcome after a Washington winter. But she had decided to do something novel. Having never been to Alaska, Conway had plumped for the cabin in the forest. Sitka was more than thirty miles away, Washington a million.

Baranof Island, with its bears, mountain goats and deer, but not many people, was a perfect setting to work most things out. The problem was, she now knew, it took more than a setting to sort out a future.

Conway had decided not to take a gun on the trip, not even her service issue weapon. She knew enough to realize that a wounded grizzly would be the greatest threat to a tenderfoot idiot with a popgun. So she had trudged along the trails with nothing more than a long, thick stick.

Her favored route was a path that tumbled the quarter mile from the cabin down to the river that flowed into the sound a mile to the west. She had taken care on her walks to make noise so as to alert any animal in the vicinity. She had felt nervous, alive and vulnerable. It was, she thought, a little ruefully, not unlike being on the job.

So the rain had been timely.

The cabin did not have a landline. And although she had brought her cell phone, she had neglected to recharge it. This had added significantly to her solitude.

Conway made little effort to conjure up a dinner that night. She nibbled, cuddled into her bed and fell asleep over the Alaska tome a little after nine. The next day, the fifth, broke clear and cold, the rain having blown into Canada.

Not knowing why, or giving it much thought, Conway had recharged her phone overnight and had slipped it into a pocket before heading down to the water on her first walk of the new day. She made for the large rock on the water's edge at the end of the trail. It had served as her vantage point and it had been from this spot that she had picked out the bears, perhaps a quarter mile distant on the other side of the water.

None were in sight this morning.

She had been sitting for twenty minutes or so before her mind acknowledged what her ears were telling her. Her cell jingle was shattering the morning stillness.

"Yes," she said, making no effort to disguise her annoyance.

"Miss Conway, ma'am," the voice in the phone was apologetic.

She recognized it. It was the young cop in Sitka. She had checked in with local law enforcement as a courtesy before hitching a ride from a local boat owner to the cabin.

"Have you been trying to reach me? Is there anything wrong?"

"No, ma'am," came the response. "Nothing wrong, but your office in Washington has been on to us. I think they were trying to raise you as of yesterday."

"My phone was powered down. Did they say anything specific? Is there some situation or emergency?"

"No emergency so far as I know ma'am," came the response. "And no details either. They just asked us to get in contact with you. If need be, they suggested we send someone down, but I got you first with this call."

"Well, I'm obliged to you," said Conway, a tad formally. "I'll be sure to give them a call. If I have problems, I'll get back to you, and if you could call them for me, that would be great."

"No problem," said the officer. "I'll be on most of the day. You have our number."

"Thanks," Conway said and she flipped the phone closed.

She had expected this. Her geek squad would not be able to get through more than a few days before getting overly excited about some story in an obscure newspaper in a country that wasn't in the latest atlases. Either that or it would be elevated internet chatter with bombastic threats against the United States, its citizens, perhaps the president.

She would not hurry to make a call. Later in the day would do fine. She had a full week and that was official.

It was at this moment that she noticed something in the corner of her left eye. Conway had always been optically observant. It had served her well in her training and in her work, most of which to date had involved protecting visiting diplomats.

The bear was huge, and it was only about a hundred yards away. The animal was standing at the water's edge, staring across to the other side, just as she was.

With a start, Conway realized that she and the bear had probably covered parallel paths to the water. She had arrived at the edge just a few minutes ahead of her clawed companion.

Conway did not move. She glanced at the ground around the rock. She was sitting at perhaps four feet above the shingle. It was not much of a fortress. She could slide down one side and be out of view of the animal, but decided against it. Slowly she turned her head. She did not want to stare straight at the beast fearing that it would sense some sort of provocation.

But the bear seemed unconcerned. He did not move. She guessed it was a male because it seemed especially big. She had seen brown bears at the zoo, and this one was right up there with the biggest of them.

She regretted not bringing her gun. Then she decided again that it had been the right thing to do. Under no circumstances could she imagine shooting such a magnificent creature. This was, after all, the bear's home. She was the intruder.

And so for what seemed like an age, Conway stared across the water, the bear held in the corner of her eye. Perhaps, she thought, it was just taking a drink. But no, the water here was too salty. It was, she decided, just out for its morning stroll and would turn on its paws and in a few moments and vanish back into the trees.

But no, the bear was moving towards her. She froze. For a moment a vision of the mermaid in Copenhagen's harbor flashed through her mind. Bears would not harm a mermaid. She would be one atop her rock, a US Secret Service undercover mermaid.

She was perspiring in the cold. The bear was walking in her direction although its head was still turned sideways towards the water.

Conway glanced over her shoulder towards the trees. She could make a run for it and hope to lose the bear in the woods. But everything she had read had advised against running. There was the play dead option, but it was a bit limited on top of the rock.

The bear was less than fifty yards away when it stopped. It raised its nose in the air, sniffing the wind. It did this for a several seconds before turning and walking slowly towards the trees. Conway felt her body loosen, the tension flowing out. She wanted to laugh aloud but stifled it. The bear had detected a human presence, or an odor that it did not appreciate.

Of course, Conway thought, she had not showered for a couple of days because it had been impossible to get the water in the cabin up to a temperature that could even be called warm. She must be smelling like some old trapper, Grizzly Adams in old L.L. Beans.

She did not move from the rock. She wanted to give the bear time to be well on its way. And it was time, she decided, to be on hers. It was time, she thought, to get back to the world.

Perhaps she had been unsettled by the sudden collision of tranquility with a life changing, or life ending, moment. But it occurred to Conway that Washington and that wider world had been unusually quiet of late as well. And yet, or perhaps because of this, Cleo Conway had a gut sense that something, somewhere, was going down. And it would beat a path to her boss, the president of the United States.

32

"I THOUGHT YOU WERE HAVING ME ON," Bailey said.

"Yes, I'm standing outside the place. Cranmer and Cromwell, Solicitors and Commissioners of Oaths. Must get a few laughs anytime they turn up in court. Are you sure this isn't a put on?"

Bailey winced. Henderson, at the other end of the cell phone, was shouting something across the newsroom at an unidentified victim.

Bailey fiddled in his pocket, looking for his cigarettes. He was out, and there was nowhere in the immediate vicinity where he could load up again.

Henderson had been right. This little corner of London really was off the map. How had Henderson put it? Missed by time, the Luftwaffe and the wrecker's ball. Not half. Bailey prided himself on his street knowledge. He reckoned he could match any cabbie but this nook on the South Bank of the Thames had somehow eluded him.

"Okay," Bailey said into the phone. "I keep going down the street, take the first left, then a right, and the pub should be in plain sight, right?"

He nodded as the confirmation came through from Henderson.

"I'll call you back," Bailey said before flipping the phone closed.

All right, he thought, Cranmer and Cromwell. What next, Raleigh and Drake?

He walked slowly. There was no traffic as the street had long been cordoned off for pedestrians.

The instruction from Henderson to seek out a pub called, of all things, The Hangman's Noose, had broken a dull torpor that had set in at the paper over the past week. The initial fuss and uproar over the dead priests had subsided and had been replaced by a par for the course sex scandal involving a leading opposition politician.

Plaice, it seemed, had been assigned to other cases, and Samantha was off learning how to shoot guns. The dead priests tale was stuck in neutral.

Then came the call from Henderson and the instruction to go and meet Sydney Small. Bailey was taken aback. He had not seen Sydney Small's byline for a long time. He thought Small, indisputably a legend in the *Post*, had either pegged it, or had parked himself in an old geezer home. Henderson had taken a certain pleasure in correcting Bailey.

"If you bothered to read beyond your stories you would realize that Sydney Small is very much alive and still up to his tonsils in royal muck," he had snorted.

"Yes, the stories have been a bit thin on the ground lately, but don't underestimate Small. This has happened before. Just when you think he's gone off the boil for good he comes up with a whopper."

But of course Bailey understood this. Sydney Small was larger than life because of his apparent absence from it. He was a virtual unknown in the newsroom. Only Henderson and a couple of the more grizzled denizens of the place could claim to have ever clapped eyes on the *Post*'s royal correspondent. He was, as a newsroom wag had once famously said, like Jesus: blessed were those who had not seen, yet believed.

So Bailey was about to secure a great rarity in *Post* lore, a scoop, a head to head with the man who, as one story had it, was so close to one female royal that it was said he had fathered a child with her.

"Sydney will be on the throne yet," said Henderson with what almost passed as a smile after Bailey had quizzed him on a yarn that seemed tall even by the *Post*'s standards.

With Cranmer and Cromwell astern, Bailey made his way slowly along the narrow street. There were not a lot of people about, and those that were seemed to be just passing through on the way to somewhere else. Sure enough, there were not many businesses in the immediate vicinity to detain a passerby, and the street was mostly composed of small mews flats, most of them needing a little paint and something other than dirt for their flower boxes.

Bailey took the left turn as instructed and proceeded for about twenty yards before reaching the right turn into what was little more than an alleyway. Henderson had told him that the alley was a dead end, but at the far end of it was the pub. Bailey could see the sign, a small wooden one that, as he got closer, revealed itself as a painted affair depicting a gallows atop a green hill. At least nobody was swinging from the rope, Bailey thought.

He paused for a moment at the door. Henderson had warned him that Small could be a tricky customer and that there were certain protocols that were, as he put it, advisable when dealing with the man.

Stepping inside, Bailey had to adjust his eyes to a gloomy room with few of the comforts that people expected when they forked over for a pint at the end of a day's work. What he noticed first was the silence. No jukebox, no telly. There was a radio on somewhere but the volume was low. A barman who looked like he might have been taking a break from hanging someone himself was slowly turning a drying cloth inside a beer glass.

"Morning," said Bailey. I'm looking for..."

Before he could finish, the barman nodded to his right. The bar was horseshoe in shape, but the seating alcoves stretched behind the glass mirror that marked its rear. Bailey walked around, his eyes getting used to the dim light. The radio, he noticed, was playing classical music. The sound didn't quite match the sight of the hangman on station behind the bar.

As he cleared the turn of the bar Bailey stared towards the tables at the far reaches of the room. To say he was taken aback would be an understatement. For a split second, he glanced back at the hangman, but the man just nodded again, thus confirming that the sole patron of the place had indeed been expecting the newcomer.

"Sydney," said Bailey. "Sydney Small."

Bailey hoped that Small had not noticed the slight stammer that had accompanied his salute.

"I'm..." But before he could finish, Small had raised his hand.

"Of course, you are. No need for introductions, Mr. Bailey. Sit down, have a drink. Dennis."

The hangman put down the glass and awaited Bailey's pleasure.

Bailey made a pretense of glancing at his watch. Frankly, he didn't really care what time of the day he had a sup, but he was being cautious. How close was Small to Henderson, who could be a bit of a stickler over drinking on the job?

Oh, bloody hell, Bailey thought.

"I'll have a Guinness," he said in the direction of Dennis the hangman. "A half."

Small, shaking his head, let out a low chuckle. "Oh, have full one," he said. "Promise I won't mention a word to Henderson, the old puritan."

"No, half will be fine. For now," Bailey responded.

The man sitting across the table from him, and drinking what appeared to be a gin and tonic, was nothing like the compact, agitated chronicler of royal shenanigans that he, and just about everybody else working at the *Post* for less than a decade, had imagined. Sydney Small looked like someone he would cover in his own reporting. He was not small. Indeed, he appeared to Bailey to extend well over six feet. Up to six three, he estimated.

Small had a long face with high cheek bones, a slight flush on his countenance that may or may not have been the gin. He was dressed immaculately in a tweed jacket and pressed pants. His brown leather shoes looked straight out of the box. All he was missing, Bailey thought, was a Fedora and a cigarette holder. But there was no sign that Small smoked, and a hat would merely have distracted from his swept-back mane of slightly dirty, blond hair.

Sydney Small, in short, looked like a toff, a rake, a royal rake. He might have stepped out of the owner's enclosure at Ascot. Of course, Bailey thought, as he glanced at Small's newspaper. It was turned to the racing section. Small seemed to read Bailey's mind.

"Just keeping up with the gee-gees. If one is going to cover the palace with any effectiveness at all, it's a head start to know a thing or two about the nags and the form," he said.

"Have you discussed horses with the queen?" Bailey asked.

"Oh, absolutely. I give her tips. She doesn't act on them, of course, but more than once I've been able to warm her up with a gentle 'I told you so.'"

"No kidding," said Bailey, his mind wandering a bit as he tried to remember precisely why he was sitting in the pub with a guy who looked like he had walked off a Noel Coward set.

"Any tips for today then?"

"I'd hang on to your money today, old boy. Nothing but half-knackered trotters on the loose. Ah ,your beer has arrived."

"Stout," said Bailey.

Small ignored the correction and closed his paper. He shuffled the pages so as to restore the tabloid as closely as possible to its off-the-press neatness. He was silent for a few seconds. He took a sip of his drink, carefully placed the glass back on the table and leaned forward slightly.

"Everyone, and I mean everyone in this world is capable of murder. Wouldn't you agree?" he said.

Bailey, about to drink some of his dark brew hesitated and nodded his head one side to the other.

"There are very few saints, and that's for sure," he said.

"Quite so," said Small. "I've been reading your stories about these dead priests. You've not pointed to any apparent link, but it's a bit of a stretch to suggest that there is none at all, don't you think?

"If I backed four winners back to back, even at different meetings, I would put it down to a little knowledge and a lot of luck. But four dead men of the cloth, all out of the same stable, so to speak, well, it can hardly be just all bad luck. Somebody, somewhere, must have a little knowledge."

Bailey could follow Small's line of thinking, but what was drawing him closer into the exchange was that Small seemed to be looking beyond him as he spoke, and beyond hangman. He seemed nervous in spite of the cool, debonair exterior

"Expecting someone else?" Bailey ventured.

"Not at all, not at all," said Small, straightening up and meeting the challenge with a full smile.

"What if I was to tell you that there might be a connection between all these four dead men, one that defied the odds book, at least in one crucial respect?"

"I'd say it's your story, not mine, Sydney."

"You're very generous, Mr. Bailey," Small replied.

"My name's Nick, and we are colleagues."

"As yes, that we are," said Small, his half smile returning for a second. "Some stories are for sharing, Nick, and this, I am certain, is one of them. Listen, I know it's early and you've been most conscientious, but I think you might want to get something stronger than that."

Small was staring intently at Bailey's half-pint glass.

"You think so?"

"I know so," said Small. "Dennis!"

33

"As you can see, ladies and gentlemen, the president is down. Bill Mellon is on top of him and others are covering the immediate area, but really people, this is all too little, too late."

"How's Bill doing?"

The question, from the rear of the darkened room, went some way towards cutting through the tension. For a moment at least, the focus of concern was on one of their own, one who at least had survived the debacle on the South Lawn.

"Bill is still in the ICU. His prognosis is touch-and-go. I suggest if any of you have any religious affiliation, you say a prayer. Also, I would suggest that if you have no religious affiliation, you also say a prayer. Anyway, at this point, as you can well see, we have only partial control of the situation."

Several heads nodded in agreement.

"We have not actually determined what has transpired and how the action against the president was effected. The visiting head of state is down, off camera to the left. We'll come to him in a few moments. At this juncture, the First Lady is in the White House, in the bathroom. She missed the whole thing."

"Lady luck," a voice in the gloom muttered.

"Screw that, no such thing." Pete Asher snarled.

The image on the screen froze. The camera, which had been mounted on a press podium at the edge of the open-sided tent, was focused on the prone body of the president who was stretched out on the ground, his body sprawled sideways on to the camera lens, his head turned away, his arms outstretched. Agent Mellon was draped across the president's back. Their bodies formed an X, the epicenter of the biggest presidential security breach since the Kennedy assassination.

The image on the screen changed to a more distant shot. A number of cameras had been on the podium, and although most of them had been pointed in the direction of the president at the precise moment of the attack, one or two had been taking wider-angle pictures of the crowd under the tent canopy.

"I'm stopping it here for a moment, and I want you all to study it closely."

Asher was the senior agent in the room, acting the part of director and editor for the initial post mortem into what was now, quite evidently, a total collapse of the service's shield around the president.

"Look at that. Everybody's either running around like headless chickens, flat on the ground, or standing frozen. But who's this guy?"

Just to the rear and right side of the president, a man was walking rapidly towards the edge of the picture. The camera did not follow him out of the frame.

Asher pressed the rewind button. The man came into view again. The image was somewhat blurred, and the man was in view for only a couple of seconds. He appeared to be middle-aged, of medium height, fair-haired, no different in general appearance to a number of people at the South Lawn reception, indeed similar in appearance to a large percentage of the American male population. But it was not his physical characteristics that were pulling the assembled agents to the edges of their seats.

"He appears calm. He is paying no attention to the president. He is walking deliberately and purposefully away from ground zero."

"Sir, he also has his hand in his suit pocket. Look, just there."

"Yeah, you're right. It was ninety degrees out there, hotter under the tent. Why put your hand in your pocket? Maybe there's something in his pocket."

The man had now disappeared off-screen again. Asher allowed the film to play forward, and as it did so, there were shots from other cameras. But the mysterious man was not seen again. Still, all in the room knew that after the attack and the deaths, everyone who had attended the White House South Lawn reception would have been searched and vetted before being allowed leave the presidential mansion, no matter what the individual's status.

The recording had reached the three-minute-mark, and most of that time had elapsed since the president had gone down. This was enough time to vacate the grounds under ordinary circumstances. It was not a long walk from the lawn to the nearest gate over by the East Wing. But these were not ordinary circumstances.

Asher lowered the tone of his voice, his words coming out slowly and deliberately.

"So, assuming this guy got out of the White House, what do I want to know about him?

There was no response in the room as all present knew that Asher himself would deliver it.

"I want an enhancement of the video segment with this guy in sight. I want to know who this guy is. I want to know why he was at the reception. I want to know the color of his damn underwear. If this guy ever screwed up his knots in the Boy Scouts, I want to know which knots and why."

The sitting agents were already thinking in those terms anyway. Tough words were the only way to vent frustration at a moment when all in the room were reflecting on their own helplessness in the face of a ruthless and seemingly flawless assault on the president of the United States and others in his vicinity, not least the distinguished leader of a close ally.

"You know," said Asher, "this is worse than Kennedy. Kennedy was in a public place in an open car. This was the White House, the one place where we are supposed to have absolute control."

There were more nodded heads and murmurs of agreement but Asher ignored them. He had been thinking about Kennedy. His uncle had been in the Secret Service back in the 1960s, so he had heard stories. Some of them had even managed to avoid inclusion in the never-ending avalanche of conspiracy books which had followed the findings of the Warren Commission.

Jesus, the Kennedy business would be a child's puzzle compared to this one, Asher thought. His eyes returned to the screen. The image of the man walking off camera, indifferent, or oblivious, to the mayhem all about him, was frozen. It had indeed taken several minutes to lock down the White House after the attack on the president. He could have made his escape. Others involved in setting up the attack may have left as well during the course of the reception, before it had actually taken place.

Asher chewed his bottom lip. "Christ, what a mess," he said out loud to no one in particular. "If this was anything but an exercise, we would all be shaking hands at Wal-Mart, bet on it."

At the mention of the e-word the tension in the room lifted, if only a little. Asher glanced at his watch.

"We'll break for lunch and get back together at two. We're going to look at this blockbuster again, and this time I want you to see the things you clearly didn't see first time. Don't talk about the film, guess or speculate over your salads, or whatever it is you need to keep body and soul in one piece. Stick to baseball and the weather. Each one of you will be asked to answer a series of written questions, and I want to hear it from each one of you separately. Now git, you've got just under an hour."

Had the trainee agents moved any faster to the door no assassin on earth would have been able to outpace them. Asher watched them leave. Rookies, he thought. God help us.

His eyes were on the door, and they had remained fixed on the silhouetted figure who had appeared after the last of the lunch crowd had vanished from sight.

"Well, look who it is," Asher said. "Special Agent Conway. Welcome back to the world."

"Thanks, Pete. I see you're getting ready for the big one again. How are they doing?"

"Oh, they'll be fine I guess. They seem bright enough, not that I'm going to inflate their egos any more than they already are. I would say the president has a fair chance with any one of them."

"I guess that's as much as we can expect these days," Conway replied.

Asher walked up the slightly inclined walkway between the rows of chairs. Conway waited in the doorway.

"Let's step outside. I need some air," said Asher.

Outside the screening room the corridor was brightly lit, bare and antiseptic. But bright lights took nothing away from Cleo Conway. She had been breaking hearts at the service for years. Time actually seemed to be her friend.

"How was Alaska?"

"It was quiet," Conway replied.

That was about it for Conway's vacation, now thousands of miles away and a million years ago.

The two walked to the end of the corridor, turned left and boarded an elevator that took them up to the ground floor. Seconds later they were standing in the early season humidity that had draped itself over Murray Drive.

"Jeanie and the kids doing okay?"

Asher nodded. "Fine, he said. "Kristen is a real teen now, though. It would take at least two of our best people to keep tabs on her, and believe me, sometimes I'm tempted."

"She'll grow out of it," Conway said. "I did."

"Yeah. Anyway, it's good to see you back, Cleo. You've doubled the experience quotient around here by simply showing up."

Conway smiled. "You're a tease, Pete," she said. "What have you got lined up for me?"

"In the next couple of days, nothing much. Just settle back in. I know it's been rough. Tidy your desk, go work on that body of yours and then be ready for what's coming down the pike."

"And what might that be?" said Conway. "What's stirring in our beautiful world?"

Asher drew a deep breath and let it out.

"The threat level seems low right now. Leaving aside the China and Taiwan situation, there's the usual stuff in the Middle East, the generic sundry bad guys. And there's something rumbling again in Central Asia, and maybe Sri Lanka."

"Which of the 'stans? And I thought Sri Lanka was all quiet and peaceful again."

Conway had always scored well in the geography tests that had been part of high school social studies. As a kid she had enjoyed pouring over maps and globes, old and new. Her father had praised her interest saying that people who grew up on large landmasses were always on the right track if they were curious about other, smaller, places in the world.

And what else on earth was there apart from oceans, Conway had always replied.

Her father's response had been a standing joke between the two of them: "Why Cleo, small landmasses and large islands of course."

The vision of her father vanished as Asher rumbled on, his deep voice occasionally throwing out hints of his equally deep southern birth.

"Well, they've been arguing over their peace process as you know," he said. "Remember the assassination of the Indian prime minister, what was his name? Gandhi, Rajiv Gandhi. It's a long time ago but do you recall something unusual about it?"

"Yes, I do," said Conway. "The lead assassin was a woman, a Tamil separatist. She was an early-day female suicide bomber, comparatively rare for the time. Why Sri Lanka? Isn't that one place we've actually avoided getting our fingers dirty, at least in relative terms?"

"You're right," Asher responded. "But we have word, by way of our friends over at Langley, that there is a kind of school for women assassins doing a thriving business somewhere at the northern end of the island. This school seems to be graduating more than just locals. In fact it's turning into something of an assassination academy, just for the ladies, and one with the kind of global prospectus that is making people around here nervous."

"Is it an al-Qaeda op?"

"Not so far as we know, and different religious perspectives would be in play between the Tamils and the qaeda crowd," Asher replied.

"Nevertheless we can't get a precise handle on just who is behind it. All we know right now is that it exists, is being protected by the local bad guys and is beginning to graduate its brightest stars."

"And we think they might be eyeballing us," said Conway.

"Maybe so, maybe not. But we can't take the chance," said Asher.

"And as part of our response to a threat that we must assume is clear and present, you're going to be assigned to the first team."

"The First Lady?"

"Never accuse me of being sexist," said Asher, a half-smile breaking across his weathered countenance. "We'll throw in the president as well. Just for the hell of it."

He took only a half-step back when Conway planted a kiss on his cheek.

"Where is he right now?" she said nodding in the direction of the nearby White House.

"Not in town," said Asher. "He's giving a speech in Chicago and attending a fundraiser."

"I'm already there," said Cleo Conway.

34

Manning stopped a few yards short of the front door. He was early for work, though he knew that there would be a couple of his colleagues already at their desks. He gazed at the building. Embassies held secrets and spawned tales but Washington, he had long concluded, was in a league of its own, most especially since the arrival of the new ambassador.

He was on his third overseas posting, and it was easily his most important thus far. The embassy itself hinted at the prestige that came with a Washington assignment. But not too loudly, he had decided. Manning operated his own rough grading system for embassy compounds, their exteriors and interiors.

While most in Washington were roughly appropriate, he felt, some were grandiose and excessive. One or two were downright outrageous given the economic circumstances of the nations they represented.

Manning reckoned that a country's sense of self, or just its sense, could be fairly assessed by what lay behind an embassy's front gate. Ireland's embassy did not have a gate. It had been found wanting for a few other details in the recent time when the Republic had transformed itself from being a small nation on the western fringe of Europe to being a rather rich small nation occupying a kind of bridge between Europe and the United States.

Despite the darker economic outlook, the end of the Hibernian Dream as one colleague had put it, the embassy's move would go ahead as it was deemed time for a larger diplomatic outpost than the Sheridan Circle quarters, one that would more accurately reflect the country's progress, its admittedly stalled ambition, and its hoped-for return to better days. That was the argument in favor at any rate.

This he had learned just a few days ago in a briefing given to top-level diplomatic staff by the ambassador. The news had not taken Manning or his colleagues entirely by surprise. What had taken them off guard was the announcement by the ambassador that a new building had already been located and paid for.

This almost Teutonic efficiency had raised eyebrows and set tongues wagging. Where was it, they asked, but the ambassador had replied that she could not give the location away just yet because a few papers had yet to be signed. She didn't want to put a hex on the deal, she had said.

"Hex, me arse. You just like keeping your little secrets," said Manning, glancing at his watch.

The structure that was soon to be the former embassy was, to the more educated eye, a four-floor, semi-detached Louis XVI-style limestone house built in 1906. It stood on a fan-shaped lot across from the traffic circle that was home to the bronze image of General Philip, "Little Phil" Sheridan, a Civil War hero of the Union who had been born of Irish parents, had come into the world on a ship crossing the Atlantic, or had been born in Ireland and carried onto a ship within days of his arrival on earth. Records were a little unclear with regard to baby Sheridan. The destruction wrought by the adult Sheridan on the forces of the Confederacy had, however, been more than well documented.

The previous ambassador had been a bit of a Civil War buff and had regaled visitors to the embassy with Little Phil stories. His successor had merely inquired who the silly little man on the horse was. She had also made it clear that she wasn't interested in any answer.

The embassy's first floor was for receptions, and the new ambassador had plenty of questions about such affairs. Moreover, she expected detailed answers. The first floor had once included the ambassador's office, but with all the confusion over moving, that sanctum had been moved up another level. The building currently housed roughly twenty people, about half of them being accredited diplomats. The overall number of occupants had been edging up in recent months, and with the impending move, more were now anticipated. America was once and again Ireland's best friend in the world, and there would be a need for more Irish hands to pump American ones.

Manning rather liked the soon to be ex-embassy, even though it did seem more suited to diplomacy in the age of horse and buggy. He was particularly curious about what secrets, real and potential, it might have gathered down the years. His lingering paranoia, which had been bolstered by the encounter atop the mountain, had tempted him in the direction of a little more eavesdropping than usual. He had idly considered what might be gained from bugging the place, particularly the ambassador's office. He had done a little private research on the web about listening devices. The embassy, so far as he could gather, had not been swept for bugs in a long time, if ever.

Typically Irish, he thought. Too trusting by far. The British, he knew, would turn a place upside down before moving into it. And they would turn it upside down again once they had set up shop. The British expected to be bugged. They hoped that others would try. It was an acknowledgement that you still counted for something in the world.

Manning was unaware of it, as was everyone else, but the Sheridan Square offices had been bugged once. Not by the British, although they had considered it and once halfheartedly attempted it, but by the Russians in their former guise as the Soviets.

Back in the early 1970s, the KGB had succeeded in planting a device in a phone in the then first secretary's office. Moscow at the time was keenly interested in the events in Northern Ireland. Tapping into the unstated sentiments of the Irish government had been considered a key element in the formulation of Moscow's strategy for the Troubles, how to take advantage and, perhaps, foment even deeper discord.

The Soviets had monitored Irish chat, both in the building and on the phone for about six months. The listeners had discovered that some rural Irish accents could be difficult to decipher, that diplomats were sometimes less than subtle in their romantic dalliances and that there was, not infrequently, vigorous debate in the embassy with regard to Northern Ireland and what to do about Irish American supporters of the IRA. The phone was eventually changed and the bug went into the garbage with it. The KGB did not attempt to replace its device.

Now, three decades later, the embassy was throwing things out again in anticipation of the move to new and better digs. So much stuff and so little room, the ambassador would say as she supervised the clearing out of anything she declared to be sinful clutter. Nobody dared point out that the new place would actually have more room.

The ambassador had also made it abundantly clear that with new quarters firmly established she was going to take on the British in the social stakes. As the peace process had lumbered on, not always in the direction anticipated or hoped for in Dublin, Her Majesty's diplomats had stepped up a kind of hearts, minds and stomachs campaign aimed at convincing anyone who cared that London's intentions were in the right place and its way of moving the Irish situation forward, was, naturally, the most advantageous to all. The tactic had been pursued with vigor at the spacious British Ambassador's residence on Massachusetts Avenue.

By way of a barely subtle response, it had been decided in Dublin that Sheridan Circle, and the nearby but separate ambassador's residence on S Street, would both go on the block. What would then be sought was a building and compound large enough to combine both residence and embassy. The British would no longer be allowed to go unchallenged in the never-ending game of ear bending.

This was, more or less, the official rumor.

One or two of Manning's colleagues had, rather unkindly he thought, suggested that the appointment of Phillipa Evans as ambassador had been necessitated by her well known, or at least well rumored, private lifestyle and the many connections it brought with it.

Whatever the reason for the shipping out, it didn't really matter all that much to Manning. He wasn't sure if he wanted to remain a diplomat for much longer anyway. He reckoned he would never make ambassador to a first rate capital such as Washington, no matter how evident his style or talent.

Manning had walked to work. He had left his sleeping wife and daughter at the Georgetown house and had covered the distance with an even, steady stride. There would be few mornings as cool as this once the month turned. Already, the city on a swamp was beginning to heat up as spring advanced.

A few minutes and ritual greetings later, Manning walked slowly up the winding staircase that led to the ambassador's office. Ambassador and her first secretary had agreed to set aside time to discuss the grand move.

It was perhaps a coincidence, perhaps not, he thought but the transfer of the embassy from its present location to its new, decidedly upscale address, was about to occur, serendipitously some were saying, under the gaze of an ambassador who was herself known to be something of a mover in matters including, but not entirely confined to, real estate. The thought made Manning smile.

The stairs duly conquered, as if some mountain's precipitous ridge or col, Manning stood at the door of the ambassador's office. He tapped gently before turning the handle and stepping smartly into the perfumed preserve of his superior. She was, however, absent from the room. It was a couple of minutes beyond their scheduled meeting so Manning decided to wait. Might as well get it over, he thought.

The office was unrecognizable from the form it had taken under the new occupant's predecessor, and this, to just about everybody, had seemed more than a little over the top with the decision to vacate now revealed.

Still, the lady's style was above reproach, all had agreed. Manning walked over to the sideboard that was crowded with framed photographs. Some were professional, but most were family snapshots, Phillipa with siblings, parents and cousins, her husband, who always seemed to be in another country doing business, a few of mother with daughter at various ages. There seemed to have been quite a few garden parties at a large country house. Most of the recent photos were of Evans on the job.

Evans was, no doubt about it, a woman of stunning good looks. She was close to fifty, for sure, or might have even reached that landmark. But the years had treated her very kindly. Her upbringing had doubtless helped. Her family, more than financially comfortable, had ensured that their daughter's had been a life of few material worries.

Phillipa, so the arbitrators of such matters had concluded, could be described as latter day Anglo-Irish, though not entirely big house Protestant.

Either way, she was a vivacious, utterly worldly woman, an Irish Pamela Harriman, her chosen work a glove fit for her many evident talents. Manning was by no means the only one who had been just a little smitten.

Manning turned sharply as he heard Evans enter the room. She beamed, and he nodded and smiled in return. He was surprised, and though he would not admit it to anyone, a little disappointed that she was accompanied by a man that he had never seen before.

"Good morning, Eamonn," said Evans. "Sit down, will you? We have some serious matters to discuss."

Here we go, Manning thought as the ambassador's companion extended his hand.

35

SAMANTHA WALSH opened her eyes. It took a couple of seconds before she quite remembered where she was.

"Oh, Nick," she said. But Bailey was not in the bed beside her.

She sat up, pulling the bed covers upwards as she did so. She glanced at the clock.

"Oh, Christ," she said. But just as quickly she settled back into the mattress. She was not working today. Finally she had some time to herself after what had been an especially intense immersion in the shady art of protecting very important persons.

Walsh was vaguely unsettled by the fact that the first person she had sought out once she had obtained her free weekend was Nick Bailey. She had imagined that their affair had been casual and unlikely to progress very far. But last night had changed that, somewhat at any rate.

The sound of a door closing with a thud brought Walsh's eyes to bear on the bedroom door. Bailey tiptoed into the room, barefoot but otherwise fully dressed, with the look on his face of a boy sneaking out of school.

"It's all right. I'm awake," Walsh said.

"So you are, so you are," said Bailey. "I popped out for a quick smoke. Wasn't going to do that in here because you don't, and besides, I don't want to be accused of nailing a copper with secondhand smoke."

"Very kind of you, Nick. You should give them up. It's a disgusting habit."

Bailey ignored the jibe, walked over to a dresser, pulled open a door and extracted a pair of blue socks. He examined the socks, with his nose as well as his eyes. Seemingly satisfied, he sat in the cat-scratched jumble sale cloth chair that doubled as a clothes horse and pulled them on. Walsh watched and wondered quite what she saw in him.

"You were very lively last night," she said after a few moments. "Anyone would think you had been celibate for a year, not just a couple of weeks. Or has it been three?"

"Was it that long? Seemed like just a couple of days," Bailey replied. "Sorry I forgot to ask you last night, but how was that place? Were you shooting guns all the time or what?"

"Milton," said Walsh. "And no, we were not shooting guns all the time, though we did manage to put quite a dent in the ammunition supply."

"So," said Bailey, "there I was between the sheets last night with Deadeye Jane. Are you a decent shot?"

"I certainly wouldn't miss you from this range," said Walsh.

She slipped sideways out of the bed, walked across the room and sat down on Bailey's lap. She could feel his body grow taut and allowed him to surround her with his arms. They kissed, furiously, slowly and furiously again, before she pinned him to the back of the chair with a forearm to his windpipe.

"Now, Mr. Bailey," she said with mock seriousness, "are you going to peacefully make breakfast, or am I going to have to clap you in irons and haul you off to the clink?"

"Can I plead inability to function in a kitchen?" Bailey said, faking a choking voice.

"No pleas," said Walsh as she stood up and stretched. "Unless it's temporary insanity."

"I'm quite sane, Samantha," said Bailey. "More than I've ever been in my life." He stood up and took hold of her. She allowed him to kiss her neck and caress her hair but after a few moments gently pulled herself away. She wasn't quite sure yet. She patted her stomach and Bailey laughed.

"They say it's the way to a man's heart, but that's only half the story, not even that, just the lead paragraph," he said.

"And by the way, you've been doing a lot more at that coppers' camp than just gently squeezing triggers. I didn't know girls were allowed muscles like that. Remind me not to meet you in any dark alleyways."

Walsh and Bailey enjoyed a leisurely breakfast and were well into their second pot of tea when a ringing doorbell reminded both that there was a world beyond the flat and their nascent relationship.

"That will be the post," said Bailey.

"The postman rings the doorbell when he delivers? Nice of him," said Walsh.

"Well, yes," Bailey responded. "When he found out that I was in the newspaper game he decided that I was not to be kept waiting. Tip-offs, informers, sources and all that. He thinks I'm Woodward and Bernstein, and whopping exclusives arrive by snail mail."

"How sweet," said Walsh as she finished off a slice of toast and marmalade.

Bailey stood and moved to the door. "Back in a second," he said. "Help yourself to more toast, or anything your little heart desires for that matter."

"Cheeky boy," Walsh said. She smiled as she reached for another slice. It was strange, she thought, so peaceful, domestic and normal. Could she get used to this, a life with Nicholas Bailey?

Before she could even begin to answer her own question, Bailey had returned, shuffling in his hands an inch thick batch of envelopes along with a single magazine.

"What's the magazine?" Walsh said. "Oh, a gentleman's publication. Give us a look."

Bailey handed her the magazine, a sheepish look on his face. "A trial subscription," he said, though not with much conviction.

He glanced at the envelopes. "Usual rubbish," he said. "Except for this."

He sat back in his chair and placed the pile of post on the table. He lifted the letter of interest in front of his face and examined it intently.

"Nice handwriting. Who from? I wonder; no return address. Perhaps it's a tip-off about a scandal at Scotland Yard. Plod on the take."

Walsh ignored his dig as she devoured the toast and magazine at roughly equal speed. It was only after several minutes that she noticed the silence and sensed Bailey's concentration. Bailey was staring at the letter that she could see ran to a second page.

"Something wrong?" she said.

Bailey did not immediately reply. "I'm not quite sure."

"Something is certainly up, that's for certain. Did I mention to you that I recently met this guy, a colleague? I don't really know him personally. His name is Sydney Small, our Buckingham Palace man. A bit of a legend in his own reign. Henderson is certainly a fan, and that says something."

"You never mentioned him Nick, nor your meeting," said Walsh, putting down her toast and closing the magazine.

"Didn't I? Well, I did meet him a couple of weeks ago in a pub on the south side of the river. A real out of the way place. Never heard of it, and believe me, I've heard of most of them."

"No doubt," said Walsh.

Bailey, with a mock smile, continued, "Well, there he was, tucked into the back of the place with his glass of gin, all on his lonesome and looking like some toff in the paddock at Sandown Park. Certainly didn't quite match my mental image, though when I thought of it afterwards it made perfect sense to have a man who looked like part of the royal rat pack covering the dear noble things.

"Well, we sat and chatted for a few minutes. He was a nice bloke, don't get me wrong, and he cracked a joke or two about Henderson which helped me ease up a bit. You never know what gets back to Henderson except that everything gets back to him. Anyway, he was going on about the dead priests, certainly giving the impression that if he had not direct knowledge he had certainly formed a theory based on something firm."

Bailey stopped and looked at the letter again.

"Yes, go on," said Walsh.

"Well, he was about to get really stuck into the matter when his cell phone went off. He had a quick conversation, said something about the palace being on the line and took off. He said he would be in touch, but that I wasn't to say a word to anyone. I wouldn't have known what to say anyway, and that's where we left it. But now this letter."

"Can I read it?" Walsh said, her hand reaching across the table.

Bailey stood up, walked back to the table, passed the letter over and stood with his arms folded.

"Very bloody odd," he said, as much to himself as to Walsh who was now scanning the letter with what seemed to Bailey a well-practiced eye.

"Nice handwriting," said Bailey, but Walsh did not respond.

She read it once and then began to read it again.

"Dear Nicholas," it began. "I must apologize profusely for my rude behavior the other day in the pub. I hope you will forgive me and trust in the fact that my sudden departure was absolutely unavoidable. A matter of life and death, you might say. I had started to tell you about my theory with regard to the deaths of those unfortunate priests.

"Had I been able to tarry, I would have taken my position beyond the realm of mere theory. There is a connection between the four, though just what the common denominator is I had no clue on the day we met. I have a rather better idea now, and to tell you the truth, it rather scares me out of my wits. As a result I am having to make myself scarce for a while. Don't bother trying to find me because you will not succeed. It's a big world, and I know one or two of the darker corners.

"I must warn you that while I expect you will want to inquire more deeply into the deaths of the good fathers, there are risks involved in such work, extreme risks, so for God's sake be careful. As I stated, I have yet to fill in the complete picture. It's a bit like the first part of a steeplechase on a foggy day; one must wait until the nags come out of the murk before drawing any real conclusions as to the result. I must apologize for not being entirely clear in this correspondence, and I am sure you are asking yourself why I would be remotely interested in this matter, or even involved in a mere peripheral way. But I am involved, Nicholas, and not just around the edge of what could turn out to be a most shocking affair.

"Let me repeat: do not even think of seeking me out. Nevertheless, I suspect that you will try. A story is a story, and I well understand that. I do not trust even the Royal Mail enough to elaborate any further. But I had a sense about you, Nicholas. You're a man with a good nose, the kind that finds the most extraordinary truffles. I am not sure if I will be able to contact you again in the near future, if at all. But again, Nicholas, please watch your back. Yours faithfully, Sydney Small."

"Truffles," said Walsh. "Oink oink."

"Odd, isn't it?" said Bailey.

"Odd, indeed," said Walsh. "But there could be more to this letter than that."

"Yes, go on," said Bailey.

Walsh, reaching for the teapot bit her lip and narrowed here eyes. "What exactly is it? A hint, a lead, a guarded come-on and a warning all rolled into one. Beyond that, and most importantly, is it just gossip, information, or is it evidence of a quadruple murder?"

"That's quite a lot," said Bailey. "I should make a fresh pot before we try to decide, or do anything else."

Walsh was reading the letter again, her brow was furrowed, and the fingers of her left hand were drumming furiously on the table.

"Do you know what?" she said. "Your friend is hinting strongly at some kind of conspiracy, a murderous plot. I don't care what he says, or how good he is at losing himself. I think we should find him."

"Sí, inspector," said Bailey.

"Shut up and make the tea," the woman Bailey suspected he might be falling in love with replied, without sympathy.

36

"Eamonn, do sit down."

Evans beamed at Manning with her knock-down smile. Manning returned the gesture as best he could.

The British had been fit to be tied when Phillipa Evans had landed in Washington. She had been an instant hit on the diplomatic reception circuit. London's man was most notable for being, well London's man.

The British ambassador, Peter Price Jones, was, of course, a skilled and perfectly poised diplomat. In normal circumstances he would have been judged as ideal for the post; a little cautious perhaps and low key to the point of being borderline dull. He was solid, dependable, not one to drop the ball.

But matched against Phillipa Evans, an Irishwoman with a Welsh-sounding name, Jones, with his own Welsh-sounding name, seemed to merge with the nearest wallpaper. So did most of the rest of the in-town plenipotentiaries for that matter. Yes, Manning thought, we made the right move. The woman's a grand slam home run, a perfect game even if only half the rumors are untrue.

"Eamonn, I want you to meet Jake Voles. He's going to be helping us with our big move."

Manning extended his hand a second time and Voles, who had remained standing, took it.

His handshake was strong, and Manning, who always made a point of looking a new acquaintance straight in the face, was immediately aware of intense blue eyes looking right back into his. Almost as if there was recognition, Manning sensed, before shifting his gaze to his boss.

"Sit down, both of you, please," said Evans. "Coffee, gentlemen?"

Manning had a feeling he would be in the room for a while so he nodded in the affirmative. Evans poured him a cup from a pot she had sitting on a silver tray. Poured perfectly, with just enough cleavage showing as she leaned into the cup, Manning thought. Christ, what a flirt.

Voles nodded agreement to the offer of a cup and was similarly rewarded.

"Nice to meet you, Eamonn. Phillipa, the ambassador, tells me you are the man for all seasons in the embassy," he said.

The two men were seated on one side of the ambassador's desk, but Evans had wheeled her chair around and was clearly intent on sitting herself down beside Voles, right beside as it turned out.

"Dog's body is another term for it," Manning replied. He was smiling as he said it, his little jibe at Evans thus masked to the point of diplomatic acceptance.

"Eamonn's ability to meet and work with people is extraordinary. The Americans like him a lot. It helps, of course, when your wife is an American. Isn't that so Eamonn?"

Manning knew the game. Evans was reminding him that he was married and that she, in addition to being married herself, was out of reach. She wasn't making an innocent statement of fact, so much as teasing him.

"I've learned the lingua americana. But what about you, Jake? You're American. From around here?"

"New York born, but my family moved to California when I was fifteen. My dad was an early days Silicon Valley pioneer."

"You're in computers, too?" Manning said.

"Yes, I was, indeed still am, but not in private business. I was in the FBI," Voles replied.

"And before that Jake was in the United States Marines," Evans said. She had a slightly dazed look on her face. To Manning's eyes it appeared that the ambassador wanted to throw all decorum out the window and tear the onetime G-Man's shirt off his body.

"Did you catch many bad guys?" said Manning.

"In a way I guess I did, but I was mostly in counter intelligence, working with computers, surveillance equipment, that sort of thing."

Ah, a spook, Manning thought. Voles had the look of a man who had been places and seen things, not all of them routine. He had the feeling that he wasn't supposed to pry any deeper into G-Man's past, an idea that was confirmed when Evans came chirping in with an offer of more coffee.

"Thank you, Ambassador," Manning said with mock politeness as he reached over with his cup and saucer.

Voles was clearly older, he thought. Probably in his mid-fifties. But he looked fit. A little under six feet and about 190 pounds. He had the air of a man who carried secrets.

Evans interrupted the silent assessment.

"I've explained to Jake that what we discuss in this room remains entirely within these walls." Her demeanor had changed. She was staring purposefully at Manning, all business now.

"And that's precisely what's were going to be talking about," she added. "Walls and what you can find in them. Jake now runs his own private security and intelligence company. He's going to be helping us out with our move to the new embassy. The building is large and right now undergoing preliminary reconstruction, and there's no telling what could end up in the place.

"We're not the Americans, and we're not the Russians, I know, but we do have interests from these past few years and, Pray God, a little money left, and that means the kind of information from time to time that some people would dearly like to get their hands on. And apart from that I have heard, believe it or not, that one of our fellow European Union embassies was bugged last year by a scurrilous gossip magazine. Would you believe it?"

Manning nodded gravely. He wasn't quite sure if Voles was necessary for the embassy of a small country with little strategic significance, but he could not argue with Evans over the possibility of talk of needed potential American investments being intercepted by another country, even a European Union friend and ally.

"Of course," he said. "Welcome on board, Jake. Anything I can do to help you can depend on it," he said.

"Splendid," said Evans.

Voles nodded and smiled. "Looking forward to working with you, Eamonn.

Manning had the feeling that his role in the meeting had reached its end and stood up.

"I'll be in the office if you need me," he said to Evans. She didn't reply. She was on her feet pouring more coffee for Voles. Slowly.

Manning let out air as he gently closed the door to the ambassador's office.

A shuffling sound on the winding staircase pulled Manning back from thoughts of Evans and her machinations. Frank Nesbitt, with whom Quinn was sharing an office until the move, was walking slowly up the stairs.

"Ah, stately, plump Frank Nesbitt," Manning said.

"Only when I'm going in the other direction," Nesbitt puffed. He was no athlete. Indeed he was something of a physical shambles. Manning, nevertheless, enjoyed his company. Nesbitt had more than an average talent for seeing right through people and the wall of formalities, clipped manners and nuance of everyday diplomacy. And he could do so in three languages.

"Your wife was on the phone," said Nesbitt. He had stopped and was leaning heavily against the wall on one side of the stairwell. "She sounded a bit tired, I have to say. Have you been up to something?"

"Did you manage to tell her that I was at a wine tasting at the Romanian embassy? Something clever like that?"

"More or less," Nesbitt replied. "How about a goat's cheese lunch with the Bulgarian ambassador?

"That would do," Manning said as he began walking down the stairs. "Make sure you knock hard on the door. You wouldn't want to surprise the two of them. Phillipa had a look in her eye."

"The Look," said Nesbitt, with emphasis.

"The very same," Manning replied. "Come back to the office when you're finished in there."

"You can help me find that *Washington Post* editorial. It's in the pile somewhere, but it must be stuck under a paper clip on some other file. It bloody well always happens to something you need to get your hands on."

"Doesn't it just," said Nesbitt, turning slowly, his hand raised to knock on the ambassador's door. "What about looking for it online? Oh, never mind."

Back in the shared office, Manning sat down heavily in his chair. His banter with Nesbitt had been precisely the kind of inconsequential exchange that he hoped would form a barrier between his present and future, and his past.

The more of it the better, he thought. Yet he well knew that such thinking was more than a little wishful. They wanted more from him and they would have it. But this would be the last time, yes, the very last time. He would tell them to take a hike; he would reveal everything to Rebecca, quit diplomacy and study law or something. He could be his father, the American version, Perry Mason with a lilt.

But for now he would simply call, check in with his wife and discuss the ordinary things, dinner tonight, Jessica's violin lesson. He hit the familiar numbers on his desk phone but only heard his own voice on the recorded message.

"Hi, it's me. Nothing much to report except just met an ex-G-Man. An interesting guy and I'll tell you more this evening. Call you back later. Love you."

Manning replaced the receiver, leaned back in his chair, closed his eyes and rested his head on his cupped hands.

Evans clearly was planning for a lot of fuss and bother in the weeks ahead. Either the White House bunfight, or the move to the new embassy would, under normal circumstances, be more than enough to keep everybody busy. Both of them occurring more or less simultaneously, and on top of normal business, had all the ingredients of a logistical nightmare.

Manning sat up and ran his eyes over his notebook. His afternoon was more or less free. Evans had asked him to scan various invitation lists with a view to putting together a high level version for the White House reception, which, she had been led to understand, would be held on the South Lawn.

Cutting and splicing the various theme-based lists would be enough to pass the while. Manning already knew that one or two of the long familiar reception faces were, of late, deceased. If nothing else he would be able to deliver definite news to Evans about names and faces she would not need to remember.

Manning hit a key to reawaken his computer but as he did so his cell phone rang. He flipped it open and put the phone to his ear. He grimaced when he heard the voice, clear enough that it could be in the adjoining room.

"I thought I said you were never to call me here," Manning said in a near whisper.

"It doesn't matter if it's my cell phone," he hissed.

"Where?" he said after a short pause.

"Okay, all right. But this is positively the last time. After this I'm bloody well out."

37

THE PLANE BANKED TO THE SOUTHWEST. Far below, the ruddy brown land and lake landscape of Labrador signaled that the Atlantic had been crossed.

This British Airways 747 out of London's Heathrow was just one jet in the daily formation heading from Europe for the cities of the eastern United States and beyond. Its passenger manifest was made up of the usual assortment of people, all of them checked and vetted before being stowed in their seats for the transatlantic journey. Steven Pender did not stand out from the rest of them.

Pender was staring out of the cabin window, blinking in the glare 37,000 feet above the earth's surface. He could sense the pull of America, though the plane was still a good three hours from arrival at Kennedy. Looking away from the window he contemplated the plastic cup with the remains of what had passed for tea. His eyes returned to the news magazine on his pullout table.

The American president was pictured in the Oval Office, leaning back against the front of his desk, arms folded, the familiar determined jut to his jaw telling the world that nobody pushed him or the United States around.

The headline, "Dollars and Sense," was an allusion to the president's reputation for seeing the world as a place where American business interests came before even the most hallowed policies of departments such as State and Defense.

William T. Packer, the article confirmed, was showing once again that he valued bottom line financial issues at home more than lofty foreign policy positions that many had believed were set in stone. When it came to Taipei versus Beijing, the writer was arguing that it was a matter of where the bucks accumulated rather than stopped. Right now, they were piling up fast because of new trade deals with Beijing. As a result, the reporter opined, much of the world was beginning to take the view that Taipei might be out of the loop to the point of being screwed.

The language wasn't quite so blunt, but Pender also read things into photos. He reckoned the president's pose in the Oval Office picture said much about the man. He was, Pender had concluded, not someone to lose sleep over ditching old friends if there was a new, bigger and more powerful partner waiting in the wings. Packer was a devious operator for sure, a right ornery bastard, an enormously successful politician.

"More tea sir." It was more statement than question, and the stewardess was already leaning across the sleeping woman in the next seat, her metal teapot gripped firmly by her long fingers.

Pender was diplomatic. "Just a drop thanks." He smiled at her and she at him. She poured, but he raised his hand for her to stop before the liquid reached the top of his plastic cup.

"Thank you," he said.

Pender stared at the brew before his eyes turned to the cabin window. Yes, he thought, Packer was the kind of man who made enemies. And the more, the better. They would help provide the necessary cover for success in the upcoming operation.

Pender closed the magazine and returned to his book. His eyes stared at the page but his mind was wandering. By necessity, Pender's future, his life, would be anonymous. But it stood to be comfortable and that, he decided, was no mean compensation.

Pender was shaken from his thoughts as the aircraft shuddered. The fasten seat belts jingle carried through the cabin as the plane bobbed up and down in the unseen turbulence. The turbulence would be short lived, a crew member's reassuring voice announced on the intercom. But in the meantime the captain was advising everyone to remain seated with their seatbelts fastened.

The shaking had awakened Pender's neighbor, an impressively-sized woman who had fussed with things in her pocketbook before falling sound asleep after the dinner service. Pender had noticed that everything the woman had done since boarding the plane had been in neat and ordered segments. She had smiled at Pender when she first sat down but had said nothing since.

Now awake again, Pender reckoned, it would be time for her chat again.

"Was that turbulence? I was snoozing," the woman said, her eyes fixed on Pender's tea.

"Oh, tea. What a good idea."

Pender turned and half smiled. "I highly recommend it," he said.

"Oh, you're English," she replied at once. "I love the English. That was my third visit. What a wonderful, special country."

"There's worse, I suppose," said Pender, his eyes returning to his tea.

"I was visiting a friend," the woman said. "She lives in a very nice apartment in London, or should I say a flat as you English do."

"Apartment's fine. Everybody speaks a little American these days," Pender responded, more or less pleasantly.

"Oh, but I'm not an American," the woman said quickly. "I'm actually Canadian by birth though I have lived in the United States for most of my life. Must hold on to our heritage, I always say. I was born in a little town not too far from Toronto. And where are you from, Mister, um?"

The woman raised her eyebrows slightly awaiting Pender's revelatory response. Pender demurred.

"Ah, Toronto," he said.

The woman nodded. She wasn't giving up.

"My name is Paula Neilson," she said. "I live in New York, and I'm in banking, downtown, not far from where the World Trade Center towers once stood."

She was throwing nuggets in succession, but Pender wasn't about to give anything back in a hurry. The plane shuddered as it encountered another pocket of turbulent air. Pender lost a little of his tea.

"Funny thing, isn't it?" he said, his eyes moving to the window, "The most turbulent air is always called clear. You wouldn't think there was anything out there at all to impede our progress. It's almost a vacuum."

Paula Neilson was not about to be diverted.

"Did you say you were in Toronto? Is this your first visit to the United States?"

Pender turned and allowed himself to half smile. "No," he said simply.

Paula Neilson let out a little sigh, but just as she was beginning to drift back to her bag and its eclectic contents, Pender gave her some slack. It was his habit to be parsimonious with personal information, but, yes, he did feel a little chattier in a plane. In a plane there was nowhere to go, nothing to do other than what everybody else was doing, and nothing to do about either of those limitations. Nothing, nothing, nothing; except, of course, to mentally plan out the more obscure details of the next job or take a little time to tease one's traveling companion.

He relented.

"My name, by the way, is Stephen Pender. I have been in the States quite a few times, a dozen or more. Wonderful country, great places to see, charming people," he said.

Paula Neilson beamed.

"And I've been to Toronto. Fun town," he added for good measure.

Neilson was beside herself.

"Oh, indeed it is. I still get up there on a fairly regular basis, once or twice a year. I have cousins," she said. She was clearly, Pender reflected, fast approaching her own version of conversational full throttle.

Oh, what the heck; it would pass the time.

"Yeah," he said, "and there are some great restaurants. What's the name of that place, the French one, Gaston's?

"Oh, I'm not sure if I know that one, but certainly there are some very good ones. Yes, Toronto is a fun place. They use it all the time for movies that are supposed to be set in New York, you know."

Pender nodded and smiled.

"So I believe," he said.

The conversation stalled for several seconds but Paula Neilson wasn't about to let go now.

"So, Mr. Pender, where do you stay in New York? A hotel? With friends?"

"I have an apartment, rented for the time I'm in town," Pender replied with a slight shrug of his shoulders. "It's self-catering, a bit like a home away from home."

"Oh, yes," Neilson replied. "That makes a lot of sense. Does it have a doorman?"

"I have not been there before, but I believe not," Pender said. "It's self-catering right down to letting yourself in late at night."

He was flirting now. He had noticed that Neilson was not wearing a wedding band and might be on the trail of an adventure. He just as quickly put thoughts of one out of his mind. This was not a pleasure trip.

The woman's eyes were fixed on his. He could sense it. She was building up to something. They were interrupted by the stewardess who was reaching across Neilson again with Pender's tea cup, now almost drained, squarely in her sights. She knew a good customer when she saw one and was clearly intent on emptying her teapot and stowing the wretched thing away.

"Oh, no, thank you," Pender said in his best home county, his hand covering the cup.

The stewardess couldn't quite hide a little frown of disappointment.

Paula Neilson released another sigh, louder this time.

Jesus, Pender thought, I might have to use karate to keep all these women off.

It occurred to him that over the last few years he had not enjoyed much in the way of life's more obvious pleasures. Dalliances were awkward when on the job, sometimes too high a risk. Longer term affairs were a no-no. He had no doubt that his winning ways would work on Paula Neilson well before they landed. But she would have to wait for some future traveling companion.

Pender braced himself for the next question. He had a good idea what it would be. Neilson reached into her bag, rummaged for a few seconds and, with a small hoot of triumph, plucked a business card from its depths.

"This is me," she said. "If you ever need a quick loan to smooth your way through New York's French restaurants just give me a holler."

"Thank you," said Pender taking the card.

"Senior Associate, very impressive."

"I hate the word senior," said Neilson. "By the way, I was meaning to ask you. What is it exactly that you do, Mr. Pender, Stephen?"

Now it was Pender's turn to draw in a breath. He turned and fixed Paula Neilson with narrowed eyes and a half smile.

"Very simple," he said. "I shoot people."

38

"Found it."

Manning's voice was raspy, triumphant. He had been ever more anxiously probing a pile of briefing papers, department manuscripts, photocopied newspaper articles, features and editorials that had piled high on his desk to the point that when he sat down he could no longer see Nesbitt across the adjoining desk.

Manning stood up, clutching his prize.

"My favorite editorial." He beamed. Nesbitt smiled.

Manning was doing his best to sound cheerful. He just hoped that his colleague would not notice the effort.

"I really turned them on this one. What's his name in the *Post* editorial department must have been fresh out of preschool. Christ, he hadn't even heard of the Chequers Protocol."

Nesbitt's smile widened. "Not surprising if it didn't exist," he said.

Manning sat back in his chair and read the editorial. He knew it off by heart but it was always worth another look. It was only a couple of years old, but it seemed to speak of another age.

"Yeah," well, I was just testing him. I ended up telling him that the protocol was with a small c and small p, more of an under the table understanding between ourselves and the Brits. Either way, we had Her Majesty's minions cold on that one, Frank. First with the punch. Not every day that *The Washington Post* more or less calls the British prime minister an idiot."

"And a little more than less," said Nesbitt. "Your best day indeed. Pity it was all downhill after that."

"Nonsense," Manning snorted.

Manning and Nesbitt worked well together for the most part. Neither man was especially tidy, and that had helped smooth over the daily trial of working in a space that was not designed for a pair of diplomats who had a love of old fashioned paper files to match J. Edgar Hoover.

"Any plans for the weekend?" Manning threw out the question more or less for its own sake, just to keep the air of normalcy on an even keel.

"Well, now that you ask," said Nesbitt, "I'm thinking of heading out to western Maryland for an overnight. To Sharpsburg, that's the town, to the Antietam battlefield."

"Oh, yeah? That was a big battle wasn't it? When was it?"

"Eighteen sixty-two, September seventeenth," Nesbitt replied. "Still the bloodiest single day in American history, over 4800 dead and thousands wounded. For a little while on September 11 they thought the death toll might be surpassed but Antietam's still standing on its own. With luck it will never be surpassed."

"I should hope not," Manning said, staring at another pile of cuttings. "The fact that you're going is a good thing. What was it that guy said about forgetting history and then history repeating itself?"

Nesbitt raised his right forefinger. "'Those who do not remember the past are condemned to repeat it.' George Santayana."

Nesbitt had the bit between his teeth now and was enthusing.

"Lots of Irish involved in the battle, of course, on both sides. The Union Irish Brigade took a terrible hammering at a place called Bloody Lane. I've never been to Antietam, but I hear it's very moving. Looks much the same as it did all those years ago, and, of course, there is the monument to the Irish Brigade which we had a hand in a few years ago. It's right beside the main observation tower, General Thomas Francis Meagher, the whole thing. Frankly there are times that I wish I was alive in those days, on a horse, a gray charger, leading my regiment up and over the hill."

"No you bloody don't, Frank. You wouldn't have lasted the first volley," Manning interjected. "Taking anyone with you?"

"No, just me I'm afraid," said Nesbitt. "I'm just about the only Civil War buff here at the moment. Donal what's his name was a complete war nut but he's back in Dublin as you know. He went to just about every battlefield. I've been to Gettysburg and that's about it. But Antietam should be fascinating, absolutely fascinating."

"Oh, I'm sure it will be," said Manning. "I'd go with you but I have a few wife and daughter things, and I might have to work a bit on this White House reception business. Time, as usual, is short."

Nesbitt, as far as his companion was concerned, was good company, for the most part. His habit of sneaking cigarettes in the office was not always to Manning's liking but that was about his only vice. Nesbitt was in the act of reaching into a desk drawer for a smoke when Margaret Morris poked her head around the door.

"Anybody got any ideas for lunch?"

Nesbitt looked at Manning. "Well, Your Highness?" The two had lately taken to referring to themselves as the princes of Denmark. It was an inside joke, a mutual salute to a former occupant of the office by the name of Eoin Sharkey.

Sharkey had become a hero to some, a villain to others by telling a visiting journalist from one of the Irish American weeklies that Ireland's diplomats in Washington were just a wee bit bored. Where once they had a wee war, they now had a blessed, but also grinding and never ending peace process. Where once there had been the delicate dance of a small nation in the midst of the big players there was now a small nation jostling for attention amid the Euro trash throng.

Of course, the peace process was wonderful, Sharkey had opined. But it did take the edge off the Washington posting compared to former years. Hardly a subversive in sight and making nice with the British, our friends and partners in a political and diplomatic merry-go-round that always seemed to start and end in the same place. Sliced, diced and explained in the inevitable joint communiqué.

Ireland, Sharkey had told the reporter, had become another Denmark, and had the visiting hack any idea what that meant to a crack diplomatic team? Any bloody idea?

It had all been off the record. Supposedly. But Sharkey didn't really know this visitor so well that he could afford to be so candid. He had failed to drive the off-the-record message home strongly enough. The result had been rather spectacular. The story had not appeared as a formal, front page report, the gods be thanked, as the ambassador had put it.

But it had topped a politics-leaning gossip column and smatterings of it had made it across the Atlantic. What had staved off absolute catastrophe was the fact that only part of the paper appeared on its website while the offending column had been confined to the hard copy version. Sharkey's four year term had ended shortly after the report, and he had been routinely posted back to Dublin, though with some less than diplomatic advice from the ambassador ringing in his ear.

Manning and Nesbitt, self-crowned princes of the now hybrid Hiberno/Danish embassy, more or less agreed with Sharkey's assessment. As such, they were reduced to taking delight in any victory, however small, and no matter how great or small the vanquished foe. *The Washington Post*, certainly leaning towards great, would do for now.

At the same time, with the big move looming ever closer, both were quite happy being princes of Denmark, for now. Besides, they were still exhausted after all the St. Patrick's Day ballyhoo.

"I feel like something Greek." Margaret Morris was impatient.

"I know a guy named Zorba," Manning cracked.

Nesbitt, eyes rolling, took the bait. "Zorba who?"

"Exzorbatent," said Manning.

"Oh, God," said Nesbitt, reaching for his London Fog coat. Manning teased him about it constantly.

"Here comes the CIA. How many spooks have you caught today?" Manning would chant any time he felt like taking a dig.

Nesbitt, however, refused to take any notice. He liked his coat because, he said, it helped him merge with the natives more easily on the Metro. He reckoned there was less chance of being mugged. Muggers might think he was an FBI agent, or better still, a defense attorney.

Manning remained at his desk. "You two go along. I forgot, Rebecca made me a sandwich. We're trying to save a bit. Remember we're taking Jessica on a trip for her spring break to Disneyworld. Bring me back some of that pastry stuff, whatever they call it."

"Baklava." Nesbitt and Morris spoke almost together.

"Yeah, Balaclava,"

"We'll see you later," Nesbitt replied, ignoring Manning's half-hearted attempt at a joke. "Evans is heading out for some boozy lunch and won't be back for ages, if at all, so we'll take our time. We bloody deserve the break, lunch just for us. And so do you. No work while we're away. Do the crossword or something, write your memoirs, that's an order."

Manning saluted, mockingly, as Nesbitt and Morris walked out the door, Nesbitt closing it after himself.

Manning rose from his desk and walked to the window. A steady wind was blowing the tree branches from side to side. General Sheridan was charging across the traffic circle named after him. The view had been the same for months, but in recent days there had been the first signs of sprouting leaves.

Spring was late this year, but it was on the way, galloping up like Little Phil.

Manning turned and covered the couple of paces back to his desk. He fidgeted with a few papers and grabbed *The Washington Post.* The front page was dominated by reports of concern over Taiwan and the behavior of the Beijing leadership, both apparent and what the administration was guessing at.

This could be interesting, he thought. His embassy might not be the outpost of a great military power but, yes, it was one of the European Union's now considerable cohort. If a war over Taiwan became a distinct possibility there would be a lot of coordinating to do with other EU embassies. Europe, led by the French, would probably end up jumping in the way of both the Americans and the Chinese.

That might prove helpful, he thought. Or it could prove to be just a meaningless distraction if the two heavyweights decided to have a real showdown. What was certain was that the threat of a superpower confrontation would blow anything to do with Northern Ireland off the diplomatic grid. And that, Manning thought, was an additional complication he could well do without.

No, he needed to keep the place front and center in the administration's imagination for just a few more weeks. It would be nothing like the 1990s, Bill Clinton and all of that. But it would be a little good news in a world dominated more and more by the bad. He would use that line about remembering the past so as not to repeat it, slip it into the ambassador's speech. He would use it even if he didn't want to believe it.

Manning, above all things, wanted to forget his own past, bury it.

He bowed his head. "Balaclava," he said. "Jesus, if only they knew."

He took a deep breath. If they came at him with a demand in the middle of his work on the White House conference it would be more than he could handle.

Manning's entire body shuddered at the thought. When the sensation had passed he sat rigidly still for a few moments, straight backed in his chair. He tipped his head back and wiped his eyes. To his embarrassment, they had welled up with tears.

Maybe this time I'll just tell them to go to hell, he thought.

39

FALSHAM HAD REACHED THE FAR END of the meadow. Though the year was young the grass was well grown, and sheep were grazing only a short distance away, back toward the road leading to the house.

It was early, the ground still damp and cold. A crescent moon sat low in the western sky while in the east one of the planets, Falsham was unsure which one but thought it to be Venus, was the last of the celestial lights still visible to the eye. Even if the sun was already above the horizon it would be hidden behind a dip in the land and line of distant treetops for some minutes yet.

Falsham stopped and stared straight ahead. He could hear something working its way through the longest of the grass. Presently, the creature revealed itself to be a badger, as likely as not returning to its set for a day's rest. Falsham's eyes remained fixed on the animal as it made its way into the orchard whose trees were low to the ground and so heavy with old gnarled branches that they looked like an army of men, each of them waving a score of swords.

The trees were far enough, Falsham decided and he turned. His boots, he noted with a silent appeal for God's grace, were soaked almost to the ankles. He looked at the sky and then across the way he had just come.

The old man was still standing, leaning heavily on the stave. Behind him the stable boy held the two horses. It had been an effort to hoist Cole atop the beast to begin with and his managing to ride the horse almost to the Colchester road surely warranted the declaration of a miracle.

Cole had survived the short journey, albeit in obvious discomfort and with much muttering and praying to various saints. The stable boy, by contrast, had uttered words that were far removed from holiness. The old man did not seem to hear.

Falsham found himself smiling. They were, he thought, a rather shabby and absurd threesome: an old and dying man, a boy discontent beyond his years and he himself, who looked in certain lights like a Spanish pirate.

He had listened for a full candle the night before as the old man laid forth

his view of the perfect plot. But first he had dissected the imperfect ones, the
Bye Plot, the so-called Main Plot, the Powder Plot, all of them aimed at ending the rule and life of the king.

Cole had reasoned that the plots had failed because the central figures in
each had allowed the ring of conspirators to grow too large. There had been,
he insisted, too many plotters in places too far flung, one part not knowing
what the other was thinking and planning.

Also, Cole complained, with each knowing of the others from the start,
one betrayal, a single confession under torture, was enough to doom all. The
plotters, he argued, had also been too hasty in their preparation, too eager in
their demand for, and expectation of, absolute and immediate fruition.

A successful plot, he believed, might require many years. The plotters
would have to behave as if they had no scheme in their minds to the point
that they were above and beyond even the smallest suspicion. A plot, Cole
proclaimed at the climax of his discourse, could be the entire span of a man's
life, the entire life of a man the unfolding of the plot. Better to wait a score of
years for success than try and fail in a day, he had said.

Falsham had listened. He had raised no objection. He could find no fault
in the old man's logic. What had troubled him was the thought of his entire life
being little more than a vessel containing a slowly unwinding plan designed to
kill this one king, or possibly his successor. Falsham understood the impatience
of those who wished for speedy success. There would have to be, he thought, a
middle way. But he had made no mention of this to the old man.

Something made Falsham start, a sound, far off, but clearly audible; a fir-
ing piece. He began to walk back across the field, his left hand gripping and
releasing the handle of his sword as he counted the paces back to his starting
point.

Falsham had suggested leaving his sword at the house but Cole had
argued that he would look unnatural without it. Besides, he said, the Scottish
usurper - that was one of the kinder references he had made to the king this
past while - might use it to knight Falsham on the spot. Had he not been
handing out knighthoods up and down the realm like priests had once dispensed false indulgences?

All too many of the dubbings, Cole complained, had made sirs of itinerant Scots who had, like starving dogs, trailed their sovereign down from the
north land. But there was always the possibility that an Englishman might

find instant favor with James, even one who looked more like a cutthroat from the back alleys of Valladolid.

"I heard a noise, over beyond the trees," Falsham said when he reached Cole.

For a moment the old man did not respond. He was, again, praying.

The boy was now some distance away, holding the horses as they joined the sheep in champing the wet grass.

"O blessed Mary, virgin mother of God, look down with mercy upon England thy dowry and upon us all who hope and trust in thy benevolence. Intercede with your son who, by his power and mercy, can restore our separated brethren to the fold and the embrace of the one true shepherd and his faithful church."

"Amen," said Falsham. "I did hear something, I am certain of it. Over there," he said pointing slightly to the left of their position.

"Yes, I believe you did hear something. I believe it to be a hunting horn. Our royal stag is not far, John. Not far."

Falsham nodded and shivered. He was still finding England not quite to his liking.

"I was away too long in Spain," he said. "I have forgotten the particular chill of an English morning."

Cole, still staring straight ahead, responded with a grunt. "There are some things that can be forgot and some that can never be," he said. Then, after a short pause: "John, I do not expect you to carry through with my plan. If it fails your life will be, by all chances, forfeit. The king, or at least his agents, could well suspect you of being an accomplice and not their master's savior. If what we do is not to be seen as the act that it truly is, you must be at your most convincing. And that means my death must be convincing, quick, but as bloody as possible."

Falsham drew a deep breath. "You understand," he said, "the hardest part for me will not end with your passing. I will not be able to grieve for you before all others. Indeed, I must exult in your demise, boast about my sword's swiftness and accuracy. It is damnable, damnable."

"It is necessary, and it is on the side of right," Cole interrupted. "You will do what is necessary. Mourn me later when the throne is rightfully filled. Now one final time, John, recite to me the story that will bring you the king's favor."

Falsham sighed and shrugged. "I am my true name, John Peter Falsham" he said. "For many years I have fought in the armies of Europe as a mercenary, and that, of course, is true. I have fought on the side of the Roman faith and against it. Having learned of the sickness of my kinsman, he being you, I have returned. I find you indeed in a poor state and yet, I learn with complete surprise, that you have married and your wife is with child. I discover that she is afeared for her future and that of her child because her husband is of the old, the Romish faith. We have been drawn together in both heart and mind. She is of the new faith, as am I. Now that she is widowed, we petition your gracious majesty for the favor of a marriage and the right to raise a family in the heart of the new faith, in this house."

Falsham nodded his head for emphasis. It was, he thought, a simple plan with many simple dangers. He was about to make a small suggestion when something made his eyes turn. Looking down the road he could not see anything new or amiss. But he could hear it. And more than faintly. It was the pounding of hooves, a great many of them. He could also hear shouts and the sound of a hunting horn, very close now, and joined by another.

Cole stiffened. He raised a withered arm and extended a finger, pointing. Falsham did not need to be directed. From where the road turned to the left, a group of about a dozen riders had come into view. After just a few moments a much larger group of horsemen could be seen. There were scores of them.

"The king," Falsham said quietly, and then in a louder voice, "and his pack of mounted hounds."

"The royal pack indeed," Cole replied. "And rather more than I had expected. The dog has easily a hundred pups running with him. They cannot all stay in the house. However, I have heard it said that the king's party disperses among all the better houses in a district, the king himself staying in the grandest, and we, John, for certain possess the grandest in these parts. He must stay at Ayvebury. There is nothing else for it."

Falsham said nothing. His soldier's eye was taking in the spectacle. The first riders were clearly guards, soldiers, swordsmen. A small cluster of banners in the second group of riders was sure indication as to the location of the king, though it was not yet possible to distinguish him from the rest.

Behind the second group came a stream of riders clearing the bend. It was an impressive sight. The leading horses were now so close that he could hear the beasts snort, see the cold breath being exhaled from their nostrils, make out the faces of the closest riders.

Falsham glanced over his shoulder and what he saw was not to his liking. Their two mounts had bolted at the sight of the oncoming horde and were running across the field towards the orchard, the stable boy in reluctant pursuit.

A simple plan, he thought again, and a simple error. He should have tied the beasts to a bush or tree.

Cole did not seem to notice the fleeing nags and pursuing boy. He was transfixed by the oncoming phalanx, almost upon them.

It was no overt act on the part of any rider that made Falsham act. It was the very lack of action instead. The leading horsemen were making no effort to slow their mounts. They had neither waved, nor wavered. They did not seem to notice the two-man welcoming party at all.

"Blood of our savior," Falsham cried as the horses bore down. For a big man he could be surprisingly agile, and it was with a single step and a swing of his powerful right arm that he plucked Cole from the earth and bore him into a thicket of brambles.

The cavalcade swept past in a crescendo of hooves, metal and grunting animals. Clods of earth flew in all directions. Both men clapped eyes on the king at the same moment. He was easy enough to see when close. He and his mount, a black mare, were at the head of the second group of riders which was merging with the first. James sat erect, a little unnaturally so and in a fashion that would fast tire a man out over a long ride, Falsham thought. And he had what appeared to be a half smile on his face. This Falsham absorbed in an instant because in an instant the king had passed them by.

Cole muttered something in Latin, more a curse than a prayer to Falsham's ear. And then out loud, in English: "Scottish cur."

40

THE WINDOWS WERE ROLLED DOWN to allow the unseasonably warm air to pass through the car. The hedgerows were showing their first green but not so much that the verdant pastures of Essex were hidden from the car's occupants.

Samantha Walsh dropped a gear as the vehicle closed in on a bend. The car, a sporty model hired for the trip, took the curve with ease.

"You handle it well, I have to say," said Nick Bailey.

"And why do you have to say?" said Walsh as she pressed her foot on the pedal and took the car up to a notch over sixty. The road was now stretching out straight ahead for almost half a mile, an unusual occurrence in a part of the county known for narrow, twisting roads that were at times little more than country lanes.

"I am a police officer, need I remind you. We learn to drive as if somebody else's life depends on it. And I'll have you know that I did do an advance pursuit course. Want to see?"

"That's okay," replied Bailey. "I'm quite enjoying the countryside rolling by. As opposed to flashing."

He smiled. She smiled and patted him on the arm.

"If this was a James Bond flick you would be sitting in the ejector seat, so just count your blessings, Mr. Bailey."

"I'm stirred, not shaken."

And so it went. The two had bantered since leaving London just after the morning rush hour. As much as possible, they had taken secondary roads. The car had a satellite guidance system, but they had kept it turned off, preferring instead to follow road signs with the names of villages that sounded like they were out of a guide to a lost, yet comforting, older England.

A few miles behind them sat the village of Little Tipping Major, which, they had assumed, was the larger companion to Little Tipping Minor. In the pub where they had enjoyed lunch, Walsh and Bailey had been disappointed to hear that Major was in fact all alone in the world though they were not the first visitors to ask about Minor.

The village itself was a biscuit box classic. It had a green, a duck pond and several cottages with thatched roofs, a luxury these days because of sky high insurance payments, but an obvious tourist draw. Lunch had been in a rose garden behind the sole village pub, the Ploughman's Rest, and though it was too early in the season for actual roses, the two had sat for a grateful hour nibbling at ham and water cress sandwiches and sipping ale, the local brew in Bailey's case, the ginger variety for the driver.

It had been Walsh's idea to drive down to Essex. She had a few days before becoming fully immersed in her new assignment. The trip would be a nice break for both of them and might just answer the questions that had been nagging at her since that foggy night on the bridge.

By a silent compact they had not actually discussed the reason for their journey while on the road. But that reason was becoming harder to ignore as the miles fell away. Their destination was now only six distant.

The straight run quickly behind them, Walsh slowed at a particularly nasty turn. Her caution was well timed as a truck came roaring into view, moving at well over the speed limit.

"Go get him! Book him, Danno," Bailey shouted above the rush of the slipstream coming in the passenger side window, a wind now tainted with a whiff of farm animals packed into the truck.

Walsh contented herself with a smile.

"We should be there any minute," Bailey said. "There will be a red brick wall on the left hand side and a gate about a quarter of a mile after you first see it. It's the only large estate for quite a distance around here. A rather significant acreage, over a thousand, along with a farm, woodland, the lot."

"Maybe we should just move in. I always fancied myself as a country lady," said Walsh, smiling.

"You'd go bonkers in a fortnight," said Bailey. "I know I would anyway."

It was as he delivered his prediction that Bailey spotted the beginning of the wall. Walsh saw it too and eased even more off the pedal.

"So how are we going to play this?" Bailey asked. "I mean this is not an official visit by the London plod, and they might find a copper and reporter combo a bit odd. Suspicious. Know what I mean?"

"Just leave it to me," Walsh replied. "When we meet whoever comes out to see us just stay in the background a bit. Look like the heavy."

"Oh, I can do that alright," said Bailey. "I'm a regular Henry Cooper."

Walsh laughed aloud. "Who? Look, you're just going to have to do," she said. "You know what they say on the nature programs about when you come up again some wild animal while hiking in the woods. Just puff yourself up a bit and look mean. Anyway, I'll keep the attention focused on me. Just watch."

Bailey shook his head in doubt but he had no time to argue as Walsh turned the wheels and took the car into what was a long driveway leading to a large house still visible behind a screen of trees that were only beginning to bud. The avenue was lined with large trees. Beech, Bailey reckoned.

One thing he noticed was the condition of the place. Unlike a lot of old country houses, this one looked prosperous. The paving on the drive was near perfect and the iron railings that separated it from the fields on either side had been recently painted. The trees, too, appeared to be properly pruned, and as the car came closer to the house, he could make out long, neat shrubbery beds and clusters of rhododendron bushes.

This place was fully maintained and clearly had money. Whoever these guys were, Bailey thought, they were not one of those vows of poverty crowds.

"Nice quarters. I'm in the wrong business," he said, as much to himself as Walsh.

They passed through a second wide open wrought iron gate and into a spacious courtyard. There was a moat and a stone bridge across it leading into an inner enclosure. Walsh stopped the car, the tires making a crunching sound against the gravel.

"I reckon we shouldn't be too forward. I'm sure they've heard us and will send someone out," she said.

Bailey looked towards the bridge. She was right. Already a man was walking across it in their direction. Walsh and Bailey both got out of the car.

"You stay with the car until I give you the signal," Walsh said. As she spoke she quickly opened a couple of buttons on her blouse.

"Puffing yourself up," Bailey said with a grin. "Crafty, very crafty. The old padres will be going weak at the knees."

"They might," Walsh replied before walking towards their greeter, an elderly man who Bailey thought likely a little beyond being impressed by Walsh's ample assets.

Bailey stood by the car trying to look like, as Walsh had put it, the heavy. As he figured she would, Walsh uttered the first words of the encounter. She would take the lead as much as possible. This was her style, a copper's style.

"We came down from London," he heard her tell the man. "I'm Detective Sergeant Samantha Walsh," she added as she produced her warrant card.

Very smart, Bailey thought. She covered both of us with the word "we," and yet she never said I was another copper.

The old man said something in reply that Bailey could not quite make out, but as soon as he had spoken, he began to walk back towards the house. Walsh, apparently invited to follow, also began walking towards the bridge. Without looking back she gave a hand signal to the effect that Bailey should follow.

Bailey moved at a fast clip. He caught up by the time they had entered the inner courtyard, an enclosure paved in gray flagstone and dominated in the center by a six foot statue of what Bailey took to be a saint.

"St. Anselm," the old man said, unprompted, as he passed the statue. They entered the house through a solid-looking wood double door. It took a moment to adjust eyes to the somewhat gloomy interior, but when he could properly make out his surroundings, Bailey could see that they were standing in a spacious hall with dark wooden staircases at each end. The paneled walls were dotted with framed photographs and several oils of stern looking clerics.

"Please wait here a moment. I shall fetch someone to meet you," said the old man before limping off to his left and down a corridor illuminated by sunlight coming through a series of stain glass windows.

"Nice digs," said Bailey. "Nice boobs, too."

"Shut up," Walsh responded, a suddenly sharp, authoritative edge to her voice.

Bailey bowed in mock salute. Walsh was turning in a circle taking in the immediate interior.

"All four dead priests studied in this place at one time or another," she said. "All their deaths have been officially explained and seem to fit into a random series of unconnected events. But the four are not entirely unconnected. They were all here, here in this seminary. That's not random, not as far as I'm concerned."

"Yeah, I'm with you on that. Watch out, here comes our man," Bailey responded.

Along the corridor a man dressed in black trousers with a maroon sweater was walking towards them. He seemed to glide along wooden floors that gave off the whiff of a recent polishing. Several feet from Walsh and Bailey he extended a hand to Bailey but Walsh quickly stepped into his way.

"We came down from London," she said somewhat curtly. "I am Detective Sergeant Samantha Walsh, Metropolitan Police."

"And your companion?" came the reply in a tone that, while, polite, was clearly expecting an answer.

"Bailey. How do you do?" It was now Bailey's turn to step into the front line. He extended his hand. It was an attempt to steer aside any further questioning. Bailey wanted to avoid presenting himself as a police officer if he possibly could.

"It's the detective inspector who is asking the questions today," he said to the man, clearly a priest though he was not wearing the Roman collar.

"Really?" the priest said with an emphasis on the first syllable.

Christ, Bailey thought, maybe he's rumbled us. But the priest did not inquire further as to the relationship between his visitors.

"Very pleased to meet both of you. How can I be off assistance? My name is Father John. Would you like some tea, a tour of the house perhaps?"

"A short tour would be fine, but no need for tea," said Walsh. "And I hope you don't mind answering a few questions as we see the house."

"No bother at all," said Father John. "But if you don't mind I have a question or two myself. What is it precisely that brings the London police to Ayvebury? I say precisely because I have an idea in a general sense. Our poor fathers. Please be careful on the floors. They have just been polished, and we would not want an accident, would we?"

"Certainly not," said Walsh. "We've had quite enough of those."

41

MANNING PAUSED AT THE BOTTOM OF THE STEPS leading
to his front door. He could not shake the sense that he was being followed,
but every time he had turned to check there had been no sign of anyone, or
of anything untoward. It was dark, so surveillance would be all the easier, he
thought. But no, he was being paranoid. He stared back along N Street. The
only noticeable sound was of a gaggle of college students bundling into a house
a few doors away.

He turned his eyes to the front door of his home, and that of his wife and
daughter. It had been left to Rebecca, an only child, by her deceased parents.

A funny thing, he thought, and not for the first time. He had met his
American wife while she was on vacation in Ireland. She was a native Wash-
ingtonian, and wouldn't you know it, he was later posted to D.C. It was fate,
in the stars, they had both concluded. Then they got married.

Manning had been posted to a couple of other cities in the intervening years as well as doing time back on home turf. Then he had returned to
the American capital with a promotion, his wife, and their daughter, Jessica.
And now he was wondering if he might quit diplomacy and settle down in
Georgetown.

He had stayed late at the embassy, not so much to work but to clear his
head and gather himself. It had not been easy between them these past few
months. They had discussed having another child. But Rebecca was working so
damn hard for the prosperous of Georgetown and suburban Maryland, though
admittedly pulling in plenty of money from her interior design business.

Rebecca Epstein Manning was, for certain, one of the hottest interior
designers in town. And because of this they had finally agreed that their
daughter Jessica would have to wait a little while longer for a sibling. By way
of compensation she had been given a kitten which had now grown into a
rather large cat.

Manning reached into his pocket for his keys. Opening the front door
he stepped into the hallway. There was a light on in the kitchen at the rear of

the house. Rebecca was working again. She must have heard him walk in the door, or sensed his presence in the hallway.

"I'm back here," she said.

"Be there in a second," Manning replied. He took off his coat and his Washington Nationals baseball hat and threw them over the coat stand.

Jessica, he surmised, was probably in her room, reading under her bed-covers. The thought made him smile as he walked down the narrow hallway to the kitchen.

It reminded him of somewhere, this kitchen. He stared at the rear window as he entered it and understood why he had felt that he was being followed. It was not a person that was tracking him but a memory.

The face flickered in the glass of the window that looked into the back yard. He saw it for only a split second. A grinning mouth, eyes wide open, nose and everything else hidden by the black balaclava. The grin changed to a laugh, a crazy laugh. And then it vanished.

"Eamonn?"

"What?"

"Are you okay? You look like you've just seen a ghost," Rebecca said, putting down a pencil with which she had been sketching on a sheet of construction paper.

"A ghost, where? Oh, sorry. I was miles away, just thinking about something I had forgotten to do today."

"Must have been a pretty serious 'to do.'" Rebecca was sitting back in the chair at one end of the pine table, eyeing him doubtfully.

"You've been working too hard lately, Eamonn. Jessica is beginning to forget what you look like."

"Well, you've not exactly been idle yourself," he responded, and with an edge to his voice that he had not quite intended.

"True, but in case you haven't noticed, I'm bringing a lot more of my work home with me. It isn't easy keeping a business going when you have to uproot every so often and head for the ends of the earth."

Manning ignored his wife's half-hearted jibe and made for the fridge.

"It's in the oven," said Rebecca. "Grab it and sit down."

Manning obeyed. He wasn't quite sure what the 'it' was. His wife could be adventurous with her cooking, although mostly it came out well enough.

"Take a seat," Rebecca said. "And it's moussaka by the way."

Manning nodded and began to eat. His wife had already poured a glass of water for him. He wanted to get up for a beer, or glass of wine, but thought better of it.

"I'm assuming you're still thinking of quitting the embassy and getting a job here," she said. "Well, I've been making a few calls and one of them was to Josh Zoellick. He would be delighted for you to come on board. He reckons you're just the type of guy he needs for his overseas operation. It would be right up your alley, Eamonn. Diplomacy with a tangible result."

"You mean money."

"Yes, that, too."

He had met Zoellick at a party thrown by one of Rebecca's clients. Her family had known the Zoellicks for ages, Rebecca had assured him afterwards. He could not quite make out what the man did for a living, but it seemed to have something to do with international real estate sales. It had been a loud party.

"He's particularly interested in the fact that you speak decent French. There might be a bit of travel to France involved, but that's no hardship. You could take Jessica and me along from time to time, and it would be easy to skip from France over to Ireland to see your mom," Rebecca said.

There was no argument with that, Manning thought.

"I'm offering you a way out, and you know you want out," Rebecca continued.

"If you don't like it you can always use it as a steppingstone to something else. We know loads of people in this town, but if you don't make the move, we'll be saying bye-bye to the lot of them by the end of the summer. And that means Jessica moving school again."

"I know," Manning said, his mouth full of moussaka.

He pulled at his tie, now in a tight knot that would take some undoing. It had little planes on it. Nesbitt referred to it as his flights of fancy tie.

"You're right," Manning said, this time surprised at the certainty of his response. "But Zoellick will have to wait a bit. There's no leaving the embassy this side of the big move and a trade and investment conference on Northern Ireland that looks like taking place in May. You know as well as I do that quitting the diplomatic corps isn't just a matter of quitting. It's more a case of surgical extraction."

"I know that, Eamonn. And Josh is more than willing to wait until summer, even the fall. He's a good guy. And he'll pay well."

Rebecca had picked up her pencil again.

"How's Jess?"

Rebecca smiled. It was that smile, the one that curled upwards from the edges of her mouth. Upwards and forever. He had gone weak at the knees the first time he had seen her smiling. He was only a few feet from her in that crowded pub in wherever it was.

A friend had once advised Manning to start up a conversation with a woman by remarking on something she was wearing. Jewelry, he had advised, was especially good for breaking the ice. Bumping into this woman, obviously a Yank, had been easy. The next few minutes could have gone either way. Manning had pointed to the Star of David that Rebecca was wearing around her neck. The last time he had seen one of those, he had said, was on a flag in Jerusalem.

Rebecca had turned quickly and with what looked like a frown on her face. She seemed to look right through him and for a moment Manning had feared his move had fallen flat. Then she spoke.

"And did it seem to you that the flag was flying in its rightful place?" she had said. He had been on his game enough to know that this was a loaded rhetorical question and he had just smiled by way of response.

"Earth to Eamonn. Come back to me," she said now. "Jess is just fine, and her cold seems to have gone. She's probably still awake reading so why don't you go up and give her a kiss goodnight, evict the kitty and then turn the light off. It's getting late."

Manning nodded again and stood up. "That moussaka was good. The Greeks bear some gifts that don't need scrutiny."

He walked into the hallway again and turned up the narrow stairway that broadened at the summit. He stepped along the landing to a second set of stairs leading to the top floor. He bounded up, suddenly energized by the thought of his daughter's greeting.

As Rebecca had rightly predicted, Jessica was tucked into a book though she was sitting up with the bedside lamp on. The cat, Claws by way of name as well as temperament, bolted through the door as Manning walked in.

"Hi, Daddy."

"Hi, Sweet Pea. What's the book?"

"Well, it's about this girl in England who is sent to the country during the war and she has lots of adventures."

"Sounds great, but look at the time."

Manning pointed at the Mickey Mouse clock on the lowboy chest of drawers beside Jessica's bed. It was a few minutes after nine.

"School in the morning, kiddo. Our friend in the English countryside, what's her name?"

"Emily."

"Well, Emily will just have to bide her wee until tomorrow night. She would have been in bed early herself because of the blackout."

"I know about the blackout, but what's bide her whatever it is, Dad? Sometimes I don't understand you at all. It's that funny accent of yours."

Manning smiled.

"There's nothing wrong with my accent. You're the one with the accent."

"No, I'm not," she protested, giggling as she did so.

Manning reached for the bedside lamp and flicked the switch. Leaning over his daughter he gave her a gentle kiss on her forehead.

"Now get some sleep," he said.

"Goodnight, Dad."

"Night, Jess."

Manning stood over the bed for a moment before taking a couple of steps to the window. Pulling the closed curtain aside he looked down on the street below. A chilly wind that had been in the forecast was now sweeping along N Street. One man was out walking a dog, his head bowed. Manning glanced up and down the street and below the window for as far in as he could see. It was quiet. He stepped away from the bed. Jessica had turned on her side and seemed to be asleep already.

"Dad?"

"Yes?"

"Can we go to Somerset someday?"

"Only if you get some sleep first."

"Okay."

Manning left the room, pulling the door closed behind him. Even at her gentle age, Jessica Louise Manning enjoyed her privacy.

As he reached the bottom of the lower stairs, he glanced down the hall to the kitchen. Rebecca was still sketching. He walked across the hall and through a sliding double door into the main living room.

It was tastefully lit by strategically placed lamps and reading lights. And there were books, lots of them, on shelves attached to two of the walls. The observant visitor might have noticed an apparent his and hers partition, one wall being dominated by tomes dealing with art, design and travel, the other by volumes mostly dealing with military history and political biography.

This was something of a deception. Rebecca's reading tastes were extremely general and her knowledge of military history had been one of the attributes that had attracted him to her in the first place. Her father had been in the United States Army, and Rebecca had grown up just across the Potomac in the part of town known as Generals' Row.

Manning slumped into a reclining chair and leaned over the side to pick up his current book from the floor. It was about the siege of Stalingrad, a tale of military woe to beat most of them. He began reading where he had left off and immediately he was back in the Kessel.

Nodding off was easy enough but nothing was easy inside the vision that confronted him in his half-sleep. It was of an endless blasted landscape with out of it rising an army of skeletal figures clothed in white camouflage, an army of the dead advancing steadily towards him, the last invader alive.

Rebecca's voice set the ghostly host to flight.

"Eamonn, go to bed, you need some sleep."

She was standing over him, a stern expression on her face, but there was also concern in her voice.

"Yeah, okay, good idea. What happened? I just started to read."

"That was an hour ago."

"I know things have been a bit crazy lately," he said, "but when all this stuff is over, we can take it easier. It's going to be a headache, because it looks like it's going to involve the president and British prime minister and maybe the Irish one, too, the Taoiseach."

"Love that word," Rebecca said. "Sounds like a rude t-shirt."

Manning rose from the chair. He moved to kiss his wife but she allowed him only the briefest touch on the lips.

"Go to bed. I'll be up soon. I'm nearly done," she said.

Manning shrugged and with a loud yawn walked towards the stairs.

"The word means leader. But you already know that," he said as he reached the halfway point on the staircase.

There was no reply. Rebecca had already returned to the kitchen and her world of Georgetown's more select, if not entirely discreet, interiors.

Manning stopped and breathed in deeply. When he had got out of the movement, when he had escaped, he had vowed never to commit any violent act in his life again. But there was no hiding from it. He would kill anyone who threatened his family. He would do it quickly, efficiently and without remorse.

He was, he knew in his heart, no lifer diplomat.

42

SAM J. HOCHBERG considered himself to be fit, at least for his age. But he was having a hard time keeping up with the long striding Secret Service agent who was escorting him to Cleo Conway's office.

"Son," he said, trying not to sound too winded, "slow down a mite. It's been a few years since I led fixed bayonet charges."

The agent stopped abruptly and turned to face the senior senator from North Dakota.

"Sorry, Senator. We're here now anyway, sir," he said, pointing to a door on the left side of the corridor.

The agent tapped lightly and then opened the door. Hochberg's eyes rested on the slim, athletic frame of Cleo Conway who was standing behind her desk in the cramped cubbyhole that somebody had decided to call an office. Conway nodded to the agent who closed the door quietly.

"Good to see you Cleo. How was Alaska?"

"Oh, it was great, Senator. Just what the doctor ordered and all that, but I'm glad to be back. I have a new assignment."

"Yes, I know. Congratulations. The president will be in good hands. And for God's sake don't bother with 'Senator.' I was a friend of your father's, and he called me names I couldn't repeat in any company, polite or otherwise."

Conway half smiled. She motioned to Hochberg to sit in the only other chair in the room apart from her own.

"Coffee? Tea? Juice? Water?"

Hochberg frowned. "I gave up coffee, tea is for wimps, I get more than enough juice on the Hill and water will only have me limping to the bathroom. Anything stronger? Only half joking."

"You haven't changed," said Conway, her smile widening. "Dad always said you were impossible."

"It's the only qualification I needed for this job. Keeps the damn lobbyists at bay. Nice that you have an office. Last time I was here you were in a cubicle beside some guy who looked like he had seen one too many Clint Eastwood movies."

"That would be Special Agent Davis," said Conway. "He's traveling overseas at the moment, with the Secretary of State."

"Ah, yes, the Vietnam visit. That's a big one, especially given what the Chinese are up to. Your father and I loved that country, even when we were destroying it in order to save it."

"Yes, I remember the stories," Conway replied. "The two of you seemed to have had your own private war over there."

"Nothing private about it at all," Hochberg snorted. "Everybody was welcome, even Charlie, though we could never guarantee the warmest of welcomes. Your dad was one hell of a soldier, Cleo. Never saw the like in my life. He couldn't even spell fear."

"Yeah, so I've heard."

"Anyway," Hochberg continued, "I'm sorry it's taken so long for me to get over here and see this little operation you've been running, and I guess I'm just glad to have made it before you hand it over to someone else. I assume your successor agrees with you that Globe, Globe, whatever you call it..."

"Globescan," Conway interjected.

"Okay, Globescan. Who the hell dreams up these names? Anyway, well, I believe the question is whether or not he thinks it's worth another round of funding from my committee."

"Yes, he does, and he's very hopeful that I'll be able to twist your arm a little and perhaps pony up a million or two more," Conway said, drumming her fingers on the desk for emphasis.

"Does he now?" said Hochberg, folding his arms and leaning back in his chair. "Lucky for you it's an off year or we would have some nit-picking congressman roaring about earmarks and special funding and how to save the taxpayer's dime. Anyway, I'm sure we can lay hands on your money. It can be your parting gift to Globespin."

Conway laughed. "I think they're over at the FBI," she said. "Anyway do you want to meet the wunderkinds? I believe they have been fed and won't be dangerous for another couple of hours."

"That's while I'm here," said Hochberg. "I've heard a bit about these guys but remind me. My mind forgets a lot these days."

"Certainly," said Conway, rising from her chair. "As everybody knows, the United States enjoyed the services of sixteen various intelligence agencies on September 11, but not one of them saw those specific attacks coming even though there were clues in abundance.

"Indeed, it had taken years before anyone had even suspected the existence of a group called al Qaeda. After the attacks, and as the war on terrorism gathered momentum, it was felt that we had to look at the world through a different lens, in fact a number of different lenses. Money was no object, of course, and various agencies revamped their intelligence gathering operations. One or two, the Secret Service included, were allowed to start up new projects. Homeland Security grew money on trees so it was simply a matter of matching ideas with dollars.

"Given that we in the service are very much in the front line when it comes to protecting our leaders from attacks by assassins and terrorists, it was felt that we had to get ahead of the game. So we set up this unit manned by, well, geeks I suppose you could call them. They are computer nerds, linguists and others of varied background who like nothing more than trawling the internet for chatter, hacking into websites, that kind of thing"

Hochberg nodded. "Some of them have records for that kind of thing," he said.

"Yes, they do," Conway replied. "But this is not a time to be too fussy. Anyway, some of them do speak foreign languages, including Arabic, Pashto and Farsi. They would be doing this sort of thing anyway so it was felt that for a relatively small outlay we could bring them in here, give them a decent level of security clearance and set them to work. We have had moderate success thus far and have been able to intercept, or have intercepted, a couple of radical groups who might have done harm to some of our people.

"By the way, they don't like to be called geeks or nerds or anything like that. Their name for themselves is 'the plot patrol.'"

"Gimme a break," Hochberg responded. "How many of them are there?"

"Thirty-two. They work in teams of four in overlapping shifts, and at least one team is on duty at all times. It's a twenty four seven operation."

Hochberg rose from his chair. "Can I have a peek at the, eh, 'plot patrol?'"

"Of course," said Conway. "Please follow me."

"I have to say," Hochberg said moments later as the two walked down a brightly lit interior hallway, "you took a risk with this job. National Security is one of those absolutes. If things go badly wrong, they look for scapegoats.

It isn't very fair, but that's the way it works. Did you ever think that this little plot patrol was a setup?

"We do indeed have sixteen intelligence agencies at last count and each one of them expert in passing the buck. Your operation here looks like a ripe target to me. Just as well you're moving on to a comparatively simple job. At least when you're protecting the president you have a chance of taking a bullet, surviving it and being hailed as a national hero. It's a lot simpler."

"I'll bear that in mind," Conway replied.

"I'm being serious," said Hochberg, "and I have your best interests at heart. But some of these computer lunatics spend their every waking hour digging into everyone else's business on those machines and planting viruses all over the place just for the hell of it. So no sense in them stopping now just because Uncle Sam is signing the paycheck. Are you sure they are working for us and not someone else?"

Conway stopped, turned and faced Hochberg. "Go on," she said.

"I will," said Hochberg, frowning. "Sure, we might learn something new about some bunch of terrorists in an asshole corner of the world the American people never heard of because your people can speak the local lingo. But the way it's going to go, maybe not now, but when they get bored, is that your plot people will be scanning my bank records to make sure that I'm not up to my ass in bribes from the feed industry, or the league of chicken farmers. That's the beauty of this set up, Cleo. A bunch of crazies in the back room who can be denied and thrown to the wolves if the press manages to run around the very smart and very beautiful agent in the front office."

"Oh, please, Senator," Conway said, her face flushing.

"Don't you see?" said Hochberg. "That's why that old buzzard in the director's office picked you. You are one of the brightest agents to grace this building in years; your qualifications are top dollar. But you're also young, inexperienced and gorgeous on camera. He covered himself every which way. I am aware that Homeland Security wasn't particularly enthusiastic about Globescan to begin with. But the prevailing view was that your operation could be a convenient foil. That's the way the process operates in our lousy post-9/11 world. Homeland Security isn't being entirely malicious, but everyone's ass is on the line now.

"It was easier dealing with the Soviets in the old days. By God it will be easier dealing with the Chinese if this Taiwan mess gets really out of hand. At least they present a big fat target."

"I appreciate your honesty with me, Senator," Conway replied. "I guess I had a feeling all along that this could turn into Mission Impossible. But it is water under the bridge now. And you know, I'm glad I took the job, this one and the upcoming one."

"I understand," said Hochberg, softly. "Your father always had to go for it, too, and most of the time he hit the target. Now tell me, what is your assessment of your situation here, and what's the worst and best that we can expect of Globescan? Jesus, what genius thought up a name like that anyway, sounds about as exciting as a Georgetown fundraising tea party."

Conway smiled.

"I wouldn't know much about Georgetown parties, but I do have an idea of the politics behind law enforcement, and I am under no illusions as to the potential for problems with Globescan. As you know, and I'm assuming you've read all the briefing papers, even if we tumble the biggest terrorist plot of the century so far we don't get any of the public credit. That goes back into the Homeland Security mainstream to be shared by all the major league intelligence agencies.

"Okay, maybe we get a pat on the back, but there's going to be no fame and glory, no glowing reports in *The Washington Post* and *New York Times*. Nothing. That, I hope, is appreciated on the Hill, in the relevant government departments, and in the White House."

Hochberg lowered his head slightly but did not indicate agreement or disagreement.

"We depend heavily here on intuition and hunches," Conway continued. "On the surface, we are not doing anything really differently than the FBI, CIA or NSA. If anything, we are just replicating their gathering and sifting of data, only we tend to go a bit beyond the normal parameters. And we look at things in a different way, from outside the box.

"I see us being more like one of those old time big city police departments, but one staffed by the kind of people who would be laughed out of a precinct house for being too jittery and spooked all the time. We combine technology and a gut sense of the big bad world as it funnels itself through cyberspace. As one of the guys here put it, we're more giga savvy than street smart.

"Anyway, we have had no problem remaining in the background, and we've been dutifully dull and boring to the point where the press has long since lost interest. That suits us fine. But it must be understood that we might just come with the goods in a way that no other agency could. I like to think of Globescan's work being like the discovery of penicillin."

"I know what you're saying," Hochberg cut in. "But if you somehow actually hit on something, or think you've found something, and it's prevented by virtue of our people simply taking precautions or changing procedures, how do we really know that US interests were a target in the first place?"

"Exactly, Senator. We're an intelligence agency in the purest sense. We're dealing in intangibles. We might never know the effects of our work. Unlike politicians, we can't quote statistics or take credit for a new factory in a district. We can't arrest people and get our name on the evening news. And unlike, say, the CIA, we can't be at least partly our own judges. We have neither the power nor the independence for that. We are hostages to fortune and misfortune. We are almost like a religion. People are going to have to accept our little miracles as a matter of faith. We don't see God, we just assume, we hope and we pray. And like God, we won't be coming down to earth to have everyone bow at our feet just because we've parted the ocean to reveal some nasty bunch of bad guys with America in their crosshairs."

Conway took a deep breath. She had delivered more or less verbatim what she had rehearsed for Hochberg's visit.

"You want somebody to speak for your guys," said Hochberg. "You want someone to explain to, well, members of my committee for example, the nature of the work done here, its importance and its results, even if it sounds wacky and there are no obvious results to see."

"Most especially now that I'm packing my bags, Senator."

"That's a tall order, Special Agent Conway."

"My father specialized in them."

Hochberg smiled and shook his head. "*Touché,*" he said. And then, in a deadpan pose. "Let me mull it over."

"Okay, Senator, but first you can look it over. Behind this door is our national intelligence version of the petri dish."

"Lead on," said Hochberg. "This should be interesting. And stop calling me Senator."

43

Bailey and walsh had stopped short of London. Before being sucked back into the city's maw they had spotted an inn called The Ruff and Reeve. All it had taken to make the decision to stop and stay was a single, mutual glance.

After checking in, they had settled into a formidable country style dinner, washed down with local ale.

They had just started their main course when Bailey got a phone call. Putting down his knife and fork with an annoyed look on his face, he spoke one word grumpily into his sliver of a phone: "yes."

But his annoyance evaporated in a couple of seconds. Walsh caught her companion's raised eyebrows and the look of surprise and satisfaction on his face as the person at the other end of the line continued to speak of something that was clearly of interest. After about a full minute during which he had not spoken at all, Bailey snapped his phone shut.

"Well, well," he said.

"Well, what?"

"Remember that report in the Italian paper about Murray, Cardinal Murray, the one that suggested his demise wasn't entirely an act of God? Well, the same paper has come out with another report claiming his eminence was knocked off. No hard facts, but claiming a knowledgeable source."

"Who told you that? Who was on the phone?" said Walsh, her knife and fork now resting on a side plate.

"Old Roger Cheese," said Bailey.

"Who?"

"Not quite his real name," Bailey continued. "It's actually Cheesman or Cheesborough or something, but he's been known as Roger Cheese for eons. And that's about how long he's been at the *Post*. He's our religious affairs man, and don't laugh, we do have one, even if we are godless. He works a lot from home these days but he has come up with a few good ones over the years. I think Henderson and he are old friends so that's how he's been able to hang on. Christ, he's nearly as old as Christianity."

"And what did he say?" said Walsh.

"Nothing in detail, but he did say that he would make a few calls. He has a gut sense that there might be something to this Murray theory after all. He said he would come into the office next week and let me know what he has dug up. Old Roger Cheese. I thought he had popped his cork."

Walsh smiled. "Eat your dinner or you will," she said.

But before Bailey could again attack his steak and kidney pie, Walsh reached across the table and placed her hand on his left arm.

"But right after you do clean your plate," he said, "I want you spit out what has been going through your mind ever since we left Ayvebury. You saw something there, I can tell."

Bailey, his mouth full, began to speak but Walsh shook her head. "Eat," she commanded.

And he did; she, too. They splurged, ordered a bottle of wine to follow the ale, had desserts, and traded stories from each other's childhood.

To anyone's gaze they were lovers but in truth they were both still holding back. Each, however, could sense the other's growing confidence while a sense of trust, though still in its infancy, was opening doors to other things.

"Aren't you going to have a cigarette?" said Walsh as they finished the last of the wine.

"Gave them up," replied Bailey, examining the wine bottle label.

"Since when?"

"Today."

"Oh, Christ," said Walsh, "I'm spending the night with a junkie going through cold turkey. Maybe we should get a second room."

It was a little after ten when they adjourned to a room that was modestly furnished, clean and warm. It had a television but they ignored it. Both were exhausted and it was a race into bed. They lay in each other's arms, saying nothing and forgoing lovemaking by a silent agreement that was almost as intimate.

It was well after midnight when he heard it. Bailey shot up in the bed. Walsh, her back to him, was sleeping soundly. He gave her a nudge, then more of a Push, and she stirred.

"Somebody's in trouble," Bailey said. "Jesus, someone's being murdered."

"Relax for God's sake," said Walsh, turning and half sitting up. "It's a fox."

"What?"

"A fox," Walsh repeated. "I used to spend time in the country when I was a child. My mother's cousin had a farm. They make noises like that, and you're right, sounds like someone is being murdered, but trust me, it's a fox."

The sound pierced the night again. "Are you sure?" Sounds like someone is giving up the ghost."

"Go back to sleep, Nick. We're not going to have much time for any when we get back to London."

Bailey tried, but even after the fox wandered off into a more distant corner of its territory and could not be heard again, he lay awake, his mind turning over various versions of a story beginning with four dead priests, an equally deceased prince of the church, and a rambling old house in the country in which, he was certain, there were answers. The only problem was, he was still only at the stage of formulating the questions.

He had not been in the least surprised to discover Sydney Small in one of the framed photographs in the part of Ayvebury that served as a wood-paneled gallery of yesteryear filled with pictures of old boys, now much older in life or long gone. Small had told him about his flirtation with Holy Orders during their meeting at the pub. In the photo, which was of a cricket eleven, Small had been seated on the left of the front row. The quality of the photograph had not been great to begin with, and it had faded as a result of years of direct sunlight through a nearby window.

Bailey wondered if Small might be in mortal danger, like the priests clearly were up until the moment that death snuffed out all things mortal. Perhaps, he thought, Small was already dead. Apart from the letters, there had not been any word from the man since they had talked over drinks. Bailey shuddered at the idea. Unlike his companion, now apparently asleep, he was not a police officer, a paid professional investigator of murderous deeds. Investigating homicidal deaths could, sooner or later, bring a reporter into close proximity to killers.

Nevertheless, he wasn't a danger freak, and the idea of being a gangland or war correspondent had never appealed. When it came to reporting death, Bailey preferred the accidental kind, better again the celebrity version, obituary writing and the like. Murder most foul was quite something else. He was, he easily admitted to himself in the fox-free stillness, a bit of a coward.

Walsh stirred and her hand fell across Bailey's face. Gently, he lifted her arm and folded it across her stomach. She was asleep on her back. There was an outdoor light over the door of the inn that had two wings at right angles to one another. It was at the far end of the other wing but it cast its light far enough to penetrate the bedroom through a gap where the window curtains failed to quite meet. It was just enough to make out Samantha Walsh's form. He could hear her breathing. It was slow-paced and rather deep.

She was physically fit, in far better shape than he was. Already, he was feeling a little self-conscious about his physique, or lack of it. It had been the reason that he had decided to give up the smokes, though right now he was craving one.

Nicotine craving, was, as much as the mysteries of Ayvebury, the reason why he was now wide awake, his mind turning over hard questions, crazy theories and some scary possible answers. And as he turned them all over, Bailey finally managed to turn the real world into dreams. But those dreams were all too like the real world again, and, when he woke up with a start, it was still dark, though less silent. The wind had picked up and a hard rain was beating against the window.

"Get up," Bailey said in a loud whisper. He was shaking Walsh who had turned on her side, her back now turned towards him.

She protested with a groan and a muttered question about the time. Bailey persisted.

"We've got to get back," he said, this time with full voice.

"But it's still the middle of the night," Walsh replied, emphasizing the last word.

Bailey, sitting up, rubbed his eyes and tried to make sense of it. He wasn't sure if it had come to him in a dream, or as he lay awake. But the idea was holding firm now that he was most assuredly awake. He was thinking back to the day before, to Ayvebury. He was seeing the photo again. The face, not quite in full view because the photographer had badly framed the shot, was still there. He could see it when he shut his eyes, indeed more clearly when he did so.

He looked at the bedside digital clock, its numbers illuminated. It was just gone four. Dawn was still an hour away at least, and the room was just a blend of dark and darker. He closed his eyes and saw the face again.

Walsh was sitting up now, waiting for him to insist that she get dressed. Bailey said nothing but dropped his feet to the floor and stood up, tense and rigid.

He turned.

Walsh, too, was now standing and reaching for clothes that she had tossed on the floor in her hurry to get into bed. The light was sufficient to illuminate her taut physique. It was a figure for the beach as much as the beat, Bailey thought.

Bailey busied himself getting dressed. He had precipitated the end of the night's slumber but already it was clear that Walsh would be ready to vacate The Ruff and Reeve before he would be.

"Jesus," he muttered. He could not find one of his socks.

Ten minutes later the two, both clutching coffees from the all night pot in the entrance lobby, threw themselves and their overnight bags into the car. The landlady, apparently an insomniac, had been up and sitting at the front desk. She seemed unsurprised that another young couple had suddenly reawakened to the fact that the reality of a new day was entirely different to the fuzzy romance of the evening before.

She took the sudden departure in her stride. "Mind yourselves," she said, as Walsh and Bailey bundled out the door. She sighed and returned her gaze to the pages of a well-thumbed cookery magazine.

"Are you sure?" Walsh demanded of Bailey as she turned the key in the ignition, switched on the headlights and wipers and turned the car to exit the forecourt.

"I'm sure. And I'm sure that it's the reason that Sydney Small wanted to see me. The man was afraid. He tried to hide it but he was afraid of something, or someone. And now I think I know who it was, though not what it was all about."

"Yes, but how does it all fit together? How does he fit into this?"

"I don't know," said Bailey. They had reached the end of the narrow lane leading from the inn to the junction with the road that would take them to the motorway. The rain was by now close to torrential.

"Ayvebury or London?" said Walsh. She was revving the engine, trying to rid it of the pre-dawn dampness even as she took large gulps of black coffee from her plastic cup.

"Save me yours," she said, pointing at Bailey's cup. "Where to?"

"London," Bailey commanded. "And drive like a bloody copper!"

44

A<small>T ABOUT THE SAME MOMENT</small> that Walsh and Bailey were grinding to a halt on a rain soaked London outer ring road, Cleo Conway punched a selection of numbered buttons that opened the door into the petri dish.

As he stepped into the room behind Conway, Hochberg glanced around and made some quick calculations.

"It's a good thing that we have the CIA after all," he muttered.

Conway ignored him.

"Senator, welcome to Globescan. I know it's not much to look at but there's a lot in here that can't be seen, or immediately assessed in the usual way."

"Like a clean desktop," Hochberg growled.

Conway was already walking towards a long desk where two of the room's five occupants were seated. One was staring at a screen, the other at a newspaper that looked like it had been used as the lining for an old packing trunk. The room was dominated in its center by a four rectangular tables pulled together. It was covered in books and sheets of paper. An extension cord running from the table to the floor indicated the presence, somewhere, of a telephone.

The walls of the room, which was lit by irregularly spaced desk lamps, were fronted by additional desks which were covered with more books, loose document sheets and discarded paper cups and plates.

"Senator, I would like you to meet Greg and Steve, while over there we have Lynn, Dave and Josh."

Lynn, Dave and Josh, all staring intently at monitors, simply raised their hands. Greg and Steve, by contrast, stood and offered theirs.

"Welcome, Senator. Must be finally getting warmer in North Dakota," said Greg.

"Depends on what you mean by warm, son," Hochberg replied.

"Never been there myself but I've always wanted to see the Badlands," said Steve, a wide smile on his boyish face.

"That's South Dakota," Hochberg responded in a tone suggesting that this was not the first time he had to straighten people out on their Dakotas geography.

Steve continued smiling. He seemed oblivious to the correction. In fact he knew exactly where the Badlands were but he had been curious to see how, or if, the big wheel from the Hill would pounce on his error.

"Greg and Steve specialize in South Asia senator," said Conway. "That newspaper Steve is reading is in Urdu, I believe. And that website, looks like some sort of jihad hothouse, am I right, Greg?"

"Absolutely," said Greg. "If the wish list on this baby was to come true none of us would be standing here."

"Sorry about the mess, Senator," Conway interjected. "I know it doesn't give a great first impression."

"Not that big a deal," Hochberg replied. "When our country's security is the business of the day I don't care too much about appearances. No windows, views, distractions. Question is, though, how good is the view of the world in here?"

"Well, Senator," said Conway, "we didn't have much choice on location. We set up where the powers put us, not that we were exactly expecting a view of the Potomac. But the perspective on global events is pretty good. We've been able to predict a couple. In one recent case we beat the CIA to the punch by at least a week."

"That's great, Cleo, but it's no guarantee of continued funding. Beating the CIA to something can just as easily piss off people who have friends on Appropriations. You might be able to stay in business for a little longer, but unless you pull of something spectacular you won't be able to simply hide behind a wall of jihad bullshit."

"Hiding's not our business, Senator," Conway retorted, a sharper edge to her voice. "I have the fullest confidence in the people working here. I know we're going to come up with results, big results."

Hochberg lowered his eyes and looked directly at Conway. He smiled.

"Again, I just heard your father speak," he said.

"But as I said, national security is one of those absolutes, and the safety of the president is a super-duper absolute. The hawks and doves alike will not hesitate in loading it on your little menagerie if something happens. That said, you, and I mean all of you, are relatively unknown, almost innocent compared to the rest of them. Right now your best chance of keeping this little operation on the go is not being noticed. The money might just pass this way in one of those lines that slip in to bills at the last minute."

Hochberg winked to make his point, but did not wait for a response.

"Sure, we might learn something new about the nefarious affairs of terrorists in faraway places because your people can speak the local lingo. Just make sure they don't get bored, and for Pete's sake don't send the big boys on any wild goose chases. That's the beauty of this set-up, Cleo; a bunch of crazies in a back office who can be thrown to the wolves if there's another September Eleven.

"I don't believe that is why Globescan was set up, Senator," Conway said, folding her arms.

"I wouldn't necessarily use the term set-up," Hochberg said.

"I'm relieved that you're moving out of here, but I understand that this, well, operation, has been your baby and you want it to keep ticking over after you head for the big show. But from where I'm standing, you're going to need a big scoop.

Conway smiled now. Hochberg had said his piece, and now she could say hers. She was aware that Greg and Steve were merely pretending to go about their business and were listening intently to the senator. The same was true for the other three on the far side of the tables. The rule of thumb inside their little world door was find secrets, share secrets, no secrets.

Nodding towards her colleagues, Conway allowed the smile to fade and be replaced by a more serious, almost conspiratorial look.

"We predict rather than react, Senator, and we won't be afraid to stick our necks out. We have no problem remaining in the background, and we'll be dull and boring if need be, but it must be understood that we might just come with something really big that all the others miss. These guys have what it takes."

"I understand what you're saying, Cleo," Hochberg cut in.

"I'm happy you do, Senator. As I said before, we're an intelligence agency in the purest sense. We're dealing in the most rarified intangibles. We might never know the effects of our work. We can't arrest people and get our name on the evening news. And unlike, say, the CIA, we can't be at least partly our own judges. We have neither the power nor the independence for that. But I sincerely believe that everyone working here can make a real contribution to the safety of our country and our president."

"Okay, Hochberg responded. "You want someone to explain to the unenlightened, the dull and the ignorant the nature of your service, its importance and its results, even if there are no obvious results to see. And you're in a hurry because your bag is packed."

"That's about it."

"All right," said Hochberg, "So you have come up with some interesting predictions and so far haven't made fools of yourselves. But, and I'll reiterate, you need a big score, lady."

Conway said nothing. She was staring around the walls of the room. Her eyes came to rest on a map of the United States with colored pins stuck in it. One pin, a green one, was in North Carolina, where the helicopter carrying her father had crashed.

Hochberg sensed her thoughts. "Let's go," he said, "I have a few people to meet. Let me mull this over."

The farewells were as perfunctory as the greetings. This time, however, Lynn, Dave and Josh stood. They had spotted Conway's thumb making the upwards motion.

Outside in the hallway Hochberg stopped and tapped his foot on the floor.

"Usually when I walk into a room people sit up and take notice," he said. "This crowd, Chip and Dale and the gruesome threesome didn't seem to be especially bothered that the ranking member of their lifeline committee had come for a visit. I guess I can only assume that they are deep into their work, and that's fine by me. Look, Cleo, I'm sure your people are dedicated, but up on the Hill this place will, over time, become a harder sell. The budget is being squeezed from all angles. But with solid results we can hold back all your competitors and those that would see you go the way of Custer. At least for a while and until you're totally immersed in protecting the president."

"Doesn't sound like much time, Senator. I'm out of here in a couple of weeks," Conway said.

"It's no time at all. I don't have to tell you that these days, even now, every day is September Tenth. Anyway, I've got to get back for a vote, but I'll try to keep you up on what's coming your way, good, bad and indifferent. Just try to keep cover for the moment, okay? Like I said, I owe your dad, but he's not around to collect. You are."

"Thank you, Senator," Conway said. "These guys, the ones here today and the rest of them, might not look the part but they are good. Trust me."

"I'll see myself out," Hochberg replied.

A full minute after Hochberg had left, Conway had not moved. Her head turned slightly as Dave came out of the office with a single sheet of paper.

"Got some goodies here," he said. "Oh, is the big guy gone? Pity. I could have given him a hot-off-the-presses briefing on the next civil war in central Africa, about three days away now, I'd guess. Not to mention a few other odds and ends other than Taiwan, but I know we've been told to keep our noses out of that one.

"Oh, and there is this. Not particularly important for us, I reckon, but it seems that the good Christians of Europe have been at it again. There are reports in an Italian paper that the cardinal prince of all the Catholics in England, God bless them, may have died from something other than celibacy."

"File it under medieval mishaps," Conway said sharply. "And come and see me in my office in fifteen minutes. Bring the others. I have a bone to pick with all of you."

45

As CLEO CONWAY WALKED quickly back to her office, three thousand miles to the east Nick Bailey was stepping gingerly through the almost soundproof door and into the *Post* newsroom.

Despite making it back to London later than they had planned, Samantha had decided that there was still time for shopping. She needed a few new work outfits with just a little extra room to conceal a firearm. They had parted with a kiss, a lame joke from Bailey about having to frisk her for more than guns, and a promise to call each other the following day.

The afternoon was well advanced and much of what was to fill the website and the following morning's hard copy edition had already been put to bed. Bailey was pleased with himself, but also wary. He was not listed for duty but Henderson could be like a press ganger in the old Royal Navy.

So Bailey walked quickly past the cluttered desks, most of them occupied by people either coming off day shifts or starting evening ones. He glanced at a monitor. The lead story seemed to have something to do with British warships moving closer to Taiwan.

"Wow, real news," Bailey said, more or less *sotto voce*.

The *Post*, he reminded himself, was serious enough to pay due attention to a potential war on page one, and light enough to get quickly bored with the story if the shooting didn't start in a hurry. Bombings, boobs and bondage could be found cheek by jowl in most editions. It wasn't the first of these that had lately given the *Post* a modest circulation boost, but a real war's positive effect on street sales and web hits could never be denied.

Bailey, now at a faster clip, made for a door in a far corner of the newsroom. He reached it apparently unnoticed. On the far side was a dimly lit corridor with a partition wall on one side and a line of glass fronted cubicle offices on the other. One of them, he knew, was Roger Cheese's den.

Bailey slowly walked along the line, peering into each office. A couple were empty, and the others were occupied by people who were vaguely familiar.

The man he was seeking was in the very last cubicle, at the edge of the news-room's known world. As he reached the door, Bailey furrowed his brow trying to remember the man's face, even his byline. It was not Cheese of course but what, Chesby, Chesterton, Cheshire?

The scene that presented itself to Bailey was out of Dickens. The small office was piled high with books, magazines and papers. Astonishingly, there was no computer in sight, but there was a battered typewriter, a Remington. At least, Bailey laughed to himself, the phone wasn't a rotary dial.

The door was open, and Bailey knocked gently. Roger Cheese was home. He was sitting, or more precisely sprawling, in a swivel chair reading a maga-zine. On his desk was a beer glass filled with water and a paper towel with an enormous meat pie on it. Cheese did not look up but motioned with his hand, pointing to a creaky looking wooden chair.

"What can I do for you, Mr. Bailey?" he said, his accent carrying a faint hint of London's East End.

"Oh," said, Bailey, taken aback by the fact that his name had been uttered by this man who, to the best of his memory, had never appeared in the news-room while he himself had been working in it.

"Bloody London water," said Cheese, picking up his glass and staring at its contents. "It's already been drunk and pissed out ten times, you know."

"I try to stay off it," Bailey responded. "Stick to the bottled stuff."

"An outright ripoff," said Cheese, now turning to fully face his visitor. "Though I wish I had thought of the idea thirty years ago. I suppose you're here about the dearly departed cardinal and those unfortunate fathers."

"Well, yes, that would be it," Bailey replied as he eased himself into the suspect chair.

"I've been reading your stuff," said the man across the desk. Bailey esti-mated his age at anywhere between fifty and seventy. He defied a precise estimate.

"Good work, I have to say, but of course you've only been scratching the surface."

"Really?"

"Really," said Roger Cheese. "It's usually the case in church affairs, not just Roman Catholic, mind you. Simply put, the basis for events can run rather deep under the apparent surface. Obviously, I've been making a few calls. Henderson has asked be to do a backgrounder, dig up any dirt I can, connect some dots. I'm not competing with you of course, but you're in the general reporting pool and cover all sorts of stories, though I suspect this one has grabbed your interest a little more than most. I can see it in your, well, prose."

"Thanks," said Bailey. "It is a little more than run of the mill, and, well, it's been, ah, interesting. Yes, interesting."

He was thinking of Samantha more than the story, but Cheese seemed pleased. He lifted the meat pie to his mouth, took an enormous bite and proceeded to speak with his mouth full. Bailey winced, but weathered the storm. After taking another slug of the objectionable water, Cheese leaned back in his chair and folded his arms.

"Okay," he said, "I was curious about the line you had in one of your stories about the prime minister looking tense when he answered your question outside Number Ten. Are you sure of that, or were you just pumping things up a bit?"

Bailey shook his head.

"I was looking at him hard when I asked the question. I knew he would just kick for touch no matter what, so the only real answer I would get was in the look on his face. And he did tense up. Just for a moment. But I'm sure the question landed as much on his balls as in his ears. And that bugger Golding was in like a sweeper in extra time before Spencer could even get the words out. I reckon there's something dodgy about all this."

"You're sure?"

Bailey shrugged. "Sure enough for another story."

"Interesting," said Cheese, as much to himself as Bailey.

Bailey's eyes were scanning the room for hints as to his host's mindset and interests. It was plainly evident by way of the books and publications that the man was seriously attached to religion and royalty. Bailey's browsing was interrupted as Cheese rose from his chair and stretched himself. He was a big man, probably twice the size that the tiny office could comfortably accommodate. Cheese sat down again, heavily, and stared straight at Bailey.

"Now here's the thing, Mr. Bailey," he said. "Somebody, somewhere, tipped off the Italian fellow who has been throwing out the murder conspiracy stuff. That sort of thing is par for the course with the Italians, needless to say, but I know of this particular Italian chap and he's usually reliable.

"Obviously, once the story broke over there our embassy in Rome would have been on to the Foreign Office. From there it went to Downing Street.

Spencer was likely aware of the story despite his huffing and puffing. The story, by the way, is now running in *La Repubblica*. Not a bad rag, sensible, if a bit of a snooze. Anyway, you don't mess around with stuff like this. I've been making a few calls, and I'm waiting for answers. I have no problems sharing what I lay my hands on but I also want to keep enough in reserve for a good Sunday piece. Is that all right with you, Mr. Bailey, Nick?"

"Sound as a pound, Roger," Bailey replied, nodding for emphasis.

"Splendid," said Cheese, reaching again for his meat pie. He hesitated and instead drummed his fingers on the desk.

"Nick, can you keep a secret?"

"Only when I have to," Bailey responded, a tad too quickly perhaps.

"You will have to because if you don't Henderson will have your job and I'll have your life. I can't yet confirm it, but I believe the cardinal and all these dead priests had contact at one time or another with the heir to the throne. I believe, and I have no confirmation, or right now even a way to confirm it, but I think the prince was in the process of flipping, that is if he hasn't done so already."

Cheese paused, allowing his words to settle.

"I don't quite understand," said Bailey. "Flipping, flipping what?"

"Flipping, flopping," said Cheese. "From one faith to another, Church of England to Roman Catholicism. Our future king is an apostate, or is about to be, and if I can firm this up it will be the biggest royal story since Henry the Eighth said up yours to the pope."

"Jesus Christ, that's a story all right," said Bailey sitting upright in the wobbly chair so quickly that it indeed wobbled. "Does anybody else have a sniff of it?"

"Not that I can tell, but that isn't going to last so we're going to have to work very quickly and very carefully. We have to be absolutely certain or we will be go down in flames big time."

"We?" said Bailey.

Cheese looked at Bailey, his eyes narrowing a little. "Me, you, Henderson, the *Post*," he said.

Bailey began to say something but stopped. Bringing Samantha into it would only be a complication.

"So you reckon that all these dead holy men are connected with his highness kissing up with the Vatican? Sounds kind of medieval, dark ages stuff," Bailey said.

Cheese laughed. It was sound that seemed to come from the bottom of a deep well.

"You might not believe it," he said, "but history will judge us and our times very harshly, I suspect. We talk about medieval and automatically look backwards into history. Who's to say that a few hundred years from now that we won't be seen as the second medieval age, the age of high wattage but low light, the age of un-enlightenment? Look around, Mr. Bailey. Half the world thinks it's modern and progressive but is really fooling itself. The other half is in a new dark age and reveling in it."

Cheese lowered his head slightly and glared across the desk. He seemed to be staring right through Bailey.

"Very little changes," he said in a near whisper. "People still kill other people thinking they are carrying out God's will. We are up to our eyes in medieval shit, my friend. *Plus ca* bloody *change.*"

Bailey found himself nodding. "Yes, well," he said glancing at his watch. "I have some catching up to do and should get out of here before Henderson sees me as a target of opportunity."

Bailey rose and almost bounded for the door.

"I'll get back to you as soon as I dig up more," he said as he reached it.

Cheese, however, was already reading his magazine.

"By the way," said Bailey, half turning. "I have a question. How did you get the nickname Cheese?"

Roger Cheese turned and looked at Bailey for a few seconds.

"It's not a nickname," he said. "It's my real name. My parents were Jews from Eastern Europe. My father was a cheesemaker. The name was not so much adopted by him as imposed by our English hosts."

"Ah, silly me," said Bailey. "That's your name, your byline indeed. I just thought the name was a little longer. In my mind's eye, know what I mean?"

"Mind how you go," said Cheese. "Remember, it's still Anno Domini fifteen hundred out there."

The warning trailed away to silence as Bailey beat his hasty retreat.

46

ALL HE TOUCHED was the space between the sheets. And it wasn't warm.

Manning sat up and covered his face with his cupped hands. He gave himself about twenty seconds before he dared look at the clock. 8.40. Not as bad as he had expected.

Rebecca had let him sleep late and had taken Jessica to school. He rubbed the palm of his hand over his chin. The stubble might have to stay.

He reached for the bedside phone and dialed the embassy. His call went through to the answering machine. "Good," he said.

He swung his legs out of bed, grabbed his watch and gave himself two minutes for a body wash and to brush his teeth. He threw on a clean shirt, reckoned he could manage without a tie, pulled on a pair of khaki pants and matched them with a pair of his more sensible brown shoes. He grabbed a navy blazer that was draped over the back of a chair and headed downstairs.

The kitchen was illuminated by shafts of sunlight probing through trees in the back yard that were still some days away from full leaf. Ten minutes for a coffee and something to bite on and he would be in the car.

Rebecca had made a pot of coffee. She had left him a bran muffin on a plate. There was also a note: "Took Jessie to school. Call me on my cell later. Love R." Throwing some coffee in a traveling mug, Manning grabbed the muffin and made his way through the rear kitchen door, into the fenced yard and out through the door in the wooden fence.

"The winner," he said as he got into the car, this time without indulging himself in his old habit of checking under the vehicle first.

He smiled. He was feeling good. It was one of those spring mornings that made Washington worth the steamy summer and dreary winter.

"Good morning, D.C." The disc jockey on the radio was suitably season-able, too.

Yes, Manning thought, it was possible to leave a past behind, just like the alleyway behind the Georgetown row houses that made up his adopted American neighborhood, now vanishing in the rear view mirror. Yes, he could live here, maybe for keeps.

Not too many minutes later, Manning steered the car through the wrought iron gates. The wheels screeched as they dug into the gravel of the driveway. He parked beside the black SUV already pulled up outside the door of the house. He was on time, just about, but clearly the G-Man had gotten the jump on him.

Manning turned off his engine and got out of the car. He placed the palm of his hand on the SUV's hood. It was only warm. So, he thought, the G-Man had been here for a while.

Manning stepped back and gazed up at the house. It was a fine looking building, a Georgian style mansion with, as the ambassador had told him proudly, an original floor plan that included no fewer than eight bedrooms, though some had been converted into offices by the previous owners.

Manning smiled. The ambassador would probably turn them back into bedrooms, probably name one after Lincoln, or better still, Mata Hari.

He took a few steps towards the front door, remembering as he did so that he was the sole possessor of the house key. So where was Voles?

His question was immediately answered. The front door of the house opened, and the onetime FBI agent was standing just a few feet away. He caught sight of Manning and waved with his free hand. In his other hand he was carrying a bulky case. It looked like it might be a container for a large musical instrument.

"How did you get in?" Manning said, holding his hands out and raising his shoulders into a bodily question mark.

Voles smiled and reached into his pocket. He pulled out a key and held it aloft.

"The ambassador," he said. "I'm sorry, Mr. Manning, but I like to do this work alone. Secrets of the trade. By the way the house is clean. No bugs, flying, crawling or installed."

Manning stared at Voles and said nothing.

"I know what you're thinking," said Voles. "Don't take it personally. I could have insisted that nobody from your embassy showed up at all, but in fact I wanted to have a word with you."

Manning twisted his feet in the gravel and eyed Voles carefully.

"Mind if I have a look around the house?" he said.

"Well, actually, I do," Voles replied.

Manning frowned.

"Again, Mr. Manning, Eamonn, please don't take this personally. When I check out a place I prefer that nobody but my direct employer is the next person to set foot in the door. Not that I don't trust you entirely, almost entirely, but for me it's just policy. This way I can guarantee a clean environment at the point of payment. After that, well…" Voles let the word trail away.

Manning well understood the man's professional caution but wasn't going to let him off the hook that easily.

"Well. I have a key. What if I just walk into the place after you leave?"

"I won't leave until the ambassador arrives," said Voles. He looked at his watch. "She should be here in about twenty minutes. Plenty of time for you and I to have a talk."

"A talk? What have we got to discuss? No doubt you agreed a price with Evans."

Voles ignored the note of disdain in Manning's words.

"Well, I'm a curious man," he said. "In the course of my work I entertain many questions and rarely do I have a chance to, shall we say, tap into the answers. At least in the clear light of a fine spring morning."

Neither man had moved since setting eyes on each other but Voles now walked towards the back of his car. He opened the rear door and heaved the case into the trunk. There were several blankets, and Voles made sure the case was well padded.

"There we go," he said, not so much to Manning as himself. But when he closed the trunk he stared directly at the diplomat.

"Let's take a little walk." The American's tone had changed. There was no mistaking an order, and though he was taken aback, Manning shrugged as if to say where.

"There's a rather fine yard out back, garden, you would say. Twenty minutes around the borders of the lawn will do nicely," said Voles.

He was already walking in the direction of a gate in a stone wall that led to the rear of the building. Manning stared after him for a second before he began to follow.

"Nice yard. And big," Voles said.

Manning's eyes scanned the space, a leafy island with plenty of privacy. It was indeed a big chunk of real estate. He would really have to find out the price of the place now.

"I think the ambassador saw this movie about Marie Antoinette and got ideas. Apart from that she wants to take on the Brits in cocktail diplomacy," he said.

Voles looked at Manning, silently asking the question.

"It works like this," said Manning, warming to the subject, if not his companion. "In years past anytime the shit hit the fan in the Northern Ireland peace process, Her Majesty's diplomats would turn on the gin spigot. By that I mean they would entertain important people in the administration and Congress, or at least people who felt they were important.

"And I mean really entertain. Lunch at the best places in town, receptions at the ambassador's place up on Massachusetts Avenue and, the *pièce de résistance*, garden parties. You ought to see some of the Yanks go weak at the knees at one of those things, especially if the embassy hauls in some royal to conduct a tour of the flower gardens and drop the possibility of some honor from the old dear at the palace.

"The British don't have to threaten anybody with gunboats anymore. They just have to mention an honorary knighthood and the revolution's over before the first musket ball is fired. Ever been up at the British place?" Manning nodded his head slightly to one side.

"No," Voles responded.

"Well, it's quite a scene. The ambassador's residence was designed by the same guy who built New Delhi. Someone at the Indian embassy told me that. I can't remember his name."

Voles smiled. "The envoy or the architect?"

"Neither."

"Well," said Voles, "I can't quite rattle off the entire Indian embassy staff, but Edwin Lutyens was the man behind governmental Delhi. I know because I did some work for the bureau in south Asia a few years back. The British ambassador's place must be impressive indeed."

"Yeah, fit for an empire. And a bloody good party. Are you an expert on architecture? Oh, I forgot, you are, in a way."

"I suppose I am. I'm also a little curious. Isn't it all peaceful now in Northern Ireland? Why the cocktail wars?"

"Old habits," said Manning. "While there's a lot of cooperation now there's still the big question over the future of Ireland, a border or no border. In the meantime, the present heavily depends on economics. The Brits are not going to leave Northern Ireland completely hostage to ourselves in the South. It's a delicate thing, a little war of sorts, only no bombs, bullets."

"You remember those things, don't you?" said Voles.

Manning, startled, looked directly at his interrogator, but the American was gazing away from him, to his right.

"I should tell you," Voles continued, now turning to face Manning, "your security and intelligence people could easily conduct a sweep for bugs and wires but that's not the entire story. Let me paint a portrait of your country as the world intelligence community might view it."

Manning let out a sigh, feigning impatience. But he was curious.

"Briefly then, Eamonn, your intelligence community is not lacking in literal intelligence but it is yet to be clearly delineated. In the past couple of years the political department at your Department of Foreign Affairs has been given a new set of guidelines and instructions on intelligence gathering. This sort of reinvigorated intelligence gathering, we won't quite call it spying, has been happening the world over, as you know, since September 2001 and all the nasty stuff that followed.

"The political department is your polite Irish version of MI6. It's moderately effective at certain levels but is still lacking a clear definition of your nation's national interest, or a clear picture of who in the world might be either harmful, or helpful, to those interests. You are at least ten years away from having a fully functional, non-military, intelligence-gathering arm. With a little help that can be cut back to five or six. But the budget is currently too small. The entire operation is gloriously amateur. Occasionally you strike pay dirt, such as Nigeria last year."

Manning stared at Voles. "Nigeria?"

"Oh, yes. There was coup in the works but one of your people picked up word of it from some local woman he was having an affair with. Her sister was shacked up with one of the army officers heading up this little operation. Your man in Lagos rang Dublin with the news, or at least part of it. He was deliberately vague because, well, he was married.

"Anyway, the British, aware that your guys sometimes do pick up nuggets these days, were listening in on the lines even though your people probably would have passed it on to them anyway. The British have habits they will never relinquish. No doubt you understand that. Anyway, they looked into it even as they filed away a note on your man's playing around. You never know when a little dirt might come in handy. The end of it all came rather quickly after that. The British tipped off the Nigerians, the plotters were rounded up and the few lucky ones ended up with border postings with front door views of the Sahara."

"And the unlucky ones?"

Voles shrugged. "But back to your intelligence people. Your police have two main units but both are confined largely to operations on your own island. Your police security and intelligence section isn't bad, and we, I mean primarily the CIA, have had some success with them in tracking down itinerant Middle Eastern terrorist types who see Ireland as a bit of a backwater where they can work undisturbed, mainly on money laundering.

"Your military intelligence is again mostly a domestic operation and is understandably reluctant to involve itself with anything civil or political. On top of that, there is the matter of jealously. Give the job to the army and the cops will be jealous and vice versa. And where there is jealously, there are wagging tongues."

"I get the picture," Manning said, cutting Voles short. "So this is where you come in. Small, recently wealthy country on edge of Europe, militarily neutral on paper but increasingly being drawn into NATO's orbit. Intrigued at the thought of playing with the big boys but nervous about them, too. And considerable opposition to the idea of such big boys games on the domestic political front. That means a government concerned about keeping a lid on things. We don't spy on people so they don't have to spy on us. We're nice people, the funny, quaint and quirky Irish, so just bugger off and leave us alone."

"Precisely, Eamonn. But how do you know you're being left alone?"

Before Manning could reply their talk was cut short by a piercing scream. Both men made for the gate, and as they reached it, they spotted the source.

"Oh, Christ," said Manning, "it's bloody Evans. What is she doing on the ground?"

The two men hurried to where Evans had fallen. She was a heap on the ground, though a heap that would not go easily unnoticed.

"These bloody heels. God, Eamonn, I think I've broken my ankle."

Manning arrived at the scene of the disaster first. Evans, her hair tossed and falling over her eyes, stared up pitifully at her first secretary.

"Ambassador, are you okay?" Manning did his best to sound concerned. He wanted to laugh.

"I'm not sure, really. Remind me to have this place properly paved when we move in. They can't expect me to walk around the grounds in carpet slippers or rubber wellies."

"Of course not," said Manning. The ambassador, who, he concluded, must have been dropped at the gate by a cab, ignored the sarcastic tone. Manning looked around for Voles. He was standing about fifteen feet away. He nodded at Manning as if to say Evans was all his.

"Well, don't just stand there gawking, Eamonn. For God's, sake help me up."

Manning leaned over and hesitated.

"Yes, go ahead," Evans said impatiently.

Manning lifted Evans off the ground, trying not to push her already short skirt any higher above her knees.

"Strong boy," Evans said. She almost purred.

Manning glanced over his shoulder in search of support. Voles, however, had gone back to the front door of the house.

"Let's get you in the door, Ambassador. Then we can try putting a bit of weight on that ankle. It doesn't appear to be broken, although you might have to inspect the place in your stocking feet," he said.

"I've inspected quite a few places in my stocking feet," Evans replied with a look that could not easily be interpreted.

Manning did not respond. Despite the fact that Evans was a little heavier than she appeared, he was concentrating on reaching the door.

"Pity the place isn't furnished yet, Eamonn. If it was, you would quickly see the possibilities and potential of our new home."

"I'm sure it's going to look really grand," he replied. Evans was flirting with him. She was smiling at him as they reached the door.

"Carry me across the threshold," she cooed.

Manning ignored the instruction. Gently, he placed Evans back on her feet. Her ankle held, though she made a pouting face.

"Oh well," she said, "the days of gallantry would appear to be well and truly gone. Sometimes I wish I lived in a time when men knew how to treat a lady. The seventeenth century. That's my time, Eamonn. I would have done well in the palace of the Sun King, don't you think?"

"I'm sure, Ambassador, you would have dazzled old Louis himself. Mind as you go, the floors look polished enough for Versailles."

47

How, PENDER WONDERED, was it possible to compare a mile in the desert of Arabia to one on an English moor? How much energy was expended over the scorched sand as opposed to, say, the trampled grass of Clapham?

The book was resting on his lap, and he, in turn, was resting in a lazy boy chair in the apartment that was to be his domicile in New York for as long, well, as long as it took.

It had, he thought, been a campaign defined in great part by distance, the great empty spaces between Mecca and Medina, Jiddah and Aqaba, Abu ash Shahm and Damascus. Spaces spanned on the back of a dromedary.

Arabia in the Great War had been the very antithesis of the overcrowded butcher's shop, Flanders. It had been an endless place for unbounded heroes like Lawrence of Arabia.

Pender fixed his eyes on the spackled white space of the ceiling and the light fixture that looked like some instrument of medieval torture.

"No prisoners," he said, aiming his right forefinger at the offending device.

It would be a goner, he thought, if he were staying in the place long. But he wouldn't be. The plan was for a quick tour of beauty spots in the New England area while he awaited news on the White House gathering. Then it would be total attention to the operation, his very last hurrah.

Pender raised himself a little in the chair and closed the book. He knew all this was pretty typical: target or targets revealed and then days of absolutely nothing. As was usually the case, he resisted asking himself why. But it was hard not to wonder. Were the president and prime minister both targets, or were they merely testing his nerve?

Perhaps the real target was someone else, or some other persons. No, it was Spencer and Packer. Yet the question that was far bigger than why was how. And where. It could only be in Washington, the White House, the most secure address on the planet. So how was he to accomplish his task undetected?

It was only after turning the same questions over and over in his mind without being able to come up with anything approaching satisfactory answers that Pender realized that the light outside had faded. Manhattan was edging into its night. He stared out the window at the lighted apartments across the street. It took several seconds for him to realize that the phone that was ringing was his, or at least the one in the apartment.

"Hello," he said.

The voice at the other end was female, English accented and a little hesitant. When he returned the phone to its mount a few moments later, Pender smiled. The consulate, curious as always, was throwing out its welcome mat. And of course he had responded in kind, agreeing to pop in to meet with the press office team, the consul general too, of course. Tomorrow morning would be fine, he had told the woman at the other end of the line.

Pender's apartment was twenty minutes walk from the British consulate, an anonymous outpost in a Third Avenue office tower. As he covered the blocks the following morning, just before his eleven o'clock appointment, Pender allowed himself a few tourist moments, though he had decided not to take along a camera, not even a pocket digital.

He was off duty. Nevertheless, his eyes took in buildings, shafts of light and reflection in glass, people and traffic, the mood of the morning. He had slurped down two cups of instant coffee, minus his usual milk, but no food because the apartment was devoid of even a crumb. So now he was feeling hungry. Hopefully, he thought, someone would offer him breakfast at the consulate. If not, he was fully prepared to buck protocol and ask.

Rounding a street corner he saw his destination. The giveaway was an oversized union flag with the royal crest moving gently in the light breeze. Moments later, Pender walked into the foyer of the building. After announcing himself and producing his passport, as advised by the previous night's caller, he walked to the bank of elevators and took one to the appropriate floor.

Stepping out of the elevator, Pender glanced to his left. There was a reception office behind bullet proof glass and a small waiting room to one side of it. He walked up to the glass pane, waited a moment while a man in front of him was directed to an adjacent waiting area and announced himself to the young woman behind the screen. After speaking into a phone, she directed him to a sealed waiting room, a kind of airlock, between the public area and the inner offices. Pender sat and waited. He closed his eyes and took a deep breath. Jet lag would take a few days to shake.

He had known diplomats in a number of countries, not all of them Her Majesty's. A few years back, and he remembered this with a split second smile, he had been hired to assassinate one. Not a real diplomat of course, just a thug from an African country that had more or less disintegrated after years of civil war. He had not carried out his instructions, simply because somebody else had done the job before him, thus erasing the man's diplomatic immunity and, according to some accounts, just about every other aspect of his being.

"Hello. You must be Mr. Pender."

Pender, eyes still shut, had not seen the young man with the oversized red tie who had opened the inner door and was now standing just inches away with an inquisitive look on a face that, by the look of it, had yet to meet twenty-five, never mind thirty.

"That's me," said Pender, slowly getting up.

The greeter smiled in return without revealing his teeth.

"Jonathan Eccles," he said. "Press section. Very nice to meet you."

Eccles offered his hand and Pender returned the gesture. The handshake was firm to the point of being forced.

"Let's go in, shall we?" Eccles said, turning quickly to the inner door.

Pender followed Eccles into the consulate's office area, past various glass walled fiefdoms, what appeared to be a storeroom and at a point where the corridor took a sharp turn, a large office with an especially large map of the United States on the wall. The map was peppered with colored pins.

"Our secret agents, I suppose," Pender said.

Eccles did not respond. He was about to collide with a blonde woman with her back turned who was picking up a pile of files outside another office door.

"Jane, sorry, well, I'd like you to meet Mister Pender the famous photographer. Jane Hurst, this is."

"Welcome to New York," Hurst said before Eccles could finish his sentence. She had turned quickly and was now standing straight. She ignored Eccles but only, it seemed, to insult the visitor.

Pender made a quick assessment. A little over the hill, almost married but never did; in dire need of a wild night.

"You're not one of those dreadful paparazzi," she said.

"No," Pender replied. "I just shoot the anonymous, anonymously."

It would have been difficult for anyone but an especially sensitive subject of Pender's response to detect the barely noticeable hint of literal seriousness. Eccles certainly did not, but Jane Hurst adopted an odd, questioning look on her face before returning to her files. She had sensed something, but it was evident that she could not follow through on her instinctive reaction to the half smile and narrowed eyes that had accompanied Pender's reply.

"As long as you weren't chasing Princess Diana. Jonathan, be a dear and help me with these."

Eccles winced. "In a minute Jane," he said. "I have to take our guest to see Mark."

Jane Hurst nodded and darted back into her office, closing the door quickly behind her.

A few paces farther down the hall the two men came to another door that was half way ajar. Pender paused and took a look inside. It was a room larger that any so far and was filled with a long conference table. Behind a glass partition at the near end there was what appeared to be a sound studio.

"Conferences, monitoring news, recording and that sort of thing. We have just installed a new generation of video phones. An awful bloody nuisance, if you ask me. You have to look happy on the damn things even when you're pissed off," said Eccles, chattily. "But please, just a little more," he said, motioning Pender to follow.

"Ah, here we are," he said after a few more paces. They had arrived at another large corner office. The door was closed, and Eccles knocked it gently with his knuckles before opening it.

Sitting behind a desk and backed by yet another map of the United States was a slim, prematurely balding man who, in contrast to Eccles, didn't look too much short of forty.

"He's here," said Eccles, nodding for emphasis and stepping into the room so as to allow Pender free passage.

The man behind the desk jumped to his feet and positively scampered around the desk.

"Mark Robinson, head of press. Good to meet you. I've long admired your work," he said, hand outstretched.

Pender returned the gesture. "Not all of it, I'm sure," he said. "Some of my work, well, it never sees the light of day, I'm afraid."

"Oh well," said Robinson, "but what does certainly has had the most enormous impact. I can tell you that some of your photos have had a direct effect on government attitude and, dare I say it, policy in one or two instances. Picture worth a thousand words and all of that. By the way, I think we met once before."

"Could have," said Pender. "You do look a little familiar. Middle East perhaps?

"Ever in Rome?"

"Yes, a few times."

"Ah, and you attended an embassy reception on one of your visits. Do you recall, it was about five years ago?"

"Well, yes, vaguely," Pender responded. He felt uncomfortable because he was uncertain.

"Yes," said Robinson. I think we talked about churches and such. You were on a bit of a tour. You're Roman Catholic if I remember correctly."

"Just Catholic. And lapsed," said Pender, folding his arms in impatience. Robinson did not take the hint.

"Sorry. But you know where we come from, always the geographic prefix. I'm Catholic myself in fact. Lapsed as well, though. Very lapsed."

"You're in the right town then."

"Yes indeed," said Robinson, laughing. "Better than Kabul for sure. Anyway, I'm delighted you popped over. I'm aware of your interest in this Washington bash. It will be at the White House, that's confirmed now. We've put together the guest list, and invitations have been posted. You're on the press list, of course, delighted that you will be there. In the meantime, however, you'll have a little time to fill. Are you planning on staying all the while in New York?"

"No," said Pender. "I'll be heading up to New England for a few days, Maine in particular. It's for a coffee table book. A break from, well, you know."

Robinson nodded.

"Maine is wonderful, though I've not been. By the way, and you're probably the first to hear this, but the prime minister will be at the White House event as will of course the American president and perhaps the Irish prime minister, though we're not quite sure about that yet. It should be quite the occasion, memorable for sure."

Pender turned slightly and stared out the office window.

"I have not the slightest doubt that it will be."

48

"You would think that at this stage of the game we would have someone on hand to scan a room for bloody bugs."

Manning was standing beside the window staring outwards. The air outside was shimmering. It was close to a record heat wave for May.

For a few moments Nesbitt did not respond. He was scanning a speech that Evans was due to deliver at a conference.

"Well," he said eventually, "strictly speaking, if you're going to bring in spooks to your embassy, you have to clear it first with the Americans, because we're friends, not enemies you understand.

"Then there's the matter of all the technical gizmos that would be used to sweep a building. We would probably have to hire them, and that would get around. One thing the government likes is the fact that the world doesn't worry too much about us having much of an intelligence operation.

"We don't have an MI6, CIA or SDECE and that can be an advantage sometimes. You would be surprised what little gems we've picked up over the years by virtue of simply not being taken notice of. It's a case of what the butler saw rather than what the bug heard. But anyway, that's the way it is, so we hire what's his name, Mr. G-Man, Voles."

"I wasn't able to track him as he went through the building," said Manning.

"What if he's freelancing for the Brits as well? He could just as easily plant a bug for them as find one for us."

Nesbitt nodded. "That's true. But he would also know that one of us might suspect that and check his work out. He needs a good reputation to keep his business going. If he was double dealing it would eventually become apparent, and that would be the end of his work in this town. Besides, I got a look at his bill. He certainly doesn't need to double dip."

Manning shrugged his shoulders.

"Okay, nobody gets to listen in on her ladyship's midnight adventures. Meanwhile, the days are dropping like flies. This trade conference at the White

House is turning into a monster. And the hilarious thing is that the guest of honor is some Taiwanese guy who might not have a country by then. I hope his money is in Switzerland. June thirteenth, that's not much more than a month away. I assume that downstairs and our British and American friends got the invitations out."

Nesbitt looked up. "I believe they went out last week actually. But you're right. I hardly see this affair going on if mainland Chinese troops are swarming through the streets of Taipei. Why would the guy possibly be thinking of Belfast? Why is he thinking of it in the first place?"

"I would think that's obvious," said Manning, half turning towards his colleague. "He's moving his operations out of Taiwan to London. I'll bet he's in line for British citizenship if he hasn't got it already. The rich always get to flee before the storm. It must be getting pretty hairy at State, and across the river. The Americans are getting very worked up over all of this."

"As you would expect," said Nesbitt. "Still, it must be exciting for their diplomats. I hope it doesn't sound perverse, but I envy them in a way in times like this. Maybe we'll end up in a war with Andorra, or Lichtenstein. Battle of the mice."

Manning let out a snort. "I can't speak for Lichtenstein but I met a guy from Andorra in Brussels a few years back. I would not underestimate a people who have spent history scrunched up between the French and the Spanish. We could easily lose that scrap."

Nesbitt did not respond. He had set down the text of the ambassador's speech and had moved on to *The Washington Post*.

"Jesus, this Taiwan business is getting serious," he said. "It seems to be running away from everybody. The Chinese look like they are gearing up to level Taipei with missiles, and the Yanks are calling up every aircraft carrier they can muster.

"It's hard to know what to make of it. I see here they are not even talking to each other on the Security Council. The Brits are four square behind the Americans of course, but the French are being awkward and the Russians are just sitting on their hands. This thing could really go off; world war bloody three."

"Yeah," said Manning. "I'm sure the Americans are sorely pissed off with the Taiwanese for pushing this independence idea to the edge. They would rather things went on as they were, *ad infinitum.*"

"The Security Council is convening tonight," said Nesbitt, turning to an inside page. "Pity we're not on it at the moment. That would be fun for the boys and girls up in New York. They would be eyewitnesses to history. Where were you, daddy, when the world ended?"

"It's not going to go that far," Manning said. "This is going to be like the Cuban Missile Crisis. The Chinese will back down."

Nesbitt, his head almost hidden behind the open newspaper, let out a low humming noise. It was his way of neither agreeing, nor disagreeing.

"I'm not so sure you're right," he said. "Stranger things have happened. Put it this way, the Chinese unleash a salvo of rockets. Say they demolish a few high profile buildings in Taipei, the stock market and a big bank or two. What do you think all the moneybags tycoons in the place are going to do then?

"They'll be right up the arses of every politician who clings to even the barest notion of independence. Next thing, somebody proposes a revised referendum with two questions: Independence, or a Hong Kong-style deal with twenty years of near absolute autonomy, preservation of the capitalist system and eventual union with the motherland, and everyone's happy.

"Let's face it, all the original Kuomintang guys are either dead or pickled. As long as they can go on making money I don't think the real movers and shakers in Taiwan are going to lose much sleep at night. What they want is to be independent from the kind of uncertainty that has hung over the place for years. And the Americans would be delighted with all this. They would be off the hook, and a major stumbling block to even more trade with China would be kicked back into the Ming Dynasty. I think the Chinese know exactly what they are at, and I think they will get what they want. Okay, so there's no out and out war, but the Olympics are ancient history, Beijing is on to a far bigger big project, reunification, and I think they are going to get it. We could have done this years ago with Northern Ireland if we had a four-million-man army."

Manning was laughing. "You know, Frank, I really think the world's nations should elect you dictator. Planet Earth would be a better place with you giving the orders. Even Evans might be convinced after a few days of *Pax Nesbitt*. But I'm still not so sure. You might be underestimating Packer."

"He's a tough bastard all right, and maybe just a little crazy," said Nesbitt. "And his people in Congress are wearing a lot of war paint. I would agree that he might just ram himself into the middle of the Taiwan Straits and force the Chinese to back off. But that's expecting a lot from the Chinese. You know this whole saving face thing."

"I think he's a bluffer, though a good one," Manning responded. "Remember that coup down in central America last year? He was going to send in the cavalry one minute, and then he just ignored it, let it slide."

"That just means he might simply be smart. Doesn't like to blunder into things," Nesbitt retorted. "Besides, he never went this far in that coup. This time it's different. The US Navy is already in harm's way, and the Taiwan Straits are becoming so crammed with ships that they could start colliding any minute for sheer lack of space. I think we're looking at a dust-up, and it could go all the way, pal."

"Maybe you're right. Time to head for the hills. Speaking of dust-up. I think I see the very man right now," said Manning, his face against the window and eyes looking out to his left.

"It's Packer's helicopter, what do they call it, Marine One. Yep, there's the second one and the third can't be far behind. He's taking the long way around from Andrews or wherever. Looks like he's heading home for his lunch. Christ, must be great to have your own helicopter."

Nesbitt put down his newspaper. "I suppose it is," he said. "Check them out. If he's mounted machine guns on the sides of those things it means we're definitely going to the mattresses. I fancy a bit of lunch myself. Are you hungry?"

49

THE PRESIDENT LOOKED AT HIS WATCH. His lunch would be just about ready. If so, it would be the first thing to go off without a hitch in at least a week.

He glanced around. The White House staff members and his Secret Service detail were looking busy, preparing for the landing on the South Lawn. He closed his eyes and took in a deep breath. He wanted to tell them all to relax but knew that would be a waste of time.

William Packer liked to make people feel easy around him. It was his nature. But the job kept getting in the way. So they fussed and fidgeted as he looked on, just the slightest hint of amusement on his sun-lined face.

Marine One was second in line of the three-helicopter flight. In a few seconds, Packer knew, the lead chopper would make room for his machine to make the final approach, across the Mall, over the waving crowds and across the last few yards to the touchdown point on the green sward at the back of the executive mansion.

The crowds of tourists were moved from the White House railings every time the president took off or landed. It had been so since September 11. Packer had argued to allow folks return to the railings at all times, but the Secret Service had opposed the idea. What difference, he had argued, were a few yards?

As in just about all matters dealing with presidential security, the Service had prevailed. It had thrown up lines of defense that had to do with bullet range, line of sight and angles of fire. So the folks would stay corralled behind a line of barriers roughly forty yards from the black railings.

Packer's unhappiness with the reality of the post-9/11 presidency and its even more stringent security rules, were, however, of less importance now than the possibility of the United States and China going at each other's throat in the seas off Taiwan.

It was against the backdrop of this apocalyptic scenario that he had made the latest trip to Camp David. Packer didn't quite see the point of the journey, but he had acquiesced with the views of his top advisors that movement itself could send necessary and desired messages to the Chinese and the American public. The president huddling in the Maryland hills with his Cabinet would be just one more public strand in America's deadly serious warning to the Chinese.

The problem was that the warning would ultimately prove to be just that. The United States had no intention of going to war on behalf of the Taiwanese. At the same time, of course, the trick was to convince Beijing that the reality was otherwise; hence the massive show of force of recent days, three carrier task forces and a fourth on the way.

Packer was not given, as so many of his predecessors were, to ruminating on what past occupants of the nation's highest office would have done in the kind of tinderbox situation that he himself was now facing. He was not a presidential historian, not the type of president who would stand in front of portraits of former occupants of the White House silently asking them for sage advice, or a tip on how to get out of a political jam.

Lately, however, Packer had been thinking about John Kennedy. He had asked to see records of the meetings presided over by the young president in the heat of the Cuban Missile Crisis. In those dusty minutes he could clearly see how close the human race had come to annihilating itself. The problem was that Packer now found himself playing the role of the Russians. It was he who was bringing the missiles on ships into someone else's backyard. It was the Chinese who were looking at an offshore island with a view to what they felt was necessary regime change.

But, already, the Chinese were much more advanced down the road to conflict than the U.S. had ever been in 1962. Packer was uncomfortable with what he felt was his country's weak hand, even during the present bluffing stage. He wondered constantly if the Chinese had correctly read Washington's intentions even before the first task force had reached the Taiwan Straits.

He was all too aware of Beijing's plan. It had sent a shudder right through his body when the CIA document had been placed on his desk just a few weeks and a lifetime ago. At first he had trouble believing it, wanted to hear it straight from the mouths of the people over at Langley.

And so he had listened, impatiently, to the story behind the intelligence, the assembling of the grand conclusion from so many snippets and trickles, rumors and hard intelligence that had been pulled together over many months, some of it with the help of allied intelligence agencies such as the British

MI6 and even the French SDECE, an outfit that seemed able to work its way into some corners of the world a lot less obviously than the Brits or the Company.

The Chinese had decided that one nuke dropped on a military base as far from Taipei as possible would be enough to bring Taiwan to heel without blowing it completely into the skies. Beijing had calculated that the United States would not retaliate with nuclear weapons and would immediately shy away from a conventional war because it would simply be un-winnable.

For one thing, there was the matter of where such a war could be fought. Not on mainland Chinese soil, for sure, and not even on Taiwan. The Chinese would not land troops on the island in advance of surrender by the Taiwanese. They would simply sit back after their one nuke, brace for the global uproar, ultimately ignore it, watch the Taiwanese economy collapse, face off against the US Navy, suffer the loss of some ships if need be so as to allow Washington, ironically, a little Asian-style face saving, and then simply threaten a second nuclear attack.

At this point who would disbelieve them? Not the Americans. They would be facing the horrifying option of having to drop a nuclear missile on Chinese soil, and that, the Chinese leadership well knew, was not going to happen.

Yep, Packer had said to himself after digesting the CIA document, the bastards have us well and truly screwed.

Packer's legacy instincts kicked into overdrive. He could not appear to be weak-willed or spineless in the face of Beijing's naked aggression. So he had ordered the greatest concentration of US naval forces since the Pacific island-hopping campaign of World War II. He had gone on television talking tough and reassuring the American people that the United States would stand behind the integrity of Taiwan.

Naturally, commentators had immediately jumped on this presidential play with words. The president had stated "integrity" of Taiwan, not its sovereignty. Packer had simply ignored the press and had begun the late night meetings and shuttle trips to Camp David.

At the same time, Packer had ratcheted up several of the arguments he had been having with Congress. As much as possible, his inner team had repeated over and over, try to keep at least part of public attention on domestic issues, even as the nation was seemingly marching, or sailing, to the brink of all out war.

"How about I juggle half a dozen golf balls and eat fire at the same time?"

had been Packer's retort. But he knew they were right. And so he had shuttled back and forth on Marine One. Unknown to the American public, he had used Camp David to catch up on much needed rest as much as planning for the supposed defense of a longtime American ally.

He was exhausted, unable to switch off his mind or block out the crescendo of thoughts, mostly dark ones. The clearest thought of all was of little comfort. He should have been a country lawyer like his father.

He barely noticed the bump as the helicopter landed and the "Excuse me, Mr. President, you're home," from the aide to his left. Home was not the White House right now. It was back in Oklahoma with his beehives. The early days of the Packer administration had been dominated by headlines containing the word "buzz," allusions to the new president being as busy as a bee and suggestions from columnists aligned with the other party that his Secret Service codename should be "Drone."

He had smiled then, wondered how the press could be so obvious with its little puns. It seemed like a million years ago. And it was. The word of the moment wasn't buzz anymore. It was bomb.

Packer unclipped his seat belt and slowly stood. He instinctively stooped in the helicopter's cabin, reserving the full stretch of his six feet three inches until he walked through the door, saluted the Marine Corps guard at the bottom and waved in the general direction of the small crowd of greeters out back of the presidential mansion.

It was a ritual that had been in place for as long as the president had used helicopters. It was staple filler on the evening newscasts. It was a moment to be president without any complications. But it would be just a moment. Inside the White House, he knew, would be yet more jarring reports from the other side of the world, more decisions to be made or not made, more meetings and preparations for a full presidential news conference two days hence.

The only silver lining was lunch. He had made it known that he wanted his favorite pork chops, done just the way he liked them: medium. How he ate his pork and steak, it had lately occurred to Packer, was just about the only medium aspect to his life. All the rest was raw or overcooked.

He moved to the door, hesitated a second, activated a smile and stepped into the bright sunlight. He waved, tried to put a bit of a bounce in his step as he alighted from the helicopter, made another wave and then pointed his finger. Just in time, Packer noticed that there was nobody in his finger's line of sight, so he adjusted it slightly and allowed it rest on what was obviously a group of Secret Service people, all familiar, except the woman in the blue business suit.

Yes, of course, he remembered, the new agent.

Packer, despite his differences with the Service over the barriers beyond the South Lawn railings, felt a deep respect for those whose lives were on the line for his. He had teased members of his detail from time to time. "Sure you would want to take a bullet for a guy like me?" he quizzed more than one agent, usually when they had been freshly assigned. The blandness of the replies had never ceased to amaze him. They never went much beyond "Yes, Mr. President."

One agent had replied, "Absolutely certain, Mr. President." Stew Lewis was now his principal protector. Packer had noticed Lewis making a flanking move to his right as he walked deliberately across the grass, trying to add seconds to this neutral, consequence-free presidential moment.

Lewis was now standing with the service greeting party. Packer knew now to make a, well, beeline for it. With just a few feet to go, just before Lewis introduced the newest member of the presidential security detail, President William "Bud" Packer reached by far the most indisputable conclusion of the day, indeed all the recent days.

My God, he thought, his eyes resting on Cleo Conway, a goddess is protecting a mere mortal.

50

O N THE DAYS THAT FOLLOWED Packer's return from Camp
David the political situation deteriorated even as the water of the Taiwan Strait
became more churned up with the vessels of war.

As the fleets assembled, the politicians and military leaders in Beijing
and Washington became increasingly concerned about an accidental exchange
occurring before any irreversible decision to launch a strike was even contemplated. For its part, the United States was kept busy trying to discourage those
of its more vigorous allies, especially old Warsaw Pact nations eager to prove
their fealty to the West, from sending troops to the crisis zone.

The British, of course, were allowed to show up and promptly did so in
the form of the aircraft carrier HMS Illustrious and a supporting battle group.
The Australians, too, got a pass into the strait and sent a destroyer and, even
more ominously, a hospital ship.

The French and Italians put to sea but wisely stayed well over the horizon,
mostly in the eastern reaches of the Indian Ocean. The Russians didn't put to
sea at all, and there were barbed comments in news reports that the Russian
navy's larger ships were still too much of the rust bucket variety, this despite
a much publicized effort to bring back some of the blue water capability of
the Soviet era.

Moscow's statements to the United Nations Security Council carried a
distinct preference for Beijing's point of view, but mostly the Russian envoy
indulged in rather smug and self-congratulatory speeches about peace and
world order. The Americans and Chinese envoys largely ignored him, concentrating instead on mutual condemnation.

The Chinese delegation, at certain moments, unleashed lines that sounded
to some of the older U.N. hands like hand-me-downs from Chairman Mao.
The Taiwanese strutted vigorously. Troop convoys drove up and down the
island and navy patrol boats rushed back and forth along the island's coastline,
especially that which faced across the strait to the mainland.

Taiwan's normally raucous politicians were, by contrast, unusually quiet.

There were no fiery speeches about throwing the enemy back into the sea. One or two members of the island's parliament came out with rather sappy speeches about the glories of Chinese history, no distinction made with regard to where those glories actually took form.

The mainland media enthusiastically replayed these pronouncements from the renegade island with commentators proclaiming that the speakers reflected the true feelings of the Chinese people of Taiwan, as opposed to people who called themselves simply Taiwanese.

There was a brief uproar, admittedly of the sideline variety, when Chinese television broadcast a story apparently showing happy tourists from Taiwan visiting the Great Wall. This, the commentator stated, was a clear signal that the Chinese people of Taiwan fully supported Beijing's assertion that there was only one China, even as Beijing was gearing up to back reality with military force.

After a few days a report came out in a German newspaper that the footage was over a year old and that such a visit to the mainland by Taiwanese was now impossible anyway because Taipei had placed a ban on all non-essential travel to the mainland about two weeks before the Great Wall outing had allegedly taken place. The footage duly vanished from Chinese television screens. But there was no correction or clarification.

As the early summer in the northern hemisphere grew warmer, the prospect of a real fight over Taiwan grew hotter. In Britain, the bookmakers were offering odds on a conflagration. One pledged to pay out even in the event of nuclear Armageddon. The prices of many basic goods in the high street supermarkets began to soar.

In the *Post* newsroom, on a day when the Chinese stormed out of a Security Council meeting with a particular flourish, throwing briefing papers at the Americans, Henderson was contemplating an idea for the following morning's front page. It entailed using a mushroom cloud photo of an atomic blast along with a graph to illustrate the sky rocketing prices of the usual basic goods, bread and milk.

"Nobody drinks milk anymore," Bailey said as he stood just a couple of feet from Henderson's desk. "All the kids get these days is fizzy junk. Milk costs too much, and people think it's full of hormones."

Henderson was silent for a moment. "I drink milk," he growled. "And just because people are too stupid to take what's good for them doesn't mean that its price is no longer important. Milk stays in the mushroom cloud."

"What are you going to use for bread then? A baguette, panini? Nobody in their right mind would buy that sliced rubbish."

Henderson had summoned Bailey to his desk, though not for a lecture on British eating habits in the second decade of the twenty-first century.

"Mr. Bailey, if you want to retain any hope at all of getting on board a plane and flying to America, landing in Washington at the time that a Chinese missile hits the Pentagon, and sending back your very last story on God's earth, then I suggest that you take that seat there in your grubby hand and plonk your bloody arse in it. Now."

Bailey smiled. "*Jawohl, mein Führer.*"

Henderson shook his head and said nothing for a moment. The newsroom was relatively quiet though it would pick up sharply over the next thirty minutes or so. The interlude would be Henderson's last chance to impart meaningful instructions to his most truculent, and sharpest, reporter.

Bailey braced himself. He knew that Henderson was winding up.

"I was about to say that ordinarily you would not be going on a trip like this at a time like this. In fact, this lunatic gathering at the White House wouldn't be going on at all only the Americans and our people see some good old fashioned propaganda in this crazy rich Taiwanese geezer promising to unleash his riches on the poor old Belfast shipyards that have been little more than a tourist attraction for years.

"Obviously, then, there's a story. It's better again because the ships he wants built are warships that might someday steam into Hong Kong and take it back. That's what he's hoping for anyway.

"Again, there's a story because the prime minister and the president are side by side on the eve of what might be the third world war."

"What about the Irish prime minister, the, what do they call him?" Bailey interrupted.

"Taoiseach," said Henderson. "Tee-shock" he added by way of phonetic reinforcement.

"No, he's not going to be there. The Irish are still militarily neutral, not in NATO. Hard to believe, I know, but they don't want their man in a photo-op with the Yanks and Brits as they gear up for the big shooting match. Their Washington ambassador will be there. I hear she's quite a looker. Anyway, your job is to play this up as being an off-the-wall sideshow to the main event. If the war starts while you're within shouting distance of Packer and Spencer, ask them how we should play this thing. Is it the end, the beginning of the end, or just the end of the beginning? I doubt if they will get the joke. After that, just head for the hills."

"Do you think it will come down to a nuclear war then?"

Henderson looked straight at his interrogator. "I remember back in 1967, the Six Day War; before your time. They were all talking about how the Arab and Israeli conflict could spread to the great powers, how America and Russia could move from what was a proxy war on their behalf to a direct confrontation with each other. But that's the difference between then and now. It was a proxy war. This time two superpowers are right in the middle of it themselves, and one of them is looking at an island as its own territory. It could well end up with shooting, yes. I only hope it isn't nuclear weapons."

Bailey said nothing. Henderson, he thought, could well be right. He thought of Samantha Walsh in the same instant. She would be Washington, too. Did the Chinese have missiles that could reach the American capital? He would check it out. Henderson stood and stretched. "Mushroom cloud it is then," he said. "Maybe we should check the price of mushrooms as well."

He turned away from Bailey and motioned with his hand. "You've got a couple of days off. Use them well. Pack lightly, Washington's a sauna at this time of year."

"Yes, boss," said Bailey, his mind already racing ahead to his rendezvous on the other side of the ocean with an eccentric Taiwanese billionaire, the leaders of the free world, a sexy diplomat, and the copper he was now sure he had fallen deeply in love with.

"Oh, and by the way," said Henderson, his voice slightly raised as Bailey was walking back to his own desk, "that idiot Mercer in Sydney who's always claiming to be our stringer."

"Yeah, what about him?" said Bailey without turning around.

"Well, the MOD in its infinite wisdom has allowed just one pool TV crew on board the Illustrious. That leaves the likes of us floundering around on *terra firma* with all the action expected on the waves that we once ruled."

Bailey nodded as he sat at his desk about twenty feet from Henderson's.

"Well, Mercer, who may not be such an idiot after all, has somehow snagged a berth on that Aussie hospital ship."

"Really?" said Bailey. "What's its name?"

"Christ, I don't know. HMAS Crocodile Dundee or something."

Bailey laughed aloud. Henderson of course knew the name; he knew all the names. Perhaps, he thought, the old bastard was easing up now that the end of the world was possibly in sight. Good timing.

"Anyway," Henderson continued, "the point I'm making is that you are going to have some competition for scarce space. And if you're sending back rubbish on all the *bonhomie* on the South Lawn and he's sending back stories on bombs away, then of course there will be no space at all. For anybody."

Bailey was not laughing now, not smiling. He wasn't paying any attention to Henderson at all. He was reading an e-mail.

It was just above his e-ticket. He was reading it for the second time, and he was feeling something that he had never felt before in his life. It was cold fear. Nick Bailey was shaking.

51

THE BREEZE HAS BLOWN steadily off the water and Pender had taken full advantage of clear skies and strong light.

He had come to northern Maine to finish off the photo project before, as he thought to himself more than once, he finished off two of the world's most important political leaders. The business of taking pictures had been a comfort. Pender did not relish killing, never had. But this mission, his final one, had many peculiar aspects to it, logistical and qualitative.

Pender had learned through experience that murder was most easily justified, in a personal sense, when the bastard deserved it.

And they all had of course. His assassination missions had invariably been carried out against men, and a lone woman, who had, each of them, been responsible for many deaths. It was a simple equation, really. By eliminating one he was certain of saving many. He did not think it murder.

As he mulled over what was past, and what was now looming very large in the near future, Pender had managed to crawl over the rocks to within a few yards of the seals. They had eyed him with only the faintest hint of interest. He in return had been playing at ignoring the beasts, trying to convince them that he was simply part of the seascape.

It was a remote place, a narrow but deep inlet on the upper coast. Not many people were around, and Pender had enjoyed the calm and quiet for three days.

Of course, he had not chosen the location. The old priest had, and as he slowly pointed the lens at the nearest seal, the animal staring back at him with sad eyes, Pender wondered what was keeping him.

The third day! That had been his instruction. Be ready for him on the third day. It had sounded biblical. But now the old man was just simply late.

Pender raised his camera a few inches, his elbows resting on raw rock just above the tide line. A suddenly stronger breeze blew off the ocean, and he shivered a little. Maine, he thought, was a far cry from the heat of New York or Washington. And he liked it that way. His planned hideaway in Switzerland would be well above sea level, cool to cold most times of the year.

In the depths of winter he could head for the coast of southern France. Above all, he would need time to rid his body of tropical, forested Africa, a place that he loved and hated in near equal measure, hate having the edge. He needed to rest in a place that did not pull him too much either way. He needed to simply rest.

Pender's thoughts returned to the creature in his lens. He adjusted the focus slightly and steadied himself. He would have just a few seconds before his uncomfortable position would require adjustment. He wanted the seal to look straight at him, through him and beyond him. It would be that look of casual disinterest that some of the smarter animal species could pull off, even in the closest proximity to predatory man.

The seal was looking slightly to one side of Pender's optical crosshairs, but, for a split second, turned its head full on to the camera and flared its nostrils. Pender's right forefinger lightly touched the hair trigger button. There was a barely perceptible click and the shot was in the bag. The seal's look had been one of disdain rather than disinterest but it would do. It was a wrap, the final photo for the book. The final photo ever for all Pender cared right now.

"Nice one," he said, loudly now because stealth was no longer required.

The sound of clapping hands was just yards away.

"Nice one indeed," said the voice.

Two humans being one too many, the seal and several of its companions rolled over to one side and slipped smoothly into the water. Pender, too, rolled over and stared at the man standing on top of a rock ten yards behind his position. It was the old priest dressed in hiking gear that looked straight out of a Hillary and Tensing photograph.

"Ah, there you are," said Pender, his left hand rising in greeting. "I was beginning to wonder."

"Wonder is always something I would encourage," came the prompt reply. It was unclear for a moment as to which man would make the first move, but an especially big wave showered Pender with spume. Placing his hands around the camera to protect it from the salt water he sprang up as quickly as his stiff joints would allow and covered the distance between the two of them in a series of short steps and slight leaps.

"I wasn't sure you would make it," he said, slightly out of breath and standing on an adjoining rock.

"Oh, I've been here, or at least hereabouts, for several days," was the response. "I see you have been photographing seals. Fascinating creatures. In the old days they were considered to be the reincarnations of drowned sailors. And perhaps they are. Come, walk with me back to the beach."

Without waiting, the priest turned and with a litheness that belied his age negotiated several other rocks before dropping down onto the sand. Pender followed, a little more slowly. His camera would not take well to a tumble.

"Splendid day," the priest said, his arms spread wide. "God is smiling on the world, or at least this precious corner of it."

Pender caught up. "God might be smiling, but I'd be a little worried over what he's thinking. One of his representatives on earth plotting murder, double murder, perhaps even the multiple kind."

The older man stopped and stubbed a booted toe in the sand. "Oh come, come, Mr. Pender. Remember, we don't always call it murder. We churchmen have notched up more than two thousand years of calling it by other names."

"Call it what you like," Pender retorted. "This time around it's not some bloodsucking tin pot dictator in a jungle clearing. These guys are serious shit and seriously protected. I thought the photo covers in the envelope were a mistake. But they're not, are they? You want me to pop off the president and the prime minister, and I don't even know bloody well why."

The old man turned and faced the water. He put his hands in pockets in the front of his windbreaker, thus giving himself the appearance of a meditating monk in a habit.

"Well, I'm glad you want to know why, Mr. Pender," he said. "I can only assume that we're off the mark and the mission has been accepted in principle."

"I guess so," said Pender. "But the question why goes beyond this job. This is the last time I will work for you and your people, and I still don't quite get how you can reconcile killing with all the love-your-fellow-man stuff."

"*Judica me, Deus, et discerne causam meam de gente non sancta. Ab homine iniquo et doloso erue me.*"

The priest repeated himself, almost in a chant, before looking directly at Pender. Pender said nothing but his expression invited a translation.

"Judge me, Oh God, and plead my cause against an ungodly nation. Oh deliver me from the unjust and deceitful man.' It's a psalm, Mr. Pender. Number forty-two to be precise, and I think it should answer your question."

"It might be an answer to God. But unlike him, I'm not exactly all knowing," said Pender. "Why Spencer and why the American president?"

The old man was silent again for a few moments.

"Of course you deserve an explanation," he said eventually.

"You may or may not be aware of the deaths of four priests in England this past while. The newspapers, one in particular, has attempted to draw links between the deaths but has been unable to do so thus far in a definitive sense.

"However, there is a link, a very specific one, and it can be traced back to our prime minister."

Pender felt a slight tingling sensation in the back of his neck, not so much at the suggestion that a political leader had been up to no good, but rather because it appeared that he would this time learn a good deal more than usual about the reasons for his assignment. In the past, he had been offered little and had sought less. But those jobs were of little consequence compared to the task that was now facing him.

He could barely contain his curiosity. He wanted to interrupt with more questions as the old man continued with his outline of a plot that, if pulled off successfully, would stand out boldly, infamously, on history's pages for centuries to come.

"In the course of his life, the prime minister has belonged to more organizations than just his political party," said the priest.

"Yeah, his local cricket club, I suppose," Pender interrupted.

The priest paused, and in so doing signaled his own impatience.

"I suppose that might be the case," he said after a few seconds. "But he was also a man who worked in the shadows, in intelligence, you understand."

"Ah," said Pender, cutting across the older man again. "MI5 was it, no MI6, more Spencer's line I would think."

"I believe he dabbled in both, but also in another sphere. Let's just say there is more to British intelligence than branches Five and Six, just as there are more players in American intelligence than the sixteen or so agencies the United States admits to."

"Superb," said Pender. "The ultimate intelligence agency. Nobody knows the bloody thing even exists."

"Precisely."

The old man raised his hand, a signal that Pender was now to listen, and only listen. And so, over the course of the next hour a story that had been more than four centuries in the making was revealed by the older man to the younger.

Pender was transfixed. More than once he felt he had to pinch himself. The old priest had clearly lived his entire adult life in a world that was one foot in the seventeenth century, the other in the present, barely.

When the telling was done, the priest dropped his head, exhausted but relieved at having passed on his secrets. He was the last of his order, and he had borne them alone since the deaths of his four companions.

Now Pender shared those secrets. But why, he wondered, had he been told everything?

"Because," said the priest, "you possess the moral character and mental ardor necessary to carry on our mission."

"But I'm only interested in a payday," Pender interjected.

The old priest laughed. "You are very particular about what you accept payment for, just as we have been very particular over the years over what we pay for. Our particulars are a fine match, Mr. Pender, rest assured."

Pender said nothing for a moment.

"But why assassinate the American president? Why not just kill Spencer? Surely assassinating Packer is going to stir up the mother of a hornet's nest?"

The old priest clapped his hands. The sound, however, was almost drowned out by a massive wave that had crashed ashore with the advancing tide.

"That," he said triumphantly, "is the very essence of our plan. The assassinations will take place on the South Lawn of the White House, at the epicenter of American power. The reaction will be immense, the investigation unparalleled in American history. And it will traipse down the wrong road entirely.

"You see, the Americans will never for one minute believe that their man was merely, shall we say, collateral damage. Packer, of course, must have been the primary target, and our poor, unfortunate prime minister just, well, an unfortunate peripheral casualty having been in the wrong place at the wrong time. Not for one second will the Secret Service and the rest of them think that their man was simply history's most powerful red herring."

Pender, his eyes narrowed and his head shaking slightly from side to side, absorbed as best he could the assassination of the President of the United States as a mere ruse.

"But how in the name of Christ am I going to pull this off? This is the White House we're talking about, not some jungle clearing, or wide open public place."

The old man, joining his hands as if in prayer, smiled.

"Ah, Mr. Pender, you are off the hook on that one. You will not carry out the killing assignment. All you have to do is take the most important photograph of your life."

52

Conway remembered the first time she had stood here. It was in her early days as a trainee agent, a tour of the West Wing for the young men and women who would someday be charged with protecting all who worked within, and one in particular.

She remembered that day in detail. It was snowing, and the White House had looked like a Christmas card. Her father had once received one, signed by his president, or perhaps by an assistant, or a machine, it was impossible to tell. It didn't matter. The card had taken center stage on the living room mantle until well into the spring of the following year.

She had been standing for ten minutes after declining the offer of a chair. The Oval Office was only feet away, up a short stair, through a door and then just a turn. The waiting area was, she thought, surprisingly small, as indeed was the White House overall.

Incredible, really, so much power concentrated in a square footage that was miniscule compared to those mega mansions of the super rich.

The walls were dotted with photographs of the president with visiting dignitaries and world leaders. There were a few of the president and the First Lady, and the obligatory shot of the president and his pet dog, a Brittany Spaniel. There was a lone photo of the dog itself on the lawn just a few yards away from where Conway, her right foot tapping impatiently on the blue carpet, waited for her meeting with the man she was sworn to protect, with her own life if necessary.

Conway pulled her cell phone from her pocket and checked it. Yes, it was switched off, just as it was when she had checked it two minutes before. She made a mental note to change the ring tone to something more somber and low key than the current hip-hop jingle, something jazzy perhaps, or better again, patriotic.

A White House assistant, a ridiculously young woman in a gray suit, appeared at the top of the stair and with a less than convincing smile motioned Conway to follow her.

"The president is ready to see you now," the woman said. She had turned on her heel before even finishing her line. Conway followed, trying to be as casual as possible.

Remind me, honey, not to take a bullet for you, she thought.

She was in the Oval Office. It was full of people, standing, sitting, walking. At first she did not see Packer at all but then picked him out in a knot of people to one side of the presidential desk. The young assistant spoke to an older assistant who moved to the president's side. The senior assistant said something to Packer that was impossible to make out amid the buzz of conversation. Not for the first time, Conway wondered how and why the president was sparing time for her with the country on the brink of war.

Packer was gesticulating, waving, and as if by magic, people began to disperse in all directions. It took only a few seconds before the room was empty but for the president, Conway and an aide who had dropped some papers on the floor beside the main doorway. Once they were retrieved, he was gone. Guard and guarded were alone.

Packer, moving to the chair behind his desk, motioned to Conway to take a seat in front of it.

"Special Agent Conway, delighted you could make it," the president said in what passed for a cheerful voice under the circumstances. She could tell he was tired and under a lot of stress.

"Delighted to be here, Mr. President," she responded as she took her seat. As if I had any choice, she thought.

Packer was looking through a file, presumably her own, Conway reckoned.

"Outstanding," he said eventually. "It's fantastic that you're coming to work with me. We need more women up front and out there, though of course I don't mean necessarily in harm's way."

He was doing his best, Conway thought, forgivingly. The president, she well knew, had a reputation for being a bit overly familiar sometimes, less than discreet, at least verbally. But so far in his presidency he had not been caught in any overt act of excessive personal zeal.

Packer was staring at the file again. Conway decided to move things on a bit.

"I'm well aware, Mr. President, that this is a most pressing time. If you would like we could meet when the situation is a little more calm," she said.

Packer looked up, a slightly puzzled look on his face. "No, not at all, forgive me, but it's your fault really, your file is really right out there. You're a regular Indiana Jones in a skirt, or at least pantsuit."

Conway said nothing in response but fixed the president with her most agreeable official smile.

"I knew your father," Packer said. The effect was as he desired. Conway was taken aback, and it showed. The leader of the free world had regained control of the conversation.

"That I did not know, sir. How? Where?"

Packer, clearly pleased with himself, lowered his head and leaned over his desk in what could best be described as a conspiratorial manner.

"Well," he said, extending the final two consonants for a full two seconds, "We met each other in Vietnam. I was a young congressman, wet behind the ears on one of those fact finding missions, co-dels they call them. We were in Saigon holed up in a downtown hotel, the Carvel or Caravelle, as I recall. We were being dragged all over the place meeting with South Vietnamese officials, the president, of course, and more generals and colonels than we had in the entire United States Army. Couldn't believe how much brass they had in the ARVN. More brass than balls, that was often the problem.

"Anyway, I'm wandering. Saigon, of course, was hotter than Hades, hotter than even this town in August, so I think we were slowly going nuts. One member of our group came down with some bug and had to be shipped back stateside pronto. Just as we're about to stage our very own coup we had a trip organized by the embassy to a place much closer to the action, out of town about thirty miles or so, up near Cu Chi and the Big Red One base, you know what I mean, First Infantry Division."

Conway nodded.

"That's where I met your pa. He was working some anti-tunnel operation, though clearly, by the size of him, he wasn't going into any of them. That job was for those crazy tunnel rats. After a briefing and a tour of a couple of local hamlets, with half a regiment in tow to protect us, it was time to get back to town. Well, I was having none of that. I bent your father's ear, telling him that I wanted to stay out for the night, taste a little of the real war when the VC were roaming around after dark.

"Of course, he was having none of it but I made it easy for him, persuaded him I was sick and not able to travel on those damn bumpy roads. I told him I was a freshman congressman and half the men my age in the state were lining up to take my job if something bad happened. Took a bit of persuading, but your Daddy was up to it once I had worn him down. The rest of the group went back to Saigon, and I got to hole up in a tent with your dad. We even went out on a bit of a patrol, though I think he faked it for my benefit.

"We just went round and round the camp perimeter. Still, I got me a bit of a story to tell back home and of course legend soon took over. Within a few weeks I was reading about how I had been on patrol in Injun country and my escorting unit had come under fire.

"You know those hometown reporters, just so hungry and enthusiastic. All I had to say was it wasn't quite that bad. I didn't elaborate and only finally put the brakes down when one kid, nice fella, was writing Audi Murphy's name in a story about my ramblings in Veet-Nam, as old Lyndon called it.

"It was getting embarrassing, but the story kind of lasted. Congressman Packer on night patrol. I still have the story in a scrapbook somewhere. But, Jesus Christ, Agent Conway, Cleo, your father was such a fine soldier, and a gentleman. We didn't foul up in Vietnam because of men like him. It was because of men like me who couldn't tell a war fact from a war bond."

Packer was sitting back in his chair now, staring over and beyond Conway, lost in some long past moment, a hot night in a South East Asian clearing, a soldier with a slow, steady voice steering him safely through the darkness.

"Hell of a soldier," he said, clearly to himself.

Conway was unsure what to say, what to do. She had been trained to deal with important people right up to the president, but in a very particular, stilted way. A president speaking like this was not in the book, although one of her instructors had told her, and the rest of her class, that presidents did often bond with particular agents, for whatever reason. The agents, however, could never fully respond, get too close in return. And it was with those words ringing in her memory that Conway looked at the president and said nothing.

Packer, after a few more moments, seemed to gather himself. He sighed, stood up and walked around the desk.

"I apologize," he said. "An old man getting sentimental."

"No apology necessary, Mr. President," Conway replied. "I'm glad that my father was able to be of service."

Packer, however, had already moved past the moment.

"Come over here," he said, walking to the far side of the room and a dark wood bookcase stuffed with hardcovers, not all of them new.

"You know," he said, "every president likes to make this office reflect his interest, her interests too, of course. Some do it with paintings, some with bronzes, photos or paperweights and stuff on the desk.

"My idea was to select what I thought, or what some of my people thought, was the best biography of each occupant of this office. And here they are, all forty-five of them. The space at the end is me, a blank, ha ha. But seriously, Cleo, I hope you don't mind me calling you by your name, it comforts me to have the company. I feel these guys are with me when it counts, like now, when we face the perilous hour."

Packer was staring at the volumes, again lost in the moment.

"Obviously I'll take them with me when my time is up. Don't want to let them fall into the hands of the enemy. And I'm not necessarily talking about the other party."

Conway allowed herself a smile. It was the president's little joke. Her time was up. Packer began to walk towards the door she had entered. She remembered a photo of her father's. Kennedy speaking to television cameras, the still shot taken from a position showing the door. The Oval Office looked small in the photograph, and really, all things considered, it was small.

"Agent Conway." Packer brought her back. "I've been asked and I've agreed, wholeheartedly I might add, that you be the newest agent in my detail. Your boss, that old cowboy Dalton, will be giving you a full briefing in a few days. You'll be on duty for the first time at a South Lawn event we're having in a couple of weeks. It's all to do with Ireland and peace and investment, that kind of thing. A very clean and cleared list of guests, a home game, although I can't promise to stay behind the rope; you know me."

Conway was trying not to shake. She nodded, stupidly, she thought.

"I don't want you to get all wound up now," said Packer. "This should be an easy introduction, perhaps the easiest day you're going to get on this job for a while."

Conway, standing as straight as she could, looked into her president's eyes.

"Yes, sir," she said. "Yes, Mister President. Thank You. I will not let you down."

Packer nodded. "I know," he said. "Because right now that's exactly what your father is telling me."

53

"I THINK I'LL GO."

Nesbitt did not reply. He was hidden behind his computer screen, had been all afternoon.

"We have the school spring concert tonight. If I miss it I'll be *persona non grata* for the rest of my natural life."

Nesbitt's silence was unbroken.

"I might have to flee the country and leave this White House gig entirely in your lap," said Manning.

"Do that and I will hunt you down, remorselessly," Nesbitt replied, lifting his head and sitting up a little more in his chair so that his head appeared barely above the screen.

"But I suppose if it's the wife and the kid doing her Von Trapp thing you should indeed go and leave the weary world to me."

"You're too kind," Manning responded as he closed his briefcase with a snap.

"I'll bring you coffee in the morning, maybe even a doughnut."

"That will be an event," said Nesbitt. "By the way, don't forget, you have to meet with the Secret Service people tomorrow to give them our final invite list. They are sending someone over at 9.30, and given who we're dealing with, I'm sure the special agent, he or she, will be here right on the button."

"Yeah, and all the while talking up his sleeve," said Manning, now at the door.

"Don't stay too late, for God's sake. Her nibs will think you're the gold standard for the rest of us."

"Don't worry. I'll be history in about an hour, and it won't even be fully dark by then. There really is a fine stretch in the evenings now."

Nesbitt's final sentence was to himself. Manning had gone after closing the door quietly.

It took Manning just a few minutes to reach his car in the underground lot. It took him just a second to stop in his tracks and a second more to see that the man leaning against his car was Roger Burdin.

Manning drew in what he wanted to be deep breath. But it never got beyond the shallow point. He had known of course that Burdin would show up again. In fact he had been lately wondering why the man from Ministry of Intelligence, Branch Six, had been taking so long.

Manning, reaching the driver's door, hit his remote button. He said nothing as he got into the car. Burdin, too, was silent as he slipped in on the passenger side. Both men sat for a moment, each waiting for the other to speak. It was Burdin who broke the silence.

"Nice motor," he said. "I've always had a soft spot for American cars. They have such comfortable interiors."

"I haven't heard a word about Pender," Manning retorted. He was not in the mood for meaningless small talk.

"No, you wouldn't have, but you will tomorrow," Burdin said, turning to look directly at Manning, a half smile on his long, lined face.

"Fitzhugh will call your ambassador's office tomorrow morning asking for a favor, accommodation for the great shutterbug. He will drop in the line that he has been under your roof at one point in the not so distant past and will suggest a rematch.

"Your ambassador will ask you if that is fine by you and your lovely wife, and you will readily agree to Pender staying with you for the time he is in Washington covering the White House trade conference."

"Why not a hotel?" Manning said, an edge in his voice.

"The reason he does not want to stay in a hotel is that he had all his expensive camera gear nicked last year in what was supposed to be a posh place in Los Angeles. He simply prefers the comforts of home now, and particularly the security of knowing that his temporary residence isn't brim full of sticky fingered strangers. It's an entirely reasonable and plausible request, don't you think?"

Manning said nothing for a moment. He had inserted the key but had not switched on the engine.

"What precisely is your interest in Pender, and why are you taking such an interest in his work arrangements? What the hell is going on?" he said.

Burdin smiled and turned his eyes to the windshield. "Start the car. How about a little trip to the White House?"

Manning shrugged. "The White House, why?"

"Just bloody drive," Burdin retorted sharply. "We haven't a lot of time."

Manning steered the car out of the lot and on to a street that was in the throes of rush hour. He did not make it more than a few yards before being hemmed in by a phalanx of vehicles, mostly D.C. taxicabs.

"I am assured, am I not? that this is the last time I will have to do anything for you people," Manning said as he squeezed into a space a few cars back from a red stop light.

"Absolutely," Burdin replied. "This is it old boy; you have my word."

"Your word. Jesus Christ."

Burdin did not respond to Manning's dismissal. Instead, as the car moved with the now green light, he raised a hand and pointed a finger.

"Take a right here. Then the next right and the first left. I think you will find it the fastest way to where we are going."

The two were silent for several minutes as Manning did his best to weave through the traffic while heading in the direction suggested by his surprisingly street-wise companion.

It was Burdin who spoke first.

"Never could get used to driving on this side of the road, you know. I believe we got it right way back when. As I've heard it, a rider stayed left so that his sword arm, his right arm, was free to meet a stranger coming from the opposite direction. Can't imagine why the Yanks opted for this side, particularly given that they are so into manly action."

"I think they discovered guns and it didn't matter what side of the damn road you were on," said Manning, drawing a little satisfaction from taking the side of his wife's countrymen.

"Perhaps you're right," said Burdin. "The Americans don't exactly stand on ceremony. Look what they did to our blessed language."

Manning had found a relatively clear stretch of street and had pressed the pedal as far as he reckoned diplomatic immunity permitted.

"Ah, the open road. How are your lovely wife and daughter by the way?" asked Burdin, folding his arms and leaning back in his seat.

To Manning, it was less a question than a reminder of his vulnerability. His past life was something his family had no knowledge of, but with Burdin, the threat went well beyond the potential for mere tattle-telling. The question harbored a threat of harm that, while unspoken, was plain. Yet Manning balked at the temptation to spit out a reply, counter with a threat of his own.

He knew such a response would be futile, so he contented himself with the most nonchalant comeback he could come up with.

"Fine," he said. "I think we're here. I can't turn, or get any nearer as you know because the street is blocked off. You'll have to walk."

"Pull in just here," Burdin commanded. "Walk I will. As you know, I enjoy a good ramble."

Manning stopped in a no parking zone and turned on his warning lights. He was expecting more, and sure enough it came.

Burdin was staring at him intently now. "Listen very carefully," he said. "This is a job that will actually make you feel rather good about yourself. Your task is to make sure that people don't get hurt. You will make sure that nobody grabs or diverts Mr. Lau, the Taiwanese industrialist who, as you know, is the star guest at the conference, the man who is going to bring back shipbuilding to Belfast, of a sort at any rate.

"Above all, don't let your ambassador smother him, kidnap him. Lau will bow as a greeting. This will seem quite normal given the part of the world he comes from. He will shake some hands, maybe speak to some people, but only those that are of his choosing. You must make sure that he is given his space, is allowed to make his own moves. Do you understand?"

"Not really," said Manning. "But I think I should be able to manage that."

"Don't think, make sure you do." Burdin was already half out of the car.

"Oh, I do love Washington," he said, turning and peering back in the door.

"I wonder if our lads would ever have been able to burn the White House back in that war, 1812 wasn't it, if they had the blessed pile ringed with all these concrete flower pots."

And then he was gone, across the street and off in the direction of the presidential mansion, venue for the post conference party for which idle banter and social diversion had suddenly become an act of ominous import and mystery.

Manning shook his head and pulled back into the traffic. He wasn't thinking of socially overbearing ambassadors, or Chinese billionaires, but of his wife and daughter and of their exposure to Burdin's potential for extreme malice.

The fact that Burdin would not require him to kill someone else meant little; indeed nothing at all.

54

BAILEY WAS SHAKING HIS HEAD. His face registered something not far short of disgust. He was looking out of the only window in his bedroom at what passed for a view.

The gap between the facing brick walls was little more than an airshaft, and the only other window in the whole depressing picture, the paint around its frame having long since peeled away, was only made vaguely interesting by the fact that the curtain behind it was never opened.

His vista, by virtue of this perpetually obscured limit, presented a mystery, and from time to time Bailey had speculated as to what lay behind it. The room had been in his building before it had been subdivided, and now it was on the far side of a partition wall at the end of the hallway. The room, he had decided in more idle moments, was a drug den, a sex parlor or the hideout for a terrorist cell. He was glad that Samantha had only ever been in his room after dark and had been spared the sheer awfulness of this outlook. He would have to find a new flat.

He would also, he realized, have to tell Walsh about the email. She was, after all, a copper, and presumably not easily frightened. Neither was he, for that matter, or so he liked to believe, but the threat had been directed at both of them, and the idea of any harm coming to the woman who now dominated most of his waking thoughts was a sensation that was entirely unfamiliar, and entirely frightening.

He had never experienced such a feeling of vulnerability in a life that had been devoted, up until very recently, to what he now saw as selfish pursuits. If he had been uncertain he was no longer so. He was very much in love with this woman and would do anything in his power to keep her safe.

But what precisely was his power? As a journalist he had connections for sure, but it was Walsh who could really draw on the muscle, most especially now that she was part of the prime minister's security unit and was, as the Americans would put it, packing.

The email had looked like a story from some other media outlet and indeed the message in it was presented in the form of a news report. It was quite simple, just a few lines, but it described, without little dressing up, the death in a road crash of a newspaper reporter and a police officer, a woman. Both had succumbed to injuries sustained in the accident that had occurred on a notorious stretch of road near a town that he had little difficulty in remembering. They had stopped in the place for petrol on the way back from Ayvebury.

The report, for want of a better word, and without elaborating, had concluded with a line that police were investigating the possibility that the car had exploded before hitting a roadside wall. Both bodies had been burned beyond recognition, but a plate number had survived leading police to a near certain, though still preliminary, identification.

Bailey had been threatened a few times over the years, mostly when he was stuck into gangland stories. He had once received a bullet in the post. But these he put down to bravado and hot air. It was the absence of both, the very ordinariness of the account in the email that had made him shudder. Yes, he thought, this looked real, the sort of thing that happened every day.

He had written stories like this himself, though not, admittedly, with the revealing job descriptions that applied to both himself and Samantha. Somebody was warning him off, warning both of them off, though off what he could not hazard a guess.

Bailey turned to face the bed. His suitcase was packed, relatively neatly for a change. He had bought the bottle of whisky in advance, not wanting to deal with duty free at the airport. The less he had to think about at the airport the better. He enjoyed flying well enough, but traveling made him nervous and these days, after all the terrorist attacks and the world seemingly heading for a bloody great war, airports were places to get in and out of as quickly as possible with minimal deviation from the main plan: get on plane, fly, get off plane.

Henderson had asked him to bring a bottle with him to New York. He was being allowed a few days in the city before heading to Washington, this in order to interview a few locally based business heavies about the White House conference and prospects of Northern Ireland being the future Taiwan after Taiwan, presumably, was blown off the map by the Chinese.

The bottle was destined for George Dawes, the *Post's* man in New York. Dawes had for years inhabited that twilight world between full time correspondent and stringer. He was neither and a bit of both. He had served the paper well, being on the spot for everything from the John Lennon assassination to

various Wall Street debacles and September 11. Henderson and he were con-
temporaries and perhaps pals. The whisky, Bailey surmised, was likely appropriate for both of them. He had encased the two liter bottle in bubble wrap, socks
and underwear and was trusting it to his hard-shelled suitcase that would be
checked in for the flight.

Bailey looked at his watch. It was time to leave. He made a mental note,
several of them.

Mrs. Grimsby downstairs had the spare key, and the taxi would be outside
any minute. He closed the suitcase, slung his backpack over his shoulder and
made for the door. Yes, he said to himself, it was time for a new flat; perhaps
it might even merit the title of an apartment.

Bailey quickly glanced around the place before closing and locking the
door. "Hi ho, hi ho, it's off to America we go." He sang the line to the tune but
any hint of light heartedness, he knew, was forced.

As he walked down the stairs, his thoughts had already crossed the ocean.
It would be a time to consider things as well as work. It would be time to ponder a future together with Samantha. Given her current job, not to mention
his own, it was a stretch to imagine that there would be buckets of time in
close proximity to one another. Then again, he thought as he walked out of the
building's front door and waved at the waiting taxi, jobs could be changed.

The drive to Heathrow was excruciatingly slow. But he had made allow-
ances for delays. The driver, thankfully, was not the chatty sort. He contented
himself with listening to radio news and traffic reports after seeking permis-
sion of his passenger.

Bailey would be arriving in the States almost a week before Samantha.
She was to fly with the prime minister's party on a regular British Airways
flight into Washington's Dulles airport. Not up front with the big tickets,
she had said, ruefully, over the phone. The prime minister and his immediate
party would be up in first class while others, including Samantha and another
relatively junior officer, would be in economy. She would not be carrying her
gun on board. Her weapon would be issued to her on American soil and in
the presence of the US Secret Service.

Bailey had been intrigued by the rules and restrictions of Samantha's new
job. It seemed that nobody trusted anyone anymore. She herself had referred
to what she called the Sikh factor, a reference to the assassination many years
before of Indira Gandhi by her own Sikh bodyguards.

The vetting of protection unit officers, even those with years of a clean record with the police, now went to quite extraordinary lengths. She had asked Bailey's forgiveness when she had replied in the negative to a question as to whether or not she was involved in a steady relationship. He had made fun of it. She would be allowed to lie this once, he had replied.

She had almost screamed down the line at him in response. It wasn't a lie, she cried, merely a fudge. Steady in this day and age implied cohabitation, and they weren't cohabiting.

Fair enough, Bailey had responded, and he left it at that.

He had begun to notice an increase in the frequency of signs for Heathrow. The radio's sports announcer was discussing Arsenal's European prospects, and the driver was clearly happy about them. He had nudged up the volume.

"Arsenal supporter, are we?"

Bailey had decided to cover the last few miles with something other than thoughts of Samantha.

"All my blessed life," came the quick reply. "And yourself?"

"Oh, me, too," said Bailey. It was not the case. Though he far from being the most ardent football fan, he had always leaned towards West Ham United. He liked their style of play.

"Been to a game lately, then?" the driver prodded cheerfully, expecting an affirmative response.

Bailey hesitated for a couple of seconds.

"Not lately, though I did see the lads at Upton Park a while back. That was quite a win." Ant it was the truth. A colleague had brought him to see West Ham play Arsenal on a day that might have been the coldest since England had a written history.

"I remember that one all right. I wasn't there. Working that day. Perishing, as I recall. Here we go, next right Heathrow."

It wasn't more than a few minutes before the two had exchanged their 'thanks, mates.' Bailey had remembered to get a receipt for his expenses and had bundled his way into the terminal. The first thing that caught his eye was the police with machine guns, one of them with a dog.

What a bloody world, he thought as he began his immersion in the process of getting himself, his baggage and the bottle of Scotch from one side of the pond to the other. It all went with relative ease, and by that night, Nick Bailey was staring out of a Manhattan hotel window, more or less mesmerized. London, he had decided, came at you in parts. New York just hit you with everything it had in one go.

"Bloody fantastic," he said by way of a rehearsal line as he picked up the phone to call Samantha. He got her answering message.

On his first night of his big assignment, Nick Bailey decided two things. That he really missed having Samantha beside him, and that he wasn't going to worry because she had not been at home, nor had responded to repeated calls he had made to her mobile phone.

Nevertheless, sleep, on this first American night, came as a rescuer.

55

THERE WAS AN ORDER TO THINGS, of sorts. On some days, the instructions coming from the Secret Service were quite specific. On others, there were none. But activity was expected nonetheless.

The premise of the work at Globescan was based on the view that best results came from freely ranging activity, that crucial discoveries were uncovered in quiet hours. It was true, though never openly spoken, that the nation's security languished partly in the realm of luck and chance. And it was in response that adjunct operations like Globescan had been created in the first place. You could never have enough data nor intelligence, and the quickest way of obtaining both was setting up a new intelligence-gathering operation. It was a recipe for chaos on one level, but people slept a little better for it.

This might have been one of those quieter days but it would take a future historian with an appetite for the obscure to decide if this was absolutely the case. Either way, the input from the Service higher ups, fast flowing and demanding in the past few days, had ebbed. Today was not a red, or even an orange alert day on the office's own internal scale, but more like a cool blue, perhaps even a sleepy green. And, as a result, expectations were at the highest level for Globescan, not unlike expectant, ever-hopeful fishermen.

The lack of bites always preceded the biggest strike of all. They hoped.

In this regard, the men and women click-clacking away on keyboards and perusing obscure manifests and hate sheets were no different to the agents with the guns and shades. It, whatever it was, was not a shot away so much as only a keyboard stroke away. That's how the bad guys worked now, the Globescanners were told over and over. The internet was the trigger for all manner of unwelcome things, so it was necessary to be up to speed on what was passing through it, twenty-four seven.

Greg Spalding could recite the pep talks backwards at this stage. He stood in the doorway for a moment and took his customary deep breath.

"Showtime," he said.

Steve, his buddy and chief competitor, was on a day off. Chip and Dale were not on either. The two others in the room, Danny and Lynn, were relatively new to the job. Lynn gave him a cheery wave. Danny nodded his head without taking his eyes off a monitor. It was Thursday evening in Washington. Most of the jihadists in the world were far to the east where it was Friday. With luck, Spalding thought, they would be praying rather than plotting.

He covered the short distance to his desk in a few strides and sat down. "Ah, sweet routine," he said.

"Sweet indeed," Lynn replied.

Spalding adjusted the framed motto that Steve had given him for his last birthday. "Doubt everything, believe anything." Spalding had asked Steve the identity of the great mind that had concocted such a gem. Some master spy, a director of the CIA perhaps. Steve Peterson had claimed the mantra for himself. So there it rested on Spalding's desk, immovable, irrefutable.

"So, what have we here?" Spalding asked as his screen responded to the single key tap.

What he had was today's date in the diary of Samuel Pepys.

"And so to bed," said Spalding. "I think we'll give old Sammy a miss today."

"Who was he anyway?"

Lynn's expression was one of genuine curiosity. She was as smart as whip but rather more in the science and math line; history wasn't her *forte*.

"He was a man who kept a diary in seventeenth century England," Spalding replied. "And he gets more or less the lion's share for founding a proper English navy."

But Lynn had already moved on and was frowning as she stared at her screen.

Spalding shook his head. "And so to work," he said.

In the course of a day's labor Spalding and his colleagues were required to cover specific parts of the globe, more or less, but not entirely limited to lines on the map. In Spalding's case this was East Asia and in particular the Philippines. He had grown up on Mindanao, his parents having been Presbyterian missionaries. He spoke Spanish and Tagalog fluently and had a reasonable grasp of a couple of the more important island dialects.

Though his range of responsibility, like that of all his colleagues, was in the broadest sense global, Spalding was primarily responsible for keeping tabs on the activities of Communist and Islamic guerrilla groups in the southern reaches of the island archipelago. This responsibility extended to the monitoring of Filipino communities in the United States and Canada.

Not surprisingly, Spalding had been drawn to the growing crisis in the Taiwan Strait, a confrontation that threatened to turn any and all other present concerns into tiny potatoes. He wasn't alone in the room at having a hard time believing that there could actually be a world war started by a fight between the two Chinas, or, as one or two in the room had put it pointedly, the two parts of China.

The China crisis, however, was having one beneficial effect. It had dramatically reduced the number of visits to the office by members of Congress, politicians from countries closely allied with Washington and diplomats from those same nations who were allowed access to an operation that, while mostly under the radar as far as the media or public was concerned, fell short of top secret. With fewer such distractions, Spalding and the others had been trawling the world's trouble spots at an accelerated pace over the past couple of weeks.

Special Agent Conway's visit had been the sole intrusion, and it didn't even count as one of those, given her job.

Spalding had a particular side interest in British history. His mother had been born in Scotland, and this had drawn him first into the story of that country and beyond it to its most immediate neighbors: England first and foremost for practical purposes, Scotland for sentimental ones, and Wales and Ireland as peripheral afterthoughts. He had been to London three times and was so afforded the kind of deference in the room given those who had traveled beyond the nation's borders.

It was no surprise then that Lynn alerted Spalding to an email that contained a copy of a report from a London newspaper concerning a string of deaths involving Catholic priests and a connection, albeit a very tenuous one, to the British prime minister who, as Spalding knew, was about to be an honored guest at the White House.

"Thought you might want to take a look at that," Lynn said without looking up.

Spalding was already digesting the contents of the report in the *Post*, a paper he had picked up, along with most of the other main daily titles, during his last visit to London. The story was pumped up; that he could see. It was suggesting things between the lines above and beyond the stated facts, though those facts were certainly interesting. Four dead people, a common thread linking them, unlikely or unusual causes of death and both a geographic and chronological spread.

But it was the "we can sensationally reveal" line that made the story jump off the page as far as Spalding was concerned. It linked the victims, all four of them Catholic priests, with a school in the English countryside which once had a student who was now head of the British government. The prime minister had boarded in the place though only for a short time. He had left, or had been expelled. The story stated the former while hinting at the latter with a line saying that the reason for a mid-semester departure, or term as it was referred to, was unclear.

Spalding read the story a second time, shaking his head. The paper clearly knew more than it was immediately revealing, he thought. He hit a few keys on his computer and brought up a biography of Leonard Spencer.

"Ah, as I thought," Spalding said.

"What did you think?" Lynn was looking at him expectantly.

Spalding looked at her for a moment. She looked good today, he thought.

She raised her hands and opened her palms.

"Sorry," said Spalding. "What I was thinking was that he went to a Catholic school, but his bio lists him as Church of England, Anglican.

"So?" Lynn responded. "He had a conversion or maybe his folks thought it would do him some good. I was in Catholic school and there were kids who were various other religions. I even remember a Hindu."

"Yeah, but that's here. It's different over there, or at least was when Spencer was a kid. There's a lot of history, and though the English are not quite up there with the Irish on the Catholic, Protestant thing, they have long had their own internal version going on."

Lynn shrugged her shoulders and began working on her computer. Spalding went back to his screen. Within seconds he had a detailed report up on the British leader's Washington visit, now just days away. It carried a few lines about Northern Ireland and mentioned a Taiwanese billionaire who was going to pump money into the place. This fueled the main part of the story which had the prime minister and president meeting in conclave as the powers drifted towards what now seemed an inevitable clash in the waters separating the rich guy's island and the Chinese mainland.

But that was everybody's story. Spalding went back to the tabloid *Post* and ran searches that, after several minutes, revealed a series of reports on the deaths of the priests. One of them had been found hanging from a bridge in London that already had its name in the history books for the infamous Roberto Calvi affair.

After printing out the stories, Spalding laid them out on his desk in order. They all carried the same byline: Nick Bailey. Spalding picked up the desk phone and punched in numbers. His call was answered and after a brief exchange he replaced the receiver.

The White House press office, though only after Spalding had identified himself by name and a code number, had confirmed to him that a Nick Bailey from the London *Post* was indeed listed as an accredited correspondent and was expected to show up for the upcoming White House post-conference reception.

Spalding checked his watch. It was still early enough to get people at the office in London. He picked up the phone again and dialed the prefix and what he considered the number that offered the best chance of an instant response. If the *Post* report had sent up any flares at the embassy, or any of the US intelligence and law enforcement agencies with offshoots in the British capital, he was going to find out.

Even if the reaction were a negative, it wouldn't deter him.

Not for the first time in his career, Greg Spalding had that feeling in his gut. Something was not quite right. Something was up.

56

CLEO CONWAY DUCKED INSTINCTIVELY under the rotors of the helicopter. The lifting-off point was one of the quieter corners of Andrews Air Force Base, the main arrival and departure point for the president, just outside the nation's capital.

It was, however, Conway's first time setting foot in the place, and now she was about to get an aerial view with the added bonus of a flight from the base to the White House along the route taken by presidential parties.

A general mental picture, that's what they had said. This was on top of Conway having to pore over detailed street grids. That was the more crucial part of the exercise. If some crazy took a shot at Marine One, or one of its identical companions, she was required to know in an instant, without computerized aids, what point, intersection or landmark in the city they were flying over.

Marine One was ready to take the president and his entourage above the Washington traffic any time of any day or night. Now was the middle of the day, a sunny one with the prospect of a couple more to come.

Conway took a deep breath as she settled into her seat. There were two special agents, Philips and Rafter, already seated while a fourth position was the preserve of a Marine Corps sergeant who nodded and indicated a set of headphones. Conway put them on and the man nodded.

"Can you hear me, Special Agent?" he said.

"Loud and clear," Conway replied.

"Okay. Please check your firearm, ma'am."

Conway knew why. She had to make sure it was on safety. An accidental discharge in a helicopter was, naturally, a bad idea. Once assured, she gave the thumbs up and got an identical reply from the sergeant whose face was obscured by a visor. Very cool, she thought. The sergeant leaned through the doorway into the cockpit and waved his hand in an upward gesture.

The noise from the rotor overhead took on a higher pitch, and the helicopter gently lifted off. Conway had been in a chopper a few times but could never quite get used to the odd sensation, compared to the more familiar thrust of a jet aircraft. The helicopter, by contrast, seemed not to move at first; indeed, she could recall faster elevators. But within seconds they were a hundred feet above the ground, rising higher and turning south westwards.

All four were linked by the helicopter's voice communication system, but for the first couple of minutes, nobody said anything. Their route was a slightly roundabout one that took them initially in the direction of the Washington Navy Yard.

Conway, seated on the starboard side, pressed her eyes closed for a moment. She had not been sleeping well. No surprise, given her new assignment. Her half-asleep dreams had covered all manner of scenarios in which she might have to take a bullet for the president. She knew this to be a normal enough reaction. A few of her colleagues had made jokes, and she had forced herself to laugh. But the dreams, nevertheless, seemed real, entirely plausible. And so she had asked herself, silently and aloud, why she had not chosen another path in life, why she had not become a lawyer, a teacher, even a member of the military which, unlike the Secret Service, could stand at comparative ease in peacetime.

Conway glanced over at Philips and Rafter. Both were looking out of their side of the helicopter. Philips was from Ohio, the Cleveland area. He was an extrovert, one of the boys. Rafter was a little more of a mystery, the strong silent type. He was from out west somewhere, Wyoming or Montana, she wasn't quite sure. She had decided that he had an image to protect. She had also decided that she was more than a little attracted to him. But that's as far as it went. Conway had her rules and a primary one was no relationships on the job.

"Navy Yard." The sergeant gestured downwards with his forefinger, and all three agents stared out of the machine that had now taken a turn to its right and was dropping slightly in altitude.

The agents had closely studied street maps and were listing off buildings and intersections as the helicopter lined itself up for an approach to the White House. The Southwest Freeway and Virginia Avenue passed underneath. Conway, who was sitting facing forward on the right side, was now looking straight at the dome of the Capitol. The pilot eased slightly to his starboard and the dome filled the cockpit window.

"Sorry, no sightseeing." It was as close to humor than any of them were going to get. Conway half smiled at Philips who was opposite and had been the source of the comment. Rafter, she noticed was looking out the other side. He was also cracking his knuckles.

A little tense, she thought.

The helicopter was flying straight and level again. The Botanic Gardens passed below and moments later the Air and Space Museum, just off to the left side. The pilot continued along the southern edge of The Mall, all eyes of his passengers, including those of the sergeant, staring out at the buildings and streets below.

Conway was feeling slightly queasy now, though she was not going to give anything away. She gritted her teeth and focused her eyes on a gray cloud in the distance that was the only exception to the clear day.

"We're going to just take a loop around the monument." The sergeant, whose nametag said Holmes, was emphasizing this by twirling a raised forefinger.

"Then we will make a final approach to the South Lawn. Sorry, I forgot to mention it but we're actually going to make a brief landing on the lawn. You won't be getting out but apparently you have to follow Marine One's line of flight all the way to the target. Let me rephrase that, destination."

The loop around the monument completed, the helicopter quickly covered the remaining distance to The Ellipse and the back of the president's mansion. People were lined up against the back railing. Had it been Marine One making the approach, they would have been moved to another barrier some distance from the railing, but the chopper was merely carrying the president's protectors, not the man himself.

They were over the South Lawn now and dropping fast. At what seemed to be the final moment before collision with the Truman Balcony, the chopper shuddered slightly, hovered momentarily, turned to its right and descended to the executive sward. There was only the slightest bump on contact with the landing markers. Conway took a deep breath and closed her eyes. With luck they would stay for a few minutes.

"Would have been a harder landing than that if we had been hostile." Philips was staring at her, smiling and nodding.

"Yeah," said Conway. "We'd be history for sure." She desperately wanted to get out of the machine and suck in some air.

That didn't happen. Conway, trying to appear focused, stared out of the helicopter at a crowd of people on the lawn. They were erecting a stage and an open-sided marquis, both, as she was aware, for the trade event that would mark her debut as a member of the presidential detail.

After what seemed like an age, the sergeant announced that they were about to take off again. Conway forced a half smile, nodded and gave the thumbs up sign, something, it occurred to her, that seemed to be the thing to do in a helicopter at least once every few minutes. Philips was staring out the window. Rafter, too, though out the other side towards a cluster of trees and bushes.

Slowly, the helicopter lifted off the ground and as it did so it turned and faced south. Conway looked down at the mansion's rooftop; several faces were turned up in the helicopter's direction. She knew that even though she was in a friendly, the eyes in those faces would follow them until they were out of sight.

"We're going to proceed a ways before turning. We have a limit because of Reagan," the sergeant said. And as he said it Conway spotted a plane gliding in towards the airport on the far side of the Potomac. She also spotted a familiar landmark, one that brought back memories of her first serious kiss.

It was that school trip to the Basilica of the National Shrine of the Immaculate Conception, or the whopper church as Jimmy Turiso had insisted on calling it. Jimmy had been a determined suitor, at least for a fifteen year old.

He had argued that a kiss in a church, especially a whopper church, would mean that Cleo and Jimmy would be a match made in heaven. Luckily, and despite the quick smacker at the tail end of the guided tour line, that had not turned out to be the case. Conway and Jimmy Turiso had long parted ways. Those who kept track of alumni in general and who had kept track of Cleo Conway in particular had informed her that he lived out west somewhere and didn't stay in touch.

"Campanile and Carillon."

"What was that?" Philips was leaning towards Conway in an effort to better hear what she was saying.

"Oh, nothing. Just a memory from a long time ago," Conway replied as the helicopter began a long, looping turn on its way back to Andrews and the Secret Service car that would plunge them back into the earthbound traffic, along the highways and streets they had been silently reciting, supposedly at any rate.

She looked backwards over her shoulder in the direction of the White

House, but from this angle and distance it was almost entirely obscured by its freshly leafed-out trees. Turning, Conway considered the broad Potomac, a reason, and better than some of them as to why the nation's capital was where it was. The river had a soothing effect, and she forgot the streets and stared as the helicopter began to make a slow turn.

Beyond the river, which was high from recent rain, the line of trees signaled the beginning of the woodland that, as best as Falsham could tell, stretched all the way to the fens that lined the coast in these parts.

It was not his land, but up to the river bank on this side was now, beyond all argument and dispute, his newly acquired estate. He had pushed the mare hard in the ride from the house, and the animal was sweating and breathing heavily in the shade of an oak that, by its girth, was quite possibly above the ground in the time of Richard Lionheart.

As best he could estimate, it had taken most of two turns of the half hour glass to reach the new end to his world. Granted, he had been lost at one point, but he was more than pleased, indeed impressed with what he had secured on the word of the king, though, in a truth that could never be told, at the deliberate cost of the old man's life.

Once again a plot had resulted in bloodshed. This time, however, the shedding had been for a purpose, the creation of another plan, one that, Falsham had decided, would take time to bear fruit. Perhaps a lifetime, he thought. But in Ayvebury, and this was a comfort, he would have the perfect wellspring.

It had all proved uncommonly simple in the end. As the old man had planned it, he had feigned madness as the king and his cohort feasted that night. His rush at the royal person with dagger drawn was augmented with a shriek that had been truly alarming. Falsham had been in his allotted place and just as the king rose from his chair to meet his maker, Falsham had slashed at his friend with a long dagger.

John Falsham was expert with a blade. He had pulled its edge across the abdomen giving the old man reason to stop his lunge across the table. Quickly pulling its end back he had plunged the tip into the old man's side at a point where he knew the liver would be pierced. As his friend was already in grave health it had taken just this to fell him, and he had breathed no more than a moment before his life had gone from the room, and the world.

There had been uproar of course, and swords drawn in abundance to protect the king; but all a little late. Falsham had turned to face the king and in a loud voice had called "Your Majesty," this to focus the king's attention on him and him alone in what would prove to be a prolonged period of alarm and confusion. The king had duly fixed his eyes on Falsham, who in turn bowed low. In doing so he stared at the body of his friend and silently recited the Confiteor.

The following minutes were still unclear in Falsham's mind. Some of the king's more excitable followers had continued to make a great noise and fuss, shouting at the tops of their voices, "Protect the king!" They had made a great display of it. Others stood back, satisfied that the anger had passed. One or two had applauded, and one particularly large man had placed a hand on Falsham's shoulder. "Nobly done, sir," he had roared above the din.

One in the crowd cried "reward," doubtless an idea never too far from the minds of those in the king's inner circle.

It was only when some of the servants rushed over to lift Cole's lifeless body off the floor that Falsham again turned his eyes in the direction of the king. He bowed deeply before the royal person.

The king acknowledged this with a wave of one hand and silenced the room by raising high the other. It was at this moment that Falsham was aware of his greatest fear, that being mere thanks. But James had risen to the occasion with a speech in an accent that was for certain alien to Essex and a concluding act that witnessed the rising from bended knee of Sir John Falsham, new owner of Ayvebury and an honored servant of His Majesty who could pass the place down to his heirs, successors and so forth.

All had cheered heartily; the king confessed to a great appetite and called for venison. Sir John Falsham excused himself saying that he would personally inspect the cooking of the meat in the kitchen. He left the room and cupped his hands over his eyes. "Forgive me," he said before walking briskly towards the smell of roasting deer.

That had been the better part of a month ago and now the lord of Ayvebury was turning his horse around for a ride back to the house. His eyes caught sight of a kestrel in the meadow to his left. The falcon was hovering at about the height of four men. Suddenly it dropped into the grass, and Falsham knew it to be the end of a field mouse, or a mole perhaps.

"It's a good omen," he said. "We will pounce on this usurper king yet." He kicked hard at the mare's flanks, and she broke into a canter.

All the way back to the house, Falsham considered one thing when he wasn't bellowing at his mount, or for sheer joy.

How long, he wondered, was the life of a good omen? A year? A hundred years? More?

57

"**J**ESUS, WHO WROTE THIS THING?"

Before anyone in the room could answer, the president had raised his hand. He didn't require a response.

There were six in the Oval Office with more on the way, not least among them the defense secretary. Roger Simms, the president's national security advisor, and Maryann Blunt, the Secretary of State, sat immediately opposite the president's desk. The other three in the room were senior aides, and all were standing.

"The way I see it," said Packer, "the Reds have a copy of this on every desk that matters right now, and they might as well be all in here, because this piece of paper gives me the out that they expect us to take, am I not right, Roger?"

"Right on the mark, Mr. President. Beijing knows full well that the Taiwan Relations Act and the more recent amendments to it do not require a specific military response by the United States should the People's Republic of China launch a military attack on the Republic of China, Taiwan."

Simms had laid emphasis on the names of the Chinese capital and the formal name of the country in direct response to what he, and he well knew the State Department too, considered a pejorative.

And Packer well knew it.

"This act was drawn up when the Chinese were still running around in those Mao suits. I remember it well. I was in the House as the time, remember telling some of my friends on the Hill that we should do a Khrushchev on Taiwan, put in some nukes and aim them across the strait at the damn commies."

The world might be on the eve of destruction, but Packer wasn't above having his bit of fun, most especially at the expense of those he viewed, with great respect, sure, but also as being a little straight-laced, tight-assed. This was especially the case with Blunt, who, over the years had seemed intent on put-downs whenever he tried to loosen things up a bit in the Oval Office.

"Mr. President, at moments like this I almost regret that we didn't. If we had, the Chinese wouldn't be just thirty miles of Taipei right now and threatening to turn the town back into a rice paddy."

"Why, Maryann, you surprise me. Would have expected something like that from Roger."

"We can all have our fun, Mr. President."

Packer looked up and contemplated the Secretary of State. Damn good looking woman, he thought; single-handedly keeps the global pearl market afloat. But just that little bit too long in Harvard.

"Before I forget, Madam Secretary," he said, "but I was wondering if the Chinese, the Red Chinese, will be studying my reaction to this Taiwan guy when he turns up tomorrow for the trade conference. Crazy thing, isn't it? Here we are having a little party intended to put the pizzazz back in that Irish peace business, and the biggest wheel at the thing is a Chinese, well Taiwanese. A very rich one of course, but it's sure funny how the world works sometimes."

"Yes, Mr. President," came the simultaneous and, in Packer's mind, altogether unnecessary response from both Simms and Blunt.

"What I'm saying is that if I just shake the guy's hand and keep my distance, the head suits in Beijing will interpret that as no military response. If I put my arms around him and smile for the cameras, they won't be quite so sure. And If I give him one of those Russkie bear hugs they will be heading for the bomb shelters under Tian An Men Square. Or maybe those inscrutable oriental minds of theirs will see things in exactly the reverse of this."

Packer was taking delight in every politically incorrect term he could muster, but all in the room knew that his question had serious intent. The visit to the White House of the billionaire Mr. Lau represented a potential opportunity.

"I say squeeze the breath out of him," said Simms.

"Not too much, Blunt interjected."He is believed to be very ill, in fact, dying."

"Poor bastard," said Packer, as much to himself as the room. "I wonder if he could spare a few bucks in his will for Uncle Sam as well as the Brits and the Irish."

"Mr. President."

"My apologies, Maryann. Not in good taste."

The Secretary of State contented herself with a nod.

"Well, the question still stands," Packer said.

"Indeed, Mr. President." Packer turned his eyes on Simms. "My hunch is that you just shake his hand, don't smile and have what will appear as serious and reassuring words. Use hand gestures. Make it look as if you're giving him some sort of commitment and then pose for the cameras. Don't smile, look grave."

Packer leaned back in his swivel chair and said nothing for about twenty seconds.

"Fuck it, I'm going to give the bastard a hug. If he's one foot above the earth and heading for six below, he could do with one. I hear he collects photographs of himself with world leaders. It's his hobby, and I'm his first American president. I'm going to make sure he remembers the moment, at least for as long as he's with the rest of the living."

"Very well, Mr. President. And just let me say that that's exactly how I figured you would do it."

"I know you did, Roger. But seriously, I'm going to play this as I see it. Leave it to my gut, to the moment."

"Very well, Mr. President. In the meantime."

Packer raised his hand. "Yes, I know, our special friend. Where's he staying? The Mayflower?"

"Actually, no. He's spending the night at the British ambassador's residence."

"What, not on American soil?" It was mock indignation, but he played it well. All in the room understood. The president liked his little jokes.

"You know," Packer continued, "maybe I'll give old Spencer a hug, too. He's a prissy sort; doesn't like to be touched. Yeah, a little ball-breaking would warm up the day. We're talking before the lawn, right? We'll have to, of course, with this China mess. Remind me, how many ships have the Brits sent again?"

"Seven," said Simms.

Packer leaned back and counted seven on his fingers. "Seven, the magnificent seven. Should be twice that. The Chinese won't be too impressed. I'll have to hug old Spence good and hard, twist his arm a bit, too. Any other business? I need a bathroom check."

"No, Mr. President. You have a free half hour," said one of the aides standing to the rear of the seated secretaries.

"Good then," said Packer. "I think best in the bathroom as you know with my copy of 'Pole and Gun' or whatever it's called. We'll convene again in an hour. Platz should be here by then," he added in reference to the Secretary for Defense.

"Don't declare war or anything," he said as he rose from his chair.

"If he does, I'll be hammering on your bathroom door," said Maryann Blunt with a smile and a nod towards Simms.

"It won't be locked," said Packer, stretching and grinning in that boyish way that had landed him the support of a majority of voters, including many who were not sure of Packer as a leader on everyday political and economic issues, never mind a situation that could lead to a global conflagration.

Just a few miles from the Oval Office, in a side chapel in the national shrine admired from the skies by Cleo Conway, the old priest was sitting and thinking. He had done with praying, and his knees ached.

The chapel was adorned with the names of saints, ancient Irish ones from an island that had once produced holy men as if on a medieval conveyor belt. The production line had long come to a halt, gone into reverse according to some clerics from the island that had passed, very occasionally, through Ayvebury. But Ireland wasn't his concern. It was merely his device.

As he tried to imagine the event of the day that was to follow this one, the priest's mind wandered from his home and place of solace to London and across the water to Washington. Pulling together all the strands of the plan had been difficult, yes, but the timing and physical separation of key players now looked complete. Tomorrow, as the prime minister, the fallen angel of the whole affair, carried out his business at the White House, the heir to the throne would make his announcement in London that he had embraced the old faith.

And not just that. He would proclaim his sincerely held belief that the faith of his ancestors, before Henry, of course, and indeed the faith of some of his near relatives even now, was the only chance that Christendom had in the face of a world so changed, so fast changing, so close to its possible end.

The four priests had done their work well with the man who would be king. But they had paid with their lives as Spencer, a zealot who would have made a Tudor blush, worked at every level, down as low as murder, to prevent what would be the second great reformation in the glorious story that was England.

With Spencer in Washington and the overwhelming distraction of a possible war with China to keep his murderous mind distracted and fully occupied, the announcement in London would be made with a relative lack of immediate impact, and, more critically, potentially violent reaction.

The heir would, of course, be at pains to pay homage to the faith he had been born into and in which he had been raised and, yes, which he was now renouncing. But he would contend, with the most diplomatic language he could muster, that it was simply not up to the great struggle that lay ahead.

Knowing full well the uproar that his statement would cause, the decision had been made to deliver it away from any royal ground. It would be unleashed to the world on a visit to a model organic farm, in Essex as it happened, and only a dozen miles from Ayvebury.

The old priest smiled at the thought. He clasped his hands together, got down on his knees one more time and bowed his head.

"Thy will be done," he said to the empty chapel.

58

S PECIAL AGENT CLEO CONWAY took a deep breath. It did little to relieve her pent up tension.

But she smiled nevertheless as she passed through the security check at the main gate of the White House. Smiled on the outside, grimaced within. Nerves, she thought, normal nerves. It was her first day on the job with the president. She would be fine when she teamed up with the others and taken her orders from the lead agent in the presidential detail, the legendary Dutch Dalton.

Conway stood for a moment inside the gate and looked down to her shoes. She was looking good on the outside. She had to give herself some credit on that account. Her charcoal pantsuit was made of a blend of fibers that the sales assistant had sworn would keep her cool on an early summer's day, even in Washington.

She glanced at her lapel pin, the right pattern for the day and the guarantee of absolute access, right up to the president's side. Her father would be proud, she thought, and she took another lungful of the now noticeably humid air.

Slowly at first, and then a little more deliberately, though not quickly, she walked up the driveway towards the main door of the mansion. There were only a couple of people in sight, a television crew by the looks of things, over by the West Wing.

Still, she knew that eyes would be watching. They always were. And she also expected the uniformed guard who stepped out from behind one of the pillars just as she reached the portico. He nodded and held the door for her, and she was inside where the air conditioning offered immediate relief.

Conway glanced at her watch. She was only a couple of minutes late, and that wasn't too bad, considering. Dalton wasn't the type to make a scene. He usually expressed his dissatisfaction with a look. Right now she could take on of those looks and deal with it. Maybe he wouldn't notice. But he did.

Dalton and the other agents were gathered just outside the back under the Truman Balcony. Dalton was pointing at some bushes and speaking with that slow stateless drawl of his. When he spotted Conway he, too, glanced at his watch and frowned. But he left it at that.

"Special Agent Conway, good morning," he said. And that was it.

"Good morning, sir," Conway responded. "Sorry for being late, but. . ."

"The traffic," Dalton interjected. "Anyway, I was saying. Heck, I won't say it. Rafter is taking his damn time in the bathroom. Maybe somebody should fetch him."

"Here he comes, sir," said Conway, feeling relieved to have the focus placed on someone else.

Dalton said nothing as Rafter merged with the clutch of special agents that would be the main security contingent on and around the South Lawn for the event later in the day. Conway glanced around the lawn, her gaze moving in an arc from left to right. Judging by the number of cameras already in place, and technicians fussing around them, the press turnout was going to be huge. This had nothing to do with the reason for the gathering of course. Ireland was all well and good, but the presence of the president and prime minister with war possible at any moment was the primary reason for a maximum media turnout.

It would be hectic, maybe a little crazy, Conway thought, and as she did, Dalton's words confirmed her belief.

"It's going to be nuts here this afternoon. And to make it worse, you can be damn certain that the president is going to bust through the rope and do the tango with everyone in reach, especially the good looking women."

Dalton was old school, and Conway knew well enough to ignore much of his social observations. That he was good at his job, some said the best, was more than enough to give him a pass.

"Okay," Dalton continued, "you all have your assignments. We meet inside in thirty minutes, and then we'll take over from the current crew. Do what you have to do meantime, get a coffee, use the bathroom."

At this, he turned and walked briskly back into the building. Conway, uncertain for a moment, decided that a rest room stop was a good idea. Rafter, standing beside her and seeming to read her mind, pointed with his finger.

"It's over there," he said. "Just through the room with all the books, presidential papers by the look of them"

"Thanks, I know," Conway replied. As she turned to walk away, her cell phone began to vibrate.

The agents, they would have been interested to know, were being more than casually observed. Pender, at times with his eyes, and for moments through a lens, had been watching the pep talk delivered by Dalton. Pender had entered the grounds at the earliest permissible time and a lot sooner than he would have done at a normal shoot. But this was not a normal shoot, and he had smiled at the pun. He assumed there would be no shooting at all unless one of the Secret Service agents had turned rogue, or suddenly flipped his lid. No, he thought, it wouldn't be bullets.

He knew only what the old priest had told him. He was aware of the Irish diplomat's role, too, or at least some of it. And like his own, it seemed pretty simple. Manning had to set up the photograph for Pender. It was to have only three subjects, the president, the prime minister and the Taiwanese guy. This was an absolute. Manning was to make sure that his ambassador and the visiting Irish politicians, no doubt camera happy, were steered off into another corner, though with the promise of inclusion in the next picture.

Manning, obviously, would be aware of Pender's presence. They had lived for a few days under the same roof in the shadow of that mountain. Pender reckoned that Manning even knew of the photographer's own limited but crucial part in what was to be a delicate choreography with a fatal twist of historical dimensions.

"Unbelievable," Pender said, turning a knob on his tripod for the tenth time.

But he had witnessed the unbelievable before, participated in it, caused it to happen. This, however, was something entirely different from all his previous assignments. Still, there was no arguing with the money. This was the mother of all paydays, and he would even make money on the climactic photo, along with everyone else of course. No matter, the more the merrier. An army of photographers and cameramen was perfect cover.

And cover was what precisely the old priest had in mind. He, too, was watching the preliminary proceedings from outside the railings that were designed to keep the uninvited off the White House grounds.

For the time being, tourists and passersby were being allowed approach the black painted fence, but all would be corralled farther away once the South Lawn ceremonies got underway.

No matter, the old man thought. He would not be lingering for the moment of truth. He was intent on enjoying a leisurely afternoon at the Smithsonian. He had only once before visited Washington, and that had been many years ago. And he had spent most of that sojourn confined to Georgetown University on a spiritual retreat.

Slowly, he turned away and fixed his eyes on the National Monument. He would walk there first and then proceed to the museum. There was nothing more he could do. He could neither interfere with, guide nor affect the ultimate outcome of events on the South Lawn. In a few hours, his plan, his plot, would be executed. Or it would fail.

Reaching into his coat, he took out the pocket watch that had belonged to his father, whose tenure at Ayvebury had seen the house turn from a family home into a place of spiritual learning, a repository of universal truth. It was a reliable instrument. If it was wound at the required intervals, though not too tightly, it would keep precise time. It was, the old priest thought, not unlike faith itself, sturdy, reliable, working at all times and always blessed with an answer, that being the hour of the day.

He stared at the watch face and calculated the course of events based on the time difference between Washington and London. If all went to plan, or roughly close to it, the prince would be making his announcement just minutes before the scheduled climax of the trade conference which, of course, included a speech by the prime minister.

Reporters on hand would be made aware instantly of the enormous story breaking in London. Questions would fly, and Spencer would know that he had failed. With this knowledge, and before he could plan any retaliation, the South Lawn Plot would reach its own high point, thus giving the reporters more news than they could conceive in their wildest dreams.

And then? Well, assuming the plan was carried out with watch-like precision, the investigation would proceed down an entirely incorrect path. The Americans would assume their president had been the primary target, the British prime minister merely collateral damage, as the Americans themselves liked to put it. And the investigation would lead immediately to the perpetrator, Mr. Lau. The Secret Service would become aware of his fury over the selling out of his island home, not yet a known fact but one that was, well, lying just over the horizon. The fact that Mr. Lau was terminally ill would ensure that the assassination and simultaneous suicide was an open and shut case.

It all seemed logical enough, though the old priest was acutely aware that the best plans could go awry. But assuming all was in place, why would it not succeed?

For a little reassurance, he said yet another silent prayer. Not just for the desired outcome, but the most perfect outcome. That there would be no additional injuries or fatalities. Morality demanded sacrifice, but not excessive loss of life. With this thought in mind, the old priest fixed his eyes on the monument and began to walk.

59

Bailey had not slept very well despite the comfort of the room in the hotel with the oh-so-English name. He was standing in the lobby, contemplating breakfast, a light one, or maybe the whole hog, the full English with trimmings.

It would be the main decision of a day that appeared to be set in stone. From the hotel he would go to the White House and there cover the conference which really wasn't much of a conference at all now, only a series of private meetings involving the Taiwanese billionaire and various officials followed by a South Lawn reception. The conference had been pegged back at the last minute because of the looming threat of war. The party, however, was a go, assuming the world didn't end in the meantime.

Global Armageddon apart, Bailey also had to consider the statements by the political leaders, most especially the prime minister and the president. And they looked as if they were going to be a little too close to deadline for absolute comfort given the five-hour time difference. He would have to work fast

Bailey's lack of sleep had mostly to do with the constant stream of text messages from Henderson, the latest being an instruction to call. Henderson clearly had been in the office from an early hour and was agitated by something more than just the narrow window of time for the story from Washington.

No, Bailey thought, Henderson didn't give a fiddler's about the conference, not when he had the possible war to end all wars waiting in the wings for the front page, perhaps the last ever front page, the final edition of all final editions.

The conference made it into the frame because of its cast of characters, not its content or purpose.

Bailey had this just about worked out when his phone went off. He had set it on vibrate so as not to alarm the locals with his ringer, a little ditty from that long ago punk band, the Sex Pistols.

He was about to parry Henderson's latest onslaught when the voice at the other end cut him dead.

"Hey," he said. It was Samantha.

"And good morning to you. Yes, I understand, but let's try to have a quick get together at the White House. I'm not sure how much rope they are giving us, but you could probably scout us out before you bring Spencer over for a chat. Okay, all right, bye."

Bailey had stopped short of pledging his undying love, or had rather been stopped short by Samantha who just had to dash, or words to that effect.

Perhaps it was the lingering echo of her voice but when his phone went off again he had hit the on button before the second vibration. It wasn't Samantha, and it wasn't even Henderson. It was George Dawes giving him a head's up. Henderson wanted Dawes to pad out the story from New York, especially if the conference ran behind schedule. Bailey indicated his agreement.

"No problem, mate," he said. "And make sure you get your byline."

There was one more thing. Henderson, apparently tied up at a meeting, had passed on a phone number belonging to a man named Sydney Small. Henderson, said Dawes, had given clear instruction that Bailey should call the number as soon as he got it. And that was now.

"Loud and clear, George," said Bailey. "I'll call you from the White House and let you know how we are getting along."

Bailey stared at his phone. Sydney Small, the man of many mysteries, the man who had told him in the pub that he would lay every last quid he had on the fact that the prime minister was up to his eyeballs in something that was no good, indeed downright nasty, and that the man was a danger to the lives and limbs of a lot of people, some of them rather prominent.

How, Bailey had asked Small, did he come across all this and what reason did he have to believe that the prime minister was dodgy, even dangerous?

Small had clammed up under this questioning. It was clear he wanted to send Bailey out on some line of investigation but equally evident that he did not fully trust the reporter. His parting line, after he had stood Bailey another drink, was to deliver some odd line about the royal family, or at least the prince, being in the line of Spencer's fire.

And now he wanted Bailey to call him.

"Christ," said Bailey, loudly enough to turn a couple of heads in the foyer. And then rather more quietly though he felt compelled to speak the words, "The world's about to nuke itself, and I'm in the middle of some plot out of bloody Shakespeare."

And that about said it. It was all a bit much, but it had helped him make one decision. If the world was going to end he wasn't going to meet his maker while hungry. Bailey walked across the lobby and into the restaurant. It would be a full on breakfast, a heart attack on a plate.

Manning had gulped a cup of coffee and considered himself lucky. He had slept poorly, almost not at all. Then he had nodded off within minutes of the alarm going off. It had been a rude awakening.

It was Rebecca's turn to get Jessica to school so Manning had been able to make his progress undisturbed through his necessary ablutions. The breakfast part of his normal ritual had to be sacrificed to the god of nattiness. Evans would be on her toes today, her eyes searching for any stain on her country's reputation.

Manning had allowed Rebecca to choose his tie. She had also picked out a blue shirt that made for a contrast with his usual white. The suit was a sober dark blue. He would be the sharpest looking man at the White House, Rebecca had assured him.

That might not matter much, of course. Today would be judged at a variety of levels with personal appearance somewhere between dollars and cents bagged for the old country, or at least its northern part, and suitable dinner invitations collected by Evans. Manning comforted himself with the thought that the gig was mainly an Anglo-American affair with the Irish tagging along for the party.

Beyond these considerations, there was just darkness. His main task was to keep Evans and the visiting ministers well away from the American president, British prime minister and the mega rich Chinese guy, Lau, and most especially from the location on the South Lawn where the three were to be photographed.

That was all there was to it, he had been assured. Nothing more than a little diplomatic choreography at the crucial moment and his past life would be his, and his alone, for the rest of his days. Manning had wondered long and hard of course. Could these people be trusted? Would his so-called terrorist past be finally buried?

At the end of all the thinking he had concluded that he had really no choice. He had to trust the bastards, those inside the British security services, and those who lurked in other shadowy corners.

As he sat at the kitchen table staring into his black coffee, Manning tried to imagine a freedom he had never really known in his adult life. He wanted to feel optimism, something beyond just hope. But he had also made a decision.

If he was betrayed, he would have to take action, act like the fighter he had once been. How he would pull that off in his present circumstances was far from clear. And the coffee gave him no answers. As he promised he would do, Manning loaded the dishwasher. Funny, he thought, how the mundane tasks in life could tie in so closely to those that decided the course of a life.

His course today was set, that of all future days still uncertain. He would go to the office for a while, check his emails and snail mail. And he would tease Nesbitt because he was he was bogged down in the office with work and would be missing the big shindig at the White House. Evans was not expected at the embassy. She was having lunch with the visiting ministers before heading to the White House. That would make the early part of the day a little easier. The end, he assumed, would not be easy because clearly something big was going down at 1600 Pennsylvania Avenue. It would make headlines and history. And he would be there for it. Knowing this he had a plan for the preceding hours. To his colleagues at the embassy he would appear in a good form. He would make light of all things, seemingly not having a care in the world because as sure as the day was getting warmer by the minute, he would be one of many people answering the questions of federal investigators by sundown.

"Here we go," he said as he left by the back door.

Packer had asked to be left alone for a few minutes. He liked doing this, sorting out his thoughts on a day that would be dominated by pleasantries and ritual. He wasn't much for this kind of stuff. He enjoyed policy meetings and big speeches. And he had always been lucky enough to have the common touch. He genuinely liked campaigning, meeting folks. He knew that he gave the Secret Service nightmares by the way that he would constantly push against the security boundaries around him, but what the hell. He was the president, not some untouchable holy man.

Packer's unease with pomp had always been at a higher pitch when dealing with the British. Yes, the special relationship, what was left of it, demanded a little extra, and it had been a thrill meeting royalty. But there always had been that strain of having to be on his extra best behavior for the Brits. It was, perhaps, the First Lady's fault. She was infatuated with all things British to the point that had he been George Washington he would have had her arrested as a loyalist. Packer laughed out loud at the memory of one royal encounter when he had suddenly been overtaken by a near overwhelming desire to fart. Only the fact that his wife was within range of the fallout prevented the kind of fusillade that had last been directed at the British at the Battle of New Orleans.

Today would be another temptation. He had never particularly liked Spencer, had much preferred his predecessor. There was something about the guy, though he could never quite work out what. One thing he did know for certain, and that was the visitors, the Brits and the Irish, would go on and on about the Washington weather to the point that he would almost feel the need to apologize. And it was beginning to cook a bit outside. Good enough for them, Packer thought. He would nod in agreement and offer sympathy of course, but he knew that once again that inner voice would be telling them to go take a swim in the Potomac.

Packer's thoughts of swimming and a renewed war, this time against suffocating etiquette, were interrupted by his secretary's voice.

"Oh yes, the Secret Service detail," he responded. "A couple of new ones, too. Send them in."

60

As it transpired, it was Special Agent Rafter who was assigned the president's belt. And he, Rafter that is, was none too pleased. The duty was simple enough. The agent stood directly behind the president as he worked the rope line, a hand firmly around the president's belt, not the top of his pants. The belt would be worn slightly loose to facilitate the grip.

In the event of any threatening incident, if anyone lunged or struck out at the president, the agent would tug sharply on the belt. The president would then be bundled to safety by other agents as the agent who did the tugging, and others, blocked the assailant, or assailants. The move had been practiced over and over, though had never been carried out during the Packer presidency.

Packer, however, had posed another problem for the Secret Service. He had a habit of breaking out of his protective corral and plunging into a crowd. Bad enough this would happen with the already security checked attendees during a White House event, but the president had broken loose on the road as well. It was a nightmare as far as the Service was concerned, but no effort to dissuade the president had been successful, thus far.

In the event of the president passing beyond the end of the line on the South Lawn, Rafter would stay with him and instead of clinging to the belt would hang on grimly to the tail end of the president's suit jacket. The president had acquiesced in this tactic, though only after joking that he would, as a consequence, confine himself to cheap suits so as to avoid expensive repair bills being foisted on the American taxpayer.

There was one, quite specific, reason for assigning Rafter to the belt. The president was a big man. So, too, was Rafter, a onetime football player with prospects who had famously charged in for a touchdown in a high school game with at least four opponents hanging off him. There had been a photo in the window of the town newspaper office for months afterward. Rafter had earned the nickname "Hulk" for his moment of glory. The old timers in the town had agreed that the young man would make something of himself. And their prediction had borne out. Hulk's hand was on the President of the United States and the president's safety hinged on its firmness.

There was more to Rafter's life story, of course, and part of it was the hand of an elderly English priest which, as it transpired, was now directing its course on the day that the onetime football star had been assigned the nation's first belt.

Rafter's life had veered back and forth after high school. He had attended college in the state system and had graduated with a most unlikely degree in Greek and Roman Civilization. It had been suggested that his interest had been spurred less by the civilization part of his studies than by a reverence for the Spartans at Thermopylae and the exploits of gladiators in the Coliseum, this apparently sparked by a senior year trip to Italy during high school.

Either way, several of Rafter's classmates had proceeded into military careers armed with the tactical theories of Alexander the Great, Caesar and Scipio. Rafter's long march had brought him to the ranks to the United States Secret Service.

What had marched with him was a taste for gambling that he had managed to unload for a while in his early days in the Service, but which had lately made a comeback.

It was tripwire with the potential to end his career, and it would definitely be uncovered in one of, if not precisely the next, security review that all agents had to undergo.

So, it was not all that difficult to accept the money along with the bundle of assurances that his role in the coming drama would be a minor one, that the president absolutely would not be harmed, and that in fact his part in the outcome would earn him a commendation, if not more.

Despite all his exterior toughness, Rafter was vulnerable to the approach from the man with the clipped Brit accent. He had wavered, naturally, but the huge advance, deposited in an offshore account in the name of a fictional company that the bank recognized as being owned by an American businessman named Smith, had brought Rafter onside.

As a member of the Secret Service, he could only admire his suitor's attention to detail, right down the excellent fake passport that was the key to the money that would resolve all his financial issues while leaving plenty more for a comfortable retirement.

And all he had to do was plant a piece of paper in a book, between page 100 and 101.

Rafter was contemplating his new riches when the voice of Cleo Conway rushed through the wire into his receiving ear. Conway said but two words. And in response to her "Let's go," Rafter finished his task in the bathroom and hurried outside into the heat of the day and into the eyes of a gathering crowd on the lawn, one which invariably was as curious, though idly so, about the agents in their trim suits and shades as the agents, in an active, professional sense, were about the faces that made up the throng.

Rafter took one look and decided that what lay ahead would have been a breeze if not for the event that had been described to him by the old padre.

Jesus Christ, he thought, some of them are going to fucking faint.

Pender, through his camera lens, had spotted Manning in the crowd that was now beginning to fill the area of the South Lawn assigned to the reception. The diplomat looked tense. He had not noticed Pender but then again, people at these things rarely noticed the faces behind the cameras.

There was about thirty minutes to go before the formalities began, though, as yet, no sign of the guest of honor, the Taiwanese guy. Pender was curious as to what the old priest had in mind, but all he knew, all he wanted to know, was that he was to capture what would be the climactic moment, the biggest story for years barring the outbreak of global war, which, of course, was also possible.

But not, Pender hoped, in the next hour. All he wanted was his shot, his money and his escape into anonymity. As he was mulling over the security of the Swiss banking system in the event of thermonuclear warfare (he reckoned Swiss bankers would come through the thing along with rats and cockroaches,) he noticed in the corner of his non-lens eye a kerfuffle about twenty yards to his left. Some of the reporters who had been mingling with guests were gathered around someone, recorders and notebooks now in action. Pender noted the gathering but stayed put. He stared though his lens again looking for Manning, but now there was no sign of the Irishman.

"Where are you, Mr. First Secretary?" he whispered. And in a sweep of the crowd he found him again, in a knot of suits. The Taiwanese savior of the Irish peace had arrived. Now, Pender, thought, if only Belfast isn't on some target list for a Beijing rocket, all would be fine.

Bailey was juggling. He wanted to get everything on tape but was equally determined to get key lines down on paper so he could fire them across without having to keep pressing rewind and play. Colleagues laughed at him about his tapes, called him a dinosaur. But he didn't trust digital recorders.

His phone had nearly blown out of his pocket. He could tell at this stage of his career when a call was coming from the office, and he reckoned he could also sense the size of the story. And this one, on any day, was a whopper.

Henderson had given him the main lines. The heir to the throne had just staged a press conference in which he had declared himself a Roman Catholic, had denounced the Act of Settlement which barred members of the Roman church from ascending to the throne. Crucially, however, he had not renounced his claim to the throne. By not doing so he had added exponentially to a constitutional crisis just as the prime minister was about to have his big White House moment.

Bailey had felt almost giddy. It was for moments like this that he had become a reporter. What was now happening had reminded him of a mantra which went along the lines that you had to be good to be lucky in the news business. This was proof enough. He was good, damn bloody good.

The scrum around the young man with the nametag that identified him as Roger Jones from the embassy was made up almost entirely of British reporters and one or two photographers who had drifted over from their corral. There were a couple of Yanks and Bailey had heard an Irish accent. The Irish, he knew, were nuts about the royals, and what had now transpired was certain to elbow the ceremonial check presentation down even Irish news lists.

Jones, who looked like he still should be in university, had clearly been pushed out as a stopgap, a sacrificial lamb for the braying hounds of the press. Spencer, thought Bailey, was a smart bastard. A diplomat could only say so much under the circumstances and would buy time while the Downing Street crowd inside the presidential mansion cobbled together a response to the obvious uproar that was enveloping the United Kingdom, 3,000 miles to the east.

"The bloody Chinese must be thrilled with this," said one reporter. It was a statement, not a question, but it was directed at Jones who had by now broken out into quite a sweat.

"I cannot comment on Chinese reaction," said Jones gamely. But he was sweating blood right now, and the reporters could smell it.

"Is the prime minister going to pull out of the ceremony now? And if not, can we speak with him before it actually starts?"

The question, both barrels, seemed to knock Jones backwards.

"I cannot comment, I mean, I cannot say. Ladies and gentlemen, if you will excuse me, I have to go back inside the White House. I'm sure there will be more from, ah, the prime minister's own spokesman soon, very soon."

Jones turned and made a move to leave but could make very little progress. The pack moved with him as he struggled to make his way back to the
nearest door. Bailey, however, did not move. Something had hit him with all
the subtlety of a cruise missile.

That face, he thought, the one in the photograph in the old house in Essex,
Ayvebury. It had indeed been the prime minister's, years ago, when Spencer
was about the same age as the harried Jones. The old priest, the dead priests.
There was a connection to the prince, there had to be. He dropped his recorder
in his pocket and started thumping numbers on his phone. Henderson would
know. The man had an unerring instinct for stitching together seemingly random occurrences. He would lay it out for Henderson and Henderson would
know that there had been murders, that the reason for them was connected
somehow to the next king and that the prime minister could very well be up
to his tonsils in the entire affair.

"Sweet Jesus," said Bailey, just as Henderson's voice barked at the other
end of the signal.

Henderson told him to hold on and as he did so Bailey could hear him
shouting at someone, something about being short-staffed and if he wanted
to pull guys off soccer and cricket for the biggest story in years he was bloody
well going to do so.

Bailey smiled. He could imagine the scene in the newsroom as Henderson
went into full battle mode. He was glad to be removed from it, if not exactly
away.

Henderson, turning his mind to Washington now, was a little calmer.

"Just throw me everything you can get," he said.

"Don't let Spencer off the hook. This is a full-blown crisis no matter what
he says, and if he calls the prince a nutter I want the word nutter in the story.
Don't hold back, don't sit on anything, call me in an hour."

And he was gone.

Roger Jones had made it back into the White House, and Bailey's colleagues were dispersing to the shade of various trees to call through to their
offices.

Bailey, too, was on his phone again, this time to Samantha who was inside
with Spencer. He wasn't surprised when he only got her message. She would be
hooked up by now to her copper colleagues as they prepared to escort Spencer
to the microphones.

"Sod it," he said. He would have to get word to her by some means.

Samantha Walsh didn't know it, but she was protecting a man who might well have had a hand in four murders.

He glanced at his watch. Fifteen minutes to kickoff.

As if on cue, some juiced up Irish traditional band had just launched itself into a frenzy on the stage set up just to one side of the speaking podium.

Bailey shook his head. He started to laugh. He needed a drink.

61

M<small>ANNING HAD HIS RADAR TURNED ON FULL</small>. The ambassador was running late. For the moment Lau was occupied by a group of officials from the various interested parties. There was a man he knew from Belfast in the thick of it, acting as a kind of impresario. Everybody wanted a piece of the Taiwanese billionaire, and from him. The Belfast official was grimly sticking to his man, holding him by the arm. Lau, for his part, looked a little out of it. His health was not good.

Manning heard the ambassador before he saw her, and in turning to match eye contact with that unmistakable voice, he caught a momentary glimpse of the photographer, Pender. Whatever was going to go down it was clear that Pender would play a role. Just precisely what it would be he could only guess at; only he preferred not to guess at all.

"Madam Ambassador," Manning said in a familiar tone that only the most alert would conclude was ever so slightly mocking.

"Well," came the reply, "at least everyone turned up. Any sight of the president and the prime minister and, oh there he is, poor Mr. Lau. I hear he's not too well."

"Not the best," said Manning. "Before we do anything else, we should meet with the minister. His plane was a little late but he arrived a few minutes ago. He's over under that open sided tent."

Evans looked at Manning, her eyes narrowed. She was about to pronounce rather than merely say something.

"I'll go over and say hello, of course, but after that it's your job, Eamonn, to keep that dreadful man away from me. I'm determined to enjoy myself here today. It's a splendid opportunity."

Her words fell below audible level. Phillipa Evans had spotted someone worth her attention and was gone. The minister would simply have to wait.

Conway was breathing slowly in and out in an effort to relax. Jim Schrull, one of the two most senior agents on the presidential detail had noticed her nervousness and had nodded in an affirming way. Jack Garraty, the other old hand, had winked at her. The president referred to them as his Jack and Joker.

Packer was fond of cards, and throughout his term there had been late night card games in the family quarters whenever the state of the country, or the world, allowed for a couple of hours of poker, or a version that the president had himself concocted and liked to call Oklahoma Throw 'Em.

"Wouldn't want Texas to get all the glory," he had told a reporter who had inquired about what had become known in some corners of the press as the president's Canasta Cabinet.

"About ten minutes to lift off," Schrull said as he fiddled with his earpiece. "The big man is in the bathroom freshening up."

Conway noticed that Rafter was flexing the fingers on his left hand. He would hold the president's belt with that hand so would be standing slightly behind and to the president's right. Schrull would be just ahead of the president as he moved down the greeting line with Garraty to Packer's right. Conway was on point, a few feet beyond Schrull. She was the scout.

Other agents would be scanning the crowd but Conway, Schrull, Rafter and Garraty would be the infield group.

It had been decided that the president would do his meet and greet routine before joining the Irish visitors for the photo-op with Henry Lau, who, for all intents and purposes, was the main guest of honor. Then the president would be pictured alone with Lau. It would be his little favor to a dying man.

It was all simple enough, Conway thought. She continued to hold on to this thought as her cell phone, which she had kept in her pocket and had set to vibrate mode, erupted for a second time. She reached for it and, taking a quick glance at the caller's number, put it to her ear. "Yes," she hissed.

Bailey, along with the rest of the British press corps, traveling and American-based, had by now wandered back into the general melee. He thought for a moment about approaching the Taiwanese star of the show, Lau, but thought better of it as the man was at that moment being smothered by a rather loud woman in an outfit that more than matched the heat of the day. Bailey got close enough to hear the woman issue an invitation to visit Dublin before seeking out the shade of a tree.

He was, he knew, going to have to focus all his attention on Spencer. To hell with all the rest of it, he thought. He found himself shivering despite the temperature that must have been pushing ninety degrees. And as if to confirm this his eye caught sight of a soaring thunderhead which looked for all the world like an atomic mushroom cloud over the city.

Bugger, he thought, that thing better hold off until after the ceremony. Spencer, he knew, would probably seize upon any excuse to duck back into the shelter of the president's house.

As a young man, Henry Lau had indulged himself in various martial arts disciplines. He was drawing upon all his mental and physical reserves, though only in part due to the verbal assault from the Irish ambassador to the United States. She had apparently enjoyed her visit to China a few years back, a sojourn that had taken in Beijing, Shanghai, Xian and those magnificent terra cotta soldiers and Hong Kong, oh wonderful Hong Kong.

Lau smiled and nodded as best he could, but he was in a losing battle. Because of the task he would in minutes have to perform he had gone without his full dosage of painkillers; indeed he had taken nothing at all beyond a couple of aspirin. Soon, he knew, the pain would be unbearable. For most people that point would have already passed. But Henry Lau wasn't everybody, an idea he allowed swirl around in his mind for the past several hours. It was becoming harder to remain focused on it, however, and this woman was threatening to break down his final reserves.

"Madam, sadly I have never been to these places you speak of since my childhood. I have never been to the China some refer to as the mainland. Now, if you will excuse me, I do need to visit the bathroom."

To the sound of an "oh dear" and the sight of a determined refocusing of attention on another victim standing nearby, Lau bowed his head and with the aid of his walking stick made for what he had been told by a White House assistant was the bathroom just inside a door at the rear of the mansion.

Lau continued to smile and nod at people as he walked, whether others acknowledged him or not. He had traveled to the White House alone, save for a driver who would soon hear some shocking news concerning his charge.

In moments, he had reached the air-conditioned interior of the house and followed a sign that led into a room off of which was one of the world's most exclusive pit stops. Lau could not help but smile, though he did not veer for an instant from his target. It was a book at the end of a row of books, third shelf from the top. The anteroom was lined with shelves carrying volumes of presidential papers. The book that he sought was packed with the thoughts, words and deeds of Richard Nixon, and it was right beside the bathroom door.

Lau glanced around. Another guest was staring at others books across the room, and he was aware of a couple of people talking excitedly in the bathroom.

Lau withdrew the volume and inserted the crook of his stick in his suit pocket. He flipped through the pages until he reached page one hundred. It was here that the blank piece of paper had been inserted by the American Secret Service agent in the employ of the English secret agent, Burdin. There was nothing remarkable about the paper. It was a little darker than the pages in the book but there was nothing to indicate that it had the potential to kill.

Lau carefully took the page and folded it. This he could do. The substance that it had been coated with, seemingly one of the most deadly potions concocted by the old KGB's Executive Action Department V, was at this point inert. It only became effective when brought into contact with liquid, which, Lau thought, was somehow appropriate given that Department V's work, which centered more or less on murder, sabotage and kidnapping, was collectively referred to as, in the jargon of the time, wet affairs.

Lau placed the page gently in his pocket and glanced into the bathroom. The man who was talking was stuffing paper towels adorned with the presidential seal into his pocket. The man he was babbling to was in a cubicle.

Lau turned, grabbed his stick and with all the strength he was still able to draw upon, made his way back to the South Lawn and its chattering horde.

Everything was working. Everything would work. His people would have their revenge at the very point of being betrayed.

62

CONWAY DABBED HER BROW WITH A TISSUE. She was still inside so her discomfort had nothing to do with the heat. It had been the cell phone call from the Globescan office. She didn't quite know what to make of it. Neither did her caller and the rest of them in the office, although they were trying to stitch things together.

The bottom line, based on information coming in from Britain through media, official and intelligence channels, was that the prince's defection, for want of a better word, was somehow tied to a series of murders of Catholic priests and that there was a connection, unclear and unproven, to the office of the prime minister, to Number 10 Downing Street.

Conway was staring at the door. The president and Spencer were due to appear at any second after their private conversation in the West Wing. And as she considered whether not to tell her superiors about the storm breaking about the guest of honor's head, the two men came into view, Packer leading Spencer by the arm and pointing at portraits of presidents and patriots, one or two of whom had distinguished themselves battling the prime minister's predecessors.

"And as you know, Mr. Prime Minister, we might be rolling out the cannon again in the next couple of days."

To Conway's ear, Packer's already booming voice seemed to have risen a few decibels. Clearly, she thought, the president's adrenaline was up. It would mean that he would be extra lively with the crowd and would no doubt bust through the rope.

She tapped her earphone, nodded to the other agents who would be taking the lead with her and stepped in front of the president and Spencer. Dalton, she knew, would be bringing up the rear along with Rafter, the president's belt buddy.

Conway had decided not to wear sunglasses on her debut and, as it turned out, they were unnecessary. It had turned cloudy, although the heat of the afternoon was a slap to the senses as soon as they were clear of the building and its circulated, cool air.

The crowd was milling about the lawn with many taking refuge under the canopy where drinks were being served. There were no chairs. The ceremony was to be a truncated one given the situation on the far side of the globe. Sometimes, Conway thought, geopolitics had its virtues. A couple of short speeches, the presentation of a ceremonial check, photos and some flesh-pressing and her debut would be over.

She walked slowly towards the steps leading up to the stage, ignoring the band's hailing to the chief and taking in the people lining the velvet rope. They were applauding and cheering, some were overly excited; none appeared to be threatening.

Walking in front of the stage, Conway kept her eyes looking left. Dalton and Rafter would be mounting the stage with the president. She was to stand with her back to the presidential podium. And as she did so she noticed some in the crowd were staring at her. This, of course, was potentially distracting so she gave into the inevitable, reached into her suit pocket and extracted her Ray Bans.

Now I look the part, she thought, and as she did so, Packer began to speak.

Pender had his lens focused on Lau. The news from Britain had made its way from the reporters to the photographers with the inevitable result. Most of the cameras were pointed towards Spencer, a few at the president. But Pender had Lau in his sights. He was sitting behind the president staring out over the crowd and into the distance. He didn't look too well. But, of course, he wasn't. Pender checked his watch. It was almost four, the appointed hour for the presentation and ceremonial handshakes. He shook his head and rolled his eyes as a rumble of thunder to his rear grew louder.

"But, of course," he said as he reached for a camera cover though, as yet, it had not started to rain.

The changing weather seemed to energize the various White House aides and the security teams hovering around both leaders. Packer, his long arms extended, began to herd his guests off the podium towards a spot on the lawn where a green mat had been placed.

Lau moved with surprising agility despite the walking cane, Pender observed. The group descended from the podium and took its position for what the program had described as the ceremonial presentation of a check, or a presentation of a ceremonial check, Pender could not quite remember which.

The president was all smiles. Spencer looked grim because this was the point that reporters would get to ask questions. Lau seemed to be smiling, or trying to. The three lined up at their designated spot, fifteen feet from the camera positions.

"This is a great day. Despite the cloud hanging over our world, this is proof positive that the work of peace goes on. I hope it will inspire others to embrace that path of peace," Packer said to a smattering of applause.

It was a clear reference to the Chinese, and Pender noticed Lau nodding. The man was no longer smiling.

Pender lifted his head momentarily to get his bearings. Spencer was on his left, Lau was in the middle, and Packer was on his right. On either side, but just outside what would be the frame of the coming photographs were two women, one a buffed looking Secret Service agent standing to Packer's left. A smaller woman with short blonde hair was standing a little behind and to Spencer's right. Another man was a standing right behind Packer but would not figure once Pender had zoomed in on his big three.

"Here we go," he said as his eye returned to his camera.

He would later tell a friend that the next few seconds seemed to last minutes with the added effect that they would rewind in his mind's eye, over and over. Packer was talking and gesticulating with his hands, Spencer was nodding. Lau was leaning over on his stick and seemingly putting something in his mouth.

Now he was standing straight, a look of amazement on his face, or so it seemed. He began to convulse even as the thunder exploded overhead and the South Lawn was struck with a rain shower and blast of wind that was tropical in its suddenness and intensity.

The other photographers around him were pushing equipment into bags but Pender kept shooting, even as Lau hit the ground and Packer fell into the arms of the agent, the woman, who caught him before he hit the ground. Spencer was on his knees, the other woman, presumably part of his police protection unit, had her hands around his torso but she wasn't pulling him up; rather she was crumpled over the prime minister.

Pandemonium followed with people screaming and agents running in from the sides. Paramedics appeared within seconds and the entire scene became enveloped in a strange sepia light as the storm cloud began to give way to the sun. Somebody shouted that the president had been struck by lightning.

Pender finally lifted his head. He had the shot. He had completed his assignment. He jammed his camera into his bag and moved to the back of the stands. He knew that he would not leave the White House for many hours and that his photos would be considered evidence. No matter, they would be all over the world before then anyway, and Lau would have his immortality.

Pender glanced up. The sun was breaking through and the great house, witness to so much history, though never an assassination, seemed to almost shimmer in the new light. There were flower boxes on the circular balcony overlooking the South Lawn, the one named after Truman. Pender stared at the balcony, the red blooms. He knew he would remember the moment for ever.

63

A LIGHT RAIN WAS FALLING by the time Falsham reached the house. Now that he was responsible for considerable lands and a small army of tenant farmers he knew he had to take note of such things. Spring rains would be a gift from God, assuming they did not exceed his need to the point that the land in use ended up like the marshes just a few miles distant.

Dismounting from his horse, Falsham went down on a knee and placed his gloved hand flat on the bare soil that had been churned up by the hooves of horses, his and others. Then he removed the glove and placed his bare hand on the same spot.

Mine, he thought. It was an idea that Falsham still found difficult to fully comprehend. He had spent most of his life as a wandering soldier. He had wandered through Europe's monarchies and wars as if in a dream. He had listened to old men's tales in Flanders and Spain where the shadow of the Moor still stretched back to North Africa and beyond to the Holy Land, a place of mystery, sanctity and the abode of long dead crusaders and warrior bands such as the Assassins.

He had, he now knew, taken his comparative freedom very much as God given. Now he would have to stay in one place though his imagination would, in turn, have to range far and wide in response to the instructions of the old man whose dying wish had been for Falsham and his heirs see England's throne once again in union with mother church.

Falsham sighed. If only, he thought, life would be but one course, and a simple one.

Standing now, he noticed the young boy who had emerged from the stable yard to fetch the horse. The boy was clutching something, a folded piece of paper. Falsham nodded and the boy reached for the horse even as he held out the paper with a muttered "My lord."

Falsham smiled at the salute but his lightness of mood quickly receded as he read the contents of the message. His presence was required in London, and urgently. For an instant, Falsham thought of taking a fresh horse and setting out at once but just as quickly decided against it. He would take a night at Ayvebury and be "my lord" for its duration. He would set out in the morning.

Falsham was convinced, or had convinced himself, that the path to the old faith, or at least what the heretics considered the old faith, was open and clear. What caused him uncertainty was its length. His mission might take a year or years, perhaps many years. But he had no doubt of its ultimate success. God would not fail those in the right.

The rain was heavier now, and Falsham turned towards the great house, his house. He would need heirs. What was bequeathed to him, the house and its great lands, would always attract avaricious eyes; this he knew for certain.

"Oh, for simplicity in life," Falsham said as he entered the stable yard. But he knew that such a life was not to be. God had other demands of him.

64

Bailey's jaw still hurt. The Secret Service agent had caught him full with a straight arm blow as he had dashed free of the reporters roped in area once it was evident that Samantha was in trouble.

Funny, but he had felt no pain at the moment of impact. Nor indeed for some time afterwards. It had started to throb on the flight back to London, and it sure was throbbing now.

He had been given a few days off to recover. Well earned, Henderson had said, which was about as generous as the man would ever get with his words.

But even Henderson knew this to be an understatement. The story, the stories, had been nothing less than sensations, the biggest in years, a perfect storm of news that had demanded extra print runs. And who said newspapers were history?

"Ouch," said Bailey as he stifled a yawn. He was still jet lagged, still trying to put it all together, the changes in his life and the changed world.

At least, he thought, there still was a world. As soon as it became apparent that President Packer would be incapacitated for some days, the Chinese had taken fright and had agreed to United Nations-sponsored talks to resolve the crisis. They regarded the vice president, Jorgensen, as a dangerous lunatic.

And the man had looked dangerous in front of the cameras, accusing the Chinese of trying to assassinate the president. It didn't seem to matter that Lau, dead at least ten times over by virtue of the chemical concoction he had absorbed, was Taiwanese and a bitter foe of the mainland government.

It seemed, though it had not been confirmed, that Lau was of the view, or somehow aware, that Packer was about to sell out Taiwan by turning around the American fleet just as it came within striking range of Chinese warships in the strait. The Sunday papers had been full of this stuff, but so many stories were floating around that the truth, whatever it was, was drowning in words and verbiage.

Packer was reportedly on the mend, though with the prospects of some facial nerve damage. He was lucky. He had come within a breath of a toxic blockbuster. Ten times more powerful than Sarin, more deadly by far than Ricin, the reports had claimed, but with a life in free air of just seconds and a density that made it ineffective outside a range of just a few feet, at least when unleashed in the quantity that someone had managed to coat a piece of paper with.

The Americans were fit to be tied about that one and obviously going full bore after anyone and everyone who might have been in the plot to assassinate the president. It didn't help their mood that one of their Secret Service agents, a man standing directly behind Packer and whose name Bailey could not remember at such an early hour, had taken the full brunt of the nerve gas cloud and had succumbed on the spot. He was being given a hero's funeral.

Too bad about the agent, Bailey thought. He had absorbed a witch's brew apparently mixed in a lab in one of the former Soviet Central Asian republics. At least the end was quick. Rafter, that was his name.

Everything else was a bit clearer. A woman in Packer's detail had survived with little more than a headache. The gust of wind and sudden downpour had lessened the toxic effect of the poison vapor, thus deciding the final outcome of the attack, now being called "The South Lawn Plot" on one of the television news channels.

Spencer had taken a gulp of the poison but tried to joke afterwards that three or four gin and tonics would have had a more painful effect. The attempt at humor had, rightly, fallen flat and he had been brutally treated in the tabloids, including the *Post*, which had managed to embrace sensitivity for about a day.

Samantha had taken in a little more, but had more or less retained consciousness throughout. She was being proclaimed an all-British hero for the speed that she had moved, once it became apparent that something was badly amiss.

She was the "plucky policewoman" who had risen above and beyond on her very first assignment with the prime minister.

Bailey had sent flowers to her hospital bed. That had been easy enough but it was his marriage proposal that was causing his jaw to ache that little bit more. This was not the way he had planned things. A proposal would only come after a long period of consideration. His mother had been a little unfair when she had once suggested that long in his case would be a lifetime.

But he had thought about it and seemed like the right thing to do. He had not realized how much in love he was until he had seen Samantha slumped over Spencer. And it was that feeling for her that had propelled him from the pack of journalists into the outstretched arm of a Secret Service agent with the tree trunk arm. They had told him afterwards that he was lucky it had been an arm and not a bullet.

That blow, of course, had been just the first of a series of shocks. With all hell breaking loose on both sides of the Atlantic and the prime minister in the middle of it in all respects, it had been open season on Spencer. It turned out that he was not at all far removed from the circumstances surrounding the prince's theological leap.

More stories had surfaced linking Spencer to the order of priests that had been instructing his royal highness in his new Catholicism. Spencer, as a young man, had been Catholic, at one point in early training for the priesthood when he left the seminary, a country house in Essex, after some kind of row or incident.

Reports of sexual abuse had been given short shrift, but there were indications of some kind of doctrinal clash. In what was to become a political trademark of the man, Spencer apparently took exception to some key spiritual aspects of his training and would consider no compromise on these issues. Rather, he had instigated something approaching a latter day reformation within the walls of the seminary.

Such heresy, combined with the man's known volcanic temper, had reportedly caused uproar. He had departed soon afterwards with his former hosts apparently all too eager to brush the episode under the pews. The story had never surfaced throughout decades of the man's political career, but it was doing so now.

"Jesus," Bailey said, forcing himself to sit up. As he did so the phone on the bedside table erupted. It always seemed to erupt rather than just ring when Henderson called, and, sure enough, the office number was showing.

"You said to take a few days off," Bailey said after he plucked the receiver off its charger.

"Yes," he added. "What?"

In response to Henderson's instruction, delivered in a lower, slower voice than usual, the kind that could not be ignored under any circumstance, Bailey's hand moved to the radio. He had it turned to a London news radio station and the familiar newsreader's voice, only this time there was an even more fevered pitch about it than usual.

He pressed a button. His physical state required the mellower BBC.

"Initial reports have described a chaotic scene in which the prime minister was apparently stabbed fatally in the chest by a homeless man that he had taken time to speak with during a visit to Clapham Common, where a new section of replanted parkland was being opened to the public.

"Downing Street has cautioned against rash speculation, but a caller to the BBC said that, in what appeared to have been an extraordinary lapse in security, the prime minister, who survived the recent White House attack, approached the homeless man to speak with him, despite the fact that the man had apparently not been vetted by police officers in the PM's detail.

"Officers shot the man when he lunged at the prime minister's private secretary seconds after Mr. Spencer was struck down. The assailant's condition is unconfirmed, but the caller to the BBC said he believed the man was dead at the scene.

"There is an additional unconfirmed report, from an unrelated source, that the attacker may have been a member of the military at some point and had the necessary training to inflict a fatal wound with a single blow. This was deduced because the assailant, and again this has to be fully confirmed, was in possession of a Victoria Cross, the nation's highest award for military gallantry.

"The cabinet, meanwhile, led by the home secretary, is in emergency session and an official statement is expected at any time.

"Leonard Spencer served a little over three years as head of the government and was no stranger to controversy. Even as he was attending the White House event, his name was linked in sensational reports to a series of deaths of Roman Catholic priests. Those priests in turn have been named possible participants in the religious instruction of the heir to the throne that resulted in his conversion to the Roman Catholic faith, His Highness' unequivocal condemnation of the 1701 Act of Settlement, and what many are describing as the most serious constitutional crisis to affect the realm since the abdication of Edward the Eighth."

Bailey's finger moved to press another button, but a stabbing pain made him withdraw his hand and grab his jaw. As it happened, the newsreader had even more to impart, details that would sow the seeds of what would become an enduring mystery.

"In a development that will be viewed as deeply ironic, the prime minister was attended at the scene by a man initially identified as an Anglican clergyman but who, according to reports just in, is in fact a Roman Catholic priest. He has been unofficially named as Father John Falsham. The priest gave the prime minister last rites, seemingly at the request of his private secretary, Peter Golding, who, though deeply shocked, was uninjured by the attacker."

Bailey's finger struck this time, and as it did so, the phone went again.

"Yes, yes, I'm coming in," he said before Henderson could fire off his summons.

Bailey rolled out of his bed. He felt unsteady on his feet. This was big, more than big, he thought. Big, and a lucky break for Samantha who was not on duty with Spencer's protection detail at the climactic moment, being on leave to recover from Washington.

Bailey shook his head. A headline inspired by a statement from some Oxbridge historian commenting on the constitutional mess came to mind, and not for the first time since the debacle on the White House South Lawn.

All history is recent, the headline had stated.

"And God knows so is my bleedin' holiday," said Bailey, reaching for his shirt.

Acknowledgments

This story has taken a while and, of necessity, it has required more than one hand to see it complete. I would like to thank my wife Lisa for her love and support from start to finish and our three children, Kate, Liz and Jack, for their patience and long unsatisfied curiosity. Well, here it is, kids!

A particular thanks to John O'Mahony for telling me at the very start that this story might actually work. Over time, the advice and encouragement of friends and colleagues has been invaluable. I would like to especially thank Joan Higgins, Isolde Motley, Bob Sloan, Peter Quinn, Terry Golway, Sean and Colum McCann, Malachy McCourt, Dan Barry, Jim Mulvaney and Barbara Fischkin. A salute to Bryian O'Dwyer for that never to be forgotten day on the lawn. Light in a president's darkest hour.

Trish O'Hare at GemmaMedia, like the cavalry of yore, timed her arrival in the process perfectly. She was quickly followed by Suzanne Heiser, whose imagination and artistry brought forward a cover that brilliantly captures the tale inside it.

A bow to John Banville, Pete Hamill, Tom Fleming and the much missed Frank McCourt. Thanks also to my colleagues over the years at the *Irish Echo* and a thought for those journalists and diplomats everywhere who daily strive to bring sanity and clarity to a world that sorely needs it.

Ray O'Hanlon, Ossining, New York

ABOUT THE AUTHOR

R̲ᴀʏ ᴏ'ʜᴀɴʟᴏɴ is editor of *The Irish Echo*, the USA's most widely read Irish American newspaper, based in New York. Over the course of a distinguished newspaper career spanning more than thirty years, he has reported from three continents and has appeared on "CBS' 60 Minutes," "ABC World News Tonight" and "PBS NewsHour with Jim Lehrer." In addition to his work as a reporter and editor, O'Hanlon is a frequent contributor to media reporting on Ireland, Irish American affairs and Anglo-Irish relations. His book, *The New Irish Americans* (Roberts Rinehart, 1998,) was the recipient of a Washington Irving Book Award.

A native of Dublin and a keen reader of American, Irish and British history, O'Hanlon lives with his wife Lisa and their three children in Ossining, New York.